EIGHT MILLION GODS

八百万の神

Baen Books
by Wen Spencer

Elfhome Series:
Tinker
Wolf Who Rules
Elfhome

Endless Blue

Eight Million Gods

EIGHT MILLION GODS
八百万の神

WEN SPENCER

BAEN

EIGHT MILLION GODS

Copyright © 2013 by Wen Spencer.

A Baen Book

Baen Publishing Enterprises
P.O. Box 1403
Riverdale, NY 10471
www.baen.com

ISBN: 978-14516-3898-1

Cover art by Tom Kidd

First Baen printing, June 2013

Distributed by Simon & Schuster
1230 Avenue of the Americas
New York, NY 10020

Library of Congress Cataloging-in-Publication Data

Spencer, Wen.
 Eight million gods / by Wen Spencer.
     pages cm
 ISBN 978-1-4516-3898-1 (hc)
1. Women novelists--Fiction. 2. Americans--Japan--Fiction. 3. Obsessive-compulsive disorder--Fiction. 4. Murder--Investigation--Fiction. 5. Fantasy fiction. 6. Mystery fiction. I. Title.
 PS3619.P4665E37 2013
 813'.6--dc23
                                    2013001232

Printed in the United States of America

10 9 8 7 6 5 4 3 2 1

✠ Dedication ✠

To June Drexler Robertson
We met when I was an awkward teenager.
Through thick and thin, you've always supported me.
Thank you for your friendship.
I value it greatly.

❖ Acknowledgements ❖

Thanks to the many people who made this book
possible: Ann Cecil, Joshua Frydman, Nancy Janda,
Deleyan Lee, Laurel Jamieson Lohrey, Susan Petroulas,
Hope Erica Ring M.D., Traci Scroggins, June Drexler
Robertson, Cheryl C. Whitemore, PsyD.

Special thanks to David G. Kosak
for stuffing himself into the trunk of a BMW Z4 to
prove it could be done.

✠ Contents ✠

✥ 1 ✥
Bounce

"Your mission, if you choose to accept it, is escape your powerful, control-freak mother," Nikki whispered to the mirror hung on the back of the apartment's door.

"Miss Delany," the policeman said on the other side of the door. "I have a court order for your commitment to a psychiatric center for evaluation. Please open the door."

Considering Nikki was in a flannel Hello Kitty sleeping shirt, her hair looked like a rat's nest, and her roommate's fox terriers were barking up a storm, escaping was truly going to be mission impossible. Taking off nearly naked was not an option; she was going to have to be clever. She grabbed a hair tie from the hall closet doorknob and stalled as she fought with her long blonde hair. "Under the New York State Mental Hygiene Law, Article Nine, Hospitalization of the Mentally Ill, I have the right to appropriate personal clothing and safe storage of personal property. Do you understand my rights?"

For some weird reason, quoting law to some policemen was like hitting Superman with kryptonite. They just couldn't cope with material from their home planet. She totally lucked out—there was complete silence from the other side of the door. Score!

She did a mad loop around the tiny living room that currently doubled as her bedroom, snatching up clothing. Bra. Sweater. Blue jeans. She dashed back to the door, dropped the clothes on the floor, and stripped quickly. Over Yip and Yap, she could hear her mother arguing with the policeman—probably telling him to grow a pair of balls and just break down the door. It was a really good thing that the officer was waffling before he even got in the door.

"Please, miss, open the door or I'm going to have to break it down."

Nikki had learned young that escalation to force was a bad thing; it led to restraints. She had taught herself how to escape a straightjacket, but it involved dislocating a shoulder. She *really* wanted to avoid that if possible. Opening the door while nude, however, would be very bad.

"Okay, okay!" she cried to give herself more time. "There's lots of locks and they stick, so be patient!"

Luckily, like any good New York City apartment, the door did have multiple locks. She fumbled loudly with them between yanking on pieces of clothing. Of course her bra ended up inside out, but she could just suffer. At least the sweater pulled on without a problem. The jeans attempted to be an octopus of alternating reverse and right-side-out legs. Panic was trying to set in, which would be very bad. While she wasn't dangerously insane like her mother would like the legal system to believe, to the causal observer her hypergraphia certainly made her seem crazy. If she didn't have pen and paper in hand, her compulsion would make her write on walls with anything available. Time to go to her happy place. She took a deep breath and imagined ocean waves against white sand. Wind through palm trees. Colorful drinks with paper umbrellas.

"Miss Delany?" The officer knocked again.

"I'm opening the door!" She hopped in the foyer, tugging on the jeans one leg at time. "This last lock is sticking!" She gave the top lock a half twist, zipped up her jeans, and looked into the mirror. A Ford model at a fashion shoot she wasn't, but she'd pass as a normal, *sane* coed about to head out to class. "As always," she whispered, "this message will self-destruct in five minutes. Cue the *Mission Impossible* theme music."

She jerked open the door.

The policeman seemed impossibly young, although that could be because he was only about five-six. The clean shave, buzz cut, and wide eyes did not help either, effectively rendering him about twelve years old in appearance. His name badge identified him as H. Russell.

Behind him, her mother was trying to gracefully shove him aside.

"Officer Russell." Nikki backed away from the door, heading for Sheila's bedroom as fast as she could, hands in plain sight. She still needed something on her feet, her wallet, and something warm, since it was freezing cold for early May. "I need a minute to get shoes on and gather my things."

Yip and Yap decided that her coming down the hallway meant that they were getting out of their crate and fell silent.

"Nikki, I don't have time for you to get your things." Her mother was in full queen-warrior-senator mode in a black Chanel business skirt suit, more diamonds than some African nations, and Prada three-inch heels. "I've got a limo outside. Just put on some slippers and come quietly."

Nikki locked down on the first ten things that wanted out. She focused on the policeman instead. *Look, Officer Russell, I'm cooperating. I'm sane. You can just stand there and be embarrassed for me.*

"Let me pack one bag of my clothes," she pleaded aloud. "I'm crashing here. My name isn't on the lease. If I just walk out, my roommate doesn't have to let anyone back in to collect my stuff."

The truth was she didn't truly "own" anything. Somewhere far back in her childhood, she had a faint memory of having a bedroom full of things that were hers and hers alone, an entire room full of privacy. Currently everything "hers" was actually stuff she permanently borrowed from her roommate, Sheila.

"I will buy you new stuff." Her mother closed fast, her heels clicking menacingly on the hardwood floor.

They hit the bedroom door at the same time, and Yip and Yap went ballistic at the sight of a brand-new person to play with. Instantly Nikki was alone in the room. The fox terriers were the main reasons she was crashing with Sheila instead of other friends; her mother was terrified of dogs. She wanted every advantage she could use against her mother, just in case of days like this. Nikki hurriedly yanked open "her" drawer in Sheila's dresser and grabbed her wallet and passport.

A quick check confirmed her wallet had everything she needed to start life over. Again. Next time in Japan. That had been her plan since she was fifteen, only she wasn't supposed to leave for another six months. This wouldn't be the first time, though, that her mother had screwed up her plans. Nikki shoved her wallet and passport into her jeans' back pocket and grabbed a pair of socks.

Officer Russell appeared in the door as she sat on Sheila's bed to put on her shoes. Sheila's perfume still hung in the air, making Nikki aware that she was about to vanish out of her roommate's life without a decent good-bye. *This is so fucking unfair!*

Fair or not, it was what she had to work with. How was she going to get out of this? She pulled on her running shoes. She needed time to think, so she grabbed Sheila's gym bag and made a show of stuffing clothing into it. Yip and Yap would make sure that her mother stayed as far as possible from the bedroom, but Officer Russell was firmly anchored in the doorway.

"This is for your own good," her mother called from the living room, nearly shouting to be heard over the barking. "You're not stable enough to live alone."

Nikki breathed out a laugh. This was going to be one of those conversations where the whole point was to influence the interloper, not the person actually addressed. Her mother realized that Officer Russell was the main thing blocking Nikki now and was trying to shift him to her mother's side. Nikki hadn't been totally aware of winning him over but trusted her mother's judgment.

"I don't live alone," Nikki pointed out to both her mother and Officer Russell. "I have a roommate."

"She posts homosexual erotica on the Internet," her mother countered. "Some of it involves underage boys."

Nikki heart leapt slightly in fear. "You did a background check on Sheila?"

"My teenage daughter disappears to go live with a complete stranger she met on the Internet. Yes, I had a background check done on the woman."

"I turned twenty last month, Mother." Nikki picked up her lip balm and used it on her lips one last time. Her hypergraphia begged her to scribble an entire random scene onto the dresser mirror. She controlled the urge and only wrote "Bounce" onto the glass.

There, this time she let her roommate know that she hadn't been murdered in a back alley. Poor Julie had actually reported her missing before the FBI let her know that Nikki had been involuntarily committed to a mental hospital. *And wasn't that fun to escape from?*

Did her mother know about her plans to flee to Japan? The biggest problem with her plan was how easy it was for a senator to track a US citizen via a passport. Provided, of course, they knew to look. Up to now, Nikki been careful not to cross any borders. She had used a spy level of caution in getting a copy of her birth certificate and applying for her passport. She had researched methods of getting out the country quietly and how movements of citizens were reported. If her mother didn't have her flagged, then she could hopscotch to Japan. If she did . . .

Nikki closed her eyes. *Breath deep. Happy place.* A desert island, far, far away from her mother. Away from the closed-in spaces of a mental hospital. Nikki, a laptop, Internet connection, and nothing but white sand, shifting shadows, and the dazzle of sun off the ocean.

"Are you okay?" Officer Russell stepped closer, and Yip and Yap howled their disappointment that the second new person wasn't letting them out of their crate.

Nikki nodded, opening her eyes. "Just trying to remember if I'd forgotten anything." *Like getting out of this apartment a free woman.* Still, she needed to find out first what her mother knew. She made a show of opening drawers and going through the contents.

"Sheila writes stories based on Twilight," Nikki called to her mother. "You know—vampires and werewolves? They're not real people. It's called fan fiction, and it's all on a password-protected forum. You have to register with a valid e-mail account and verify you're over eighteen to read the stories."

"And you think this makes a site secure?"

She knew it didn't. The question was, in digging through Sheila's private websites, did her mother's people find Nikki's? Did it matter? If Sheila broadcasted Nikki's "Bounce" command, everything would be abandoned and everyone would move to the new site.

Nikki took a deep breath and tightened her hands against taking out the lip balm and this time writing on the walls. Fighting with her mother would get her into more trouble. She needed to run, not stand and try to win this argument she had no hope of winning. She never won. Right now, she needed to be clever and quick.

There was a fire escape outside the window. She had tested it out—once. The open steelwork triggered her mild fear of heights. If she could get a head start, she could be to the subway station before Officer Russell caught her. She needed him out of the room.

"Here." She pushed the gym bag into his hands. "Oh, my pills. Can you grab them from the medicine cabinet?" She pointed toward the bathroom and scooped up coins from the dresser top. The one time she attended high school, she lived in dorms. There was a prank that involved the heavy room doors and coins. She had never tried it out on the apartment doors.

"Pills?" Officer Russell's eyes went a little wider.

"Medicine. Mental patient. I know you guys are all a little jumpy about mixing the two. My birth control is in the medicine cabinet with some of my roommate's prescriptions."

"Y-y-yeah."

She followed him across the hall.

"Birth control?" her mother cried from living room—as far as possible from the dogs as she could get while staying within supervision range of the bathroom.

"Trust me," Nikki said. "None of us want you to be a grandmother."

Officer Russell snickered and opened up the crowded cabinet. "Whoa."

"It's in the back," she said unhelpfully, pulled shut the door, and pushed coins into the space between the wood and the jamb.

"Hey!" Officer Russell yelped as he found the door wedged shut tight.

"Nikki!" her mother shouted.

Three steps and Nikki was in Shiela's bedroom. She hit the latch on the dog kennel even as her mother cried, "You stupid idiot! I told you that she was dangerous!"

Yip and Yap came bounding out, nearly levitating with their excitement. They ignored Nikki; she was familiar and thus boring. Barking madly, they charged toward the living room. Nikki slammed shut the bedroom door and flicked the lock. Two more steps and she was to the window and then out onto the fire escape.

Nikki's heart lurched as she forced herself out onto the steel catwalk and then down the rickety ladder. She couldn't let her fear of heights slow her down. She hit the street and started to run. She didn't stop running until she was in Japan.

2
The OMG Baseball Bat

She was living in Japan. Osaka, Japan, to be exact. Two months and it still startled her in a way she found weirdly uncomfortable. She had moved dozens of times before in the States, from suburban mental hospitals, to a dormitory at a private high school in the middle of nowhere, to walk-up apartments in gritty inner-city neighborhoods. Never before had she constantly felt like she was being hit in the head with a baseball bat labeled "OMG."

Some days it seemed like everything triggered the feeling. Waking up lying on a futon on the floor. *Whack!* Going pee at a public restroom by squatting over a ceramic trough. *Whack!* Wandering up and down the levels of a bookstore with thousands of interesting-looking books without being able to read a single word. *Whack!* Walking through an entire shopping district, surrounded by people, and unable to guess or even ask where to buy a basic cooking knife. *Whack!* One minute she would be steaming along, enjoying the adventure of living on her own, and then the "OMG" baseball bat of cultural shock would catch her smack between the eyes.

By lunchtime, she was slightly punch-drunk by the number of hits she'd taken. The only reason she didn't suggest meeting at KFC or McDonald's was somehow the combination of familiar and uniquely Japanese that the two food chains represented would have been more unsettling than the little hole-in-the-wall traditional *okonomiyaki* shop. At least the act of taking off her sandals in the restaurant's foyer, putting them in one of the many cubbyholes, bowing to the waitress, and stepping down into the sitting area around a grill-topped table was now comfortingly familiar despite being totally foreign.

Nikki waved off the menu that the waitress was trying to offer her. "*Sumimasen*," Nikki tried to remember the Japanese word for "menu." "English—English . . ."

"Ah!" The waitress smiled as she realized what Nikki was trying for. "English menu. *Hai*! One minute."

The waitress disappeared into the impossibly small kitchen hidden behind a half-wall where a cook was already standing.

Her best friend, Miriam Frydman, laughed in greeting. "One of those kinds of days?"

"God, yes." Nikki tossed her backpack onto the seat beside her. "There are days I could just kill my mother. All this would be easier if I'd been able to stick to our plan and learn Japanese."

Nikki had met Miriam the only time she attended "normal" high school. Not that you could really call Foxcroft "normal" as it was an expensive private boarding school. Miriam always had a fascination for all things Japanese. Nikki just wanted to have half the planet between her and her mother. She and Miriam had come up with the detailed plan that would have had both of them fluent in Japanese, employed by the same company, and sharing an apartment together. Her mother, though, had yanked Nikki out of school in her senior year and ruined every later attempt to keep to the plan.

Miriam tilted her head and squinted in deep thought. Her bright pink-dyed hair, gathered into quirky pigtails, and her high-school outfit were both part of her own battle with all things Japanese. She'd confessed that she had come to the conclusion that as a *gaijin*—an "outsider"—she would never fully fit in, so she had decided to stand out. Nikki would never have the courage to dye her hair or wear anything as short as Miriam's miniskirt, but Miriam was fearless. "Nah, I think you'd still be reeling even if you'd learned Japanese first. I felt the same way for the first six months. Really? The toilets alone break all language barriers when it comes to cultural shock." She slid her glass slightly closer to Nikki's side. "A stiff drink does help."

Nikki snorted. "I'm actually tempted. Much as a drug addiction scares the willies out of me, knowing that something like valium would make it—make it *seem* better—for a while . . ."

Miriam dragged the glass back to her side of the table. "My bad. Sorry."

The waitress came back with a sketchily translated menu and slightly better phrased "What do you want?"

They picked their *okonomiyaki* toppings, Nikki pointing to her selection on the English menu and Miriam ordering from the Japanese one.

Nikki tentatively added her drink order. "*Mazu?*"

The word got a muffled giggle from Miriam and a blank stare from the waitress.

From behind the hand covering her mouth, Miriam murmured, "Water is *mizu*."

Nikki winced, wondering what she had actually said to the waitress. Hopefully nothing obscene. "*Mizu kudasai*."

The waitress smiled. "Ah, yes, water!"

"*Mizu. Mizu.*" Nikki repeated softly after the waitress left. Miriam might be right and being fluent might not stop the cultural shock, but she was tired of being clueless of what was being said around her. Her whole life had been a series of being completely helpless and at her mother's mercy or heavily dependent on the kindness of friends. "The plan" was for them to live together, but Miriam was locked into a lease for another four months at a place where she couldn't have a roommate. For the first time, Nikki was living alone, buying her own clothes, and cooking her own food. She loved being independent, but constantly being lost and confused the moment she ventured out of her apartment was frustrating the hell out of her.

The waitress returned with their drinks and two mixing bowls with the ingredients for the *okonomiyaki*. They watched as the waitress mixed up the batter and poured it onto the hot grill. She used a large steel spatula to round the batter into a thick pancake.

Why *okonomiyaki* was considered Japanese "pizza" still mystified Nikki; it was shredded cabbage mixed with flour and topped with barbeque sauce and mayonnaise. The only similarity was that it was circular and came with countless toppings. Personally she thought of them as very weird pancakes. She had discovered early on that the shrimp came with their heads still attached and she couldn't quite deal with having her dinner stare at her with accusing eyes. The other thing that slightly creeped her out was the fact that the shaved *bonito* on top wriggled as if still alive.

Once the waitress had both "pizzas" in place, she motioned that they weren't to fiddle with the dough with the little spatulas that were in lieu of forks and spoons. "Ah—cook—don't touch."

The *shoji*-style front door slid open, triggering a call of "*Irasshaimase*" from the two employees. The new customer was one of the impossibly slender *salarymen*, looking like he would only weigh over hundred pounds if you dipped him and his two-piece suit in one of Osaka's many waterways. It still freaked Nikki out that, at five foot three, she could look down at a goodly number of the Japanese men, the newest customer included.

He took off his shoes and tucked them into a cubbyhole next to her sandals as the waitress hurried across the twenty feet between the kitchen and the foyer to greet him properly. Waitress bowed, *salaryman* bowed back. It was like watching anime come to life; a good, happy moment that Nikki desperately needed at this point.

The *salaryman* was installed in the booth beside theirs and the grill-top of his table fired up to get ready for cooking.

"So?" Miriam nudged at Nikki with her socking clad foot. "Who's dead?"

"Hmm?" Nikki studied the *salaryman* in the guise of cleaning her hands with the wet wipe. He was thin and delicate like a sparrow. She couldn't tell how old he was; he was so tiny he seemed like he should be only thirteen, but most likely he was a college graduate and in his twenties. Certainly, he made many manga storylines about boys passing as girls more believable.

Miriam nudged her hard, forcing Nikki to give up her study of the *salaryman*. "You're wearing your shirt of mourning. You only wear that after you kill someone. Who's dead?"

Nikki tented out her Goth Lolita shirt. It was the most beautiful thing she ever owned, all black silk with long sleeves, and lace everywhere. She'd bought it to cheer herself up after the Brit vanished out of the novel. Did she really only wear it after a murder? "I blogged it. Didn't you read it?"

Miriam covered her mouth as she yawned. "I had an *nomikai* Friday night. God, only the Japanese would require employees get hammered together on a regular basis. I spent most of yesterday in zombie mode. I did see your blog on doing your laundry but nothing on you killing someone off."

"I posted the murder later."

"Who did you kill?"

"The expatriate, George Wilson," Nikki told her glumly. "The idiot pervert."

Miriam laughed. "What does this make? Three love interests you've killed before even getting to the sex? You have to stop killing people."

"I've tried! I just can't stop myself. One minute George is drinking sake in his Umeda apartment, getting ready to go out, and the next he's taking an eight-hundred-dollar Blendtec blender to the guts."

"A blender?"

"Yeah, ever notice how sharp the blades are on a blender? I broke the glass container against George's head and set the blender on puree." Nikki made the sound of the blades spinning and twirled her index finger in a tight circle. "Blood all over the white countertop."

"Cool. I approve."

Nikki laughed. "I thought you would. The color contrast was stunning."

"Where did he get the blender?" Miriam pointed out the one thing that worried Nikki about the murder.

"I think he brought it from the United States. Does it really matter? It's not like it's a sword or firearm." It still geeked her out that the Japanese had more laws controlling swords than guns.

The waitress returned to flip over their pancakes. They were nice and golden on the cooked side. As Miriam asked the waitress something in Japanese, Nikki realized that the office worker was staring at her in utter horror.

Oops.

It was something she kept forgetting; since English was taught in Japanese schools from first grade up, Japanese people normally understood a lot more English than she understood Japanese. She played back their conversation and winced. How was she going to explain?

"I didn't really kill anyone. I'm a writer." Was that what the Japanese called authors? "I write books. Novels? Miriam, help."

Miriam laughed and said something that made the man bolt from the booth, grab his shoes, and run still in his stocking feet out of the store.

"What did you say?" Nikki cried.

"I told him you don't kill nice little *uke* like him, only big bad *seme*."

"Miriam! I don't kill people—real people."

The waitress returned with the *salaryman*'s drink order and eyed the empty booth with confusion.

"Ix-nay on the urder-may," Nikki said. "I don't want a burned *okonomiyaki*."

"You know, you could just delete the scene. George had real promise as a hero. Rich. Handsome. Alive."

"No, I couldn't," Nikki grumbled. "You know that. George is now dead to my hypergraphia. When characters are alive, everything just flows. All I have to do is occasionally nudge things into place with a little research on the details. Once they're dead, it's blank-page time. I don't have time to be staring at blank pages. Besides, he was turning out to be a completely sick bastard."

It had been the sale of her first novel that allowed her to continue on with their plan despite the fact she couldn't speak the language, hadn't gone to college, and had no work experience. Her advance on royalties arrived two days before her mother. It had gotten her to Japan and into an apartment, paid for a laptop and all the things she needed day-to-day, like clothes, with enough left over for her to survive for over a year. Even better, her publishers asked her to write a second novel. Unfortunately, they wanted the book within a year's time. She needed to deliver it on time because she would run out of money shortly after her deadline. It was a race to see if she could finish writing before her funds ran out.

The problem was that the novel had to meet certain standards. Because her first book was being marketed as a romantic thriller, she needed a heroine and a hero who meet, fall in love, and survive to the end. So far, all her possible romantic leads had been killed—except the one that mysteriously vanished in mid-sentence. But she suspected that he was dead, too.

"Don't worry, we'll work through it," Miriam said. "Do what you do best, and I'll fill in any missing pieces. Team Banzai go!"

Which was why Miriam was her best friend. She had always protected Nikki and gave her hope when life went to hell.

"Thanks," Nikki said.

"Okay, so we need a new romantic hero. A stud muffin for your little dormouse artist."

"She's not a dormouse, she's just emotionally scarred. George would have completely freaked her out. Him and his school girls in bondage fetish."

The *shoji* door slid open again and two more *salarymen* in dark suits ducked into the shop. These two were tall and sturdy looking.

"*Irasshaimase,*" the waitress and the cook called, welcoming the new customers.

The men scanned the shop, said something to each other as they noticed Miriam with her pink ponytails, and then focused on Nikki. There was something decidedly unfriendly about their faces.

One slipped off his shoes and headed for them like a very polite avenging angel.

"Miriam." Nikki indicated the man.

"Tanaka *desu.*" He introduced himself as Mr. Tanaka. Make that Detective Tanaka as he produced a police badge and flashed it. He continued talking.

"What's he saying?" Nikki turned to Miriam for a translation.

"Oh my God, Nikki," Miriam gasped. "He's arresting you for murder."

✠ 3 ✠
In the Kitchen,
With a Blender

Nikki liked pens. She took some comfort knowing that most writers did. Only her obsession for ink-based writing instruments was on the same level as a wino's fixation on wine. The only things she had ever stolen in her life were pens, usually cheap ones off peoples' desks. The only new pen had been a six-hundred-dollar Cartier Diabolo fountain pen with an 18K-gold nib. (One couldn't really blame her; her mother had dragged her down Rodeo Drive in some vain attempt to make Nikki presentable during an election campaign and triggered a writing fit in Neiman Marcus. She had locked herself in a bathroom stall and written out a vivisection on a fistfull of paper towels.)

What "worked" best for her hypergraphia were cheap retractable ballpoint pens supplied by oxygen companies and such to hospital staff to promote their products. It was her special brew in a brown paper bag. She could hold the compulsion off sometimes by just gripping one tight and clicking it repeatedly.

Since arriving in Osaka, she'd fallen in love with Zebra Surari emulsion ink pens with 0.5mm points in five colors. She bought them like some people bought cigarettes. She had a dozen in her backpack, mostly black, her favorite weapon, but at least one of the other four colors. She paired them with the B6-sized Campus notebook sold at

FamilyMart. Compared to what she bought in the United States, the slim notebooks were stunningly cheap, yet superior in paper quality. God, the Japanese understood writing by hand.

Handcuffed in the back of the tiny police squad car, she really wished she could think of anything except pens. And how much she *needed* one in her hand. With paper. And both were within her backpack beside her.

Maybe if she used her teeth . . .

Then again, perhaps thinking about pens was better than thinking about the mess she was in. This wasn't the United States. The police could and would hold a suspect as long as they wanted. There was one case where they arrested a man and held him for questioning for three days. He was suspected of nothing more than groping women on the train. When his parents reported him missing to the very police station that was holding him, they weren't told that he was just down the hall. In the end, the police realized that they had the wrong man and released him without apology despite media outcry.

And they suspected her of murder!

She bit down on a whimper as the need to write grew a little more desperate. She closed her eyes, took deep cleansing breaths, and tried to focus only on her happy place. Pristine white sand. Water so blue that it defied description.

The car pulled to a stop and they were at the Osaka Prefectural Police Headquarters next to the sprawling gardens of the Osaka Castle.

God, she would kill for a pen.

The police department looked much like its American counterpart—desks crowded with computers, office supplies, and paper files threatening to overrun everything. Luckily they stopped her by a desk with pens in a coffee mug. She eased around so the cup was behind her and in reach of her handcuffed hands.

"*Watashi no nihongo wa heta desu,*" she said while running her fingers blindly over the pens. It meant—hopefully—that her Japanese was bad. "*Wakarimasen.*" Which meant "I don't understand." She found a retractable pen. She gripped it tightly, and carefully, silently, clicked it. She took a deep breath and relaxed as she breathed it out. "Please. Does anyone speak English?"

The policemen were talking to each other, ignoring her. She silently clicked the pen a few more times, trying to decide what to do. If this were the American police, she would ask for a lawyer and refuse to talk to the police until someone showed up, probably from the public defender's office. All the anecdotal evidence, though, seemed to suggest that Japanese citizens didn't automatically have the right to an attorney. If she asked for someone from the American consulate, would they call the embassy for her? Did she want someone?

No. And definitely not. She clicked the pen again.

Detective Tanaka took her by the arm and led her to an interrogation room. At least that's what it looked like: a tiny room with just a steel table and four chairs. She didn't wait for him to point at one of the chairs. She slid in one without being told.

The detective put her backpack on the table and settled into the chair across from her. Silently, they eyed each other. It reminded her of meeting a new psychiatrist. The quiet weighing in of battle spirit before the subtle and non-so-subtle word games started.

He was tall, solidly built for a Japanese man, and good-looking. Brown hair and brown eyes went without saying, although his haircut wasn't the drama excess she was used to in J-pop idols and male nightclub hosts. He seemed fairly young to be a detective. Was he one of those guys that got ahead merely because he acted the arrogant alpha male? No, he didn't have the self-centered air that they had. He was searching her face, his dark eyebrows arched in mild confusion. Maybe he was the rare type of man that was as intelligent as he was good-looking. Maybe he did criminal profiling and he was realizing that she really didn't fit the type that killed men with blenders. If she could keep from scribbling madly on the walls, she might even be able to convince him of that.

"I don't speak Japanese." She said it slowly but not loudly. Loudly only annoyed people. "Please. English. *Kudasai.*"

"*Chotto matte kudasi.*" He stood up and took out a key ring. She realized that he was going to take off her handcuffs. She managed to slip her stolen pen up her sleeve and tucked it into her watchband before he reached her side.

"*Arigato go—go—goazimasu.*" She purposely stumbled with the "thank you very much."

As she rubbed her wrists, he took his seat again. Okay, not being handcuffed was good, maybe. It meant Tanka didn't consider her dangerous. If she lost control of her hypergraphia, however, her hands would be free to disobey.

They had taken her wallet and passport at the restaurant. He took them out now and studied her passport and tourist visa papers. He sounded out her name. "Nikki Delany."

Nikki nodded. "*Hai.*"

He produced latex gloves out of his coat pocket and pulled them on. Oh, joy. He was treating her backpack as evidence. He cautiously unzipped the bag as if suspecting she had poisonous snakes inside. She winced as she remembered the contents: an extremely graphic *yaoi* manga, a package of fireworks, more pens than God, a fresh notebook, and one very large knife. In the USA, everything but the pen and paper would get her into trouble. At least in Japan, they'd only be concerned with the knife.

He pulled out the sealed plastic package of the fireworks she'd bought at 7-11 that morning. As she'd expected, he put it to the side with only a slight look of confusion.

A paper fan she forgot she'd collected followed. It was one of the traditional non-folding fans called an *uchiwa*. She had recently started to decorate the walls of her apartment with them because they were given out for free. This one had a beautiful woodblock print of a sparrow sitting on a flowering tree on one side and an advertisement on the back, although she couldn't tell for what. It stated "lead the value" in English and then "*kanji*" underneath identifying the company. She had asked the man handing it out for a translation. He'd misunderstood and demonstrated fanning himself. It triggered one of the many cultural shocks of the morning.

Detective Tanaka laid the fan aside and took out the *yaoi* manga. She liked the series because it explained the world of manga production, but the cover made clear that the plot followed the romance of two men. She was laboring over translating a page a day in an attempt to learn Japanese on her own. Tanaka's confused look grew deeper.

He took out the notebook she had bought that morning. He flipped through it, noting all the pages were blank, and put it down. Her hands were moving toward it before she stopped herself. Tanaka eyed her hands and then the notebook.

Jerking her hands back would be bad. Considering how twitchy her fingers felt, picking up the notebook would be very bad. She froze. Her Japanese utterly failed her. "Good paper. Very good paper."

Finally he hit the cleaverlike *nakiri* with the gleaming black blade.

She had done endless research on knives in her quest to learn how to cook Japanese style. She knew for example that the nakiri of Osaka were called *kamagata nakiri* and had a rounded corner instead of the Tokyo rectangular shape. She had not a clue how to say "cut vegetables."

"*Daikon.*" She named one Japanese vegetable she knew, the large radish root and mimed cutting one up. "Chop, chop, chop." How did you say cook? "*Shabu shabu.*" Technically it was a dish, but the name came from the sound of the food being cooked. She was fairly sure you chopped up vegetables for it.

"Ah." He made a little noise of understanding but was careful to put the knife onto the chair beside him, out of her reach.

The door opened and the little tiny *salaryman* from the restaurant paused in the doorway, clutching a folder to his chest.

"You!" Nikki pointed at him, and he nearly jumped back out of the room. "You speak English!"

Tanaka snickered. "Yes. He speaks English. This is Aki Yoshida."

She didn't know if she was more pissed or relieved. She settled on relieved because pissed usually caused problems. "This is a mistake. I write novels. Like this." She tapped the manga. She really hoped that Yoshida didn't pair Miriam's taunt at the restaurant with the cover art of a half-naked, big-eyed *uke* staring up at his leering *seme*. "I'm here in Japan researching locations for a novel I'm writing. That's what we were talking about in the restaurant. One of my characters had been murdered. I wrote about killing . . ."

Tanaka was in full confusion. She had outstripped his understanding of English. She tucked her hands under the table, reached up her sleeve to her stolen pen and clicked it. *Breath deep.* Click. *White sands.* Click. *Blue ocean.* Click.

"I didn't kill anyone." She stuck to plain and simple.

Yoshida nervously eyed the knife on the chair on the police side of the table. Tanaka said something to him and pointed to the fourth chair. The little policeman edged closer to Nikki, grabbed the chair, and dragged it quickly away from her side.

"I'm a forensic scientist," Yoshida said. "I studied at California State University."

So he should understand English very well, but he didn't look any less scared.

"I write novels," she tried again, slower. "I was talking about my book. My characters are not real people."

Yoshida opened the folder that he was carrying and pushed a picture toward her. It was a blond man, fairly good-looking if one overlooked the fact that he was obviously very dead.

"Do you know this man?" Tanaka asked.

"No." *They had a dead body! They had a real dead body!* Clickclickclickclickclick.

"He is American," Tanaka said. "His name is Gregory Winston."

"I don't know him!" Okay, that was eerily close to her character George Wilson's name. She fought the urge to reach for her notebook. Now was not the time to break down. "Crazy" was too close to "homicidal" in most people's dictionary.

"He had an apartment in Umeda," Tanaka said.

Just like George Wilson.

"I don't know him," Nikki said. How do you prove that you don't know someone—especially after they're dead? "Really, I've only been in Japan for two months. I barely know anyone."

"Did you meet him in the United States? Maybe you were lovers?"

"No! I've never seen that man before in my life!" She was going to lose it soon.

Tanaka motioned to Yoshida, and the little police officer took out another photograph and put it beside the picture of the dead man. It was a Blendtec blender covered in blood, still set on puree.

She upset her chair, tripped over it, and came up against the wall before she realized that she had recoiled as fast as she could from the photograph. Her mouth was open and something loud and not very sane sounding was struggling to push its way out. She slapped her hand back over her mouth to keep it in.

"You recognize this?" Tanaka asked.

Nikki nodded and then realized that it made her very guilty looking and shook her head.

"Which is it? Yes or no?"

She found herself in the corner, still trying to backpedal away from the photograph. She took her hands away to explain how she "recognized" the blender but didn't *recognize* it.

"I wrote a story. I made up a man. I made him an American living here in Osaka for business because I'm writing a book set here in Osaka. I said he lived in Umeda so he could see the Ferris wheel on the top of Hep Five. Honest to God. I made it all up."

Shit, she was babbling. She needed to shut up. "I was eating ramen for lunch and thought 'George Wilson will be killed by a blender' and started to write it. I don't know why a blender. I didn't even know anything about blenders. That's just how the muse works." *Stop talking.* "I had to look them up on the Internet. They're really a stupid murder weapon. Their cords are only this long, you always put on the jar before you put on the blades, and I don't know if you can buy them in Japan." *Stop talking! Just stop!* "I spent all yesterday doing research on them. I ended up on youtube.com watching the Blendtec 'will it blend' videos. They put weird shit in blenders and reduce them down to scrap. You know—marbles and cell phones. It felt right; it was the kind of blender George would own."

She slapped her hands over her mouth. Obviously, she had lost Tanaka long ago, and Yoshida was frowning in concentration to understand what she had said. She wasn't sure if that was a good thing or a bad thing.

Yoshida started to talk in Japanese to Tanaka. Maybe translating. Maybe suggesting that they put her in a mental hospital. She really wished she understood Japanese better. She closed her eyes and thought of tropical beaches—someplace where people spoke English—with no blenders.

Cigarette smoke made her open her eyes. Tanaka had taken out a pack of Lucky Strikes and lit one. He was listening to Yoshida, but he was watching her with puzzled eyes. He held out the pack as an offering. Nikki shook her head. He took a portable ashtray, known as a *keitai haizara*, out of his pocket and placed it beside him.

"Where were you last night?" Tanaka asked when Yoshida finished. "With people? They can say you were with them?"

Could she talk without babbling? She slid her hand off her mouth and tried to stay focused on not babbling and sounding guilty as hell. Her hands fluttered around, looking for the pen she'd been holding. "Saturdays I do chores. I cleaned my apartment, did laundry, and wrote." The pen wasn't in her pocket or up her sleeve. She scanned the floor and spotted it beside her overturned chair. She edged over and scooped up the pen as she righted her chair. She pushed the chair toward the table while keeping to a sane, safe subject. "There's a FamilyMart across the street. I went to it three—no—four times. Nakamura was working yesterday; she wants to be a JAL flight attendant, so she likes to practice her English with me. First time I bought panda blood-flavored cookies . . ."

"*Nani?*" Tanaka exclaimed.

Yoshida shrugged.

"Panda blood-flavored?" Tanaka asked.

Nikki sat down, her right hand holding the pen hidden in her lap. She put her left out on the table to distract the policemen. "I don't know what they're called." Nikki quietly clicked the ballpoint and tried not to think about the huge gaps of time she spent in her apartment alone yesterday. "The bag has a picture of a panda on the front. The cookies were squishy, and they have some kind of red filling. I thought it would be cherry or raspberry or something, but it was something icky that I've never had before. I didn't like them. I posted about them on my blog, and someone commented that they were panda blood-flavored."

Yoshida condensed her ranting down to four words.

"You went three more times?" Tanaka asked.

"Second time I bought the ramen for lunch and got yen coins for the washing machines in the lobby of my apartment building. I went home and ate and wrote." The visits had been hours apart. She had been alone, lost in her writing. Click. Click. Click. "I posted the scene, started my laundry, and then went back to FamilyMart."

By then, she was in the fact-checking phase of writing, trying to fill in all the details that the muse had left out. In the scene, it had just been "the blender" and the action had been confusing, mostly because of her own ignorance of the kitchen appliance. Somehow she had lived twenty years without seeing one in person. She had found the Blendtec videos, and it felt right, but none of her searches were pulling up where you could buy them in Japan.

"I'm out of rice and stuff," she said. "I had planned to go food shopping, but I wanted to keep working—polishing the scene—so I got three rice balls for dinner."

She also showed Nakamura some Blendtec videos on her laptop and asked the girl if she had ever seen any for sale. *So not going to mention that.* She realized, though, that she had proof of the third visit. She couldn't tax-deduct food, so normally she didn't keep food receipts. Since she had taken the laptop with her in her backpack, though, she had tucked away the sales slip as she pulled out her computer. "I kept the receipt. It's in the little zippered pocket in the front."

Tanaka unzipped the compartment and pulled out the little slips of paper. Nikki had kept the receipts of her morning shopping because the manga, and possibly both the fireworks and the knife, were all deductible. She would have to check with the Team Banzai members. Tanaka sorted through the receipts and found the one that recorded her trip to the FamilyMart. He uttered one of the Japanese wordless sounds of surprise and slid the slip to Yoshida, who produced a plastic evidence bag and bagged it.

"How long did you talk with her?" Tanaka asked.

This sounded good, like maybe she had an alibi. "I was there fifteen minutes. Maybe twenty minutes. I didn't know what I wanted to eat for dinner. I like to try new stuff, but the panda blood-flavored cookies made me not want to experiment."

She had desperately wanted peanut butter sandwiches, but none of the local food stores carried the tiny jars of Skippy, which was the only way the spread was sold in Japan. She didn't want to make a special trip across town to buy some. "In the end, I got the rice balls because they're a safe bet. I like the salmon-stuffed ones. Then I looked at the manga until no one was there so I could ask Nakamura questions."

Yoshida translated or speculated or talked about the weather. He didn't mention rice balls, which were called *onigiri*, so she wasn't sure what he actually talked to Tanaka about.

Tanaka nodded to whatever Yoshida told him, watching Nikki through his cigarette smoke. "Last time you went?"

"About ten minutes later." She checked on her laundry and then went back to the convenience store without going back up to her apartment. "I wanted to ask Nakamura more questions, but she had gotten off work. I decided to buy something to drink, but I didn't want soda. I looked at the drinks for five or ten minutes. I bought something I thought was grape juice—I don't know what it was—it tasted horrible." She pointed at the pile of receipts. "I think it might have been sake. I kept the receipt to show my friend."

Tanaka shuffled through the papers again and found that she indeed had kept the receipt. She took it as a very good sign that he seemed slightly dismayed by it. He tapped his fingers beside it for a few minutes before asking, "Who else did you talk to about the blender?"

They were considering the possibility that someone else had murdered George's doppelganger. Relief went through Nikki, as she had a trump card on top of the receipts. "I blogged it."

Tanaka glanced to Yoshida, who said something long and detailed. Surely the Japanese knew about blogging. Yoshida got up and left.

"We start again." Tanaka stubbed out his butt and tapped another cigarette out of the pack. His dark eyes studied her closely. "Why are you in Japan?"

"I'm writing a novel set in Japan," she said truthfully. "I came to do research for the book."

"On a tourist visa?"

"I don't qualify for other types of visas. I have another thirty days on my visa." At which time she planned to visit South Korea with Miriam for the weekend and renew the tourist visa upon their return flight. It was the trips out of Japan and back to renew her visa that made her budget so tight. She had been trying to set up a different, longer visa, when her mother forced her early flight. If she could get a three-year artist visa, then her money would stretch further.

Tanaka considered her as he took a long drag on his cigarette and blew out the smoke. "You write about murder?"

Yes? No? If they looked at her blog, they would see it was all she wrote about lately. "Sometimes."

"Sometimes," Tanaka echoed. He studied her another minute. "You do not know this man?"

Nikki shook her head.

"But you wrote of a man being killed with a blender?"

Nikki winced and gave a tiny nod.

"This man—this made-up man—he was American?"

Nikki nodded again.

"And he lived in Umeda where he could see the Ferris wheel?"

She had babbled that out? Yes, she had. "Yes, he did."

Yoshida came back with a laptop, which he pushed toward her. He had a browser up in English. A Tachikoma robotic tank from *Ghost in the Shell* anime peeked around the window from a screensaver. The little forensic scientist was an anime fan.

"Your blog. Show it to us, please." Tanaka pointed at the laptop.

Nikki typed in the address for her author website. She used a pen name in an effort to keep her writing secret from her mother. She had suspected she might want to be able to prove that she was really the author of the book, so she had included photographs of herself, albeit hidden under a secret directory. "Look, see, this is my website."

"Ah!" Tanaka studied the secret pictures closely. "Very sexy."

Nikki blushed. Sheila's brother, Doug, had been the photographer, so Sheila had taken the opportunity to play dress-up and matchmaker. Nikki ended up in a tight leather dress, three-inch stiletto boots, and more hairspray and makeup than she had ever used in her entire life. On the bright side, she doubted her mother would recognize her. On the downside, it had led to a short "thing" with Doug that ended like most of her dating attempts. She was just too creepy for most guys to take for more than a few days.

She went up a level to the public front page that featured her first novel. Luckily, her publisher hadn't gone with the cover that was splattered with blood. "This is my book. I wrote it."

See, I'm a writer, really I am!

Nikki dropped down to her blog, and they read over her Saturday together. Yoshida translated for Tanaka, animating parts with his bird-delicate hands. First post of the day was about the panda-blood cookies. In the second, she ranted on about her love/hate relationship with the Japanese concept of laundry. Hanging everything on bamboo poles on the balcony of her apartment was alternately charming and annoying as hell. Third post was a snippet from her day's work. It was a short chunk of the scene, really just a teasing of fiction. Blood splattering across white countertops. The whirl of a blender. The killer leaning over the dead body, dripping with cast-off blood.

Tanaka gave a slight cry of dismay and pointed at the comment counter. "One hundred and five comments?"

"I have a lot of fans," Nikki temporized. There had been only thirty comments that morning. What had made them triple in number? She scanned anxiously ahead as Tanaka scrolled through them.

Comment thirty-one was from Miriam, using her handle of "SexyNinja." She had posted from her phone "OMG, ThirdEye has been arrested for murder!" Nikki locked down on a groan. Miriam must have gone to Nikki's blog to read the snippet and then posted to it by mistake instead of to the Team Banzai secret forum. There were a half-dozen posts of "Who did she kill?" that did nothing to establish her credibility with the police. Pixii then turned the thread's focus with "George Wilson with a blender!" and that started people posting her memorable murders. The most recent post stated simply, "Dupont, Louisiana, population 1,965." Nikki winced; her friends were not helping. When the list updated with "Dupont, Louisiana, population zero," she reached out and tapped back to the snippet.

Tanaka had been discussing something with Yoshida in Japanese. He turned to her and stated in English, "You posted your blog four hours before Gregory Winston was murdered. The first comments were minutes later."

She nodded, unsure if this was good news or bad.

"Do you have access to the data on who reads this?" Yoshida asked.

"Yes." She logged on to her online analytic software.

Tanaka gave another cry of dismay as the world map showed her hits. "You have fans in Japan?"

"Yes." When she first started to write, she couldn't lock down on any one set of characters and follow their lives to any meaningful end. She'd been depressed by her failures until she started to post them with names changed to that of the anime and manga characters they most resembled. The fan fiction community embraced unfinished work. Thus her audience was worldwide, as the world map clearly showed.

"These hits." Tanaka pointed at Japan on the map. "How many are from Osaka?"

She drilled down a level to get hits from Osaka. On average, there were three dozen hits a day. She frowned at the number. She hadn't checked her statistics for months. She knew that some were Miriam checking in on her. Pixii would have registered as Nara. They didn't account for all of the hits. Who else was reading her blog from Osaka?

"Did you post other things about this character before this?" Tanaka asked. "What he looked like? Where he lived?"

"Yes, lots of stuff." Her muse poured out a rough story. There was always the need, however, for her to fill in details to knit the bare bones into a logical narrative. In the past, she often ended up with writer's block over specifics. Who was this person? What did they look like? What was their name? Where was this scene taking place? How did the character get there? And most importantly, how did this fit in with the rest of the book?

She constantly had to dig through the Internet, looking for the stupidest information. Little things that most readers would never know if she got wrong. How many people that read *Dupont* would know if she got the type of bleachers wrong at the high school football field? Yet she'd been stalled for a week until she found a random photo on someone's Facebook page that was set as public.

She discovered if she visited the story's setting, she could quickly pick out most of the details to flesh out the rough scene. It was the main reason she set the book in Japan. (It also meant she could tax-deduct all of her travel and any entrance fees.) Knowing that many of her readers loved all things Japanese as a by-product of being fans of anime and manga, she blogged extensively about her research trips to promote both books. "I could show you the posts."

She worked back through her blog to find the public debate with herself over where George Wilson should live. She'd locked onto the Umeda district quickly but wasn't sure where. There were the twin towers of the Umeda Sky Building with the rooftop observatory suspended between them. She toured the skyscrapers and had been impressed with the panoramic views, but it hadn't felt right. The Japanese had a love affair with Ferris wheels and thus they appeared often in anime. The HEP Five building had one on its rooftop. For some reason she felt as if George's apartment should feature a window that framed the Ferris wheel until it was larger than life. She decided to work backwards by taking a ride on the Ferris wheel to see which apartment buildings had a view of the structure. Of course only a handful of her readers would ever know if she got it right—but she would be stuck until she figured it out for herself. She couldn't afford the delay.

What she hadn't realized was that her fear of heights would kick in on the Ferris wheel. She'd been fine during her visit to the rooftop of the Umeda Sky Building; her only shaky moment had been on the steep escalators that crossed from one tower to the other, seventy-eight floors above the street. It hadn't helped that Miriam decided to torture Nikki on the Ferris wheel.

Nikki had uploaded a video she had shot during the ride. It was embarrassing, but she did make the funniest squeaking noises every time Miriam made the car sway. She had edited in a pointer to the video so viewers could see the building that she eventually picked out.

Tanaka shook his head through the entire video. When it ended, he said, "So, everyone knows that your character lives in that building?"

She nodded, and then it hit her. She looked down at the photograph of the dead man. "He lived in the same building?"

Tanaka nodded. "Miss Delany, is it possible that you have a very disturbed fan?"

⚜ 4 ⚜
Little Bighorn

Nikki wasn't sure if having a psycho fan was a good thing. Actually she was fairly certain it was a bad thing, but at least it meant she was off the hook for the murder of Gregory Winston. At least, that's what she assumed for a few minutes. The police, however, showed no signs of planning to let her go.

Just as it was becoming clear that they meant to hold her, the door opened and a female police officer stepped into the room. She bowed, apologized for interrupting with *"Gomenasai."* The reason for her interruption was hovering right behind her, a man in a hand-tailored, pinstripe suit whose appearance screamed "American." He was tall and broad, as only a steak-fed male could be.

The American went through the elaborate formal introduction with Tanaka and Yoshida. Business cards were exchanged and carefully studied.

Nikki knew a handshake was coming—politicians lived on their handshake—so she tucked away her stolen pen and braced herself.

"Miss Delany? I'm Terrence Walcott." He bowed first, out of habit, which meant he'd been in Japan for a long time. He had a very faint Southern accent, which was ironic, because Osaka natives had a similar slight drawl to their Japanese. He held out his hand. She gave him a "we are close allies" firm shake that ended with her left hand covering their joined hands, just for a few seconds, enough to imply a warmth and intimacy of close association. She read it striking home with a slight shift in his face.

"I'm with the consulate here in Osaka," he said. "I'm sorry we have to meet under such circumstances. We had a call—" He paused to change what he was going to say. "I understand you were arrested in the murder of Gregory Winston?"

Miriam must have found out that there was an actual murder attached to Nikki's arrest. Only something as serious as Nikki being railroaded for murder would have made Miriam call the American embassy. What exactly had Miriam told them? Not the whole truth, or the man would have addressed Nikki as a senator's only child, not as one of the questionable masses. Judging by what he almost said, Miriam only told them enough to get him to the police.

Nikki doubted that she could keep Walcott from finding out who her mother was eventually, but she certainly wasn't going to tell him at this point. She kept to what he needed to know to get her released. "I'm a published author researching a novel already under contract that is set in Japan. I never met Gregory Winston. I was never in the building where he lived. I have an alibi for the time of his death. I was in Otemae at the time of the murder. I've already presented proof of that."

He nodded along with her bullet points. "Please, Miss Delany, let me get caught up and then I'll see about getting them to release you."

Walcott and Tanaka engaged in an epic Japanese conversation with occasional tangents with Yoshida riddled with English computer terms. Obviously they were telling Walcott about her website. They didn't actually tell him the url or her pen name. She took out her stolen pen and clicked it quietly, trying not to think of standard embassy protocol that basically would fire off a signal flare through the US State Department with her present location.

At the end, Walcott turned to her and asked, "Miss Delany, have you had previous problems with stalkers?"

Only my mother. "No."

"The police say Gregory Winston's neighbors called 119 before he was actually killed. There was a fight that started with someone coming to his door and ringing his doorbell. The call has his screams recorded in the background. The police know the exact time of his death, and you were in Otemae during this time. Officer Yoshida says that the attacker was much taller than you."

It never even occurred to her to ask anything about the actual murder. She simply assumed they wouldn't tell her. Then again, they probably wouldn't have told *her*.

"And I'm still here—why?"

"They're not discounting that you might know the attacker."

"I don't know anyone in Japan." Wait, Yoshida and Tanaka had seen Miriam. "Except for the girl I was having lunch with." Shit, she couldn't let them think that Miriam had anything to do with this. "And she's only an inch or two taller than me." And could totally kick ass when it came to fighting. "I've been posting information on my character George for three weeks. If some nutcase reads my blog, they could have already picked out Gregory as the closest matchup to my character a long time ago. One of the reasons I put George in Umeda was because of the number of expats living there. The police said I posted that snippet four hours before Gregory Winston was killed. That would give this psycho fan enough time to get to George's—to Winston's apartment and murder him."

"Do you have any fans that may be that crazy?"

She stopped and gave it a long, honest consideration. She was writer; written words revealed more to her than to the normal person. Had she ever read any blog comments that even suggested homicidal tendencies? Any off-the-wall remarks on her twitter feed? Nothing came to mind. "No. I don't know who is reading my blog here in Osaka. I honestly wasn't aware of the number of hits. I used to compulsively check my stats before my first novel sold; it was a way to stroke my ego. I stopped needing that kind of egoboo when I got my first check."

Walcott nodded and turned back to the policeman and the discussion continued in Japanese. Nikki closed her eyes, and thought of tropical beaches, and clicked her stolen pen. She needed to write soon or she was going to explode. Maybe she should ask to go to the bathroom and . . .

Oh damn, this was Japan; public restrooms didn't have toilet paper or paper towels. She flinched as the "OMG" baseball bat of cultural shock hit her.

Walcott turned back to her, his face warning her that she wasn't going to like what he was about to say. "If you cooperate, the police will let you go. I recommend that you cooperate fully."

"And what exactly is cooperating?"

"They'll need your DNA and fingerprints to compare with unknowns found at the murder scene. And they want your password for your analytical software so they can track hits to your blog. And they want you to take down the scene."

They weren't going to find any matches to her fingerprints because she'd never been in any of the private buildings in Umeda. Same with DNA. Giving away her password was annoying, but she kept all her websites carefully compartmentalized so discovery of one wouldn't compromise the others.

Most importantly, a real man was dead and chances were good that someone with very violent antisocial tendencies had been following her every move.

"Okay. I'll cooperate."

Dusk was falling when she and Walcott finally walked out of the police headquarters. She was starving, and she desperately needed to write. For the last half hour, between chewing on her fingernails, she'd been madly clicking her pen and cycling through every single deserted-island fantasy she'd ever constructed. She needed to scrape off Walcott, find something to eat before the need to write completely took her, and then let the muse run loose.

Rush hour was starting, filling the streets with tiny cars and miniature trucks and office workers on town bicycles. The subway station was down the hill, the same direction as her apartment building, so Terrence walked with her. They were the only non-Asians on the street. Everyone moving purposely around them was short, slim, dark-haired, and dark-eyed.

"Are you going to be safe?" Mr. Walcott asked.

It was hard not to be angry with him; he was about to unknowingly bring her mother down on her. Nikki reminded herself that he did get her away from the Japanese police. *Play nice with the man; he could be an ally in the coming war.*

"Yes, I'll be fine. I'm very capable of taking care of myself." *I've been doing it off and on since I was eight.*

He looked down at her, worry written all over his face. "It's just that you've posted a lot of personal information."

Nikki laughed. "Not really!" Of course she hadn't; her mother had trained her well. "It only seems like it. Yes, I talked about getting my apartment. How small it is. That it doesn't have an oven. That it has an on-demand hot-water heater. I even posted pictures of the interior. I didn't mention that I was in Otemae neighborhood, that I'm in a building that caters to *gaijin*, or that I'm on a monthly lease. None of the photos showed the exterior of the building or even the view from my balcony. When I post that I've gone someplace—like the Hanshin department store that's in Umeda—I don't say if I took the subway or just walked across the street."

Nor could anyone trace her via her apartment IP address—as she always used an anonymous proxy service that masked her location.

"I see. That makes me feel better. Please, be very careful." He shook her hand firmly and then went down the steps into the subway.

She went to the corner. There was a rare break in the traffic, but no one moved to cross the street until the walk light came on. She had discovered quickly that the Japanese always waited for the walk light and always crossed at the corner. She had seen people stop in the middle of the night and wait on deserted street corners for the walk light to give them permission to cross. Jaywalking was simply not done. Terrence Walcott was getting on to a subway train full of people texting like mad because talking on cell phones was against the rules. No one would be eating or drinking. There was no graffiti on any of the walls, all posters were carefully placed in accordance with the law, and people carried little portable ashtrays for their cigarette butts.

How did she find—in this city full of obedient, lawful people—a person looking for inspiration to kill?

Despite her screaming need to write, she stopped at FamilyMart to pick up dinner. She had learned the hard way that the hungrier she was, the longer her hypergraphia took to burn out.

News that the strange American woman was linked to a murder must have filtered through the employees. The male cashier startled visibly when she came through the door. He watched her nervously as she picked up a basket and walked to the ready-made meals. She picked up a pre-cooked *okonomiyaki* to make up for the one left behind with Miriam. The rice balls looked good, so she got three of those. She added two of her favorite filled buns to her basket before she realized that hunger and stress were nose-diving her into a major pig-out.

But if being stalked by a killer wasn't justification for a pig-out, nothing was. Generally she avoided alcohol, but she was feeling the need for some medicine-induced calm. She studied the alcohol selection. Between her lack of experience in drinking and the labels in Japanese, she had no clue if she would like the liquid inside.

Miriam picked up on the first ring. "Where are you? Are you okay?"

"What is decent to drink here?" She turned her cell phone's camera on to the wine selection.

"Oh, good, they let you go!" Miriam said. "You would like the stuff in the little dark green bottles. It's a plum wine. It's very sweet and mild."

"Yes, I'm free." Nikki picked up the miniature bottle of wine. The label claimed that it held two hundred milliliters; she probably could down it in three swallows. Not really enough, it seemed, for self-medication. She added a second bottle to her basket and headed for the check-out counter. She picked up a Snickers and a Kit Kat as she passed through the candy aisle.

"I'm so sorry," Miriam said. "I called the consulate. I was really worried that you would end up in prison."

"It's probably the only reason I'm free." Nikki watched the clerk scan her purchases with shaking hands. What did the police say to the employees? Had they explained the blender? "They really didn't want to let me go."

"I shouldn't have teased that *salaryman*. I had no idea that he would take us so seriously!" Miriam cried. "I'm really, really sorry."

"It's not your fault." Nikki tucked her phone under her chin, dug out her change purse, and counted out thirty thousand yen to cover the major splurge. "This is more than a run-of-the-mill murder. There's a shitload more." The clerk's eyes had gone huge. Apparently he spoke English enough to understand the word "murder." "Just hold on a minute."

Nikki collected her change. She unwrapped a rice ball, took a big bite, and headed out onto the street to get the automatic door between her and the listening clerk. "I've got a psycho fan that killed a man using a blender in the apartment building that my character lived in! Get this: a Gregory Winston instead of George Wilson."

"Shit!" Miriam said. "What about the others?"

"Others?" Nikki asked.

"Well, you've killed like three men and two women so far, right? Four men if you count the Brit."

Nikki jerked to a halt, and her stomach did a sickening flip. "Oh shit! Oh shit! Oh shit!"

"Nikki?"

"Oh shit!"

"You did talk to the police about the other characters. Didn't you?"

"No! Oh shit!" The police were bound to find out. They were crawling all over her website when she left. "Wait! I didn't blog about them!"

There was a clicking of keys from Miriam's side. "Hmm, you're right. It doesn't seem as if you did. So you're good—unless . . ."

"Unless what?"

"Well—unless your psycho fan did something like hack your computer."

❈ 5 ❈
Scary Cat Dude

She couldn't hold off the need to write any longer. She dumped her FamilyMart bags right inside the door of her apartment and sat on the floor to fumble through her backpack. She needed her new notebook. Writing on the computer never satisfied the need. Pen and paper was the only way.

Luckily her hypergraphia liked the small Campus notebooks, approximately five inches by seven inches, which all the Japanese schoolchildren used in class, so they were easy to find. Despite being created for *kanji*, the lines were nearly the same as college-rule width. She was never without at least one tucked into her bag.

She found the notebook. With hands shaking, she opened it. She numbered the inside cover and dated it. The smell of ink was pure nirvana to her stressed nerves. She was able to pause, pen hovering over paper, and consider what she should write.

As Miriam pointed out, she needed a new romantic hero.

Her problem with characters dying wasn't new. That was the other damning part of the equation with her hypergraphia. If she wrote about kittens and rainbows, her mother probably wouldn't be trying to lock her up. Horrible things happened to her nice and not-so-nice and sometimes outright nasty characters. It had been a graphic disembowelment—complete with descriptions of steaming coils of intestines—that triggered her first visit to a psychiatrist. Her novel attempts were usually wastelands of death, ending abruptly as all the characters met their untimely end. The novel she had sold had been a miracle of keeping the hero and heroine alive long enough to reach a happy ending. They died soon afterwards, but she chopped that part off.

Good for her, since romantic thrillers were big. Bad for her, since it meant that her next book also had to be a romantic thriller, and her publisher had given her only a year to write it. Between the two, Nikki decided to base the heroine on herself. "Natasha" was an up-and-coming-but-still-starving artist deeply in love with Japanese culture. While Natasha was leading a very safe but somewhat uninteresting life exploring Osaka, all her hero candidates had died—violently—without even meeting Natasha. George was just the most recent. Nikki was starting to worry about making her deadline. She needed a hero. A *romantic* hero. A stud muffin.

Perhaps that was the problem. She wasn't creating heavily armed, dangerous survivors. So far all the men were nice, normal people. *Salarymen.* Unarmed cream puffs. Very dead stud muffins. She needed a hero with a gun who knew how to use it.

It was time for her to create an ass-kicking, name-taking hero.

He felt like Death. He watched over the dead, dressed in black, wrapped in his own silence that no one disturbed. To those around him on the bystander side of the yellow police tape, the murder scene was strange and new, at once horrifying and fascinating. They were the people that lived in the nearby houses, drawn by the bright carnival of police lights, and now stood watching with eyes round and hands over their mouths.

He was more familiar with death than even the Kyoto police on the other side of the barrier. The police understood the principles of snapping a neck. They recorded and documented the results with close study of murder victims. They had never reached out, grabbed tight of a living being, and given the hard twist and felt the struggling body go limp.

He was Death, but this wasn't his work. There was another killer in Kyoto. So he stood and watched.

Police had brought in harsh work lights, trying to hold off the night as they investigated the murder scene. The uniformed officers were taking pictures: bright flashes of light against the darkness. A detective in a suit was questioning a woman. The witness was wearing a sheer baby-doll top and a miniskirt that was barely decent. She was dancing in place, trying to keep warm, shaking her head.

"I told the other officer everything I know," the witness said. "Can I go? I'm freezing."

"Miss Ogawa, I just have a few more questions," the detective said. "You live near here?"

"Yes. I told the other officer." Miss Ogawa rubbed her arms. "I live just down the hill. I thought I heard my neighbor's kitten crying. I was looking for it when I saw the foot sticking out of the pile of leaves."

"What's your neighbor's name?" the detective asked.

"Fujita Yuuka," Miss Ogawa said. "She's a shrine maiden at Ikuta Shrine; the one that burned this afternoon." She pointed up the hill toward the smoldering ruins of a Shinto shrine. "Can we walk down to my apartment, where it's warm and I can answer these questions? I've been out here for hours now."

After the heat of the day, the night seemed chilly but it really wasn't that cold. More likely, she wanted to get away from the dead body. The Japanese believed strongly in ghosts.

The detective studied the house down the slope from the crime scene and then swept his gaze up the steep hillside to where the body lay. "You came all the way up here because of a cat meowing?"

The woman missed the importance of the question. It was likely that the police had determined that it was Yuuka under the thin layer of leaves. The detective was trying to figure out if Ogawa had any link to the murder.

"I heard that Mr. Fujita had been badly burned in the fire," Miss Ogawa said. "I figured that Yuuka's at the hospital with him. Poor kid. It would be bad enough to lose the shrine and her father in one blow, but her kitten, too?"

"And exactly where is the kitten now?" The detective obviously didn't believe there was a cat.

Miss Ogawa scanned the woods around them. "It ran off before I could catch it. I hope it's okay."

"When was the last time you saw Yuuka?" the detective asked.

He could tell the police that the killer had been a large man who had sexually assaulted the dead girl after he killed her. While the police wasted their time, though, questioning Miss Ogawa, he could study the primary crime scene before anyone could disturb it further.

Careful not to draw attention to himself, he turned and walked away. Once he was cloaked in darkness, he went up the hill toward the burnt shrine.

Halfway up, he found the kitten. Or perhaps more accurately, the kitten found him. In a sudden rustle of dead leaves, it came bounding out of the undergrowth and started to scale his leg with needle pricks of claws. He reached down and caught it before it reached his knees. It was a tiny orange bundle of fur and sharp claws and a rough purr.

"What do you think you're doing?" he asked it.

It gave a little squeak of meow in answer.

He shook his head and continued up the hill. He might as well take it with him. If nothing else, it gave him an alibi for poking around the smoking ruins. Besides, if he left the kitten behind, it would get lost again.

Like most temples, there was a little storefront that sold charms and fortunes that supplemented the offering income. The building had been deliberately set on fire. He could smell the kerosene used as accelerant. The ancient timbers would have gone up like paper. The fire had spread to other buildings. He stalked through the blackened landscape, cinders crackling under his feet.

His cell phone vibrated quietly, reminding him that he was on a tight leash. He stood a moment, hand clenched tight around his phone as it rang again. Another ring and it would go to voicemail and a timer would start before someone would come hunting him. He was only trusted as long as he stayed on his leash.

He took a deep breath and accepted the call. "What?"

There was silence from the other side except for measured breathing.

He growled in anger. "Someone set fire to a shrine to cover his tracks. He killed and raped a shrine maiden. Am I done here?"

"The shrine is dedicated to Taira no Atsumori. He's enshrined in a *katana*."

He studied the small, upraised building behind the main worship hall. The *honden* would have housed the god's *shintai*. Nothing was left of the building but smoldering timbers. The *katana* would have been made of the highest quality steel by one of Japan's legendary sword makers. This one was imbued with the power of a spirit worshiped as a god. It would have easily survived this fire. He should be able to sense the presence of the *kami* even if the sword was buried in the smoking ashes. "It's not here."

"Any sign of who took the *katana*?"

"From what I can tell, it was a lone male. He was a tall, heavy man. He's about six foot three. Close to two hundred pounds. He's taken a splash bath in Ralph Lauren's Polo Black to cover the fact he sweats like a pig. Between his size and grooming habits, I'm going to say he's American."

That triggered a quiet "hmm."

He waited, teeth clenched. None of this had anything to do with Simon. The trail was growing colder and colder as he was kept running in circles.

"A man matching that description was murdered in Umeda district of Osaka last night. The police report mentions that he has a number of antiques in his apartment, but they didn't catalog them."

"If he was killed for the sword, it's not going to be there." He didn't want to waste more time.

"Go to Osaka. See if this was the same man and find out if the sword is still at his apartment."

The need to write satisfied, Nikki flopped back to lie on the floor.

Ass-kicking: check. Name-taking: check. Hero? Nikki wasn't sure. The important thing was she could face the rest of the day feeling somewhat sane.

She flexed her right hand to work out the cramps, and glanced at her wristwatch. She'd been writing for two hours. Out of habit, she written in tiny little neat letters, sandwiching two rows of sentences between the faint blue lines of the notebook paper.

She finished her writing ritual by picking a Post-It Note color for the new character. For some reason, he felt like a turquoise. Lacking a name for him, she labeled his Post-It: Scary Cat Dude. She added him to the collage on her apartment wall and shifted the note for Yuuka's kitten to his story thread.

That done, she stepped back, looked at the wall, and cringed.

Her collage of Post-It Notes was one of the few organizational tools that worked for her. Her novels were seemingly random scenes of people struggling with day-to-day lives. She needed this vast tree of notes to understand why any one character was part of her story. In light of Gregory Winston's murder, though, her story tree looked like something a serial killer would produce.

There were times Nikki wished she were more in control of her writing. She had thought George was a hero. With each scene, though, he'd drifted more and more toward being a villain. In the end, he'd set the fire to the shrine and killed Yuuka. Heroes did not rape dead teenage girls. After George's binge in villainy, she hadn't felt bad about his messy death. It had felt somewhat karmic; he nearly deserved it.

But Gregory Winston hadn't.

Probably.

The police hadn't told her anything about Gregory. Nor had they mentioned any other murders in the area. The question remained if her stalker had also killed stand-ins for her dead characters. Had he killed a shrine maiden in Kyoto? Kidnapped a British man? Tortured a pregnant woman?

She pulled out her laptop and did her best to track down recent murder cases in Japan. As always, she found herself fumbling with the language barrier. Tourism sites were expertly translated, as were top stories of world importance. Gregory's death had made the news wires as "an American expatriate murdered in Osaka," but the exact details were being kept out of the media. She could find no indication that a teenage girl had been murdered in Kyoto. Yuuka's body, though, had been hidden away in her novel and found only in the newly written scene. A search for "temple fire" spammed her with hits scattered across the country. Apparently old wooden buildings had a habit of catching fire. "Kyoto," "temple," and "arson" got her hits on the Golden Pavilion, but that famous fire had been in the summer of 1950.

She wasn't even sure how to track down details matching the other murders she had written. In her scenes, the killings had been in vaguely described locations and the bodies had quietly but mysteriously "disposed."

There seemed to be only one way to find out if someone had used her story to plan a murder: go to Gregory's apartment building. What she posted was fairly vague. The actual polished scene had lots of telling details. If those details matched up, then her psychopath fan had full access to her files.

She ate the rice balls as she loaded up her backpack with everything she might need. Subway map. Umbrella. Flashlight. Lock picks. The last thing Nikki did as she left her apartment was make sure she wasn't being followed.

6
Scene of the Crime

Nikki always got lost in the Umeda Station as it tangled itself in and around several underground malls, the basements of several large department stores, and Osaka Station. None of the maps she'd found thus far covered all of the connected areas, so it remained an unknowable maze. Some of the streets around the station were only crossable via pedestrian bridges, which created their own midair maze. Nikki would surface at various exits, like a confused gopher, get her bearings, and plunge back into the labyrinth.

She finally found one of her landmarks—a literal notch in the wall serving unidentified meat on a stick with a *noren* curtain separating its standing customers from the flow of commuters. From there she found signs for HEP Five. She often suspected she had walked in a big circle, but so far she hadn't found an easier way through the network of malls and subway lines.

HEP Five was a tall, narrow shopping complex with high-end boutiques that cratered to wealthy twenty-something. George's building was east of HEP Five. She used her cell phone to guide her to the right set of doors and out onto the street.

There was a KFC at the corner, the Colonel's familiar face beaming down at her in triplicate.

Nikki's stomach was doing strange flip-flops as she headed toward George's building. She had no idea what she was walking into—or

even if she could. She might not be able to get through the building's
security. As she walked toward it, a woman used keys to unlock the
foyer door and walked into the building.

How was she going to get in?

She noticed an American man with a suitcase heading toward the
front door. She fell into step behind him, pretending to search her
purse for keys.

*Don't mind me. I live here. Just lost my key. See. Harmless. Not
wanted for murder at all.*

Amazingly, it worked. Being short and harmless-looking had its
advantages.

The lobby was typical of Osaka: a narrow slit between two
restaurants leading back to a tiny elevator.

The man with the suitcase took notice of Nikki as they stood
waiting for the elevator. She kept digging in her purse. She made the
mistake of peeking up and found him eying her with suspicion.

"I've never seen you here before."

Her heart flipped in her chest. "Um, I'm new. I just moved in the
other day."

"I didn't know anyone was selling a unit."

"I'm subletting, actually. It's a friend of a friend kind of thing."
She fell back to George's conflict line. "He was here on a sponsored
visa and got laid off from work. He's trying to line up another job,
but he had to go home to get a tourist visa, and he decided to spend
some time in the States visiting family. It was cheaper for me to
sublet than do a weekly mansion." The fact that her appartment was
in a no-deposit mansion building was another reason she was having
money problems.

"Greg Winston?" The man pointed upwards. "Up on fourteen?"

She nodded.

"That was quick." The elevator dinged, and the doors slid open.
"He was still trying to figure out what he was going to do when I left."
He motioned for her to get on first, and then wheeled in his luggage.
"I'm Stewart Robertson. I was just in the States, visiting family and
renewing my tourist visa."

"Small world," she said.

"Life as an expatriate," the man said. "Juggling truths and lies to
stay in the country."

He tapped the buttons for the third floor and the fourteenth. "Welcome to the hood. We do mixers Thursday nights, but people probably told you that already."

"Yeah, everyone's been so nice."

He got off on the third floor, saying, "See you later."

Nikki rode up to the fourteenth floor. She had never bothered to figure out what floor George lived on, just that he was high up enough to clear the other buildings between him and the HEP Five. It was really freaking her out that the killer managed to match up a man that lived not only in the right building, but had the identical visa problem.

Only Miriam knew about George's visa problems. It might be proof that the killer had access to Nikki's files. The killer could have picked Gregory just because his name was close to George. The visa trouble might have been just coincidence; all expatriates faced endless visa struggles unless they married someone who was Japanese. She only had thirty days before she ran into the problem herself. Or maybe Gregory just had the bad luck to be home while someone—like Stewart from the elevator—wasn't. Hell, her demented fan might have just rung doorbell after doorbell until a man answered.

The elevator stopped on fourteen, and the door opened. She hesitated until the door started to close again, and then she hopped out. Around the corner from the elevator, the door to 1401 had police tape across it.

At that point Nikki went into a major debate with herself. She should just leave. She was scared. She was in enough trouble with the police. Crossing a police barrier to a murder scene where she was a suspect would be dumb. She could end up in prison just for breaking and entering. True, it meant someone else would pay for her housing and food, but she was fairly sure the food would be bad and the sheets would have a low thread count. And God, the hypergraphia in a true prison might be impossible to deal with.

The only way Nikki was going to see if her psychopath had copied her novel was to see the murder scene.

She was scared, but it was scarier, though, to stay clueless to whether or not someone who could kill a man with a blender had full access to her computer files.

Oh God, I'm going into this apartment.

Nikki wasn't sure if she had won or lost the debate, but that was always the problem of fighting with herself.

She took out her lock picks. It seemed to take forever to pick the lock, even though Nikki knew it couldn't have been more than two minutes. It was the longest two minutes of her life. She kept expecting the elevator to ding, signaling someone's arrival, or one of the neighboring doors to open. But she got the door open, slipped into the unlit apartment, and shut the door without being caught.

In the dark, the coppery smell of blood pressed in on Nikki, heavy and thick as a blanket. The stench was so oppressive it seemed as if she had to be standing in blood. Fear prickled the hair on her arms, and she shifted her feet, expecting a horrible stickiness underfoot. The tile under her feet, though, was clean.

Across the apartment, framed by glass doors to the balcony, the framework of the HEP Five Ferris wheel gleamed blood red like a giant demonic spider web. It was nowhere near as romantic as she had thought it would be.

Slowly her eyes adjusted to the dark. She was in a foyer, with the kitchen directly to her right. A door to her left stood open to a bathroom dark as a cave. The apartment was all shadows and pools of darkness, evidence of violence—beyond the smell of blood—cloaked.

Nikki fumbled for the light switch, found it, and turned on the light.

More than the countertops had been white. The floor and the cabinets were white. Blood splattered everything, from the floor to the ceiling, dried to ruddy red, stark against the white.

Too scary. She turned the light off and then wiped it clean of fingerprints. It was a good thing she had just had a massive writing session, because otherwise she'd be digging for her retractable pen.

What was she doing there? What did she want to find again? Oh, yes, she was trying to see if the killer had copied elements of her book that she hadn't made public. She leaned against the door, eyes closed, trying to figure out what she had written that *could* be copied.

In the kitchen with a blender: check. But she had posted that.

A man with the initials GW living in this building: check. But that she had posted, too.

Sake cup on the counter.

Nikki fished her flashlight out of her bag to avoid turning on the overhead light again. There was no *sake* cup on the blood-splattered counter. She felt relieved until she realized that the police might have taken it as evidence.

What else could point to the killer having had access to her files? She crept through the apartment, running her flashlight over the contents. It was a clean, simple place, much as she had imagined it. Sleek modern furniture mixed with Japanese antiques in a way that Nikki wished she had the money to emulate. She would give her eyeteeth for the lacquered sword *tansu* that Gregory was using as a coffee table or the beautiful wedding kimono on the wall.

In the bedroom was a tall *tansu* with a dozen drawers standing in as a dresser. In the bottommost drawer was a coil of heavy jute rope. She eyed it without touching it. George had a sick little fetish for tying up schoolgirls; it was what truly lay behind his rape of Yuuka's body. He liked his sexual partners young and helpless. With Yuuka, he'd discovered the ultimate in helplessness was dead.

Did Gregory have the same fetish or had the killer put this here? The rope was the type used in the ancient Japanese practice of bondage called *kinbaku*. She had learned much more than she wanted while researching George's scenes. She closed the drawer without being able to decide what it meant in terms of her stalker.

She was about to give up when she saw an Isetan Department Store bag in the bedroom trash can. She stared at it, feeling sick. There wasn't an Isetan in Osaka. There was one in Kyoto, anchoring down half of the sprawling train station. George had gone to Kyoto to steal an antique samurai sword enshrined at a local temple. When he reached the train station, he realized that he had no plan on how to get the sword back to Osaka. He stopped at Isetan's and bought a case used by high school students to carry wooden practice swords to and from school.

After he'd stolen the sword and killed Yuuka, he'd taken a crowded express train back to Osaka with the case slung across his shoulders. The whole trip he felt as if he was being watched. By the time he reached Osaka, he wanted to be rid of the incriminating sword, so he left it in one of the coin lockers at the train station. It wasn't until he reached his apartment that he realized he still had the Isetan bag folded up in his pocket. He'd taken it out and tossed it in the bedroom trash can where it seemed to taunt him with his guilt.

To anyone else, it was just a simple plastic bag. To Nikki, it was like the blood on Lady Macbeth's hands. *Out, damn'd spot. Out, I say!*

Had Gregory just coincidently been at Kyoto and shopped at Isetan or had his killer left the bag in the trash, slavishly recreating her book? She used facial tissues as impromptu gloves and carefully took it out of the trash. Inside was a sales receipt. It was dated Saturday, a few hours before Gregory had been killed. She took out her phone, scanned the *kanji* of the item bought and ran it through her translation app. *Bamboo sword bag.*

She dropped the receipt in horror, and then hastily picked it back up with the tissue, fumbled to get it back into the Isetan bag, and shoved both into the bedroom trash can. A minute later, she was out of the apartment and, a minute after that, she was running away from the building.

"Who in fucking hell is this crazy! What kind of whacko would go through that much fucking trouble? Go to Kyoto, buy a bag . . ."

Oh God, what else had he done in Kyoto?

She dug out her ballpoint pen and stood clicking it and practiced her deep breathing as she tried to think in some calm, rational way.

Data on her Internet searches went onto the net and came back to her. When she was just researching her novel, she never bothered to use a proxy service to disguise her apartment's IP address. Anyone could have intercepted her searches and deduced information. She'd tried several times to pull up "Isetan Kyoto *Fukuro Shinai*" before discovering it didn't mean "bag for bamboo sword" but "bamboo sword wrapped with leather." After that, she'd searched English sites for "shinai bag." It wouldn't take much to realize that she wanted to buy the bag at Isetan in Kyoto.

What she hadn't researched on the Internet were the coin lockers. She had sacrificed half an hour and a few hundred yen to find out how they worked. The only place that the exact locker number and PIN number for the digital lock were recorded was in her password-protected documents.

She would have to cross through the train station to find her way back to the subway. She only knew one way to go. It would only take her a minute to check the locker.

If the killer had left something for her to find, then he was way beyond slightly deranged. How did she attract such a monolithic loon before her second book came out?

Nikki scurried back through the underground maze linked to Umeda Station. She wasn't sure how long the locker rental was good for. Eight hours? Only until the last train of the day? A full day? If the killer left something in a locker before he had killed Gregory, it was drawing close to twenty-four hours now.

There was so much she didn't know.

She felt like she was lost in a dark, shifting ocean. All around her were people she couldn't understand, signs she couldn't read, as she tried to find her way through the complex of malls and subway stations. So completely lost.

What the hell was she going to do when she reached Osaka Station? She had Tanaka's business card; he had pressed it on her before she left police headquarters. She could call him and ask him meet her at the station. The digital key meant she didn't have to mention her little tour of Gregory Winston's apartment. If she couldn't get into the locker, she only looked like she was histrionic.

But what if she could get into the locker? What did she tell Tanaka? How did she explain knowing the PIN? If she told Tanaka that it was in her manuscript but not posted to her blog, then he'd know she'd been hacked, and would probably get a warrant for her computer. Maybe. More likely, he'd just assume she was working with the killer.

Surely there would be security cameras on the lockers. If Tanaka checked the video from them, he would find out who used the locker last. But what if Tanaka didn't check them? What if he didn't believe the killer had hacked into her computer files? It was more logical that she knew the PIN number because she had programmed it in. She couldn't force them to check the security cameras. She could only count on them weighing the circumstantial evidence, and it made her look like an accomplice.

No. She wouldn't call the police—unless there was a dead body. A corpse would trump everything. There shouldn't be any dead bodies, though, if the killer was sticking to script. Japanese were lawful people—surely the killer would keep to her story. Of course, maybe the killer was some imported, crazed, American serial killer; they couldn't be trusted.

She was probably on a wild goose chase.

Besides, how would the killer get a dead body into the train station unnoticed?

Body parts, on the other hand, were a possibility.

Her stomach was doing cartwheels by the time she found her landmark niche restaurant. It had closed for the night, a steel gate rolled down over it. Beside it were steps up to the street level. There was probably some underground link to Osaka Station from Umeda Station since it seemed like half of Umeda was tied to the underground complex, but she hadn't found it yet. Instead she went up the steps and across an alley and into Osaka Station.

At least the coin locker that she wanted was right by the door.

She stood eyeing it nervously. The "in use" light was on. Something was in it. She went to the touch-screen control panel for the bank of lockers, hit the English button, and selected the "take out the baggage" option. It asked her for the key she used. She picked the cash payment option of "key number." It asked for the locker number and PIN number. Her hand was shaking as she keyed both in.

There was a pause, and the machine asked for eight hundred yen.

"Shit," she hissed. Did that mean the PIN was right?

Nikki dug out hundred-yen coins, dropped the first coin twice before she managed to feed it into the machine. She was short a hundred yen coin, and she mindlessly fed five-and-ten yen coins in until the machine flashed "Thank you for use" and spit three of her last coins back out at her.

The "in use" light was flashing. The door was unlocked.

"Please," she whispered. "No body parts."

She opened up the door.

George had left a *katana* in the locker. She had figured he couldn't carry a sword on the train without some kind of covering. She had picked out a light brown cotton fabric kendo travel bag with little dragonflies stamped randomly in white and red.

Something tall and skinny leaned in shadows of the locker, wrapped in a tan fabric.

Well, at least it wasn't a body part.

7
In the Shadow of the Swallowtail

Nikki had been annoyed and dismayed when George stole the antique *katana* in Kyoto. He was supposed to be her romantic interest. There he was splashing kerosene onto the back of a temple's gift shop to create a diversion for his theft.

Of course, her hypergraphia had just scribbled "the sword" into her notebook without any description. George had been too caught up in the fear and excitement of his escalating crime to even notice what he clutched in his hand. After he killed and raped Yuuka, he nearly left it lying beside her dead body as he staggered away. He came back for it only after the sirens of the fire engines brought him to his senses.

Nikki would have been stuck on the scene until she fleshed out all the little details, so she had thrown herself into researching samurai swords. She learned that the hilt of the *katana* wasn't one solid piece but nearly a dozen items carefully fitted together. The hand guard, called a *tsuba*, was a disc of metal about three inches across with a slot in the center. Each *tsuba* was a hand-crafted piece of art and often had the samurai's family crest, called a *mon*, worked into the design. After looking at dozens of web pages, she decided that the stolen *katana* had a *tsuba* made from a metal of gold and copper with a dark blue-purple patina called *shakudo*. It featured a swallowtail butterfly *mon* done in gold leaf against the purple.

Surely the killer hadn't stuck that closely to the script.

Nikki lifted out the bag, undid the ties, and shifted the fabric aside to look closer at the sword inside. Gold swallowtail wings gleamed on a violet field.

She suddenly had an intense feeling that someone was watching her. She glanced around. Hundreds of people flowed around her, coming and going through the gates to the train platforms. Focused on getting to their destinations, none of them seemed to be paying any attention to her.

"*Sumimasen,*" a *salaryman* apologized as he brushed past her. Before she realized what he was doing, he wedged a piece of luggage into the locker she had left open and shut the door. The "in use" light went on.

"Wait!" she cried.

"*Sumimasen,*" the *salaryman* apologized again, bowed, and hurried out of the train station.

She whimpered as he disappeared. She hadn't really meant to take the sword out of the locker. She glanced around for another locker and realized that hers had been the only unoccupied one. Every locker in sight had its "in use" light on. The feeling of being watched was still there, even though no one was looking at her. No one was even standing still, pretending to focus on a magazine or telephone conversation or oddly colored piece of floor. Everyone was coming and going, and she alone stood still like a rock in the ocean surf.

What the hell was she supposed to do? George had burned down a temple and killed a girl to get the *katana*. What if her monolithic loon of a fan had done the same? If she called the police, they'd probably arrest her for two murders.

But if she didn't call the police, she would still have a homicidal maniac stalking her.

She felt someone next to her, staring.

Nikki leapt to the side, bringing up the wrapped sword to block an attack.

There was no one there.

"Shit!" She was shaking. For one split second, she could have sworn there was a Japanese teenage boy standing beside her, his dark eyes furious.

She started to walk fast, blindly fleeing into the night.

She was trying not to run. Running would make her easier to track. She walked fast, weaving through the heavy crowds moving through Umeda Station. She didn't care if she was lost; all that mattered was putting distance between her and Osaka Station. She took random turns, going up escalators and down elevators and in and out of the stores.

Just when she thought she was hopelessly lost, she saw a sign for the Tanimachi subway line. She danced in place as she checked the map to figure out the cost of the ticket, fed a ten-thousand-yen bill into the ticket machine, grabbed her ticket and change, and bolted through the gate. There was a train sitting at the platform as she ran down the steps. She made the car just as the "door closing" chime sounded. There was no one else running for the train. The door closed and the train pulled out.

She slumped down on the bench seat and stared at the bundled sword still clutched in her hand. Some loon had hacked her computer, read her book, and was using it as inspiration. He had stuck a blender into Gregory Winston's stomach and set it to puree. There might be a seventeen-year-old girl dead and raped in Kyoto.

What the hell was she going to do? The police already knew she had a crazy fan. Would telling them about these new twists help them catch the man? Probably. But what could she tell them without making it seem like she had something more to do with the murders?

She could give them a copy of her manuscript on a flash drive. She could even tell them most of the truth. She believed her computer had been hacked, and she was scared. They were cops; they could fit the pieces together without her.

She would have to do something with the sword—like throw it in the canal since it now had her DNA and fingerprints on it. Hopefully it was a replica and not some real and irreplaceable antique. Surely her fan wasn't so insane that he had stolen something so valuable and then left it in a coin locker.

One thing was for certain—her life was about to get a whole lot crazier.

"Oh, this sucks," she whispered. "Bad enough that I write this shit, now I have to live it?"

She couldn't stop writing though. Even if she could magically cure her hypergraphia, she still would have to finish the novel. If she didn't, she would have to give back the money that her publisher had already paid her. All of it—even the part she'd already spent.

She didn't know how her stalker was hacking her laptop; she thought she had made it secure. She had online "friends" that were computer experts, but none of them were close and trusted. Anyone she asked for help might be the very person who had hacked her computer. She'd never met any of them face-to-face and had to hope what they told her was true. One of them could be lying.

There was the little policeman, Yoshida. She could ask him for help.

Now that she thought of it, though, it was weird that of the hundreds of restaurants in Osaka, the one he chose after processing Gregory's murder was the same one she met Miriam in to talk about her novel. She had emailed with Miriam about where to eat. Could he have intercepted those messages?

He was an anime fan. He might visit the same forums that she did. He could be one of her many online "friends" and she wouldn't know.

But he was so tiny. The police said—no—*Yoshida* said that the attacker was much taller.

She slipped her cell phone out to call Miriam and then remembered that was against the rules. She eyed the commuters around her, currently ignoring her. She considered texting her. No. That would make Miriam an accomplice to—to—to something. Tampering with evidence? On that thought, she made sure to delete her call to Miriam from her phone's log.

"You don't seriously think that a policeman hacked your computer?" She whispered to her phone the conversation she so desperately wanted to have with Miriam. "Why would Yoshida have me arrested? So we could meet while he's in a position of authority? He honestly seemed terrified of me, but that could have been an act. But why would he put a *katana* into the coin locker? How could he know I'd be crazy enough to go looking for it?"

It was only three stops to Tanimachi 4-chome in Otemae. Far too short a distance to come up with any reasonable answer. She darted off the train and hurried out of the station. If she was being followed, she only had a couple of minutes lead time to get to the safety of her apartment. She could grab her laptop, a change of clothes, and then go someplace else, someplace safe.

But where the hell was that at this time of night?

Her apartment was on the sixth floor, around the corner and down the hall from the elevator. She had never minded before that the bare concrete hallway reminded her of something out of *Ringu*.

She unlocked her door. Opened it. Then realized that the killer could be inside—waiting for her. She stood in the doorway for a moment, panting, carefully scanning the small room. She had left the sliding closet door open and the accordionlike door to the bathroom was folded. The studio apartment had no other place to hide. She stepped in, shut the door, and locked it behind her.

"Calm down, stay calm." She kicked off her sandals out of habit. "Psycho fan wants to play. Killing me would stop the game, so I'm probably safe from him. Everyone else is dead meat, but I'm—I'm—I'm scared shitless but probably safe."

She realized she was still clutching the sword in her left hand. She put it on the table and picked up one of her omnipresent pens. She paced her small studio apartment, clicking nervously.

"Does he know where I live?" She considered. "Well, if he hacked my computer, he knows everything on it. I e-mailed my new address to my editor and my agent, so, yes, he knows where I live."

The only thing that might save her was an oddity of Japanese urban planning. She was in 4-choma, or the fourth district, and anyone could find that. Her block number would have been assigned by both proximity to the city but also in the order it was settled. Finding the right block was more difficult. The houses on the block were then numbered as they were built. The first house on the block was "one." There might be a dozen houses between "one" and "two" as newer houses crowded into the spaces between the original buildings.

Because of this, even housewives had business cards with maps to their houses printed on the back.

Her crazed fan, though, had obviously been stalking her for a long time if he found a *katana* to match the one in her story. He had time to roam her neighborhood and find her apartment building.

She needed to bounce. Usually she just fled with what she was wearing. But she never had so much "her" to leave behind. Never before could she decorate the walls, buy clothes, pick out dishes and pots. Everything in the apartment was seeped with her happiness in setting up her place. The joy in her power to finally make decisions for herself.

She could be packed in thirty minutes.

She had washed her clothes on Saturday and hung them on bamboo poles across her balcony. Luckily everything was dry. She took them down, folded and then rolled them to save space. She only had one suitcase, an ultra cute Hello Kitty trolley that she had bought for her "visa renewal" trips. Maybe she should head to South Korea early.

As she packed, she backed up her novel twice onto flash drives. She could give one to the police so they would have some hope of catching her stalker.

What about the *katana*? She eyed it sitting innocently on her table, still wrapped in fabric. "I can't explain the sword."

She would figure that out later. Right now, she needed to pack as quickly as possible. Stopping to think things through would only let stress seep in, and then she would be stuck writing until her hypergraphia subsided. Of course, as her suitcase filled up, she couldn't help but notice what wasn't going to fit. All her expensive spices. Her new rice cooker. Her body-sized pillow. Her Hello Kitty duvet cover.

"No, no, don't think about it," she sang to herself. Maybe she could have Miriam pack them up and ship them. "No, that might make her a target. Better to just abandon anything I can't carry."

She caught herself chewing on her fingernails. She jerked her hand out of her mouth. Food. Wine. That's what she needed to calm down. Self-medicate away some of her stress before she ended up in a writing marathon.

She heated up the *okonomiyaki* that she had bought earlier and ate it while checking her secret forum. Miriam had posted the code word of "Prepare for bounce!" to spread the word that Nikki might need to bolt and needed someplace to crash. The replies to her post were "Team Banzai: Go!" and "Team Banzai: No Go!" as people stated their ability to offer up refuge. She scanned the replies, her stomach flip-flopping. She had built up Team Banzai over the years, working at a level of secrecy that the CIA probably would be impressed with. Surely it hadn't been compromised. Even if her computer had been hacked, her stalker wouldn't have found the key to her code words or any information on Team Banzai. She kept that information locked in her head, where her mother couldn't access it.

The part of the team that was on her side of the world had responded to the post. She scanned the "go" for people she knew were in Japan. Pixii, Jaynaynay, Cloud, and Beehgly were offering her crash space. Pixii was closest but lived out in the middle of nowhere with some old master potter. Nikki wasn't sure she would be comfortable living with a strange man. There was also the matter of simply finding the place in the middle of the night. The other three lived in studio apartments in Tokyo and worked as English teachers. She would have to cycle between their places while looking for a new place to rent.

She focused on packing instead of thinking about how all her plans were falling apart. How she was going to lose Miriam. How wonderful it been sharing life with her best friend instead of just chatting online.

Sniffling from unshed tears, she emptied her backpack so there would be room for her laptop. She still would be able to talk constantly with Miriam online, she told herself. They'd done it for years.

"Keep this up, you'll end up writing for hours." She shut down her laptop and shoved it into her backpack. She shoved her current working notebook into it too so it wouldn't tempt her. "Just focus on packing."

She distracted herself with choosing a purse. Her favorite, hands down, was the beautiful messenger bag made out of an antique silk obi. Just looking at it always made her happy. She and Miriam had found it in Kyoto while researching Shinto shrines. Generally it was too big to haul around on a daily basis, but it was perfect for a bounce. It could hold all the essentials. A handful of pens. A blank notebook. Her change purse and wallet. Her passport. Two more black pens. Her cell phone. Another blank notebook. Her iPod. Hand towel. Toilet paper. Phrase book. Two red pens.

She stood clicking a pen, frowning at her purse. What else?

Her doorbell rang.

She jerked up and stared across the room at her door. She could see the shadow of someone standing beyond the door through the crack at the bottom. Was it her psycho fan? She scanned the room quickly for a weapon and saw the *katana* on the table.

Her stalker would know she'd picked up the sword at the train station. Or would he? If he hadn't seen her pick it up, at the train station, how would he know that the contents of the locker had been switched?

She crept to the table, fumbled open the fabric case, and slid the *katana* out of its sheath as the doorbell rang again. Cautiously, she went to the door and peeked out through the spyhole.

Detective Tanaka stood outside her door. "Miss Delany? It's Detective Tanaka of the Osaka Police Department."

"Shit!" She danced backwards. "Shit! Shit! Shit!"

"Miss Delany, are you alright?" Detective Tanaka called through the door.

"I stubbed my toe!" Nikki yelled. What should she do? She realized she still had the damn *katana* gripped tight in her hand. "Shit!"

She ran in a tiny circle, looking for somewhere to hide the sword. Refrigerator? Too small. Balcony? Too open.

"Miss Delany?"

"Wait a minute! I was in the middle of changing my clothes." She slid the *katana* into the shadows next to the toilet and jerked shut the accordion-style fabric door. Anything else? Her half-packed suitcase sat out in the middle of the floor!

"Miss Delany?"

She winced as she threw her duvet over the bag. This stalker thing was completely throwing her off her game; she was smarter than this! She considered changing both hiding places when Detective Tanaka tried the door and found it locked.

"Hold on!" she shouted. She hiked up her shirt to make it seem like she had been naked and had spent the time getting dressed and not hiding a possibly stolen weapon that might have been used in a murder. "I've got to get dressed!"

She snatched up one of her many pens, clicked it twice, took a deep calming breath, and unlocked the door. "Tanaka-san." She made a show of tugging down her hiked-up shirt. "I was getting ready for bed." To explain the duvet-covered lump in the middle of the floor, she added. "I was laying out my futon."

He seemed taller, but then he hadn't loomed over her in a dim foyer before. Nor could she remember him wearing strong, musky cologne at the police station. One corner of his mouth quirked up into a tiny, dangerous smile. He barely seemed like the same man who had sat across the table from her all afternoon. It was as if he'd taken off a mask and beneath was someone a lot more dangerous than the polite civil servant.

She started to swing the door shut again, but he put out his hand and held it open. "What is it that you want, Detective?"

He sniffed deeply and scanned the room. "I need to ask you more questions about Gregory Winston."

Was there blood on her shoes? She hadn't even looked. She didn't dare glance down.

"May I come in?"

It went against all her instincts to let him into the apartment. There was the small matter, though, that she didn't think she could get the door shut without a fight. It was her experience that the less cooperative she was with authority figures, the more force they used to get what they wanted. She hated that she needed to go against her instincts to keep the stakes from being raised.

She'd found, though, that distraction worked well in situations like this. "I'm glad you're here." She stepped back from the door and out of his reach. "There's something I want to give you."

"Eh?" Tanaka stepped into her apartment and closed the door behind him.

She tried not to let that seem ominous. It probably was a Japanese custom. Bow in greeting. Take your shoes off. Close the door. Not that Tanaka had done the first two. Odd. He'd taken off his shoes at the restaurant and had bowed to her shortly before handcuffing her hands behind her back. It had struck her as absurdly polite. And why was he here without a translator? Had he just been pretending to barely follow English at the police station?

She backed away from him. "I've made a copy of the documents that I've been working on. I think it's possible that my stalker has hacked into my computer and read everything I've written."

Where had she put the flash drive? Her apartment was in complete disarray by her frenzied packing. She locked down on a yelp as she realized that she'd left the *katana*'s sheath on the table.

Someone leaned against Nikki's back and whispered into her ear, "Do not trust him. He is not who he seems."

She jerked sideways, trying to keep Tanaka in sight while looking behind her. There was no one else in the room.

"Miss Delany?" Tanaka said.

Nikki blinked at him. "I—I—I had the flash drive a moment ago. I'm not sure where I put it." She pointed at the piles of clutter strewn in a semicircle around her duvet as she had sorted through the things she wanted to take or leave. She had to keep him from noticing the sheath.

"Give him nothing," the male voice whispered again. There was definitely someone pressed close to her, his breath warm on her skin. She could see, though, in the reflection of the balcony's sliding door, that no one was standing behind her.

Nikki slapped her hand over her mouth, but a whimper of fear slipped out.

"Miss Delany?"

"Need to pee!" Nikki yelped. She fought with the bathroom's door until it was open only wide enough to allow her to slip through. She slammed it shut behind her and flipped the little catch lock.

Her mother was right. She was going insane.

What if I killed Gregory without even realizing it? Maybe I put that sword into the locker. It would explain how I knew where it was and what the PIN was more rationally than the idea of some psycho fan.

Well, good news, she wasn't being stalked by a nutcase.

Unless, of course, you can stalk yourself.

The door rattled.

What a thing to realize when cornered by a homicide detective.

"I'm going pee!" she called.

The door shuddered and somehow held.

"Tanaka-san?"

A knife blade stabbed through the fabric of the door and sliced downward.

Nikki screamed . . .

. . . and blinked down at a dead man lying crumbled outside the open bathroom door. There was a neat slit in the back of his suit coat, wide as a *katana* blade, seeping blood. She had the *katana* in her hands, the blade dripping blood.

"Oh. Oh. Oh." Something warm was trickling down her face. She glanced in the mirror over the vanity. Blood streaked her right cheek.

And her eyes were so dark brown, they were nearly black. As she stared at her reflection in shock, they shifted back to her normal blue.

"Oh. Oh." Had she just killed Detective Tanaka? She didn't remember doing it—but he was dead, and she was holding the bloody sword. She looked again at the man.

"Tanaka-san?"

The back of the man's head looked wrong for the police officer. Instead of neatly trimmed black hair, the man had grizzled brown hair with touches of red. There were two odd bumps on the top of his head.

She had to step over the body and the spreading pool of blood to get out of the bathroom. She glanced down as she did and nearly stumbled.

The body wasn't human. The bumps on the head were furred ears. There were no eyebrows over full burnt-amber eyes set in a raccoonlike mask of dark fur. The face extended out in a muzzle, ending in a black dog's nose. A mouth full of sharp teeth hung open, lips locked in a snarl.

The man-beast held a very big knife in a hand that was dark-furred and claw-tipped. It was wearing a conservative suit with patent leather shoes and an expensive wristwatch. There was a hole punched into the chest of the white button-down shirt now soaked with blood.

No one else was in the apartment.

She whimpered. Where was Tanaka? Who was this? *What* was this?

Had she just killed a man, and was her mind was trying to make it okay by seeing him as a monster? She closed her eyes for a minute and opened them again.

Still a raccoon in a business suit with a knife.

Far down the hall, the elevator stopped on her floor with a "ding." It reminded her that her neighbors might have heard the whole fight and called the police. She snatched up her backpack and shrugged it onto her shoulders.

She needed . . .

✠ 8 ✠
Blackout

The night became an odd stuttering movie with her jerking through it like a broken puppet. One minute she was in her apartment, staring down at the dead man, and the next she was walking through a crowded underground mall. She paused, feeling oddly hollow, light, and a touch feverish.

How did she get here? Had she gone into shock or something and walked out of her apartment, leaving a dead man sprawled on the floor? Did she remember to pick up her . . .

. . . and she was on a nearly empty train, speeding through the night. The overhead fluorescents turned the windows into mirrors, and she stared at her reflection as her eyes shifted from brown to blue.

What was happening to her? Had she killed Detective Tanaka? Was it really some kind of animal in a business suit on her floor or simply a delusion to make killing Tanaka acceptable? Had she snapped before he attacked her or after? Had he really attacked her or was that part of her delusion? Was this the onset of madness that her mother always braced against?

And where the hell was she going?

Over the door of the train car, a digital sign scrolled out *kanji*. She waited for the English translation to appear. Kyoto. She was heading toward Kyoto. They passed a small deserted station without slowing. She was on the express to Kyoto. It was a forty-minute trip.

What was wrong with her? Her doctors had often suspected her hypergraphia was related to temporal lobe lesions, because it was the least serious possible cause of her symptoms. Thought to be genetic in nature, the lesions ran in families and often accompanied epilepsy—which she had never showed signs of having before. Unfortunately, her doctors could never find signs of lesions, and hypergraphia was also caused by bipolar disorder, frontotemporal dementia, and schizophrenia.

So why was she blacking out? She was fairly sure that in the middle of an epileptic seizure, you couldn't operate a Japanese ticket machine. It was sad and scary to suddenly want to be bipolar, but it was the lesser of two evils at the moment.

The fabric-encased *katana* lay across her lap. Her backpack rested at her feet. She snatched up her bag. She'd been transferring things into her purse. Where was it? Surely she hadn't left it in her apartment, or worse, lost it somewhere along the way. Maybe she simply shoved everything back into her backpack. She opened it and took inventory. Her laptop was in it, her flashlight, two notebooks, five pens, but nothing else. Not even a single pack of tissues. She unzipped all the various compartments and felt down to the bottom. Nothing. Not her change purse. Not her cell phone. Not her driver's license or passport or bank card.

"Oh God." She slapped her pockets, full panic setting in. In her right jeans' pocket was a wad of hundred thousand yen, each worth around a hundred US dollars. Where had it come from? She didn't keep this much cash on hand, and she didn't have her bank card. Had she withdrawn the money and left the card in the machine? She gripped the bills tightly. She was so screwed if she'd lost her bank card. She carefully tucked the money back into her pocket.

The need to write washed over her. She fumbled with her backpack to get out her notebooks. To her dismay, the first was already filled. The second one was her current working notebook. She turned through the pages with trembling fingers, found the first blank sheet, and submerged herself into the calmness of writing.

More than ever, she needed a hero.

He was too late.
The hallway was full of the coppery richness that came only from

a full body's worth of blood spilled out onto stone. He could smell it as soon as he stepped off the elevator. The stench grew stronger as he walked cautiously down the hallway, pistol in hand. The girl's name was printed on the plaque beside the last apartment: Demming Natasha.

He sighed. Something bad had found the girl before he could.

He tried the doorknob. The door wasn't locked. He pushed it open, bracing himself for a body on the floor beyond. He wasn't disappointed, but it wasn't what he had expected. A *tanuki* lay sprawled in a pool of blood.

He stood in the doorway a moment, surprised, and then stepped into the apartment and quietly shut the door behind him.

The mix of coppery blood, musky *tanuki,* and the girl's sweetness was familiar. All three had been in Gregory Winston's apartment. It wasn't surprising that they'd come together again here, but that it was the girl who'd apparently walked away unscathed. But how? The police reports claimed that the girl was young and seemingly harmless. Appearances, though, could be misleading.

The fabric folding door to the bathroom was sliced in half. Judging by the way the *tanuki* lay and the blood trail, he had cut his way into the tiny space only to come face-to-face with his killer. The shape-shifter had been killed with a single stab wound through the heart—quick and clean. There was a bloody towel on the bathroom floor from the killer cleaning his weapon, and the *tanuki*'s wallet, emptied of cash.

To the victor go the spoils. According to the driver's license inside the wallet, the creature was using the name Harada Hayashi.

He breathed out disgust; the most dangerous of the monsters were the ones that could use the weapons of men along with their own natural talents. Either Hayashi had gotten clumsy with its excitement or there was more to this girl than reported.

There was a purse on the table with her wallet and passport, along with the impression of a long thin blade painted in blood. A Hello Kitty duvet covered a half-packed suitcase in the middle of the floor. Around it were small piles of items. The girl had been packing when the *tanuki* arrived. Where was she now?

He picked through the suitcase and things she'd left unpacked. Size-small, bright-colored T-shirts. Manga. Festival fans. Anime figures from *Gacha* vending machines. Everything hinted at a young, whimsical girl.

How could such a girl kill a cunning monster?

There was a frenzy of Post-It Notes on the wall in a kaleidoscope of colors. A turquoise-color Post-It Note caught his eye. It read "Shiva? Vishnu? Kali?" with the "Shiva" underlined multiple times. Below it were two more turquoise-colored notes. "The Brit" and "JFK to Osaka. Hotel Nikko Kansai Airport, Osaka. Walk to train station, airport to Umeda, express to Izushi, Nishimuraya Honkan." It was the exact travel itinerary for Simon before he disappeared. The last turquoise note had a variation of the smiley face, *x*s for the eyes, a squiggle for a mouth, and several question marks surrounding the face. What did that mean?

He scanned the wall for more turquoise notes. There was one off to the side, down low. It read: "Scary Cat Dude." Was that supposed to be him? Under it was a flash of pink. He lifted up the note. The Post-it Note underneath read: "Kitten."

How could she know about the kitten? He hadn't mentioned it to anyone.

He stepped back, eyes widening, to actually look at the collage in front of him. Ananth had said the police tagged Natasha as "a person of interest" in Gregory Winston's murder, which was shorthand for "we think she's involved but we can't prove it." There had been no explanation, though, in the police reports as to why they suspected the girl. He studied the other colorful scraps of paper, trying to find a pattern. Slowly, he managed to see the underlying order. It was tracking dozens of people and objects as they intertwined. Each person had a different color, although there was some overlap, since she had only a dozen or so to choose from. Several colors trailed down to end in a frowny face with *x*s for eyes. A "GW" was tracked in violet on the wall. He brought YF's pink to an end before his own color stopped with a death mask and two words: "Harada." "Blender."

Half-hidden under Gregory's death mask was another flash of pink. He lifted the frowning face to read the note: "*Katana*, Osaka Station, locker 1601, PIN 108."

That would explain why the sword hadn't been in Gregory Winston's apartment. The lockers were emptied after three days of nonpayment. The sword would be still there. Unless . . .

He glanced at the bloody blade impression on the table. It was the right shape for a *katana*. If the girl knew where Winston had hidden the sword, then she could have retrieved it and killed the *tanuki* with it. What happened, though, afterwards? Why had she left without her purse and suitcase? Did someone take her?

He sniffed, pulling in the blood-drenched air, testing it for a more elusive scent. There was a slight tinge of ozone, like lightning had passed through the room.

His phone vibrated. He growled softly and took it out to look at the number. Ananth. He glanced at the turquoise Post-It Notes on the wall. It was a tenuous lead at best, but it was the only one he'd found since arriving in Japan. He needed to find this girl. He couldn't let Ananth order him off on another wild-goose chase. He considered what to tell the Director and what to keep to himself.

He took a deep breath and answered. "Yes?"

"What did you find?"

"I'm going to need a cleanup at the girl's apartment."

"You killed her?"

He barely controlled the impulse to fling his phone against the wall. He forced himself to count to ten before answering. "No. There's a dead *tanuki* here; it's the same one that was at Gregory Winston's place. The girl isn't here. I think she bolted."

He considered offering to track her and decided against it. Ananth didn't trust him. If he seemed too eager, the Director might yank him off the hunt. He waited for the man to think through the options and come to the logical conclusion.

"Find her." Ananth ordered after a moment of silence. "But make sure you don't kill her until we've had a chance to question her."

Nikki stared at her notebook. What the hell was she writing?

Harada was the name she had given the assassin that killed George Wilson. He'd showed up at George's apartment disguised as one of George's friends. Only after George had opened the door did he realize his mistake . . .

Much like what had happened to her.

After a long discussion with her editor, Nikki had put Natasha in a nicer building than hers and given her a spacious one-bedroom penthouse with a clear view to Osaka Castle. At night, they shined great spotlights up onto the gleaming white stones and gold-edged pagodalike roofs. Surrounded by dark gardens, the castle looked as if a hole had opened up to another time.

Natasha's walls were covered with sketches and paintings, not Post-It Notes, and there was no dead body at Natasha's. Or at least, Nikki didn't think there was. She hadn't written anything about the quiet artist for almost a month. Trying to write a more glamorous version of her life was like pulling teeth, as if her whole being refused the lie. What her hypergraphia had spit out since the conversation with her editor had been utterly lacking in detail, as if Natasha lived in a white void.

This scene was full of details—only they were details of Nikki's apartment.

And the Scary Cat Dude had used Gregory Winston's name instead of George's.

First the blackouts and now this—so not good. She was blurring reality with her story; not a good sign. How much of the scene was actually suppressed memories of what happened during her blackout? It would explain the mysterious hundred thousands of yen in her jacket pocket.

The train started to slow down, and the loudspeaker announced, "Kyoto *desu*, Kyoto *desu*."

9
Burn Out

As soon as the doors opened on the train, Nikki hurried from the platform toward the lobby of Kyoto Station. She had only two hours before the local trains stopped running. She needed to go back to Osaka to get her passport, credit cards, and anything else vital that she had left behind. An express would take forty minutes, and a local would take nearly an hour. It would leave her only an hour to get to her apartment and back to the Osaka train station to catch the sleeper to Tokyo. Her stomach was doing flip-flops over the idea of returning to her apartment with the dead body. Part of her very active imagination envisioned bugs crawling in and out of his mouth, but she knew in the enclosed apartment it would be days before that could start. She focused on the diminishing time before she would be stuck in Osaka without a place to spend the night. Miriam was the only person she knew in Osaka, and she wasn't going to bring this mess down on her head.

Kyoto Station was a vast modern structure built to be a visual re-creation of the valley that Kyoto nestled in. The lobby was a six-story-high rectangle under an umbrella of steel and glass. The occasional pigeon testified that despite seeming enclosed, one side was open to the elements. The wedge-shaped Isetan Department Store actually started three floors under the station and formed a mountainous slope up and out of the lobby that you could walk up

73

the side of—provided you wanted to hike more than ten floors to the roof-top garden.

The lobby was crowded with people hurrying home from cram school and office socialized drinking. Nikki wove through the sea of Asians, aware that she was the only *gaijin* in sight. The far wall of the lobby was one massive bank of automated ticket machines. Despite the number of machines, lines were cued up.

The only money she had was the hundred thousand yen. She nervously fed one into the machine. It calmly took it and spit back nine ten thousand yen bills and a handful of coins. She gathered them up and headed to the gate to scan the big digital board showing train departures. She wanted an express but she would take . . .

. . . she was in a taxi on the outskirts of a town.

The driver was a typical Japanese taxi driver: a middle-aged man in a uniform and white gloves. The car was spotless, and he was listening to a baseball game between Osaka's Hanshin Tigers and the Yokohama Bay Stars.

Why was it that every little piece of the puzzle seemed so orderly and sane and yet the big picture was filled with blood and chaos? Was the order serving to magnify the disorder?

At least she still had her backpack and the money in her jeans' pocket, and of course, the *katana*. It was only her sanity that she was losing.

The taxi stopped. They were on a steep hillside, the orange *torii* posts of a shrine gleaming in the headlights. The driver said something in Japanese and tapped the digital display of his meter that showed eight hundred yen. Apparently he thought this was where she wanted to go.

She had asked to come here? Where the hell was here? She could see stumbling into a taxi and asking for a hotel, but what was this?

"*Nani?*" She pointed at the *torii.*

The driver answered in a flood of Japanese.

"Do—do you speak English?" she cried, interrupting him.

"Eh?"

"English?" She couldn't even think of the phrase in Japanese. "Where are we? Is this Kyoto? Osaka?"

"Kyoto. *Hai.*" The driver nodded and then pointed at the gates in his headlights. "Ikuta Shrine."

Had she asked to go to a shrine? In the middle of the night?
"No, I don't want . . ."

. . . she was standing under a streetlamp in front of the shrine,
alone, the taxi no longer in sight.

"Stop doing that!" she shouted. "It's scaring me."

It started to rain. It was a light drizzle, but it washed away what
little strength she had left. She walked in a small circle within the pool
of light, eyeing the dark landscape around her. There was the shrine
. . . and not much else. The street ended under the streetlight. Down
the hill, on either side of the road, were tall blank walls, over ten feet
high, giving no clue to what lay beyond them. She seemed miles out
of the town center with no idea where the nearest subway station
might be or if the subway would still be running by the time she got
there. Her wristwatch said it was nearly midnight. All told, she'd lost
almost four hours to the blackouts.

"This day really, really sucks. What the hell am I even doing here?"

There was nothing to be done but go into the shrine. Something
locked in her unconscious had brought her the whole way out here;
she might as well find out what. Sniffling back tears, she took out her
flashlight, turned it on, and walked into the temple grounds.

The gravel path disappeared into a grove of tall trees, cloaked in
darkness. In the distance, there was the glimmer of a spotlight. She
could smell smoke, and the odor grew stronger as she went deeper
into the shrine's grounds. Dread grew in her chest as if the dark and
cold were seeping into her, tainted with wood smoke.

Her hypergraphia had spilled out scenes about a little Shinto
shrine on the edge of Kyoto. While the daughter who worked as a
shrine maiden had been vividly depicted as a wonderfully sweet and
vibrant girl, everything else had been full of holes. Nikki had spent
days exploring the temples of Kyoto, soaking up details to fill in what
was missing from the scenes. While she visited dozens, she hadn't
been to this one.

Or had she?

What if she'd been having blackouts all along? What if she'd been
living some dual existence, stealing ideas from reality and disguising
them as fiction? What if the "flow" of hypergraphia was uncorking the
bottled-up memories and letting them come out?

It made horrible, terrible sense. When she wrote, she always felt like she'd dashed through some massive elaborate stage, carefully only tracking what the point-of-view character saw and felt and ignoring everything else. She disregarded everything the character hadn't focused on, and thus lost important details that she needed to fill in later.

What if the reason her settings always felt so real was because they *were* real?

Did she write the vivid scene of George setting fire to the shrine because she'd been here before? Had she found the fuel can sitting in the storage shed, the door unlocked because this was peaceful Japan and no sane person would steal from the gods?

She had written about the sloshing sound the kerosene had made inside the can as George splashed it on the back of the gift shop. The smell of the thick fumes as the dry wood soaked in the liquid. The heat of the fire as it "woofed" to life with a single flick of a lighter.

Beyond the deep shadows of the trees, there was a courtyard lit by a jury-rigged floodlight. The light shone on a jumble of blackened timbers. Only burnt skeletal remains were left of what had stood for a thousand years, but she recognized the buildings all the same. To the left was the gift shop that sold charms. To the right was the raised stage of the *kaguraden* where Yuuka would dance with the other shrine maidens, pretending to be so solemn and serene when she was giggling inside.

Straight ahead was the *haiden,* or hall of worship, where Yuuka had been cleaning the day of the fire. Beyond it stood the *honden*, a small, upraised building with a steep gabled roof. The *honden* was the most scared part of the temple and closed to the public. Yuuka's father only opened its doors on certain festival days. The *katana* had been kept within the *honden*; George had set the fire to gain entrance to it.

"Oh, no," Nikki whispered. "No."

"I didn't know he'd burned it," someone said behind her.

She spun around, blinking away tears and raindrops. A boy stood in the pool of light. He looked fifteen or sixteen and was fiercely beautiful, with raven-winged eyebrows and eyes so dark they were nearly black. His hair was pulled back into a ponytail that was twisted up into a topknot. He was dressed in a somber blue kimono, black *tabi* socks, and *geta* sandals.

"Wh-wh-what?" She glanced around, trying to fit him into the destruction around her. What was a teenage boy doing here in the middle of the night, dressed as a samurai?

"I didn't know that he set fire to my shrine."

"I-I-I'm sorry. Your family owns this shrine?"

"For eighty generations, yes, they have served me. I do not know what will happen to it now. There are no sons to inherit it; Misa was to marry a boy from Nara. Ichiro would have adopted him as a son and passed the shrine to him."

Nikki frowned, trying to understand who this boy was and if she had somehow greatly wronged him. Currently everything was refusing logic and order and she was floundering lost. "She's dead?" Nikki was no longer sure who "she" was though. Yuuka? Misa? Were they the same girl?

"Yes," the boy said bitterly. "He killed her and raped her and hid her body in the dead leaves."

Nikki closed her eyes against the vivid memory of George's fear and anger suddenly turning to lust and need. *Oh God, what have I done?*

The rain turned to a heavy downpour, and she stood there, uncaring, weeping.

"Come." The boy took her by the arm. "The storehouse wasn't touched by the fire."

He led her into the darkness.

In the back corner of the shrine area there was an old Edo-period storehouse with stark white walls. Unlike the storage shed, it had a massive padlock that looked centuries old. Apparently, though, it was not truly locked, as the boy tugged the padlock off without producing a key.

"I'm Taira no Atsumori," he said. "You may call me Atsumori-kami. My name is written with the *kanji* for honest and then the *kanji* for prosperity."

The double doors creaked open and he walked into the cavelike darkness.

"I have a light." Nikki turned on her flashlight. The walls seemed a foot thick, and the only window set above the door was tightly shuttered. How could Atsumori see anything? She could hear him, though, opening up wooden drawers somewhere in the back.

"There is a lantern here," Atsumori said. There was a flare of light, brilliant against the black, and when she could see again, he had a small old stone dish, filled with oil, with a burning wick draped over the edge.

"Yeah, that looks safe." She edged into the building. The light danced off tall *tansu* with metal-reinforced drawers and high rafters strung with paper festival lanterns. There was no sign of electric outlets or overhead lights.

"I can protect you here." The boy rooted through the drawers of the cabinets. "Once we leave the shrine, though, I will be dependent on you."

"What?" She felt like she had come in at the end of a conversation.

He handed her a fine linen towel. "You can dry yourself with this."

Nikki buried her face in the towel. It smelled of pine and cedar, like it had been stored with potpourri. "I'm Nikki Delany. I'm so sorry about everything that happened." She felt tears welling up again as she thought of all the madness she had accidently spilled out onto this serene place. "I—I don't know how this all happened. I don't even know how I got here."

"I brought you here."

Nikki laughed into the towel. "No, no, I mean—I don't remember how I got to this shrine."

"I brought you," the boy said with quiet intensity. "I killed the *tanuki* that attacked you in your home and brought you here."

Nikki lowered the towel to stare at the boy. He was sitting on the floor in the pool of light cast by the oil lantern. He watched her with calm detachment. He couldn't have said what he just said—one of them must be misunderstanding the situation. She played the conversation back. And ran through it a second time when it came to the same illogical end.

"What?" she said.

"I have been with you since you found my *katana* at the train station."

Nikki buried her face back into the towel, trying to rationalize the situation. It would be so comforting to believe someone else had killed the man in her apartment. She had thought she'd seen a boy who looked like Atsumori glaring furiously at her at the train station. She had felt like she'd been followed from Osaka Station back to her apartment, but there hadn't been space in her closet-sized bathroom for both of them without her noticing. One of them was probably stark raving mad, and, unfortunately, it was her.

"I don't understand," she mumbled into the towel.

"The sword is my *shintai*. Where it goes, I am forced to follow. When I realized I could easily take over your body, I used you to bring it back to my shrine."

With her eyes covered, she recognized his voice. She had heard him murmur a warning at her apartment. When she looked, though, there had been no one behind her. She had been alone with the killer.

It was possible that she was also completely alone in the storage building.

She gripped the towel tightly and whimpered. If she was so totally gone that she was seeing him in such vivid detail, she couldn't imagine how she could prove to herself that he was really there or not.

"Are you afraid of me?"

"I'm afraid of myself. I'm afraid that I've gone crazy." *I'm afraid that I've killed people—lots of people.* "None of this makes sense. I don't know if you're even here. Look at you. I'm soaked to the skin and you're still dry."

"Of course I'm dry. I am a *kami*." He cocked his head. "Do you not know of these things? Of *kami* and *shintai* and the function of shrines such as this one?"

"*Kami* are gods." She knew that the word wasn't an exact translation; they were actually the essence of nature or something that English didn't have a word to explain. The phrase "eight million gods" was to indicate that the *kami* were beyond counting. "I—I don't know what a *shintai* is." Was it a good thing that the boy claiming to be a god was using a term that she didn't know? It could mean that he was actually sitting beside her—but it left her with a person who believed he was a god.

"A *shintai* is the object I reside in. The *katana* is my *shintai*. I am where it is; hence I was in Osaka when you found it."

"Why didn't I see you then?"

"I am not as powerful as Amaterasu Omikami or even Sarutahiko Okami. I am limited in how much I can manifest outside of holy ground."

Nikki recognized the name of the sun goddess, Amaterasu. The sun goddess was the queen of the gods, holding a position in the Shinto pantheon much like Zeus. Her brother was Susanoo, god of the storms, and they engaged in sibling rivalry that rocked the world. Nikki didn't know the god Sarutahiko. More proof that she wasn't crazy—maybe. "You said you killed the man who attacked me?"

"I am sorry. I was forced to take over your body. He would have killed you otherwise."

"All good." She wasn't sure where she stood on the crazy thing anymore. If her blackouts were caused by possession, it would certainly explain how she ended up at a burned-out Shinto shrine in the middle of the night.

"Who was the man at your apartment? Why is he searching for us?"

"Who?"

He reached over and opened her backpack and took out her notebooks. "You wrote about a man searching for us at your apartment." He opened her newest notebook to the scene that she had written on the train.

"That—that's just a story I'm making up." Nikki blushed. She normally didn't let anyone but Miriam see her notebooks. "Those people aren't real."

Atsumori cocked his head. "You do not know what you are?"

"I'm a writer. I make up stories—like *The Tale of Genji*?" She assumed he would know of the most famous Japanese novel ever written, since it was over a thousand years old.

"You are an oracle. What you are writing is the truth."

"No, no, no." Nikki shook her head. "I write crazy, impossible things—like demons eating children."

He looked slightly confused. "But demons do eat children."

A childhood's worth of therapy was quickly unraveling. "I make things up."

"You knew where my *shintai* was hidden. You knew how to undo the lock."

Nikki pressed a hand to her mouth as she took it a step further back. She had known everything about Gregory from the fact that his window framed the HEP Five Ferris wheel to the problems he had with his visa. Denial leaked out from under her fingertips. "No."

Atsumori opened the other notebook. "'*Sunlight. The fresh green smell of the new* tatami. *The hushed quiet of the* haiden. *The silent dance of the kitten as Maru warred with the dappled sunlight. She found herself smiling, as if all the peace and love of the shrine filled her up and spilled over.'"* He closed the notebook. "Misa loved this place. You wrote the truth."

Nikki stared in horror at the notebook. "No, that can't be right. I never thought of her as real."

"She was."

Was. Even if she denied Atsumori's existence, the sword and burned shrine were proof that Yuuka . . . Misa had been real. Nikki had cried when she wrote the girl's murder but she nevertheless wrote it in full gory detail. And there was Gregory, dead by a blender. She had been so proud of his death scene that she posted it online hours before he was killed.

Everything she wrote was real? She didn't want it to be true. She knew her characters better than her few so-called "friends" and certainly better than any of her family members. She loved them. She cried as she wrote their slow and painful deaths. And they all died. She never had a character survive to "happily ever after." Tears started to burn in her eyes and she fought to keep from crying. She had bawled uncontrollably when she thought that her characters were no more than figments of her imagination. If she started to cry now, she wouldn't be able to stop. As she dug through her backpack, looking for tissues, she couldn't stop thinking about all her recent characters. How easy it had been to "think" in terms of the foreign Japanese culture. Little things like how a character would spell out their name in *kanji* when they met someone new.

"*I liked this part,*" Miriam had said after fact-checking Yuuka's introduction. "*But you used the wrong* kanji. *Her name would be Misa using those* kanji."

Nikki started to weep. Misa been so excited about the upcoming Gion Matsuri. She had gotten a new *yukata* to wear out to the festival. Nikki had come to Kyoto and toured Isetan and watched girls pick out *yukatas* in the kimono department. Had Misa been one of the girls Nikki spied on? Had Misa been the cute little high school girl trying on the white *yukata* with the scattering of pink flowers that Nikki took reference pictures of? The girl had felt *right* for Misa. She had been so cute and full of life. To think of her dead and dumped in the bushes by Gregory Winston . . .

Oh God, she'd written five deaths already, and there were a dozen other people who had "this will not end well" written all over them. All of them real people. All of them she knew better than she knew Miriam.

With that, she started to keen.

"What is wrong?" Atsumori asked.

"They're all going to die. I used to try and stop them from dying, but death is like this juggernaut. It just plows through everything I put up to slow it down and nails them hard. I've even tried switching characters to who I thought were nice and good and careful people and they do things like drive over the neighbor's toddler by mistake, or drop their hammer off a six-story roof onto a bypasser's head, or kill a teenage girl and burn down her family's shrine. I knew the moment that George—Gregory—walked up to the temple gate that he was going to kill Misa—somehow. Characters crossing paths always ends badly. It's like the Ghostbusters—don't cross the streams. Oh God, oh God, and I wrote myself into this novel!"

✠ 10 ✠
Boy God

The boy god or possible delusion was still sitting patiently beside Nikki when she woke up hours later. She was fairly sure she had been arrested, which meant Gregory was dead, so she'd probably been to his bloody apartment, so it was possible she'd found the *katana* at the train station. After that, it was a bobsled ride downward into either madness or divine possession. She still hadn't decided which.

"You don't sleep?" she asked to fill the silence.

"Sometimes. Although it's not as you would call sleep. I lose focus on your world. It is how the *gaijin* could wreak havoc on my temple."

She stretched, aching, having slept on the stone floor in slightly damp clothes. She didn't even have a change of clothing. At least with the money she—Atsumori—had stolen from Harada, she could buy more clothes. She was at a loss as to what . . .

. . . she was standing on a street corner in the rain, waiting for the light to change. Her backpack and the fabric-encased *katana* were slung on her right shoulder.

"Stop doing that!" Nikki cried, startling an old woman standing beside her.

Embarrassed, Nikki turned around and went into the FamilyMart on the corner. She made it a point to never have less than two notebooks and a full dozen pens. She kept to black ink only; her hypergraphia *needed* black. The other colors had been to soothe her writer's heart. At the moment her writer's heart was crying in the corner and had no interest in pens except as a medical device.

Clicking one of the ballpoints nervously, she moved on to her other drug—junk food. She got four salmon rice balls, a box of Meiji chocolate-covered almonds, a slice of chiffon cake, a bag of pepper-flavored potato chips, a sandwich that looked like it might be egg salad, and two bottles of Coke. After considering the state of her life, she added a coin purse, panty liners, two pairs of socks, six packs of tissues, and a folding umbrella. She caught glimpses of Atsumori moving through the aisles like a dark thundercloud, horribly out of place in the bright, squeaky-clean convenience store. Otherwise, he was invisible to her and obviously everyone else. She was considering alcohol when she sensed him close beside her.

"Don't just take me places without asking," she whispered. "I really, really hate that. If you keep doing that—I'll—I'll—" She clicked her pen. She hated that her options were so limited. But she couldn't stand being used that way. It reminded her of being locked up in the sanitarium by her mother. Threatened with drugs and straightjackets if she wasn't compliant and "good." "I won't be used like that."

"I'm sorry. I did not consider that it would bother you now that you know the cause."

"It does." She picked a mini bottle of plum wine off the shelf and stomped to the cashier to pay for everything. It bothered her even more that there really was no way to stop him. He probably could keep hold of her as long as he wanted. Hours. Days. Weeks. "Just tell me where you want to go."

"*Eh?*" the cashier asked, wide-eyed.

"*Kyoto desu?*" She asked the first "where" question that came to mind. "*Is this Kyoto?*" pushed the limit of her Japanese.

"*Hai!*"

So they were still in Kyoto; Atsumori hadn't taken her out of the city. Yet. She had things she wanted to do before she let Atsumori drag her all over Japan. The first was finding a bathroom. "*Toire wa doko desuka?*"

"*Toire.*" The cashier considered and then pointed across the street. "Subway station."

She glanced to where he was pointing and saw the steps leading down into a subway station and probably a public restroom. *"Arigato!"*

Her panty liners were given special treatment. They were discreetly packed into a separate brown paper bag that the Japanese used only for feminine products. The package nearly screamed "cooties."

Outside she said to Atsumori, "I'm going to the bathroom." Hopefully alone but she doubted it. "And then to have something to eat. Then I'll go wherever you want."

Nikki found a pay phone at Kyoto Station and fed it hundred yen coins, praying that she wouldn't have to deal with a Japanese-speaking operator. She wrote out some stock phrases in case the person who answered the phone didn't speak English.

After three rings, the other end picked up with a meek, *"Moshi moshi."*

"Pixii, *desu?"* Nikki read off her cheat sheet. "Is Pixii" was the closest she could figure out to "Is Pixii there?"

A very Japanese "eh?" of surprised confusion was the only reply.

She tried to calmly repeat the question. Slower. "Pixii, desu?"

"Hai?" The other person sounded like they were in grade school. *"Donata desu ka?"*

Nikki wasn't sure, but she thought the person had asked "Who's calling?"

The one and only time she actually met Pixii was at an East Coast anime convention four years ago. Nikki had been traveling with a pack of teenage girls and somehow ended up responsible for cleaning up after all the naïve stupidity that implied. Pixii had been dressed up as a magical girl from some anime that Nikki didn't recognize. The only thing Nikki remembered clearly from the meeting was that Pixii could beat the snot out of any man who thought scantily clad girls doing cosplay were sluts, and then administer first aid to the wounds she inflicted.

Was this really Pixii?

Well, Nikki wasn't going to get anywhere if they kept to Japanese. "This is ThirdEye," Nikki identified herself reluctantly.

"Third! Oh my God, are you okay? Where are you? What

happened? SexyNinja has been going nuts! She says she tried calling you all last night and you never called her back!"

Nikki breathed out relief. Yes, she remembered now. Talking to Pixii was like having a conversation with a five-year-old on a sugar rush. Her voice was naturally little-girl cute, she was shorter than Nikki's five foot three, and, much to Pixii's disgust, she didn't need a bra. She looked and sounded like she was twelve years old, but in truth she was thirty, a veteran combat medic, and had a doctorate in arts and archeology.

"I'm fine," Nikki said. "I lost my cell phone yesterday. I need a place to crash. Can you put me up for a while?"

"Yeah! Team Banzai: *go!* It will be great." And then the brain caught up to the mouth. "Um, so, what happened? Why did you disappear? We expected you to post last night."

Nikki winced. This was so much more than just an overbearing mother. Of all her friends, Pixii was the one who could cope best with Nikki being either dangerously insane or merely possessed. "Things got crazy. I have some things to do, then I'm heading to your place."

"Oh! Do you need the directions again? My place is kind of impossible to find."

Which was one of the other reasons Nikki had chosen Pixii to crash with. "I've got them memorized. I'll call you again when I get to Nara."

"Great! Just keep your eye out for the little shrine alongside the road. The driveway back to the house can be tricky to spot. You might have to stop at the shrine and . . . oh shit, I need to go check the kiln!" And Pixii abruptly hung up.

Atsumori wanted to go to the Fushimi Inari Shrine. Luckily Nikki had planned a trip to visit it and knew that there was a train that stopped right in front of the shrine, otherwise Atsumori would have had her walk several miles in the rain. With his help reading signs, they found their way through the multiple train systems of Kyoto to the JR Nara line.

"Why are we going there?" she asked as they settled on the train. *We.* She laughed bitterly. To a causal observer, she was completely alone.

"Misa's death has desecrated my *shintai*. Until it's purified, I'm greatly limited in what I can do. We are going to the shrine to have my *katana* blessed."

"*Katana*" and "death" made her remember the scene she had written the night before. "Did I—you—we actually clean your blade?" Somehow that sounded slightly pornographic.

"Of course."

"And this blessing—it will—deal with—killing Harada, too?"

"He was a *tanuki*. He was *yokai*."

"And that means?"

"*Yokai* are not humans. They are not animals. They are spirits. They do not exist as you understand life."

"Harada bled all over the place."

"That was not his real body. He could take the shape of a small girl or a dog or even a teapot."

"Teapot?"

"In that case, instead of blood, he would have spilled tea."

Click. Click. Click.

"Who was that man?" Atsumori murmured in her ear.

Nikki looked around the train car, but she was alone, not even Atsumori was in sight. She could feel him, though, as if he was sitting beside her. "What man?"

"Last night on the train, you wrote about a man searching your home."

Nikki sighed. Thanks to a childhood spent in psychiatric treatment, she knew all the symptoms of schizophrenia and had always been secretly proud that she showed no signs of the disorder. She was now exhibiting almost all of them—if Atsumori wasn't actually sitting beside her, invisible to everyone. Then again, schizophrenics usually had self-referential delusions. The logic looped neatly around so it was nearly impossible to prove that their belief was false.

She couldn't help but see her current situation as classic symptoms. If *tanuki* could take on any appearance, then everything that had happened at her apartment made sense. She had opened the door to a magical creature that only looked like Detective Tanaka. It knew—somehow—that she would cooperate with the police. The *tanuki* shifted its appearance again as it attacked her to that of an animal wearing a business suit. Why, she didn't know. *Obviously changing into a teapot wouldn't have been helpful.*

If Gregory Winston, Misa, and Harada were all real people—or at least things that passed as people—then Scary Cat Dude was a real person, too.

"I don't know who he is. I've only written one other scene with him. He seems to be working with a powerful organization, like maybe the government or underworld."

"Underworld? With demons?"

"With criminals." She frowned as "demons" rolled around in her mind. Her hypergraphia liked the idea that Scary Cat Dude was linked to something otherworldly. Normally she would embrace such a notion, but then, normally, everything in her books stayed fiction. The burned-down shrine and the dead bodies were inescapable truth.

"He was at the shrine?" Atsumori asked.

"Yes." She flipped back through her notebook. She hadn't had a chance to type in the scene. "That was his first scene." She read over the pages, aware that Atsumori seemed to be scanning them with her. Did Japanese gods read English? She supposed it wouldn't be very godlike if they couldn't.

Atsumori thought aloud with a deep "Hmm."

Nikki really wished that if she could hear him, she could also see him. "What?"

"The *tanuki*, it killed the *gaijin?*"

"Yes, Harada killed . . ." She was now confusing her character name with the real man. Which was which? Not a good sign. ". . . him. In my story, the *gaijin* worked for an American insurance company." Was it true for the real man, too? She hated the idea of assuming what she wrote as fiction to be the whole truth. The fiction, though, explained why a businessman would suddenly become a criminal overnight. The real man kept rope in his bedroom dresser. "He had some kinks that would be illegal in the United States. He liked the image clubs in Dontonbori."

An image club had a variety of fantasy settings, and their prostitutes would dress up in costumes. As long as full penetration didn't take place, it was perfectly legal. He liked his women as young as possible, in a school uniform, either in a subway car or a classroom.

"He kept pushing the limits of the law until he found a *yakuza*-run image club that let him go beyond them."

The club had brought him into the orbit of Harada and various other characters in her book. They gave him a twelve-year-old Chinese girl and enough rope to hang himself with.

"They took videos of him with a child. It would have gotten him arrested here in Japan, but in the United States, he would have been labeled as a monster for the rest of his life."

"So it was these *yakuza* that sent him to my shrine?" Atsumori asked.

She nodded. "They told him to get a camera and pretend to be a tourist. To walk around and take pictures. He could go where no Japanese could. Where no Japanese would. He didn't believe in *kami*; he wasn't afraid of their wrath. They talked as if he would be safe from the *kami*."

"Humans like him are rare. If Misa had not taken my *shintai* off the shrine grounds, I would have only been able to protect her indirectly. I couldn't stop him. Not before he killed her. Nor afterwards. He was like scrabbling against polished stone."

"Harada had heard of the fire at the shrine and guessed that Gregory had set it. He went to Gregory's place disguised and, once inside the apartment, demanded the sword." The scene had confused her, as Gregory had started out treating Harada as an old friend that he was trying to brush off and then realized that he was talking to the *tanuki*. Until Harada broke the blender's glass pitcher against Gregory's head, the scene had been all dialogue and no description. Then everything had been Gregory—his pain, his screams, his blood. There hadn't been anything about his killer. She hadn't even been sure that Harada was a "he." It was as if she knew describing him would be useless, that she knew that he could utterly change his appearance.

Self-referential delusions, she reminded herself. She clicked her ballpoint.

The great entrance of the Inari Shrine was within a stone's throw of the tiny train station. As Nikki walked under the towering gate, Atsumori appeared beside her. It was weirdly comforting to be able to see him. In the timeless entrance plaza, he looked proper for the setting despite the sober kimono and topknot.

The shrine was the biggest she had ever seen. There were dozens of buildings within sight, gilded and brightly painted. A large bronze statue of a fox sat beside stairs leading up to the main temple, a red bib tied about its neck. It seemed to frown down at her, a large granary key in its mouth. Originally the god of rice, Inari had moved into the modern day by becoming the god of success and prosperity in business. The lavish temple was proof of the Japanese's belief in the god. There had been two Inari shrines within walking distance of Nikki's apartment in Otemae. She had toured them with curiosity but without reverence. She didn't believe in her mothers' one god; her childhood had been too unjust for there to be a benevolent, protecting spirit. She certainly hadn't believed in the complex Japanese mythology. Why a mischievous fox as the god of business? It seemed at once charming, childlike, and completely random.

If the *kami* Atsumori was real, and evidence was amounting that she wasn't completely delusional, what of Inari?

"Please, pray." Atsumori motioned to the front of the main shrine building. There were nearly a score of sturdy ropes leading up to bells hung overhead. Obviously he meant for her to pray like the Japanese did.

She fished out her coin purse and peered into it. How much should she offer? Normally people offered five- and ten-yen coins—basically the equivalent of nickel and dimes. She'd used up all her small coins making the phone call to Pixii. She only had one-yen and five-hundred-yen coins. Dropping four pennies into the offering box seemed insulting, while tossing five dollars in seemed too extravagant; but if there was a slim chance that Inari was going to answer her prayer, she wanted to be on his good side. She read once that the offering boxes were constructed so that the noise of coins falling would be loud, drawing the god's attention. Thinking of how Atsumori had slept through Misa's death, she dropped a five-hundred-yen coin into the box, shook the rope forcefully to ring the bell loudly, and then clapped her hands as hard as she could.

"Please help us purify Atsumori's *shintai*." She bowed.

Atsumori bowed along side her.

After a minute of silence, she asked. "Now what?"

"Five hundred yen for a purification?"

She jerked around, yelping in surprise.

A handsome Japanese boy grinned down at her. His hair was cut and styled into wild spikes, and he wore a high school uniform with disheveled grace. "Five hundred yen not nearly enough."

"How much is it?"

"What do you have?" He had her backpack off her shoulder and unzipped before she even realized he was reaching for it.

"Give that back!"

He pushed the paper bag containing the panty liners into her outstretched hands. "Don't need that. Hmm, this is interesting."

He was pulling her computer out of her backpack.

"No!" She dropped the panty liners and jerked her computer out of his hands. Hugging it to her chest, she backed away from it. "This isn't for trade, *baka*." It was one of the few Japanese insults that she knew. "We have yen. We can pay for it. Just tell us how much."

"What's the fun of that?" He strolled away, still rooting through her backpack.

"Hey!" She snatched up her panty liners and chased after him. "That is mine."

"That's up for debate." He waved one of two rice balls she had saved for her lunch in the air before biting into it.

"It is not! That is my backpack, my belongings, my lunch!"

"Yet you come begging for a purification."

"I was not begging."

"Yes, we were," Atsumori murmured.

Nikki glared at him.

"I asked you to pray to Inari for help," Atsumori said. "Prayer is to ask earnestly for help from one greater than yourself. That is begging."

"I don't want to argue semantics right now," Nikki whispered to Atsumori. "Can we have this discussion at some other time?"

"No, we're having it now," the boy mumbled around the remains of her rice ball. "You should always understand the nature of the relationship that you're entering into before you commit to it."

"Give me back my backpack, and then we'll have this conversation."

He stole the second rice ball and the mini bottle of wine out of her backpack and then tossed it to her. "Number one: humans are like rocks."

"What?" Nikki carefully tucked her computer back into place and zipped her backpack shut.

"I'm defining the nature of the relationship." The boy beckoned, continuing up the staircase out of the grand square. "Humans can be porous as sand or solid as granite."

"You mean in terms of a *kami* affecting them?"

"Exactly. Number two: *kami* are like water. They flow. How well they can flow into a human depends on how porous the human is."

"What does this have to do with purifying the *katana*?"

The boy laughed and twisted the lid off the wine. "Everything." He took a swig. "Or nothing. That is what you need to decide."

The stairs led up and up through countless bright red *torii* spaced less than a foot apart. It was one thing to know from the guidebooks that they numbered over ten thousand, but it was another thing to see them marching up the mountainside, seemingly without end. It felt like some odd twist to reality.

"I don't understand," Nikki said.

"Number one: humans are like rocks."

"You said that."

"It bears repeating until you understand it. Most humans are somewhat porous, but they're not easy for a *kami* to flow into. Most humans need to perform rituals to open themselves up for a *kami* to enter. Some humans are solid as granite; not even Susanoo can push his way into them. A handful of humans are like sand."

Atsumori had taken her over without a ritual.

"I'm like sand?" Nikki said.

"Are you?" The boy smiled innocently.

Nikki considered the boy. Who was he? What was he? Could he see and hear Atsumori—or had he merely reacted to her side of the conversation? "I don't know."

The boy took another swig of wine. "I would think that would be a very dangerous thing to not know about oneself."

"How is it dangerous?

"Number two: *kami* are like water." He laughed at the look of disgust she gave him, and then he sobered. "Have you ever seen what water can do to rocks?"

They had been steadily climbing the gentle wooded slope of the mountain flanking Kyoto. The path weaved back and forth through the trees, nearly continuously flanked by the red-painted *torii*. It had rained that morning, and the water dripped from the leaves.

They were suddenly overrun by a dozen high school girls in tan skirts and blazers coming down the mountain. The girls went by as silently and shyly as a herd of deer. Atsumori and the boy had stepped off the path, so there was no way to judge if the girls had seen either one.

Was their guide a *kami* pretending to be a high school student? Or was he a human possessed by a god? Or just a kid messing with Nikki's head? The only godlike thing about the boy was that he spoke English as fluently as Atsumori.

Of course, that all looped back to the possibility that she might be alone, wandering around lost. Certainly she had no idea where they were headed except "up."

"Where are we going?" Nikki asked.

The boy drifted out into the middle of the path, walking backwards as he spoke. "A shrine maiden will have to do the purification. After it is done, your angry friend will be free to wreak his revenge, whether you want to join in or not."

"Revenge?" Nikki turned to look at Atsumori.

"I will not force you," Atsumori said quietly. "The *gaijin* was merely a tool that could be safely used. If we do not deal with the *yakuza* . . ."

"No." Nikki stopped walking.

" . . . they will be free to use someone else to take my *shintai*."

She unslung the *katana* from her shoulder.

Atsumori's eyes went wide. "Please, I beg you, do not abandon me."

Their guide took three quick steps back, distancing himself from her. "No, I cannot take it."

Nikki considered just laying the sword down and trying to walk away. Would Atsumori let her? Could she actually do it? He'd been trapped with the locker at the crowded train station, hundreds of thousands of people walking past him and not one able to help him. Here he would be stuck on the path until someone came: a high school student, a priest, or a random businessman. He would be at their mercy. Knowing the lawfulness of the Japanese, the sword would be taken to the local police station.

"Nikki, please. For a thousand years, my family has guarded my *shintai*. Those men sent a *gaijin* to kill my beloved child and burn down my home. They sent a *tanuki* to kill you and take me back. We cannot just ignore them and hope they will leave us both alone."

She glanced to their guide, who took another step back.

It would be like walking away from a man without legs as he pleaded with her for help. How far could Atsumori follow her, begging her to come back? All the way down the mountain to the shrine's gate?

Meanwhile, the police would recognize the *katana* as the one stolen from Misa and probably dust it for prints and check for blood. They'd find Harada's blood and Nikki's fingerprints. Thanks to Gregory's murder, her prints were in the Japanese database.

The sword was real. Atsumori might be nothing more than her own madness. Leaving the sword would not distance herself from her own insanity.

"Fine." She shouldered the *katana* again. "But you will not use me to kill the *yakuza*."

Atsumori studied the ground for a moment, his jaw set. "I will not force you."

Somehow they had circled back to the first courtyard of the shrine. A heavy downpour started, clearing the plaza as people darted for cover. Most gathered in the little gift shop along the left wall of the square. Their guide dashed to the *kaguraden*. Nikki followed, annoyed that they had walked up and down the mountain for no reason—unless the reason was just to give her time to understand how completely screwed she was.

The open stage of the *kaguraden* was worn bare by hundreds of years of use. The sliding doors of the back wall had been painted with a mural nearly worn off. Only the suggestion of green treetops and mountain ranges remained. Shrine maidens in brilliant red trousers and crisp white short kimono tops had gathered along with musicians in kimonos. They went still in surprise as Nikki came up the stairs, dripping wet.

The oldest of the shrine maidens padded up to Nikki. "You wait." She pointed across the square to the gift shop crowded with tourists.

"*Sumimasen,*" Nikki bowed and apologized.

"Akane, she is my honored guest," the boy said in English.

The woman gasped slightly, her hand going to her mouth. She whispered something in Japanese.

It triggered an oddly stilted conversation.

"She has a sword that needs to be purified," the boy continued in English. "Burn what she is wearing."

"What?" Nikki cried.

The woman asked a question.

"You smell of blood," the boy said. "You will need to be purified as well as the sword."

"I'm a size eight. Do you know how hard it is to find jeans in Japan for me? Girls are like little twigs here!"

"You can wear a *yukata*."

Nikki squeaked in protest. "I—I—I stand out enough."

The woman asked another question in Japanese.

"You're a blond-haired, blue-eyed female, traveling alone," the boy said. "You couldn't stand out any more than if you wore a monkey suit. A *yukata* won't make a difference."

Nikki noticed that none of the shrine maidens was actually looking at the boy as he spoke. Most of them were staring at Nikki as if she'd grown two heads. She supposed that a dripping-wet woman with a sword would get that reaction. She wished she understood what the shrine maiden was saying to confirm that she wasn't the only one seeing the boy.

"You can stop at Isetan at the station," the boy said. "I promise you there will be a pair your size."

Could he promise that because he was Inari, god of good fortune? Or was he just a schoolboy saying whatever he needed to say to get her to cooperate?

The shrine maiden said something in Japanese, and the others stirred out of their confusion. Before she even knew what was happening, she was led back to a prehistoric bath and four women were attempting to strip her.

"No, no, no!" She smacked away their hands as she flashed suddenly to her first compliancy hearing, where her mother had done everything in her power to put Nikki's hypergraphia into overdrive. For some stupid reason, the laws allowed "emergency hospitalization" for seventy-two hours before a commitment hearing. "Harrowing" didn't even come close to describing the showers that the orderlies put her through for three days prior to the hearing. She swung up the *katana* to block their attempts, gripping the hilt in a way that should translate in any language. "Don't touch me! Don't fucking touch . . ."

. . . she was kneeling in the *kaguraden* as the shrine maidens danced around her to drum and flute. She was dressed in a white *yukata,* smelling faintly of soap. Her hair was gathered into a ponytail, still damp against the back of her neck. The *katana* lay on the worn wooden floor in front of her. Atsumori knelt beside her.

"I told you not to do that," she growled and started to rise.

"That was not me." Atsumori spoke in a rush, motioning for her to stay kneeling. "Lord Inari did not want you to harm his servants. You should not have threatened them with the *katana.*"

She glared at him but gravity and her knees forced her to sink back into a kneeling position. "You should have stopped him."

"I cannot." Atsumori bowed his head to the floor. "I know I told you that I would protect you, but the truth is that I am not a match in power to Lord Inari. He is a god. I am a simple samurai."

Or a complex psychosis brought on by years of abuse.

She glanced about her for some indication that someone else was aware of Atsumori.

The shrine maidens were dancing in solemn practiced moves in a circle around her to the beat of a deep drum. A flute thrilled through a thin, wavering melody. The maidens held in their hands a wand decorated with zig-zagging folded paper streamers that they occasionally waved over her head. Despite the music and the rustle of the wand, the ceremony was strangely quiet. She felt an odd crawl of electricity snake over her body, making all the fine hairs on her arms stand up.

Her fingers fidgeted, overwhelmed by all the weirdness and stress of the day. The need to write was beginning again. She clenched her hands tight.

"I can't take much more of this craziness," she whispered. "After this, we go to Osaka, get my passport and bank card, and go to Nara. Agreed? No attacking *yakuza* on our own."

"I will not force you," Atsumori said.

Which was not the same as agreeing, but she would have to be content. There was a good chance that she was merely arguing with herself.

11
The Cleaners

The annoying boy, who may or may not have been the god Inari, had disappeared, leaving her with only the shrine maidens, who were in awe of her. They whispered to her shyly in a mix of Japanese and mangled English. With Atsumori translating, she managed to understand that the white *yukata* was actually just for bathing and they wanted to swap it for a rich purple one with white rabbits. The outfit came complete with a wide *obi* belt that was white with pink cherry blossoms, white *tabi* socks, and sandals. Knowing that *yukatas* could run anywhere from fifty dollars to several hundred, she felt odd accepting it, but apparently her own clothes had already been burned. Even her bra and panties were gone. As she suspected, she'd been too wide in the hip for the underwear that the shrine maidens tried to provide. She felt weirdly naked.

"Lord Inari said you could buy clothes at Isetan." Atsumori vanished into thin air as she left holy ground.

She paused a moment, slightly dismayed by his disappearance, and then marched resolutely toward the small train station that was not much bigger than a ticket machine sheltered by a lean-to. "We're going back to Osaka. I need my passport and bank card."

Nikki felt like she was losing it. She'd spent so long being told that she was insane while everything around her was normal, that this roller-coaster ride through impossibilities was shaking her to her core.

It did not help that she'd lost almost everything she owned. Nor that she was the only non-Japanese person she'd seen all day. Or that the only person that she could easily communicate with might only exist in her own madness.

She clung to what she knew was undeniable truth. Gregory Winston was dead. The shrine had burned. Misa was dead. Wait, scratch that. She didn't know for sure that Misa/Yuuka was dead, because so far her only source for that was Atsumori.

She could nearly hear her doctors murmuring, "You're weaving a web of deception to support the implausible."

Of course, they were denying that her mother was being unfair to keep her locked up for basically a harmless illness. Not once had she ever threatened anyone or done anything that could be dangerous to herself. Of course, that could be different if she ever actually took the medicines that the doctors prescribed for conditions she didn't have—anti-depression medicine given to a mentally healthy person made them suicidal.

"No, that's what my mother wants: for me to admit I'm crazy and meekly take the pills and sit in a white room all day, stoned out of my mind."

She'd fought through years and years of being outnumbered, against any number of quacks who wanted to milk her mother for money, with the entire social machine at their backs. What a few gods and the Japanese underworld compared to that?

It did not help, though, that her stress-induced hypergraphia made it so hard to believe she was completely sane. Even if she could stop the hypergraphia, she still *needed* to write, because it was the only way she had to make money—unless, of course, she started prostitution or returned to the United States.

"I'm not going back." She realized that she was chewing on her fingernails and jerked her hand away from her mouth. She pulled out her notebook and found a pen. She flipped past the two last scenes, both featuring her new possible hero, the Scary Cat Dude. At some point she wanted to type them into her computer, but not now. Retyping scenes didn't satisfy her hypergraphia. She would get the need out of her system and then go back to Osaka, get her passport . . .

Had the Scary Cat Dude really been to her apartment?

If she wasn't writing the truth, then there was still a dead body—possibly—in her apartment—that might or might not be a supernatural monster or a police detective. She took a deep breath and let it out.

She would assume that everything was true. A *tanuki* came to her apartment disguised as Detective Tanaka and she . . . Atsumori had killed him. Scary Cat Dude had been to her apartment. He had made arrangements for the dead body to be removed. The important question was: did Scary Cat Dude take her passport and bank card? In the scene she'd written, he hadn't, but she had stopped writing before he left her place. He could have taken her purse, or he might have left it there for even scarier people to find. Or maybe "the cleaners" would take everything she owned out of the apartment. How thorough were these cleaners?

She laughed bitterly as she realized that she couldn't believe any of it had happened as she wrote it. It was all horribly ironic that she felt like she would need to be insane to believe the proof that she had never been crazy. She scrubbed at her face, trying to figure out what to do about her passport. If Scary Cat Dude or his cleaners had taken her purse, then going back to the apartment would be pointlessly dangerous. Everyone who was looking for her apparently knew where she lived: the police, the *yakuza*, and the mystery organization.

The only way of knowing was to extend the scene, but then the only reason for doing that was if she believed that she was writing the truth.

She eyed her notebook. All she had to do was write and believe. The last was going to be the hardest part.

He took pictures of the girl's Post-It Note wall as he quickly dissembled the collage of multiple-colored pieces of paper. Ananth had sent him to the apartment merely because she was a person of interest to the police and their leads had dried up. There had been no mention of her being a Talent. At this moment, he seemed to be the only person who realized she might have powers, and he intended to keep it that way. If the truth came out, someone else would be assigned to find the girl and he'd be back to chasing dead ends.

After he took down the Post-It Notes, he searched through her luggage for any traces of her writing. She had packed a dozen notebooks full of small but beautifully fluid handwriting. At the top of every page was a person's name, their color code, and whether the notes had been retyped into her computer. He stuffed the notebooks into a plastic shopping bag. He also found a flash drive in the zippered compartment of her suitcase. He shuffled quickly through the various loose flyers scattered throughout the room and he took any that had handwriting on them. He searched her purse; it yielded another flash drive, her passport, and her wallet with a New York State driver's license. He put all three into his coat pocket; he didn't want her leaving the country.

The door opened behind him, and he had his gun leveled at the new arrival before he recognized the fashionably scruffy man. "What are you doing here, Chevalier?"

He used Japanese since the Frenchman acted as if his limited French was a sign of a mental defect. What's more, Chevalier viewed any conversation in English as confirmation.

Chevalier waved an unlit cigarillo to take in the small room, the *tanuki*'s body, and the hallway behind him. "I'm babysitting this gathering of monsters." The Frenchman put the cigarillo into his mouth and muttered around it. "It's clear, *mon petit monstre.*"

Denjiro Sato drifted into the room, radiating his normal noble disdain toward everyone and everything. His first name meant "good ancestor" and he was proud of his bloodline that he could trace back to the supposedly divine bloodline of the Japanese emperors. Ironically, though, Sato was one of the most common last names in Japan. Sato acknowledged their presence with a cold look and then crouched down to examine the dead *tanuki*.

It would be easy to believe that someone had paired the two out of a twisted sense of humor. Chevalier and Sato were polar opposites. Chevalier's habit of leaning against any surface that would support his weight disguised his six-and-a-half-foot height. He had the French elegantly messy look down to a science, from his artfully tousled hair to his tailor-fitted suit with the half-buttoned shirt. He favored thin, leaf-wrapped mini cigars that reeked more than normal cigarettes. Scents clung to him, mapping out a day of coffee, cigarillos, soot, and blood. Apparently the pair had been following in his wake, cleaning up dangerous evidence. It was obviously fraying Chevalier's temper. The man didn't like being reminded that his greatest worth came from being dense as a rock. It often reduced him to glorified babysitter for more dangerous Talents like Sato.

On the other hand, if Sato was annoyed by the situation, it was hidden under his normal mask of aloofness. Nothing marked its day on him. Every strand of his long black hair was in place. His *salaryman* shirt and suit were neatly buttoned despite the heat. He would seem more regal, though, if he wasn't only five foot five. Face locked into neutral, Sato carefully searched the *tanuki's* pockets.

"Why are you still here, *Monsieur Minou?*" Chevalier spoke without taking the cigarillo out of his mouth, a ready excuse for his perfect Japanese. "Weren't you told to find the girl?"

It was tempting to shoot the man just for the insulting nickname, but he wasn't sure if he could take Sato. He holstered his gun. "I'm working on it. It looks to me that she's bolted." He nudged the abandoned suitcase as proof. "I'm trying to figure out where she'll run to."

Chevalier laughed as if the idea of him doing deductive reasoning was amusing. "*Pour penser, il faut un cerveau.*" The Frenchman leaned against the door and took out a lighter.

"Don't," he growled at the man.

"Ah, right, the legendary nose." Chevalier lit the thin cigarillo anyway. "A *tanuki* in an Armani suit knockoff? What's this world coming to, *Monsieur Minou?* All the monsters acting like they're human." The Frenchman grinned as he breathed out smoke; he was like a schoolboy poking at a caged lion with a stick, so pleased with his own courage.

Sato also ignored the baiting. He was probably well used to the taunting. "What's this girl's connection to Winston?"

"She's American." He volunteered the information only because they would probably already know it. Chevalier snorted, confirming his guess. "I don't know any other the connection."

"You didn't find anything to link her to him?" Chevalier asked.

"The *tanuki*." He fed them more information that they already knew. He was taking point on the search only because there were no solid leads. He would only stay in the point while the risk of an ambush outweighed finding anything useful. "Its scent was all through Winston's apartment. It had to have been the one that left the smeared paw prints in the fresh blood. It killed Winston last night and then came here tonight for the girl."

Sato gave him a long, measuring look. "It was killed by the *katana*."

"I could tell the killer used a blade," he admitted and added truthfully, "I didn't find a weapon other than the *tanuki*'s knife. You sure that it was the *katana* from the shrine?"

Anger flashed through Sato's eyes, but the man kept it off his face. "Of course I'm sure."

He nodded as if it were new information to him. "The *tanuki* must have found a connection between Winston and the girl before it killed him."

"Or it was just following the police reports like we are." Chevalier idly opened the refrigerator beside him, eyed the contents, and took out a can of Coca-Cola. "It would explain the time delay between killing Winston and attacking the girl."

He hadn't considered that possibility. *Yokai* were solitary creatures that coexisted alongside humans on the same level as house spiders, cockroaches, and feral cats. If the *tanuki* had information from police reports, then most likely it was working with humans, something they'd never seen before. It would explain, though, the number of robberies that they were investigating. "The *tanuki* came looking for the *katana*."

Chevalier laughed as he cracked open the Coke. "And found it the hard way."

Sato stepped across the body, carefully avoiding the pool of blood to retrieve the *tanuki*'s wallet from the bathroom. Before he could examine it, though, Chevalier snapped his fingers and held out his hand. Sato gave the Frenchman a long hard look and tossed the wallet to him.

Chevalier juggled Coke, cigarillo, and wallet to check its contents. The Frenchman grunted as he found the billfold empty. "Did you loot him?"

"Whoever killed him did. I'm assuming it was the girl."

Chevalier grunted again, unconvinced. "Really, why are you still here? Shouldn't you be trying to find this girl?"

"She's had at least an hour's head start, and we're one block from the subway." He gave the room one last scan to see if he missed anything. If he found anything new, he would have to share the information. Once he left, though, something important might be destroyed in the cleaning process. What was the lesser of the two evils? "She's got cash to travel. Using the automated ticket system, she could head for any point in Japan without leaving a paper trail."

Chevalier tucked the wallet into the breast pocket of his suit. "I'll have our people pull surveillance camera footage, starting with this station."

Normally he would have already made the call himself. *Kami* couldn't be photographed, though, not even when they were housed within a human. If the god enshrined in the *katana* was possessing the girl, then not a single security camera in the city would pick her up.

Sato placed his hand on the folding door. The cut fabric melded together, returning to whole. The patina of wear vanished from the door, and the smell of newness flooded the apartment. "It will take me hours to erase all this."

That was his cue to leave. Sato would remove all evidence that a fight had taken place: the broken door, the pool of blood, and the dead body. He would leave the bric-a-brac of Nikki Delany's life for the police to puzzle over, trying to understand why the American girl had suddenly gone missing.

Annoyingly, Chevalier chose to follow, carrying his stolen Coke. "What's in the bag?"

The top layer were flyers, so he took one out and handed it to the man. "They're tour books and flyers from places she's been. She's either going to head for friends or go someplace she's been to before."

It was a flyer for the Gion Matsuri, the month-long festival in Kyoto. Pictures dominated the glossy advertisement but the information was all in Japanese. How fluent was she? It could be a factor in where she might hide. Her elegant cursive handwriting flowed around a picture of the float procession.

Chevalier read the English words aloud. "'In 869, the entire country was struck by a plague. Emperor Seiwa sent an envoy to the Yasaka Shrine in Kyoto to pray to the god Susanoo to end the country's suffering. He ordered the creation of sixty-six halberds, one for each province, to be erected at the palace's garden and then had the portable shrines carried by strong young men from the temple to the palace garden. For more than a thousand years, Kyoto has celebrated

Gion Matsuri. It is one of the three largest festivals in all of Japan. It infuriates Kenichi's princess.' Why?"

Chevalier raised an eyebrow in question. "Who is Kenichi?"

"I don't know," he said truthfully enough.

Down on the street, with Chevalier's smoke dulling his senses, there was no trace of Nikki's scent. He wanted away from the man so he could examine in peace the flash drive he had found. He unlocked his car with his remote and slid in behind the wheel.

Chevalier climbed in the passenger side without asking permission.

He gripped the steering wheel tight, trying to hold in his anger. "Aren't you supposed to be watching Sato?"

"He doesn't like me crowding him while he works. He's a good little monster; he'll stay put."

The steering wheel was starting to bend, so he eased back on his grip. "You do know that he can make you vanish with a touch of his hand?"

Chevalier laughed. "No, no, he can't hurt me. That is why I'm his babysitter. I'm impenetrable to such things that go bump in the night. The monsters, they cannot touch me."

"I can touch you."

Chevalier laughed. "Ah, yes, *Monsieur Minou*, I am not bulletproof, and you are heavily armed. But you also know that if you go rogue, all the monster hunters will come crashing down on your head. Then who would be left to find Simon, *mon ami?*"

He hated that the answer was no one.

"I am worried—What the hell? Do you have something living in your—" Chevalier suddenly yelped as Misa's kitten latched all four sets of claws into his ankle. Swearing, Chevalier stomped down hard, and there was a cry of pain.

His gun was out and at Chevalier's head before the man could stomp a second time. "Hurt it again, and I'll kill you."

"Are you fucking insane?"

"Get out."

After the Frenchman scrambled out of the car, he pulled away quickly. He wanted to put distance between him and the desire to put a bullet into Chevalier's brain. At the first light, he reached down and fished the kitten out of the passenger leg well.

It gave a piteous cry as he ran fingertips over it, searching out where it was hurt. Luckily, Chevalier's aim was off as always. He'd only gotten the kitten's tail.

"Let this be a lesson. Don't jump something that is bigger than you."

His phone rang. That would be Ananth whipping him back into line.

He answered his phone with, "He left Sato unguarded, pushed into my space, and kicked my cat. I didn't shoot him. I could have shot him, dumped his body, and let everyone think Sato had slipped his leash."

"I'm giving you a chance. Stop pulling guns on people or I'll have you put down."

He clenched down on a growl. The kitten climbed up to his shoulder to rumble counterpoint in his other ear.

"You find anything at the girl's apartment which could tell us where she's taking the *katana*?" Ananth asked.

"No." He had the feeling that it was the other way around. The *katana* was taking Nikki Delany someplace. If the *kami* possessed her too long, though, it would kill her. If all the abandoned pieces of her life told a true story, her death would be sad. "I'll call you if I find her."

Nikki sat back in the seat, biting down on a groan. If she was writing the truth, then Scary Cat Dude had her wallet and passport. If.

She still needed to go to her apartment. She needed to see for herself what the truth really was.

✠ 12 ✠
Erased

She got through Umeda in record time as Atsumori guided her. "How do you know your way around better than me?"

"I am a god and you are not." Atsumori used her mouth to speak. It was a weirdly uncomfortable feeling, and she decided not to ask any more questions.

She dithered on the corner across from her building, pretending to study the selection of drinks in the vending machine. It was a Coke machine with all the familiar soda logos sporting *kanji* lettering. Her focus, though, was on her balcony. The light was off in her apartment—the last she could clearly remember, it had been on. She didn't have her keys. If whoever turned off the light also locked the door—Atsumori, the Scary Cat Dude, the police—then she had no way to get in without talking to the landlord. If the landlord unlocked the door herself, there was way the woman would miss the dead body on the floor.

If it was still on the floor.

Maybe the light bulb had burned out.

She wasn't accomplishing anything out on the corner. This was the first real concrete proof that what she wrote wasn't a forgotten news report wrapped in insanity. She had to go and see the truth for herself. The bloody insanity or the clean impossibility. She steeled herself to walk across the street and into her building.

The lobby was empty. A security camera on the elevator fed video to a monitor opposite the elevator's door. Nikki glanced at the screen as she pushed the call button. The elevator car was up on the ninth floor. Its doors were closing, whoever had gotten off was already out of sight.

There was a long pause as the electronics considered possible directions, and then slowly the car started down to the lobby.

"Come on, come on." Nikki whispered to it, trying to watch both the monitor and the lobby door at the same time.

She was aware of a tension shimmering through her body; Atsumori was readying for a fight. The ritual at Inari's shrine had apparently eliminated all barriers between them. She felt him merging with her and she no longer blacked out. It was weirdly uncomfortable—like she suddenly had been made a glove—but she preferred it to losing consciousness.

She wanted to tell him to stay out of her, but she was afraid that she might need him.

The elevator doors opened. A mirror hung on the back wall of the car, probably in an attempt to make the tiny space seem bigger. Her reflection had Atsumori's fierce brown eyes. She stepped into the elevator and turned around so she wasn't facing the mirror. For some odd reason, the security camera hadn't caught her entering. According to the video monitor, the elevator was empty.

Keeping an eye on the monitor, she stepped closer to the camera and then raised her hand up to cover its lens. The monitor still showed an empty car with the doors standing open.

She smacked the camera lens. "I'm here! Show me!"

The monitor continued to deny her existence as it showed the doors closing.

Had someone looped the video feed? She hit the "Open" button, and the screen showed the doors reopening. No. According to the monitor—or maybe just her perception of the monitor she just wasn't *there*. Which had gone crazy: *her* or the universe?

The frightening truth was that it made more sense for it to be her.

She punched the "6" button and rode up to her floor. The dead body of a man she had killed shouldn't be comforting, but part of her really hoped that was what she would find in her apartment. It would be there, real and undeniable. If it was gone she would be faced with two possibilities: that there had never been a dead man, or that she had written a true account of some secret organization quietly covering up a murder. The first was so much more logical and reasonable than the second.

She felt like she was racing around and around the question of whether she was crazy. It had always been comforting to run through the symptoms of schizophrenia and not find any of them in herself. The last few days had rattled her confidence. Delusions of being possessed, hearing voices, and believing in secret conspiracies were classic symptoms. She knew that schizophrenic patients could weave a tight fabric of delusions that even a sane person couldn't unravel because of the interdependent logic. "Invisible aliens controlled people via messages hidden in cellphone signals" was impossible to disprove, since the aliens were invisible and the messages concealed. "Japanese spirits living in swords" wasn't that far removed from invisible aliens.

Was her very attempt to cling to the claim of sanity proof that she was insane?

The elevator dinged as it stopped on the sixth floor. After a pause, the door rolled open. She stepped out, her footsteps loud in the bare concrete hallway.

At her door, she hesitated. Which did she really want? Dead body or clean room? Proof that she'd been attacked or complete lack of evidence?

Taking a deep breath, she opened the door.

The room held the new *tatami* smell of freshly cut hay. The bathroom door was closed; there was no hole cut through the fabric. The room was cleaner even than when she moved in and certainly the neatest it had ever been while she was living there. Everything was carefully put into place. Her Post-It Notes were all missing, and the wall looked newly painted.

"Damn you," she whispered.

Fighting to control her anger, she stepped into her apartment and closed the door.

"What is wrong?" Atsumori asked.

"I almost died here. I killed a man. And they erased it all until only the absence of dirt stands as evidence."

"Who are they?"

"I don't know."

Her keys sat on her table, in full view of the door, beside her purse. Anyone else would have thought she had just stepped out for some harmless errand—like taking out the trash—and just never came back. Whispering curses, she snatched up her purse and rooted through it. The useful clutter of her life—her iPod, packs of tissues, and city maps—was all there. Her passport, driver's license, and credit cards were all gone.

The Scary Cat Dude had taken them. Somehow, she had to get them back.

✢ 13 ✢
The Castle

Still shaking with anger, Nikki stripped off her borrowed *yukata*, pulled on underwear, dressed in jeans and a T-shirt, quickly packed her suitcase with the rest of her clothes, and then fled. She had planned to go straight to the train station and go to Nara, where Pixii lived. She couldn't leave, though, until she managed to get back her passport and wallet.

Osaka Castle sat in the heart of the city, a pocket left over from the past, surrounded by a nearly half-square-mile park. Around it was a deep moat filled with jade-green water. Wide stone ramps led up to great iron-clad wood gates looking big enough for elephants to pass through. A cobblestone road wound uphill, between walls of massive stones fitted together like the building blocks belonging to a giant child. Beyond a second gate were a dojo and a Shinto shrine and yet a third gate leading to a courtyard at the foot of the towering castle. Dusk was racing toward night. She'd been to the castle enough times to know that the little gift shops and food stands in the stone courtyard were still open but the entire park area would be practically deserted. She hit the stand selling fried octopus dumplings, *takoyaki,* and then retreated to the shrine to think.

Who were these bastards? What right did they have to come into her apartment and erase all evidence that she had fought for her life against a supernatural monster? Okay, maybe it was a good thing that

111

they'd taken away the body. A dead raccoon dog in a business suit would have been hard to explain to the landlord.

Why did the *tanuki* attack her?

In her novel, Harada worked for a *yakuza* crime boss. Harada had heard about the shrine fire, gone to Gregory Winston's apartment to collect the *katana*, and lost his temper when Gregory told him that he didn't have the sword. How did Harada end up at her apartment? Had he followed her from the train station? No, he'd come disguised as Tanaka, so he must have known the detective had questioned her. It suggested that the *yakuza* had access the police records but not necessarily police cooperation, or Tanaka would have come himself.

When had Harada taken over Tanaka's identity?

It was possible that the person who arrested her had been Harada all along. Once she considered the possibility, though, it seemed more likely that she had been questioned originally by the real Tanaka. Harada would never have taken her to the police station in the first place.

"What's wrong?" Atsumori interrupted her thoughts.

She blinked, and realized she was sitting with a *takoyaki* halfway to her mouth. "Huh?"

"You—you made a noise."

"Oh, um, I thought of something."

She had chosen to hide at the Hokoku Shrine inside the castle's compound so she could see Atsumori when he spoke to her. She didn't need her sanity rattled any more than it already was. They were in the back of the shrine in a secluded rock garden, well out of sight of the gate. The boy god had been pacing restlessly around the small grassy islands that the rocks sat on. It felt like they had slipped into a twilight world, the setting sun spilling gold light over the rock garden and the thick castle walls secluding them from the distant traffic. The only sounds she could hear were his footsteps crunching on the gravel and the caws of the crows.

"What did you think of?" he asked.

She gave a bitter laugh and lowered her chopsticks, resting the octopus dumpling back with its brethren. "Oh, it just occurred to me that if I had done the sane thing, I wouldn't have had you with me when Harada came to my apartment. I would have been sitting there, sorting through all the bric-a-brac of my life, thinking that the only person I needed to stay one step ahead of was my mother."

He frowned slightly. "You are running from your mother?"

"She thinks I'm crazy." She laughed bitterly again. "If I tried to explain any of the last twenty hours to her, she would know I'm crazy."

"You are not insane."

"Says the god," Nikki murmured and picked the *takoyaki* back up with her chopsticks. "Are you hungry? Do you eat?"

"I feed upon the spirit of the offering."

She winced. Put that way, it made him sound like a vampire. She understood what he really meant. Maybe. She believed that he was nourished not by the food but the goodwill behind it. "Here. You can have the rest of these." The *takoyaki* were good but rich and slathered with sauce and mayonnaise. They were only sold in eight packs as a traditional pun on the fact that octopi had eight tentacles. "I'm stuffed."

He came to sit beside her, the *takoyaki* on his lap as if he was about to open them up and eat them. She lay back on the stone patio and watched the sunlight fade out of the sky.

Good news: she didn't have a homicidal stalker hacking her data files, and the slightly unhinged shape-changing assassin was dead. There were, however, two organizations moving through the shadows, both possibly criminal in nature, looking for the *katana*. The *yakuza* had proven that they were willing to kill to get it. The other one had a weird "James Bond" feel to it—as if the British Secret Service were employing Frenchmen and monsters.

Scary Cat Dude was right in thinking that, with cash, she could make her way to any point in Japan without leaving a paper trail. She could most likely bolt to Tokyo without fear of trouble following.

While she had a thousand dollars worth of yen in hand, she would need access to her bank accounts sooner or later. Without proof of identification, she couldn't replace her bank card. And there was the small technicality that she was only legally in the country for another thirty days.

She needed to get her passport back. In the United States, she could have breezed through life without it. In Japan, though, everyone who looked at her knew that she didn't belong. Everything from the shape of her eyes to the color of her hair marked her as a foreigner.

So how did she go about contacting Scary Cat Dude?

He had a cell phone. If she could find out his number, she could call him. She didn't know his real name, but he *was* one of her characters. She might be able to write a scene where he tells someone his phone number.

She sat up, dug out her notebook and pen and, in the gathering darkness, started to write.

It took him the rest of the day to find out anything new about Nikki Delany. She hid everything about herself behind an impenetrable wall of secrecy. Both her phone and her flash drive were protected with passwords. In the case of the flash drive, it was ten characters of upper-and lower-case letters mixed heavily with numbers. He needed to call in a favor to have both passwords cracked. The flash drive contained word-processing documents; the handwritten information in the notebooks typed in and embellished. There was nothing of her: no address book or e-mails or calendar.

The prepaid cell phone had been decorated with cherry-blossom stickers and a half-dozen overly cute charms dangling from straps. It looked like a phone that any Japanese teenage girl would be carrying. It was utterly devoid, though, of any personal data. There were no numbers in the contact list. The incoming and outgoing call logs were all scrubbed clean. If he hadn't taken it from her purse, he wouldn't have been able to guess it belonged to her.

Who was this girl? Why was she so careful?

The phone did have dozens of photos, but only of manhole covers, vending machines, and bicycle chains. He thumbed through a collection of links, sprockets, and chain guards from various city bikes, wondering at her fascination. What did they have to do with a *kami* enshrined in a stolen *katana* and a dead *tanuki*?

He was about to abandon the phone when it rang. He read the caller ID as he waited for the call to drop to voice mail. It was a local number. Nikki Delany knew at least one person in Osaka.

Luckily Miriam Frydman wasn't as secretive as Nikki Delany. By the start of evening rush hour, he knew her life history. Miriam was the second child of four siblings, but the only one who attended a boarding school. That hint of her being a problem child was smoothed over by the fact that she had no criminal record, had graduated from high school with honors, and had been accepted to Princeton University's East Asian Studies Department. She was in Japan on a work visa, employed as a translator by the gaming company Capcom, and living in Osaka. By his standards, she was squeaky clean.

Miriam called Nikki's phone a dozen more times; she obviously didn't know that Nikki had abandoned her ID and cell phone at her apartment. If that was the case, she also didn't know that Nikki had bolted. Most likely, Miriam's next step would be to visit Nikki's apartment. Sooner or later, the people who sent the *tanuki* after Nikki would be looking for their "man." It would be best if squeaky clean didn't cross paths with monsters—human or otherwise.

He caught up to Miriam as she stepped onto the subway train. She sensed him before she saw him moving toward her and shied away, scanning the other passengers with wide frightened eyes until she spotted him. And then her eyes went even wider, as if she knew what he was.

He should have guessed that Miriam Frydman would be a Sensitive. Talents like Nikki Delany were like metaphysical bonfires to spiritual moths.

"Ms. Miriam Frydman, I'm with the FBI." He flashed a badge to prove it, but she didn't believe him. Even a normal person would have trouble lying to a Sensitive.

She edged toward the door, trying to flee. "I didn't think the FBI had jurisdiction overseas."

"The FBI investigates any murder of an American citizen abroad." He stuck as close to the truth as he could. "I'm looking into the murder of Gregory Winston on Saturday night."

She hit the closed door, and her eyes widened even more. "I don't know anything about it. Really. My friend is writing a horror novel, and some psycho fan copied one of the murders from the book."

"Yes, I know." He knew that Nikki Delany had written Gregory's murder hours before it happened. It was the most recent file saved on her flash drive. The wall of Post-It Notes was an accurate portrayal of the current condition of Nikki's work. The novel wasn't one solid manuscript, but hundreds of scenes labeled by the "character's" initials and a seemingly random numbering scheme. For some reason, though, she had changed everyone's name. So far, he hadn't been able to identify what name she'd given Simon.

"We think that Ms. Delany might be in danger," he said truthfully. "Do you know where she is?"

The next station was announced, and she relaxed slightly with the promise of escape. "She's probably doing research for her book. During the week, she visits locations she's using for her novel. She goes out to Kobe, Kyoto, and such by train."

In other words, she could be anywhere. "Is she fluent in Japanese?"

"No, but you really don't need to be to get around."

The train was slowing down as it entered the next station. All around them, people shifted, readying themselves for the doors to open. Miriam's relief grew more evident on her face.

"Ms. Frydman, we believe Ms. Delany is in danger." All evidence of the struggle in the apartment had been erased, so he stayed vague about the location. "She was attacked by a man armed with a knife last night in Otamae."

"What? Was she hurt?"

"We don't know. We found her phone. We know you've been calling her."

Miriam whispered a curse. "I'm going to her place now."

"I would advise against that. She's not at her apartment. You might make yourself a target if you go looking for her."

"I don't fucking care! She's my best friend. She's in this mess because I talked her into moving to Japan!"

"You can help her by telling me where she might go to be safe. Does she know anyone else in Japan?"

There was someone else; he saw the thought flash across Miriam's face. The girl, however, only shook her head.

He put his hand on the door behind her and leaned over. He hated having to terrorize her, but better him than someone who would actually hurt her. "We think that Gregory Winston might be related to a murder in Kyoto. A sixteen-year-old girl was killed and then raped."

Miriam went pale at the news. "Was—was she a shrine maiden?"

He nodded. Nikki must have shared her writing with Miriam.

"And someone set fire to her family shrine?" she asked.

"Yes."

"Oh God!" Miriam gasped. The level of her shock was measured by the fact that the train pulled into the station and the door opened without her seeming to notice. She flinched hard as he caught her arm and pulled her onto the platform. "This isn't the right stop."

"You're not to go to her apartment. She's not there, but he might be."

She frowned up at him, nearly vibrating with fear and anger. "Let me see your ID again."

He gave it to her, and she studied it closely.

"What is it with government employees?" she grumbled. "Every one I've ever met has never told the whole and honest truth."

"People don't want the truth. It's big and scary. It has sharp teeth, and it's hiding under the bed, just waiting for the lights to go out."

She jerked her gaze up from his badge to glare at him. "Lying doesn't make the monsters go away."

Had she spent her childhood terrorized by things no one else could see? The boarding school made more sense now. Her parents must have given up and written her off as impossible to deal with. Let someone else deal with the child who insisted that monsters were real.

"No, it doesn't make them go away." He sighed. He'd had this argument countless times with Simon; the irony was that he normally took Miriam's side. "Just—just sometimes it's easy to be wrong." He couldn't tell her about the *tanuki* and *kami,* if for no other reason than that he wasn't sure what had happened in Nikki Delany's apartment on Sunday night. He was fairly sure, though, that Nikki was in over her head. "Ms. Delany might have been taken by force. There's no way I can know for sure without checking the places where she might hide. If she was taken, I need to find her—quickly."

She sensed he was telling the truth, but she still didn't trust him. She hunched her shoulders against the burden of protecting her friend in the face of danger and stared down at his ID. She traced her fingertips over his badge as if she could sense the twofold truth and lie held within it.

"We've been friends since high school," she said softly. "Her mother is a control freak. Nikki just wanted to get away from her. Coming to Japan was my idea. We had this plan—we go to Princeton and come here at the same time—but everything kept going wrong. We were supposed to have an apartment together. We were supposed to watch out for each other."

"Please . . ." Asking her to trust him was impossible; all her senses had to be telling her that he was dangerous. "I can protect her. I promise you."

She flinched slightly as if he had hit her. "I don't know where she is. Her mother made it impossible for her to make friends. I'm the only person that she *knows* here in Japan."

The joy of working with Sensitives was that they were so used to being able to tell when someone was lying that they operated on the assumption that everyone had the same ability. They told shades of truths. The key word obviously was "know." There was someone that they both considered trustworthybut whom Nikki didn't know. A friend of Miriam's that Nikki had never met? An estranged family member? Whoever it was, Miriam wasn't going to tell him.

But the moment he was out of sight, she'd contact whoever it was to see if Nikki was safe. All he needed to do was give her a chance to make the call.

He pulled out the card that said "Tobias Gregson, Special Agent" and listed his cell phone number as 06-4397-2948. "Call me if you hear from her." With that, he let her flee.

Nikki frowned at the page. She could tell that the card was a lie. His name wasn't Tobias Gregson; that was a name she would pick out for some obscure literary in-joke. Gregson was a police officer in Doyle's Sherlock Holmes mysteries; Holmes thought the policeman had promise. She sensed, too, that Scary Cat Dude wasn't an FBI agent, but if someone called the FBI, they would unhappily vouch for him. He worked for someone who moved in the shadows. Maybe the CIA. It still felt more like British Secret Service, although she wasn't sure why. The phone number on the card didn't connect directly to his cell phone; he wouldn't give out his real cell phone number. Someone could track him via his phone. The number on the card, though, somehow reached him. A whole web of lies surrounded him, and yet, for some reason, he felt trustworthy.

She became aware of Atsumori leaning against her, feeling as solid as a real person, reading what she wrote.

"Is this the same man as before?" he asked. "The one that searched your apartment?"

"Yes." She realized that Atsumori might not approve of her plan and had the ability to stop her. "I was worried about my friend, Miriam, but he kept her from going to my apartment. She's safe. I need to go to the bathroom."

She put away her notepad and stood up. He rose with her. Not good. She liked Atsumori as far as boy gods went, but if handing him over to Scary Cat Dude meant Miriam would stay safe, she'd do it in a heartbeat. At least she would try. With him riding her shoulder, though, she probably couldn't.

"I really want some privacy to pee. I'm just going up to the gift shop to use the one in the courtyard. I should go quickly—I don't know if they lock those for the night."

She tucked his *katana* up into the eves of the shrine. "I'll be right back."

She half-expected him to possess and stop her, but he didn't. She walked away trying not to feel like she was betraying him.

She went to the bathroom first, rehearsing what she was going to say. Then, with heart pounding, she fumbled coins into the pay phone and dialed Scary Cat Dude's number. There were some odd clicks, and then it rang.

"*Moshi moshi.*" He had a voice like distant thunder, a deep menacing rumble.

"Scary Cat Dude, is that you?"

He breathed out a huff of surprise. "Nikki Delany?"

"You have my wallet and passport."

"I do."

The important stuff established, they listened to each other breathe. She was hoping he would say, "I'll give it back" to make things simple.

"I want them," Nikki said. "Needed" was more accurate, but it was a weaker position.

"You have the *katana*."

"I know where it's hidden."

They listened again to the rhythm of the other's breathing. He was in a room or a parked car, no other sound leaking into the conversation. What was he learning from her silence? Dusk had given way to full night; the cicadas finally quiet. The sound of distant traffic was muted by the thick stone walls of the castle.

It started to rain, the raindrops glittering as they fell into the pool of light around the phone booth. Beyond Nikki's island of brightness, the darkness seemed to close in.

"Are you still there?" Nikki hunched against the falling rain.

"Stay where you are. I'll be right there." He hung up.

She cursed as she realized that he hadn't asked where she was. He got her position that quickly? Part of her just wanted to run and keep running. If she was going to get her passport back, though, she needed to stick to the plan.

Nikki didn't know where he was when she called him, but it must have been close. It was only a few minutes before he ghosted out of the darkness into her island of light. She recognized him even though she had never considered what he looked like; the angular shape of his face, his long black hair, and the way he moved reminded her of a lion. He looked very scary-sexy in a black trench coat.

She had one moment of intense relief until she noticed the gun in his hand.

He gave her an odd look, as if she'd confused him and surprised him at the same time. "What are you doing standing in the rain?"

"You told me to stay put." Her teeth started to chatter.

He scanned the darkness around them for hidden dangers, finding nothing. He studied her again, still looking confounded. Then he looked away, set his shoulder, and said, with his voice full of ridicule, "You should have taken shelter."

"I didn't want to risk you not finding me."

"Here, take my coat." He took off his long black trench coat, a dozen sizes too big for her, and handed it to her, still warm from his body. She slipped it on and wrapped her arms around her, trapping in the heat, feeling guilty as the rain started to fall harder.

"Where's the *katana*?" He had made his gun disappear behind his back when he took off his coat. He produced it again like a magic act.

It took all her courage to say, "Give me my passport and wallet."

He considered her long and hard. He reached into his back pocket and pulled out her belongs, including her phone, and held them out to her.

Sniffling in the cold rain, she glanced inside her passport to verify it was hers and then checked to make sure her bank card, credit card, and driver's license were still inside her wallet.

"Where's the *katana*?"

"Why do you want it? Aren't there freaking gods everywhere here in Japan?"

"We want it because it's been stolen, along with other minor religious artifacts. We're working with the Japanese government to find them."

"If I just give you the *katana*, the *yakuza* will still be after me."

"The *yakuza*?" His eyebrow arched in surprise.

"That's who sent the *tanuki* to my apartment."

"If the *yakuza* are behind this, then we'll deal with them," he promised. "Where's the *katana*?"

How much could she trust him? He was supposed to be a "hero," but so had Gregory Winston and look at how that had ended. A covert international agency tracking down stolen artifacts, though, matched up with the scenes she'd written.

"It's at the shrine." She hated that it felt like she had betrayed Atsumori, but she needed Miriam to be safe from people looking for the *katana*.

"Go." He indicated that Nikki should lead.

Nikki headed toward the shrine, trying to ignore the feeling that she had made a huge mistake. She still didn't know his true name. He handled his gun as casually as another man would a cell phone. He was a tall, strongly built man; his narrow waist and flat stomach were proof that everything his T-shirt covered was all muscle. While his clothes were clean and neat, his mane of black hair and five o'clock shadow gave him an air of untamed danger that made her uneasy. Nor did it help that he didn't seem to trust her, didn't seem to like her, and had no real reason to keep her safe.

"What's your name? You know my name; it would be nice to know yours." And when he didn't answer, she shrugged. "I could keep calling you Scary Cat Dude."

"Why do you call me that?" he rumbled in a tone close to anger.

"You're scary—and you rescued Misa's kitten. I could have called you Scary Kitten Dude, but that just doesn't scan as well."

After a minute, he said, "My name is Leo Watanabe."

The name felt right. It fit him. He was telling her the truth.

They rounded the corner, and she stopped short of the *torii* gates into the shrine. "It's in the shrine. Under the eaves of the smaller building."

He started forward but stopped just beyond the gate when she remained in place. He scanned the castle grounds. "Go get it."

She shook her head. "I don't think that would be wise."

"We have to get back to my car, quickly," he said. "Get the sword!"

She started to back away from him but then heard the sound of running feet echoing off the great stone walls that surrounded the castle. The moat and the high walls were about to create a trap.

"Get the sword." He took cover behind the *torii* post.

She dashed toward the sword, swearing. There were scenes Nikki knew were going to end badly even before she picked up the pen. It was like a horror movie when the creepy music started to build; it signaled that the monster was lurking in the shadows, breathing harshly, about to pounce, maim, and kill. This time, though, she was the heroine, and when the violins were screaming that the moment of pain was at hand, she was the one who was about to feel it.

She snatched up the *katana* and Atsumori flowed into her and through her like a lightning strike. His anger was white static brilliance that her body couldn't possibly contain. They howled wordlessly and rushed like a storm's wind through the temple grounds and headlong into the oncoming enemy. There were six tall, lean men with sharp faces and feral grace.

"*Tanuki* dogs!" Atsumori shouted and slashed out. The sword whistled as it cut the air, and then it hit. The force translated through her arms with shocking knowledge that they had just struck with all her strength, that the blade was razor sharp, that they had just dealt a killing blow, that they'd cleaved through flesh and bone with impossible power. Nikki cried out with fear and dismay as blood sprayed over the face. She tasted it thick in her mouth.

"Delany!" Leo shouted behind her, and his gun roared in the night.

The men yipped in terror as Atsumori struck again, amputating an arm holding a gun before cutting the nearest man in half. "It's the *kami!* The *kami!*"

Atsumori whirled, ducking low, and Nikki heard a gun thunder and saw the muzzle flash inches above her head, and then they struck the gunman, slicing through his legs with a sweeping cut. A backward stab took another man in the throat.

Nikki barely registered that the other three men had been shot dead, when Atsumori lunged at Leo.

"No!" Nikki closed her eyes, trying with every fiber of her being to stop.

They jerked to a halt and stood poised, panting in the cold rain.

She opened her eyes. The blade was pressed to Leo's neck, blood trickling from the razor cut. He watched her, tense and expressionless. "Don't hurt him. Please, don't hurt him."

"Who is he?" Atsumori used her mouth to growl.

Leo's eyes narrowed, but he didn't move. Didn't speak.

"He's Leo Watanabe." She realized that the name meant nothing to Atsumori. "He's the Scary Cat Dude."

"Is that why you left me behind?" Atsumori shouted. "So I couldn't stop you from calling him?"

"We need help," Nikki said. "They'll kill me and take you. We can't take the *yakuza* alone."

Atsumori glared at the man and Leo stared coldly back.

"You trust him?" Atsumori asked.

Did she? If she said no, Atsumori would probably kill him. "He feels honest."

"I asked if you trust him!" Atsumori roared.

"Yes!" she cried. She'd been inside of Leo's head; he wanted to protect her.

"She's hurt," Leo said quietly. "If you don't let me help her, you're going to lose her."

Atsumori jerked back and looked down at her body. There was a hole in her shirt, and the fabric was dark red. Atsumori touched her shirt and then stared at their bloody fingers. "Oh, Nikki, what have I done?"

"Let me help her." Leo's voice was low and urgent.

"Keep her safe," Atsumori said.

The *kami* slipped out of her, and her legs folded like a puppet whose strings had been cut. She saw Leo leaping toward her, trying to catch her before she hit the ground, and then everything went dark.

✠ 14 ✠
Let Me Pass

They were on holy ground. It was the only way to explain why Atsumori was sitting beside her futon when she woke up. Her hand rested on the *katana,* and his fingers were interwoven with hers. Sunlight danced on the ceiling, reflected from something that shimmered and moved. The air was heavy with the smell of cut grass from *tatami* mats, and a cicada droned loudly somewhere close by. Her throat hurt and her side throbbed with pain.

She tried to ask where they were, but nothing came out. She swallowed, wetting her mouth and raw throat, and tried again. "Where?"

"Osaka," Atsumori said.

She pulled her hand free so she could smack him. "Where?"

"I am not sure." Atsumori admitted unhappily. "I have not dared to leave your side. I have leant you all of my strength that you could safely bear."

Guilt twisted inside of her as she remembered that she had tried to hand over his *katana* without worrying about what Leo might do with him. She laced her fingers with Atsumori again.

Someplace in Osaka, on holy ground, with one very unhappy boy god.

Presumably in the protection of the Scary Cat Dude, who was not an FBI agent, who probably was named Leo Watanabe. Maybe. He'd been so leery of her at the castle; how did he feel about her now that she had tried to whack off his head and then had a screaming fight with herself? He probably thought she was stark raving mad.

She ran her fingertips over the *katana*'s sheathe. No, if he thought she was crazy, he wouldn't have left the sword. In the scenes she wrote, he'd known all about *tanuki* and *kami*. He knew about her ability; he'd figured out that she had written Gregory's murder before it happened. He'd talked about Talents and Sensitive as if all this weirdness was normal.

Did he realize that he was one of her characters?

All his scenes were in the notebook she had with her. She hadn't typed them up. Unless he read the last few pages of her current working notebook, he couldn't know for sure. Could he guess? Well, there was the note on her wall, but he might think that was spillover from Misa or Gregory. She tried to remember what they had talked about at the castle. Had she accidently let it slip? She hadn't explained how she had his number, but she did tell him that she knew about the kitten. Would he realize what it meant?

One thing was certain: he had taken her to a shrine instead of an emergency room because he was hiding her. She supposed that it would be worrisome to some people, but the last place she wanted to be while helpless was a hospital. It was too easy for her mother to find her there.

She noticed that everything Leo had returned to her was piled next to her head. She reached up with her free hand to pick up her phone, wincing as the movement lanced through her with pain. Obviously Leo didn't know her mother—the phone was on, transmitting her location to anyone determined to find her. She deleted all the calls from the log and powered off, making it untraceable.

She drifted to sleep and woke again sometime later as a shadow moved over her face. She opened her eyes to find Leo kneeling beside her futon. She wondered if he ever shaved, as he still had two or three days' worth of stubble. He had amazing eyes; dark and expressive. He peered deep into her eyes as if he could look straight to her soul.

"That's just you right now, isn't it?" Leo asked.

"Huh?" She blinked at him.

"I'm talking to Nikki Delany, right?" Leo said. "Not the *kami* who tried to behead me."

"Oh! Yeah, I'm just me now. Sorry about the whole head-whacking thing."

He looked surprised at her word choice, and a slight smile flashed across his face. "It's—It's fine. What matters is that you trusted me." He hesitated before adding in his low, rumbling voice. "I—I need your help."

A surprisingly Japanese "Eh?" slipped out, one she would have been more pleased with if she wasn't so confounded. "Me? You're the one with a gun and the ability to speak Japanese."

"I'm looking for this man." Leo pulled a stack of Post-It Notes from his breast pocket. The top one was turquoise and read "Shiva? Vishnu? Kali?" She remembered then that he had fixated on that particular plot thread in her apartment. Of course that was back when she thought he was just a character in her novel.

"Do you know where he is?" Leo asked.

There was something very surreal about sitting in a room without a single modern fixture in sight, the cicadas drowning out all traffic noise, and considering the whereabouts of a man she hadn't thought was real.

"The Brit? No," she said. "I don't know what happened to him. His storyline just came to a dead end."

"He was killed?" Grief filled Leo's dark eyes.

"No. No. His part of the story just—stopped. He was in Izushi and in the middle of a sentence, his scene ended. I've never had that happen before."

"But you don't think he was killed?"

"Usually if a character is killed or dies, I write it out." *In full gory detail and then occasionally post it to the Internet.* "I write in third person with occational shifts to omniscient, so even after a character dies, the scene can continue. Usually I—I show what the killer does to the body afterwards."

It was really quite morbid now that she knew they were real people, real deaths, and real bodies.

Leo produced a Campus notebook and a pen, exactly like the ones she bought for herself. He held them out to her. "Can you write more about him? Where he is now? Why hasn't he called?"

She eyed the paper and pen. It had been unsettling to write about Leo as he searched for her. She didn't want to write about a real person who was possibly dead. She knew that she wasn't really responsible for her characters' deaths; she fought too many times trying to keep them alive to know that it wasn't in her control. She didn't want to write out the words that confirmed the Brit's death, knowing that he was real. "I—I don't know."

He pressed the notebook into her hands and laid the pen on top of it. She stared at it with dismay. There was a little whispering of longing to open up the tablet to the crisp blank paper, click the pen down, smell the ink, and lose herself in writing. The most horrifying part was that she knew sooner or later she would cave in to the desire. It was what kept her from being able to totally convince every doctor who ever treated her that she was sane. She couldn't stop writing.

But twenty years had given her some control over the need. "I'm not sure if he's still part of the story. It could have been he was just a witness."

"What do you mean?"

"Witnesses aren't fully fleshed characters, because they interact with only a small part of the story. They just observe a plot point that none of the main characters experiences. A witness is an old woman whose goats have been stolen for a ritual sacrifice. A cemetery caretaker who notices a grave has been dug up. A child who was in the graveyard on the wrong night and is killed. They—" She closed her mouth on the words "don't matter," because these were real people. Of course they mattered, just not to the story.

"So, sometimes witnesses live and sometimes they die?" He collected all the Post-It Notes with her coded death masks together. He ruffled the stack like a little flipbook, and the expressions stuttered past, making a film of character deaths. Some slow, some sudden, some unexpected, some not. The last face was that of "the Brit." Like Leo, he been hiding his true identity, and she hadn't been able to assign him a name. She clipped the pen to the notebook and carefully put them down.

"I can't just write about any old thing. I've tried that for school." And for her mother and for many, many doctors. "I can't get much past 'See Dick and Jane run' when I'm not focused on a horror story."

He flinched slightly at the word "horror."

She dropped her gaze to focus on the pale blue futon cover. The print had small dragonflies scattered few and far apart. She traced one with a finger. "It's just how I work. When I start a novel, all the characters, no matter how random and scattered they seem, they always connect together to one common story. A horror story, filled with death and monsters and magic."

"But not all your characters die," he growled.

She nearly said, "Most of them do," before she realized both of them were now characters in her story. She clenched the cover tight. "Some of them get out alive."

Not the ones that stayed and fought to the gory end. The ones that stopped the monster never got out without taking a deadly wound. The characters that survived were usually the ones that never even realized they were in danger. They waltzed into the story, sidestepped danger, and left well before the final fight.

"So Simon might still be alive," Leo stated.

"Who?"

He gave the Post-It Notes a slight wave to draw her attention back to the square of turquoise-colored paper. "Simon Fowler. He's the man you were tracking with these."

"I was?" She still couldn't quite wrap her brain around the idea that all her characters were real.

"He arrived in Japan two months ago and disappeared. I've been looking for him for six weeks. This note is the only clue I've found so far that indicates that something happened to him."

"Maybe he doesn't want to be found."

Leo shook his head. "He wouldn't have done that to me. Even if he wanted to vanish, he would have left me some kind of sign."

"He's your friend?" she asked cautiously, thinking of the friends she had left clueless in her wake.

"He's my father." Then, seeing her confusion, he added reluctantly, "I'm adopted."

Children fleeing from parents she could fully understand, but would a father hide from his son? Leo was some sort of assassin and certainly the type of kid you might want to hide from. It reminded her that when she was young, she'd mistaken the word "estranged" as another form of "strangled."

"Please try," Leo said.

"If he's not part of the story anymore, I won't be able to write anything." She warned him against disappointment.

"I understand, but I don't have any thing else to go on."

She sighed and picked up the pad, opened it, and clicked the pen. With the point hovering over the pristine paper, she considered her character: the Brit. She had written his scene on her flight to Japan in May. Her hypergraphia had been at full throttle. For once in her life, she had welcomed her disorder because it meant the start of the novel with the tight deadline. Nearly fifteen hours in the air, the flight seemed perfect to wallow in the writing. Somehow she decided that her first character would be on the same plane as her, heading into danger, and thus "the Brit" came into being. She'd written out dozens of pages of story before it suddenly came to a stop in midsentence. She tried several times during the flight to finish the scene but couldn't. It literally felt like he'd fallen off the face of the planet.

There had been no indication that the Brit—Simon Fowler—had planned on disappearing. Had she written anything about Leo from his father's viewpoint? There had been something about an angry storm on the other end of the phone, a person rumbling like thunder over something mildly amusing to Simon. Yes, there had been warm affection mixed with mild exasperation for Leo, but no fear. Simon would have left Leo some sign if something had unexpectedly sent him fleeing.

So where was he now? What was he doing?

The pen dipped, touched the paper, dotting it with black ink. After a minute she raised the pen and lowered it again. A second dot joined the first.

It wasn't going to work. Simon vanishing had been an inciting incident, pulling Leo to Japan so he could be part of the story that Nikki had entangled herself with when she was arrested for Gregory Winston's murder. There was no real indication that Simon had anything to do with Nikki's horror story.

She raised her pen again. A third dot. She needed some way to tie Fowler mentally to her story so that whatever weird juju her ability could trigger could be fueled. If Leo had come looking for Simon, then surely as the hero, his goal was to find his father. It was important to the plot, she told herself, to know if Simon was alive or not.

※ ※ ※

. . . fragile pale dawn shone through an open window. Like always, he was bound and gagged, but this was yet another strange bedroom. He had lost count of the beds and the mornings. Behind him was the odd omnipresent sound that had been in every hotel room: the rattle of stone against wood. As he listened intently, trying yet again to identify the mysterious noise, he heard the mechanical tones of "Toryanse" playing at some distant crosswalk. He was still in Japan but impossible to tell where. He felt impossibly tired and hollow and light. When was the last time he had eaten? He lay helpless, unable to move, as the lyrics played in his head.

> *Let me pass, let me pass*
> *What is this narrow pathway here?*
> **It's the narrow pathway of the Tenjin shrine**
> *Please allow me to pass through*
> **Those without good reason shall not pass**
> *To celebrate this child's seventh birthday*
> *I've come to dedicate my offering*
> **Going in may be fine, fine, but returning would be scary**
> *It's scary but*
> *Let me pass, let me pass*

Seventh birthday made him think of his son. Leo had to be going mad with worry. Knowing his boy, he was burning bridges to find him. He wasn't sure if he wanted him tangling with this crowd. His boy was deadly, but even he would be getting in over his head.

Simon tested his bindings. Someone knew their knots. He couldn't move an inch; still, he spent several minutes trying. The distant crosswalk started playing "Toryanse" again, and he found himself thinking of the more sinister second verse.

> *Let me pass, let me pass*
> **Here is the underworld's narrow pathway**
> **It's the narrow pathway of the demon's shrine**
> *Please allow me to pass through*
> **Those without sacrifice shall not pass**
> *To bury this child at age seven*
> *I've come to offer my services*

> ***Living may be fine, fine, but going back would be scary***
> *It's scary but*
> *Let me pass, let me pass.*

He had to get out of this nightmare, but he wasn't sure how. Every morning had been the same: trussed up like a suckling pig waiting to be roasted and served. The mystery rattle grew louder and faster. There was a small muffled explosion. Sharp stone fragments rained down on the bed, and a sudden cloud of dust drifted through the room. He had run out of . . .

Nikki blinked at the page. It had stopped in midsentence again. Why?

She clicked the pen to retract the point and realized that Leo was leaning against her back so he could read over her shoulder. His body was a strong, solid wall wrapped around hers, filling her awareness with his warm strength. His scent was like expensive musk cologne on the summer wind, light to the point of elusive.

He growled softly in anger as he pressed fingers to the paper. "This tells us nothing."

"He's alive."

"This could have been weeks ago."

She considered the scene. There was no real time marker, but she had started out wanting to know Simon's condition now. Currently it was nearly noon, judging by the play of the light and shadows. "This takes place tomorrow morning."

He sighed with relief, his breath warm across the bare skin of her neck. "What else did you not write?"

She chewed on the pen, thinking back over the impressions that hadn't made it onto paper. "It's a hotel room with two Western-style beds, not futons on the floor like it would be for a Japanese-style room. The duvet is pulled back so he's lying on sheets. The curtain wasn't drawn, but there's nothing to be seen from the bed, just open sky, not other buildings or mountains."

"So, on the coast or on the plains."

She laughed at the kernel of information. "Most of Japan." She frowned as she searched for more information that she knew but hadn't included. "He was tied in the traditional bondage method. You know. The jute rope with all the knots. The ones they use for sex?"

"*Kinbaku-bi?*" he rumbled softly into her ear, reminding her how close he was. Then, as if he wasn't sure he understood her, he translated it. "The beauty of tight binding?"

She blushed and nodded. She saw nothing sexy about being tied up, but she knew it was her own personal demon. She still had nightmares of being "restrained" in hospital beds. She focused on the scene, trying to ignore Leo. The only other impressions she could glean were of the man himself. Simon was frustrated by his helplessness, angry with himself for not being able to escape, and afraid mostly for the son he knew would come charging after him. She wouldn't be so brave in his place.

Leo stood, taking his warmth with him. She felt suddenly, horribly alone, as if Simon's desperate isolation had seeped into her. "What else?" he demanded.

She stared at the paper, trying to glean more. "I can't tell anything else. Usually the only way I can tell more is to see a photograph of the setting or visit it."

Leo growled. "If we knew which hotel he was in, we wouldn't need you to write more."

"There is that."

"What about the scene he disappeared in? Could you find out more if you visited Izushi?"

"Maybe," she said slowly. "I don't know."

"Come with me to Izushi. Help me save my father."

"What? Me?" No one had ever asked her for help. She was the person who always that needed to be saved. The helpless one.

"Please. This is the first time in six weeks that I've had proof he's still alive."

Proof? Writings of a possibly mad woman were all he had? It seemed pitiful, but even more pathetic was her sudden want to have him sit back down and let her lean on his strength. Truth was, it wasn't Simon's loneliness echoing inside of her, but her own.

"Okay," she whispered, hating her weakness. "I'll help you."

15

The Kindness of Water

After the peaceful timelessness in the shrine, Leo's black sports car, gleaming from the recent rain, looked deadly and felt horribly out of place in the zen-barren temple grounds.

Nikki's stomach was full of cold snakes. Getting into a car with a practical stranger was a huge personal "no no" for her. Only someone who was stupid as well as crazy would do it. People who got into strangers' cars never were seen again. Horrible things were done to them and their bodies were hidden away where they would never be found. She knew almost nothing about Leo except that he knew what it was like to snap a person's neck with his bare hands. It wasn't a particularly reassuring factoid.

Leo opened the passenger door for her and stood waiting, his face unreadable. The interior was as sleek and deadly looking as the exterior.

Getting dressed had been a lesson in her mortality. There was a huge bandage on her left side. She'd peeled back one corner to find a healed but angry-looking scar the width of her thumb. The clothes she'd been wearing had completely vanished except for her bra and underwear, both stained with dried blood. Every movement triggered mild pain, as if someone had carefully beaten her from head to toe.

Because of Atsumori, though, all her bruises had already faded to banana yellow.

Nikki tightened her hold on the *katana*. There wasn't room inside to swing the sword; she would be totally without Atsumori's protection. She wasn't crazy, but she might be stupid.

While she hesitated, a small furry body streaked out from under the nearest porch and scrambled up into the car's interior. It was Misa's ginger kitten, Maru.

"*Doko iku no?*" Leo growled softly.

Maru climbed up onto the passenger seat and mewed.

"*Soto soto.*" Leo pointed to the ground at his feet.

The kitten mewed again and scrambled onto the storage case between the front seats.

Leo had been desperate to find his father, impatient with all the roadblocks and lack of information. Yet he'd taken responsibility for the kitten. And if he had wanted to hurt her, he would have already done it. She'd been unconscious for hours. What's more, he could have kept the *katana* from her, leaving her completely helpless.

"It's fine." Nikki slid into the vacated seat, holding tight to the *katana*.

Leo gave her a long, hard study and then shut the door, giving in to his stubborn passengers. He walked around the car, got in, pushed the kitten into her lap so he could fasten his seat belt, and started the car with rumble.

She wanted to ask Leo questions, but there was an unwritten rule which said that once you started to ask people questions, they were free to ask back. It was the main reason she didn't seek out other expatriates. The conversations all went the same way. *What's your name? Where are you from? What brings you to Japan?*

They had already started down that dangerous road by exchanging names. To be fair, she couldn't expect him to answer to Scary Cat Dude. God forbid, if they got into another fight. Yelling, "Watch out, Scary Cat Dude!" had shades of Jugemu, the boy who nearly drowned because people had to recite out his ridiculously long name to get him help.

How much did Leo know about her? In the last scene she wrote, he hadn't been able to dig into her past. He didn't know about her years locked in mental hospitals. He didn't know how crazy her mother thought she was.

If he didn't know, she didn't want him to find out.

It seemed fairly simple. As long as she kept the door shut on personal questions, she didn't have to answer any. They could just sit in silence. It left her in a car, though, with a virtual stranger.

She studied his profile as he picked his way through the heavy traffic. His black mane and dark almond eyes said that one of his parents was definitely Asian. His accent spoke of a childhood in the United States. The car was modified for Japan, with the steering wheel on the right side of the car, but the interior smelled of him.

She could create a personality sheet for him. Whenever she had trouble getting a handle on a character, she wrote down everything she could determine about them. Place of birth. Zodiac sign. Pet peeves. Biggest fears. Anything for her hypergraphia to springboard from. Her fingers twitched at the idea. She petted the kitten as a distraction. It purred and wrapped its paws around her hand and chewed with needlesharp teeth.

"Ow, ow, ow," Nikki said.

"*Hoi.*" Leo reached over without looking. For a moment his fingers brushed over hers, strong and calloused. The kitten abandoned her and grappled Leo's hand. He scooped it up and moved it to his own lap.

Leaving nothing to occupy her hands.

"Why do you still have it with you?" she asked.

He stared at the road, muscles in his jaw tensing. After a minute of silence, she didn't think he was going to answer, but finally he said, "Despite what he thinks, he's still young and fragile. The world is a hard place to be all alone."

Was that a comment on the kitten or her?

She distracted herself by digging into her backpack and finding a notebook. Curling up in the seat so he couldn't see the page, she started to write what she wanted to know about the most. Him.

He'd been in the cage for two days without food or water. He lay on the iron bars, panting. His entire body felt like he was buried in sand. His eyes felt like sandpaper and his mouth was parched dry. He kept hearing jets and helicopters flying overhead, which meant he was near either Kona or Hilo Airport—unless they had flown him to Honolulu while he was drugged. The first day, he had howled as he tried to escape, but he was too weak for that now.

The far door of the warehouse opened, throwing a shaft of hot light through the dimness. The wind came through the open door, taunting him with the scent of recent rain. A figure stood in the doorway, sunlight gleaming off pale hair.

Behind the newcomer, the familiar voice of his captor was speaking.

" . . . confirmed that there is only this one. We haven't determined what it is."

The newcomer and Williams came striding across the concrete floor, boot steps echoing in the empty space. Leo watched them come, too tired to snarl.

This new man was tall, white, and lean with piercing blue eyes. He crouched down, carefully out of arm's reach, to stare through the bars at Leo.

"Thought you said you took him down with a tranquilizer," the newcomer said. He had an odd accent. Most of the men sounded like the people from television, even the men who looked like they could have been local Hawaiians.

"I did." Williams kept farther back, blending with the shadows.

"So what's wrong with him?"

"He's probably dehydrated."

"You haven't given him water?"

"It didn't seem necessary." Williams had been in favor of shooting Leo from the start. Voices over the radio, though, had ordered for him to be caged until "Fowler" could arrive.

Was this Fowler, then? Did this mean that they would kill him now, or was there some new torture in store?

Fowler scanned the warehouse and spotted the sink on the far wall. He walked to it and turned on the faucet. Would he actually give Leo water? His captors had so thoroughly ignored him that he was sure they were going to let him die in the cage. After filling a plastic jug, the newcomer walked back to the cage, sloshing the water loudly as he walked.

"You want some water?" Fowler trickled a little out.

Thirst moved Leo. He heaved up on his knees, pressed against the bars, one hand cupped and thrust out to catch the stream of water.

"Ah, ah." The flow stopped. "Say 'please.'"

Leo studied the man. Was this a trick? Did the man merely want him to beg before he died?

"Say 'please' and I'll give you water. You're going to die in that cage if you don't. Do you want to die?"

Leo shook his head.

Fowler shook the jug. "Say it."

It came out a whisper, but he was rewarded with a handful of water. It was cool and delicious despite a chemical tang he wasn't used to.

"What's your name?" Water sloshed loudly again, promising more.

He licked his lips. "Leo. Leo Watanabe." Another handful of water.

"How old are you?"

"Seven."

For a minute, no water was forthcoming as the man chose to look to the ninja instead.

"You shouldn't trust it to tell the truth," Williams said.

Then the water came, three handfuls' worth.

"Where are your parents?"

"Gone."

"Gone 'went away'? gone 'died'?"

He didn't want to talk about his parents. The man sloshed the water jug when he fell silent. He still was so thirsty.

He reluctantly explained. "Mom went away long ago."

"And your father?"

"Men came to our farm after New Year's. They said we didn't own the land. The king gave it to grandma's grandfather. Dad took the truck to town with papers to show that it's ours. He never came back. I've been looking for him."

"Williams." Fowler gestured, and Williams nodded and left.

The questions ended, but the water continued in handfuls until Leo was no longer thirsty.

Williams came back after the sun had set. In the darkness of the warehouse, he was just a dangerous voice. "John and Naomi Watanbe were married twelve years ago. They had no children. Naomi was killed ten years ago in a hit and run. It's lying to you."

Fowler shook his head. "Hawaii has a large number of *yokai* that followed the Japanese sugar cane and pineapple plantation workers from Japan. It's possible that an *obakemono* took the wife's place. His father isolated himself and kept the boy hidden. You can't have a birth certificate for a child born to a dead woman."

Fowler glanced toward Leo and saw that he was watching him closely. Fowler turned away and lowered his voice to a whisper. "Any word on the father's whereabouts?"

"He was in a head-on with tractor-trailer truck on January fifth. Killed instantly."

Leo wailed in distress.

"What are we going to do with it?" Williams came out of the darkness, his pistol in hand.

Fowler shifted in front of Leo, hands spread to ward off a shot. "I'll take responsibility for him."

Nikki stopped writing and peered over the notebook at Leo. He was watching the road intently as he whipped through slower traffic, the kitten asleep on his lap. She had no idea what an *obakemono* was. What did it make Leo?

Who was this man whom she trusted enough to get into a car with and be driven to parts unknown? He took her away from the multiple-lane highways lined with skyscrapers, through little towns with modern houses with metal roofs, and up into the mountains. They stopped at a quaint little town for gas and rice balls. She squatted over a ceramic gutter on the floor of the very Japanese public restroom, feeling more and more lost and alone. The only feeling that she was doing the right thing came from the patience and care that Leo had for the kitten. It had scrambled out of the car when she opened her door, heading for an empty lot beside the gas station. As she headed back to the car, the kitten was burying its feces.

Leo called a simple "*Hoi!*" that brought it running back. He'd taken a bowl out of the trunk, set it next to the car, and filled it from his own water bottle. As the kitten drank, Nikki remembered how Simon had dribbled water into Leo's outstretched palm. Like everything she wrote, it was a vivid nightmare. She was left with memories as if she had personally experienced it. Fowler framed in the doorway, haloed with the brilliant light of a Hawaiian summer. Cool water trickling over parched skin. The taste of water.

It was maddening what wasn't said or explained in the scene.

There was no mention of Leo attacking or killing people. But if he hadn't done anything, why had the platoon of soldiers ambushed him? Knocked him out, locked him up, and then ignored him for days? Why would the Williams only refer to Leo as "it"?

When Leo had talked to Miriam, he had thought about the fact that Miriam was a Sensitive. Miriam had spent most of the scene trying to escape Leo. It was implied that Miriam could sense his hidden nature.

"Are you some kind of monster?" was probably not a good opening question. Most of the other questions she could think of would reveal that she'd been writing scenes about him. Would he mind? He had recognized himself on her Post-It Note wall, but she had one notebook with his scenes. It was one thing to imagine her writing about him, but it would be another to read his own thoughts on paper. A little voice she used to call her writer's instinct told her he would be upset by the invasion of privacy.

"I got you water." Leo held out an unopened bottle that was bejeweled with condensation in the summer heat. "You need to be careful not to get dehydrated."

"Thank you." Whatever else he was that led to him being in the cage, he had still been a helpless child dying of thirst. No matter what he was now, he'd treated her with kindness.

✠ 16 ✠
The Tree of
Many Colors

Leo took her up and over the mountains to a little town called Izushi. She had researched it extensively, so she had a weird feeling of *déjà vu* as they came down off the mountains into the narrow streets. Izushi had been founded back in the dawn of time—the town had been mentioned in Japanese literature as early as 27 B.C. Like much of Japan, it put all "historic" parts of California to shame. It had seen the rise and fall of several empires. Unlike Osaka, which had been mostly bombed to rubble and rebuilt, the small town looked like a medieval Japanese village with a light sprinkling of modern technology.

Leo drove through the narrow streets, lined with the stone walls of ancient samurai houses, muttering darkly at the GPS system. The kitten stared at the moving arrow and occasionally lifted a paw to pat at the screen, changing the information.

After the third time, Leo pushed the kitten into her lap. "Keep him out of trouble."

He reprogramed the GPS and in short order they were at a beautiful inn that looked hundreds of years old. They drove through the huge fortified gate to a parking lot.

"This is the *onsen* that the Brit—Simon checked into." Nikki eyed the entrance she had studied via the website. It was a beautiful centuries-old inn. "This isn't the place he's being held. It's a more modern place."

"I know this is safe for you. I've been here twice already, questioning the staff."

Scaring the staff silly, judging by looks of the *yukata*-clad woman who went scurrying away at the sight of Leo's car.

The kitten scrambled out when Nikki opened the door. Leo called something after it as it went scampering away.

"What did you tell it?" Nikki thought of Leo in the cage and changed her pronoun. "Him?"

"To be careful of the cars."

"Why do you use Japanese with him?"

Leo shrugged and looked vaguely guilty of some crime. "He's a Japanese cat."

He surprised her by lifting her Hello Kitty suitcase out of the trunk. He must have found it while she was unconscious. His own suitcase was a simple black, hard shell. While it probably held clothes, it looked like it could contain a number of pistols, too.

They were greeted at the door by an elegant kimono-clad hostess. The woman was beautiful, with creamy skin and glossy long black hair coiled into a bun. She greeted them with a graceful bow. Nikki was instantly aware that she hadn't bathed since Inari's shrine, that her hair was oily and lank, and that she was wearing the same underclothes she'd been shot in.

One look at Nikki and, despite Leo's attempts to keep the discussion in fluid Japanese, the hostess insisted on speaking very broken English.

"*Tsuma desu.*" Leo waved a hand toward Nikki.

Nikki understood enough Japanese to translate: this is my wife. She stiffened as all the unhappy endings of her relationships collided with the word. The woman smiled gently at them, pleased with their fictional happiness.

The hostess led them to their room tucked in the back of the hotel. Apparently their room had been vacant because it was the most expensive suite in the place. Not only did it have a Japanese-style porch with wooden sandals waiting, but also a private open-air hot spring bath carved into a rock grotto. She couldn't imagine how expensive the room was. She had priced out stays at similar *onsen*-style hotels.

A standard room with access only to communal baths often ran over two hundred dollars per person a night.

"Why did you tell her that?" Nikki whispered after the woman bowed and left.

"Tell her what?"

"That we're married?"

He blanked his face. "I did not think you would understand what I was saying."

"I know enough to understand that."

"I see."

He didn't see. He couldn't understand how much she had always wanted a normal life. To go to high school. Attend the prom. Go to college. Date. Marry. She had spent eighteen years dreaming of being free of her mother, only to have it all snatched away. She'd spent the last two years running and hiding like a wanted criminal. Miriam was the only friend she would recognize face-to-face. Team Banzai was all women she had met online through a shared interest in manga and fan-written fiction. The few guys she'd met since she turned eighteen had turned tail and run after they got to know her. If it wasn't the hypergraphia or the graphic nature of what she wrote, it was all her hang-ups from growing up in mental hospitals. The only men she knew growing up were doctors or orderlies. One ordered that she be given drugs "for her own good" and the other stood over her, making sure she took them. Then there was the small issue of being tied to a bed while the woman in the next room was raped.

The likelihood of her ever getting married was slim to none.

"Don't say we're married," she said. "Just don't."

"Okay, I won't." His phone started to ring. He took it out and stared at it.

"You're not going to answer it?" she asked.

He took a deep breath and answered it. "What is it, Ananth?"

The caller apparently was one of those men who shouted at their phone. She could hear him clearly even from two feet away.

"You're to check in every eight hours," Ananth barked. "See that you do. Where are you?"

Leo closed his eyes and was silent for a minute before saying, "Izushi. I have a lead on Simon."

"You're to find Nikki Delany!" Ananth shouted.

Leo glanced at Nikki and then turned away. "This is the first lead I've had on my father in six weeks. It will only take me a few hours to check out."

The voice on the other end sounded like whatever sympathy he had for Leo had worn off weeks ago. "You're going to have to come to terms with the fact that he's most likely dead!"

"I'll believe that when I see his body. I will look for him until I find him."

"You're utterly failing to prove that you can be trusted without Simon as your handler! Shiva cannot allow you to run amuck!"

Leo pressed his fingers to the bridge of his nose. "It's late. I'm tired. I'll return to Osaka tomorrow."

There was a long silence on the other end, and then something murmured that Nikki didn't catch.

"Yes, sir." Leo put away his phone, shaking his head.

Nikki knew why he wasn't telling his organization about her—the moment he did, he would have to turn her over to the man on the phone. Any normal sane person, though, would have to ask. Would want to know. "Why didn't you tell him you found me?"

He glanced at her, worry in his dark eyes. He looked away, radiating unease. "There are things in the world that that can move unseen and kill without mercy." With seeming reluctance, he defined "things." "Monsters. Spirits. In theory, Shiva protects people from evil that a normal man would be helpless against."

"But in truth, they don't?"

He shook his head. "Shiva is self-serving when it comes to defining who is a monster and who isn't. There are people with special abilities—people like you . . . and my father. Shiva sees anyone with a gift as a possible monster—as someone to be controlled, contained, or eliminated. To protect 'normal' people."

Nikki really wished the Japanese were more into chairs. She had a sudden need to sit down. "So if they find me . . ."

"If they don't know about your ability, they'll assume you're just accidently caught up in this mess. You can't tell them about your writing—or that the *kami* can take you over. Both make you valuable and dangerous."

His scene as a child made more sense now. Shiva had captured him when he was young, decided he was monster, and would have killed him if Simon hadn't intervened.

"My father had dreams of being a doctor," Leo said. "He was in his third year at medical school when Shiva discovered him. They yanked him out of college and never let him go back. He wanted to heal children, not run around signing off on kill orders."

One of those kill orders had been for seven-year-old orphaned Leo, locked in a cage, dying of thirst. No wonder Simon had adopted him. It explained, also, why Leo was rebelling against Shiva and all the veiled threats they were leveling at him.

Her hands fluttered slightly at the thought of being caged. Shiva sounded like her mother, only with guns and literal cages instead of doctors and mental wards.

She dug into her backpack, looking for a pen. She found one and clicked it repeatedly. *Note to self: avoid being questioned by Shiva.* She had years of experience trying to convince people that she was completely normal—but so far practice hadn't made perfect.

"What do they want with me?" Atsumori murmured into her ear, reminding her that she wasn't alone with Leo. The boy god had been quiet the entire trip and she had wondered if he'd gone to sleep. Had healing Nikki exhausted him? Did gods get tired?

"Why is Shiva looking for the *katana* in the first place? What do they want with Atsumori?"

"*Kami* like him are considered 'tame monsters' and aren't dangerous if they're in the right hands. Shiva is focused more on whose hands he is in rather than having actual concern about him, especially if *yokai* like the *tanuki* at your apartment are involved."

She remembered Leo's reaction to Harada's driver's license. "Shiva will stomp on the *yakuza* for working with the *tanuki*?"

Leo nodded. "*Yokai* can't be policed by normal humans. Shiva uses tame monsters to go after the dangerous ones."

Was Leo one of the tame monsters? Shiva was sending him after her because they thought she might be dangerous. As long as Shiva continued to think that, Leo was free to "find her."

Of course, once they found Simon, she would have to explain the weirdness around her. Leo had taken down her Post-It Notes before the cleaners arrived. He'd snagged both of her flash drives and all her notebooks. That covered all the evidence in her apartment. What else?

Well there was the dead *tanuki*. Lots of dead *tanuki* if the fight at the castle was uncovered. How could she explain all the hacked-up raccoon dogs in business suits? *Click. Click. Click.*

If she said that she knew *kendo*—the Japanese style of fencing with a *katana*—she could explain using the sword to kill the *tanuki* both at the castle and at her apartment. She had taken a semester of martial arts with Miriam at Foxcroft. She was fairly sure that school records would be vague enough after nearly five years to give her wiggle room there. How had she gotten the *katana*? She could say she had lied to the police and that she knew Gregory . . .

"Shit!" she cried.

Leo whipped out his pistol so fast it seemed to materialize in his hand. He searched the room for something to shoot. "What is it?"

"The police know about my writing." She took a deep breath, trying to stay calm. *Don't lose it in front of the man with a gun.* "An officer overheard me talking about Gregory's murder with Miriam. That's why I was arrested."

He cocked his head, frowning. "That wasn't in the police reports."

"I blogged the scene. Not all of it, but enough. It was on my website until the police had me take it down."

He frowned deeper, eyes tracking as if reading over the reports in his mind. "Someone sanitized the report before I saw it."

"Shiva?"

He shook his head, holstering his pistol. "I don't think so. I was lead agent on Winston's murder. Normally, I would have been the first person from Shiva to see all police reports. I would have been the one to issue a request for the report to be sanitized."

It left an obvious candidate: her mother. Walcott must have filed a report with the State Department; naturally her mother would send her own cleaners to remove evidence of Nikki's "craziness."

Okay, she was going to completely freak out. She needed Leo gone so she could do it in private.

"I'm going to take a bath." She hoped he'd take the hint and make himself scarce. "I haven't washed for days, and I'm feeling really gross."

Leo moved toward the door, pulling out his pistol to check its clip. "I'm going to make sure this hotel is still safe. If I don't come back, take the train and keep the *katana* close to you. The god will protect you."

He was gone before she could form a good answer.

An entire page of dots did nothing to make her feel comfortable with her level of sanity, but it did relieve the stress-related need to write. Since evidence was mounting that she wasn't insane, whatever had blocked her from writing about Simon was back in place. Her hypergraphia, though, had been fed enough that she could consider the implications that her mother knew she was in Japan.

Unlike Shiva and the *yakuza,* her mother had studied her habits and had already found her weaknesses and knew how to exploit them. How had Miriam contacted the American Embassy? If she had used her cell phone, then all calls out of her cell were being tracked. Since Miriam had mistakenly posted to Nikki's public forum instead of the Team Banzai forum, it was possible that Miriam hadn't thought of using a public phone to make the call to Walcott.

In a panic, Nikki found her cell phone and checked it. She had remembered to turn it off in Osaka. Time to ditch it completely; this was why she always carried the cheapest prepaid phone she could find. She took out the battery, making it untraceable. She considered pitching it into the toilet's reservoir tank, but there was a slim chance she might still need it. She checked for her favorite hiding space: the inside lintel of the closet door. There was a narrow ledge. She chewed a stick of gum and used it to tack the phone onto the ledge. She experimented with sliding the door open and closed. Hopefully, the phone would stay hidden for years before being discovered.

By law, the *onsen* staff should have asked for her passport. Residents of Japan, however, were circumvented; Leo must have checked in with ID that claimed he was a citizen of Japan. Since he had told them Nikki was his wife, they probably assumed she was a resident. It made her feel guilty—he'd made her untraceable, and she'd snapped at him.

Of course, she could be worrying unnecessarily. Her mother didn't trust outsiders to corner her; she always supervised the capture. According to the news on Sunday morning, her mother was in D.C., defending the separation of church and state. (Her mother was weirdly agnostic. She maintained that there was a god but viewed him with a suspicion that Nikki had inherited.)

Regardless, Nikki needed to lay low for a while. It meant limited posting to even her secret forums, keeping to public phones, and being careful when she used her bank card. Both Shiva and her mother were probably monitoring her bank accounts, so withdrawing money would put her instantly on everyone's radar.

With that in mind, she counted her cash. She had fifty-two thousand yen, or in the neighborhood of six hundred dollars. She could get to Tokyo, but the combined train tickets would probably eat half her money. She should hit an ATM just before she left Osaka. Every yen she could pull out meant a longer time she could go without setting off signal flares.

She wasn't sure what to do about the *katana*. If she gave the sword to Leo, Shiva would stop looking for her. The *yakuza* wouldn't, unless Shiva killed them all.

Of course there would still be her mother to worry about. It was sad that of all the scary people chasing her, her mother frightened her the most.

When Leo searched her apartment, he had suggested that *kami* couldn't be filmed. The security system at her apartment building hadn't shown her while Atsumori was merged with her. It seemed to indicate that if she kept the *katana*, she could move invisibly through Japan. Shiva would still be chasing her, but it might be safer not to give up the sword.

Until they found Simon, though, it was a moot point. As far as anyone could tell, she'd vanished off the face of the Earth.

She was running out of time before Leo returned, and a bath actually seemed like a good idea. Hoping for some privacy, she stuck the *katana* in the closet, behind a set of rolled-up futons. Not that it actually meant that Atsumori couldn't spy on her, but it made her feel better.

There wasn't a Western-style shower. The "private" bathing area was an open-air hot tub for five. Like all Japanese baths, there was an area where one sat on a stool and washed using a hand-held shower and bucket. Only after you were clean did you step into the tub. It felt dangerous to be sitting naked among rocks out in the garden, washing her hair. Logically she knew that the garden was constructed so no one could spy on her, but she felt like someone might walk up the garden path at any minute.

Had all the unaccounted-for bruises faded since they left Osaka?

She peered at them, unsure. Under the bandage, the thumb-wide scar was still angry red but looked weeks old. It cut a groove along her rib cage just beneath her breast. The bullet had come frighteningly close to hitting her heart, but luckily it hit bone and deflected instead.

The water in the grotto was deliciously hot. She had to slowly ease into it, but once immersed, she felt like she was melting in the heat. Despite doing nothing but sitting in a car all day, she was exhausted. It was tempting to jus nod off in the heated water.

"If you stay in too long, you will faint," Atsumori murmured in her ear.

She yelped and scrambled out of the grotto, cursing, to pull on the hotel's *yukata*. "Don't do that!"

"You looked as if you were going to fall asleep."

"I would have gotten out before I did." She pulled the thin cotton *yukata* tight around her. Apparently, tucking his *katana* into the closet wasn't enough to give her privacy from the god.

There didn't seem to be a point to hiding in the bathroom to get dressed. She pulled on clean clothes as quickly as she could. Once she felt decent, she considered her dirty underclothes. Blood stained the left side of her bra and the band of her panties. She considered just throwing them out, but they were her favorite matched set. She realized that her biggest reason for not simply washing them was because Leo would see them drying.

"Oh, grow up," she muttered as she ran cold water into the sink. "So a boy will see your undies. Big deal. I'm sure he's seen lots of girls' undies."

She added shampoo to the cold water and scrubbed at the bloodstains. Considering she had woken up in the *yukata* from the Inari Shrine and not in the shirt and jeans she'd been wearing at the castle, Leo had already seen her undies.

She caught a glimpse of Atsumori out of the corner of her eye as she hung up her panties. He was smirking at her underwear.

"What?" she snapped, embarrassed.

"Why do you have her on your underthings?"

"Her" was Hello Kitty. The bra and panty were a matched set with the iconic cat on them.

"Because I can." She eyed the underwire for blood. "I never got to pick out my own clothes when I was growing up. I know my mother has excellent taste in clothes, but she only seemed to buy me ugly things. They made me feel worse about myself. It wasn't until I saw this television show about models that I began to realize why I felt so ugly all the time. These girls would be sitting around in pajamas with their hair up and no make up and they were as ugly as me. The only difference was that they got to put on pretty things and makeup and be beautiful."

"But why her? Why not beautiful underthings?"

She was slightly surprised by the question until she remembered that Misa had a slight fetish for lacy underwear. The shrine maiden probably unknowingly gave the boy god an education on such things. "Hello Kitty is beautiful by always being herself." She hung up the bra beside the matching panties. "She is not skinny and does not dye her hair, or wear fancy clothes. All she needs is to be clean with clothes that fit her well, a cute hair bow, and she's set."

She suddenly realized that it wasn't Atsumori she was seeing out the corner of her eye, but Leo. She flinched in surprise and then cursed. "Will you two stop doing that?"

Leo gazed down at his feet in silence for a minute before saying, "The hotel appears safe." He retreated into the bedroom to pace with grace. He'd brought the kitten in, and it chased him as he strode back and forth. "One of the girls is a minor Sensitive; I'm the only guest that has scared her in the last few weeks. I didn't find any signs of *tanuki* or other *yokai*."

"That's good." She turned off the bathroom light, cloaking her underwear in darkness.

"Can you try to write more?"

"I tried already." She remembered then what was in her notebook. With heart thumping hard, she dropped a towel onto the tablet to hide it. She didn't want him to see it, pick it up, flip through it, and find the scenes with him as a child. She scrambled for another distraction away from the notebook. What were some of her tricks against writer's block that might work? "Do have all my Post-It Notes?"

"What do you need those for?" He rumbled.

"Being able to see all the elements of my story sometimes helps me see places where I need witnesses." She held out her hand and twiddled her fingers in what she'd been discovering was a universal "give me" sign.

He huffed but pulled the stack of Post-it Notes from his coat's breast pocket. He passed all but Simon's to her. He stood a moment, fingering the turquoise paper like it was a lifeline to his father. And then, reluctantly, added it to the pile in her hand.

She sorted through the scraps of paper and started to stick them to the largest blank wall. The hotel room was larger than her tiny studio apartment, so she could spread out her plot tree. The wider separation between the characters made the interconnections more obvious. "These are all my characters. They're in the story for a reason—I just don't know why. Your father is part of my story, and I think more than just so I can meet you."

"Pardon?"

She blushed furiously and focused on sticking up the notes. "I need to find other characters that interact on the same plot thread as your father so I can use them as a witnesses."

"What do you mean?"

"See this cluster of characters? This is the *katana* branch." She had up three of the six colors that she knew were definitely linked to the *katana*. "Gregory—who I was calling George—killed Misa in Kyoto to steal the *katana*. Harada killed Gregory in Umeda trying to take the *katana* from him." She found Natasha's white notes and added them to the wall. "I find the *katana* and kill Harada in Otemea. If most of those people weren't dead, I could use one of them to find out about the others. Like I could use Harada to witness Gregory—only they're both dead, and my writing doesn't work on dead people."

She hadn't completely intertwined the branches in her apartment, so Leo hadn't grouped the rest of the Osaka characters with the first four. She still wasn't sure how the next few Post-It Notes were related.

"The thing is, this branch isn't the whole story, it's just one little piece of it. All these other characters aren't tied into the *katana*." She named the people as their Post-It Notes went up onto the wall, spread far apart to emphasize the lack of connections. "There's Haru and Nobu, who are eight-year-old twins that live in the Shimogyo Ward of Kyoto. Haru has been picked to be the *Chigo* or celestial child for the Gion Matsuri this year. It means he supposed to ride in the *Naginata-hoko* in the parade, but he's scared of heights and the float is three stories tall." She understood his fear completely. "Nobu is going to take his place and has been learning the dance that Haru is supposed to do on the float."

She'd picked yellow for the twins. She put them close to Misa's pink since they lived in Kyoto, too. She wasn't sure, though, if they were related in any way. Misa had been excited about the Gion Matsuri, as the month-long festival meant an increase of tourists visiting all the shrines of Kyoto. Misa hadn't been involved in the parade and the twins hadn't visited Atsumori's shrine. With the fire and Misa's death, the possibility of their stories intertwining was even more remote.

"There's Chitose; he's team captain and starting pitcher for the Tohoku High School baseball team. They're going through the regional tournament, trying to get to the National High School Baseball Championship." Chitose's color was teal. She put him close to the Osaka branch because the playoffs were held in nearby Kobe.

"And the real crazy outlier, Kayo. She's a war widow in Hiroshima with her two children and elderly father who repairs watches." Nikki stuck the pale green at the far edge of the wall. "Her scenes are all in August of 1945, a few days before the atomic bomb is dropped. She lived about a half-mile from the Aioi Bridge, which was the Allied aiming point. Talk about 'this will not end well' written all over a character."

She waved the remaining Post-It Notes at him. "I've got over three dozen characters in all, and so far only me, Greg, Misa, and Harada have intersected." She shuffled the papers to Simon's turquoise Post-It Note.

"Here's your father, in Izushi, and he's here because . . .?"

She turned to Leo for the answer.

"The Japanese government is building a hydroelectric dam to replace the nuclear power plants damaged in the 2012 tsunami," he explained. "The area is supposed to be geologically stable—well—as stable as you get for Japan—but there were several odd landslides that stopped work. They asked Shiva if they could find the underlying problem. Ananth felt that the Japanese were merely covering all the bases. They tend to be much more superstitious than, say, the Germans or the French. Then again, they have good reason. The Inquisition and other witch hunts stamped out much of the abnormal in Europe. Places like the United Kingdoms logged their virgin forests and fought the things that like to live in those dark places long ago. Japanese supported the more Buddhist and Shinto ideas of living in harmony. Live and let live."

Ananth had been the name of Leo's phone contact. As far as she could tell, he wasn't a character, but so far she'd gotten all the names wrong. "Who is Ananth?"

"The old man? He's the Director of Shiva. A bastard of a Hindu with ice water for blood."

She didn't have any non-Japanese characters beyond herself, Simon and Gregory. Nikki nodded, tucking away the information, as she tried to mesh the real reason for Simon's visit into what she remembered of her scene. She was going to have to read it again since it had been months since she'd written it. "Shiva didn't think the threat was real, so they sent your father alone?"

"He's a Sensitive, not a Talent, and he's worked with them for nearly two decades, so he's trusted to travel alone. But yes, normally I work with him as his bodyguard. Simon thought it was a good chance to show that I could work alone and talked Ananth into letting me go solo in Nova Scotia."

It meant that Leo and Simon were half a world apart when Simon disappeared. If there was any logic to her ability, then Leo hadn't started to affect "the story" until he began to investigate the *katana*. Whatever Leo was doing in Nova Scotia had nothing to do with Simon's disappearance except for the fact that he wasn't guarding over his father. Was Simon's section simply a way to show Leo's reason for being in Japan?

Like Leo, Simon had refused to be named. Miriam had nicknamed him "the Brit" because British phrases would occasionally slip into his narrative. Nikki knew that he worked for an international agency named after a Hindu god. The phrase describing Shiva as "the one who kills the forces of darkness" resonated with her. She'd even taken "ThirdEye" as her handle after fleeing New York City—an attribute often associated with Shiva.

She continued to stick Post-It Notes on the wall, tracking the progress of her characters through their day-to-day lives. Compared with the confusion of the *katana*' branch, Simon's was so bare that only three notes marked his arrival and departure from the story. Still, the fact that she had mapped his movements from New York to Osaka to Izushi was more than she would do for a simple witness. He had to be important to the overall story somehow.

What was the common thread?

"This is probably going to take a while," she told Leo.

✠ 17 ✠
To Sleep,
Perhaps to Dream

Leo left her considering her colorful plot tree, trying to sketch out a story framework around Simon so she could pinpoint him. She took out her laptop and reread his only scene. Simon's attention had been on his phone call to Leo as he arrived at the construction site. The twelve-hour time difference, the fifteen hours on the airplane, followed by a night's sleep and a morning riding on a Japanese train—which banned talking on cell phones—meant that they had been out of contact for days. Leo was "out on a job," and Simon had been worried about his safety. Knowing now that Leo was a "tame monster" for Shiva, she could understand why. Simon started the conversation speaking in code.

"It's me," he said. "How'd it go?"

His son's voice was like a summer thunderstorm, rumbling in the distance, promising violence on the landscape. "It went."

He relaxed slightly. If the job was over, then his son was home. "Are you okay?"

The reply came too fast, too angry. "I'm fine!"

He waited, scanning the valley below him where bulldozers crawled over freshly torn earth. It would be better if his son confessed freely rather than be forced to report what had happened to make him so angry.

For several minutes there was only the low growl of anger, and then a snarl of "The density estimate was bullshit. One or two? My ass! There were over twenty. I needed to do a lot of scrambling to stay in the clear. I missed a jump."

His heart stumbled slightly at the news. *The job is over*, he reminded himself, *and he's home safe*. "Did you report the discrepancy?" What he really wanted to add was, "Or did you just chib the blighter who set the density?" He had to stop being the over-protective father and let his son stand on his own.

"Yes. Written down and cc'd all the heads."

"Good boy."

"What about you?"

"Just got here." He knew his son was trying to distract him from asking more questions, which meant he would probably not be happy with the news. "How bad?"

There was a long, unhappy silence and finally, "They'll let me out of this bed by the end of the week." And then an unhappier, "Doctor is here. I've got to go."

The conversation with Leo was much more understandable now. The vagueness of the discussion was because Shiva had sent Leo off to kill monsters. Not something you would discuss over a cell phone. The information Leo had been given about the number of monsters had been wrong. He'd barely gotten out alive. Worse, he was in a hospital when his father disappeared, unable to come searching for a week or more.

After the phone call, Simon had gone down into the valley to talk with the construction supervisor. The man had been uncooperative and brushed Simon off first chance he'd gotten. Leo's father had drifted through the work site, trying to ignore the fact that his son was in a hospital, half a world away. He inspected equipment, made it a point to talk to every worker, and then climbed over the broken landscape.

Like the conversation, everything seemed to be in code. She couldn't figure out what exactly Simon had been looking for. Since his mind was on Leo, his point of view didn't include information on why he was there and what he wanted. Nikki had assumed she could fill in the details later.

What hadn't she written? There were so many details that would have been clear moments after writing them that she'd probably forgotten now.

There was a slight knock, a female voice murmured something in Japanese, and then the door to the room slid open while Nikki was still trying to come up with some kind of reply. One of the hotel staff members knelt in the doorway and murmured again in fast Japanese.

"*Na—nani?*" Nikki managed to stammer out.

The girl made a cute face as she thought deeply and then said something slowly. Nikki wasn't sure if she was still speaking Japanese or very mangled and thus unrecognizable English.

Then Atsumori's presence flowed through her, and her mouth opened and she heard herself say, "Yes, please, put out the futons, thank you."

At least, that's what Nikki heard. The girl looked startled and laughed.

"*Katajikenai,*" the girl said in a deep male voice and laughed again. "You sound like a samurai. You must have learnt Japanese from historical movies." The girl moved to the closet and slid open the door. Inside were two futons and Atsumori's *katana.*

Nikki was beside the girl before she realized that she was moving, and snatched up the *katana.* "Please, do not touch that."

She retreated to the porch, stepping into the wooden sandals, fled into the garden.

She found a gate on the other side of the garden, and without meaning to, she was out into the town. She wasn't sure if it was she who was running or Atsumori. After the third turn, she was fairly certain it wasn't her.

"Stop! Stop! Stop!" she cried.

They took six more steps and stopped just beyond the *torii* marking the entrance to a small shrine.

"What are you doing?" She caught hold of the base of a *foo* lion statue just beyond the *torii,* trying to anchor herself so he couldn't drag her away.

"Talking." Atsumori appeared beside her. "There are things we need to discuss. I am not sure we can trust this half-breed, and certainly it seems as if we've been detoured to his needs, not ours."

"Ours? There are no 'our' needs."

He looked a little stunned and hurt. "We need to find out who ordered my *shintai* stolen."

"That is your need," Nikki said.

"Have you forgotten the *tanuki* in your home?"

She was really starting to hate how she'd lost control of her life days ago. "They are after you, not me. If I didn't have your *shintai*, no one would be trying to kill me."

"You have been caught up in the flood waters. I wish it were otherwise, but that is how it is. Even if we parted, those seeking me would still hunt you down to discover where you had hidden me. I must stay with you to protect you."

She swallowed down on "Leo will protect me." Atsumori was right that she had been trusting Leo more than she should simply because he was one of her characters. She had crawled into his head and read his thoughts. He was the Scary Cat Dude who rescued kittens. He was the poor misunderstood and abused little boy, saved only by the kindness of his now-missing foster father. He was the man who didn't want to burden his father with how truly wounded he was.

Assuming—dangerously so—that every word she wrote was the truth.

"I do not think we should trust this male of yours," Atsumori said.

She laughed at the idea that Leo belonged to her. "Noted. But I think finding his father will help you and me."

"You only have his word that the man who came to this town is the same that saved him from the cage. He has your writings; he can use your truth against you."

She frowned as she searched her memory. No, not once did the man tied up think of his son as "Leo." It brought her back to the fact that she knew so little about Leo. "What is an . . ." She struggled with the word that Simon had used. "*Obakemono*?"

Atsumori relaxed slightly, nodding as if he had won some point. "An *obakemono* indicates *yokai* that can shapeshift. There are any number of them. I believe his mother must have been a *bakeneko*."

"And a *bakeneko* is . . . ?"

"If a cat's tail grows too long, its tail will split in two and the cat will become a *bakeneko*."

She nearly said "Oh, that's so stupid," but then remembered to whom she was talking. Silly as it sounded, it probably was true. She took a deep breath as the understanding canted her entire belief system on its side. She was never sure if she believed in God, but somehow confirmation (and long-delayed realization) that there were countless "gods" dancing about Japan and all the attached spiritual system was true . . .

Why was it less intimidating to think she might be insane rather than think maybe every part of Japan mythology was true? Was insanity more sane than *tanuki* and *bakeneko*?

"Nikki-chan?"

She waved aside his concern. "I'm just coping. Give me a moment." She took a couple more deep breaths. Maybe it wouldn't be so overwhelming if she weren't running from murderous *tanuki* in the company of a god . . . and Leo.

"His mother was a monster? How does that work? I mean—why didn't she kill and eat his father?"

"*Yokai* can be both good and compassionate or malicious and evil. It has been my experience that *yokai* are drawn to humans who can sense them. It is quite possible this half-breed's father was what he refers to as a Sensitive. It is not uncommon for a *bakeneko* to take the place of a loved one who has died. They can mate with humans, but their children are *yokai*."

The scene with Leo in a cage suddenly made more sense. "Oh." And the one with Miriam. "Oh."

The girl from the hotel staff had taken the futon mattresses out of the closet and unrolled them so they lay side by side, making one big bed on the *tatami* mat-covered floor. The implied intimacy set Nikki's heart beating faster.

"No, no, not going to happen." Nikki grabbed the edge of the right-most futon and dragged it to the corner. Really, what was she thinking, sharing a room with a total stranger? She remembered how Leo's hand had felt as it brushed over hers during the drive—large, strong, and oh so male—and dragged Leo's futon away from hers to the farthest point she could get it.

She stared at the mattresses for several minutes, chewing on her bottom lip. That she didn't want Leo sleeping near her was entirely too obvious by the futons' new positions. Should she go with something less blatant? Maybe she should move Leo's to the front of the door, so it seemed more like she was worried about someone coming into the room undetected. That would appeal to a herolike guy—right? The porch, though, was more open to attack.

Once she had Leo's futon out on the porch, it occurred to her that he might not even come back to the room: he knew he had until dawn to find his father alive. If he'd spent six weeks of fruitless searching, he'd only return to see if she knew anything new about his father. If that was the case, she might be pissing him off by moving his bed for no reason.

She dragged both futons back to the center of the room, inches apart instead of touching, sheets and duvet smoothed back into place. After a minute of staring down at the futons, she laid the *katana* between the two mattresses.

"Okay, find Simon and everything will be good."

Simon dreamed that he was buried, pinned under rocks and earth, massive and unyielding as a mountain. Water dripped down his checks like cold tears—spilled down his breast like raindrops sliding down glass. He strained to dig himself free, but he was bound tight. He burned with anger toward those who had thrown him down and buried him. He'd get free and show his righteous anger—but no matter how hard he pushed and wriggled, he couldn't free himself.

Nikki frowned at the page. "Really? That's it?"

She had written several chapters on one character buried underground before—poor Mary Southland. This was clearly just a nightmare. The dream world was always blurred at the edges, details lost in darkness. She had no smell of earth or feel of the crumbling dirt. She tore the page out and laid it on Leo's futon. Tucking away the rest of the incriminating notebook, she thought about the scene. Had there been anything that didn't make the page? No, there was nothing.

She lay in the dark, listening to the night noises. She closed her eyes and tried to will herself to sleep. The last thing she needed was to push herself to exhaustion on top of everything else. The day's events jumbled through her head. She rolled onto her side and pressed fingertips to the *katana*. "Atsumori?"

"Sleep, Nikki-chan." For a moment, she felt his fingers twine with hers. "I will watch over you and keep you safe."

She understood then the comfort of belief. Calm swept over her and carried her off to sleep.

✠ 18 ✠
Stalking on Paper

Japan had been the land of mini cars, mini fire trucks, mini ambulances, and even mini tractor-trailer trucks, so it shouldn't have been a surprise that the bulldozers were half-sized. They did some mysterious shuffling of dirt around a large rip in the steep river valley.

Nikki trailed after Leo as they moved through the construction site, drowning in the smell of mud and diesel and the roar of heavy equipment clanking and beeping loudly. What great fodder for her book, but she wasn't sure now if she could bear finishing the book for publication. How could she let people enjoy the death of Misa? Besides, there was the small problem that she might not be alive to finish the novel, as her characters usually died.

Leo had returned after dawn, full of angry silence. She got the distinct impression that he was furious at someone, perhaps everyone, maybe just her.

He hadn't wanted to come to the construction site. It might have been the last place anyone could place his father, but she had written him alive, in a hotel room. She didn't try to explain her artistic process, mostly because she was no longer sure of anything except for the fact there was very little "artistic" to it. She'd only recently discovered that she could "tweak" a scene by visiting where the story was set. A character walking through a familiar place, mind on some problem (or pursuing a monster), ignored the world around them. During a tweaking session, she could take her time, use her own eyes to take in everything, and yet keep the character's mindset.

Between Leo's furious silence and the roar of the heavy machinery, though, she was starting to get a headache. She was going to have to tune them out if she wanted to get in touch with Simon's thoughts. When they stopped for Leo to talk rapid-fire Japanese to yet another yellow-helmeted man, Nikki dug through her purse to find her iPod. Earbuds in, volume up high, she retreated into soothing music.

Simon had floundered through the mud—it had been even thicker that day because of a downpour the night before. Simon, though, had left the mud behind as he thought about his angry son, who cared so deeply and yet shielded his heart with fierce defenses. There had been a shift in his attention, away from the treacherous footing.

Swaying in time with the music, Nikki considered the possible directions that Simon could have gone. There were the remains of a road, cut short by the construction's sprawl, that led upriver, away from the dam site. It matched with Simon's easy, mindless walking.

Nikki picked her way through the mud to the road. There she took out her notebook and pen.

The deafening roar of the construction dropped away as he walked up the deserted road. Around him life, continued as it had for hundreds of years, ignorant of the coming flood.

Simon had taken the road. Nikki hitched the *katana* on her shoulder and headed after the man. The road matched the river, running fast and heavy beside it. A bend took them completely out of sight of the bulldozers to a small farmstead. A house stood empty, the front door invitingly open.

This was the farm of the people evacuated out of the valley. They had been there for generations, out of mind, displaced by a disaster on the other side of the island and the needs of the many. They were not that different from Leo's family. Their family farm had been given to them by the Hawaiian king and the state had tried to sell it to a private investor to raise money for public coffers.

There! Proof that the Brit was indeed Leo's father. The question remained if Simon had gone into the house. "Will you get your mind off Leo and pay attention?"

"You're thinking of me?" Leo murmured beside her.

She jumped sideways. "I told you not to do that! And no, I'm talking about your father. I'm trying to track him, and he's not cooperating at all. I think he went into the house."

"I could find no sign of him in the house." Of course Leo had checked, probably more than once.

She glanced down the road, hugging the river's bank. The farm's mini fields terraced up the hillside behind the farmhouse. There was nothing else of interest to draw Simon away from the house, and Simon had mentally linked it to Leo, so there was a good chance he'd explored it.

"What did the construction people tell you? Did anyone see him come this way?"

"The landslides stopped after Simon vanished, so they've convinced themselves that nothing was wrong in the first place. They don't want to talk about him or what could have been causing the problems."

Was it that they didn't want to seem superstitious? Or didn't they have to acknowledge that someone might have been their sacrificial lamb?

Nikki made her way through the overgrown front yard to peer through the open door. It was an old-style farmhouse, the entrance just a mudroom with a dirt floor and one center stepping stone up into the house for guests to use. "*Ojamashimasu!*"

"No one is here." Leo took her call to mean she was going in. He stalked into the dim interior.

It was a sign of how long she'd been in Japan that she was slightly dismayed that he hadn't taken off his shoes. Then again, the house was slated to be flooded. She compromised by taking off her shoes and carrying them with her as she followed Leo into the house.

It was a sturdy house, if somewhat crudely made by American standards. The ceiling was wooden, and many of the inner doors were filthy *shoji* paper. There was a surprising amount of stuff still scattered everywhere, although there were spots among the clutter that suggested someone might have taken a handful of items. There were dishes piled around the kitchen sink, although there were no lights on the instant hot water heater and flipping the light switches produced nothing.

"They have moved out—right?" Nikki asked.

Leo gave her a dark look. "The owner died. His son moved to

Osaka years ago. He dropped out of college to work at a host club in Dontonbori."

"A host? What was his name? Kenichi? Kenichi Inoue?"

His eyes narrowed tightly. "Another character?"

"Yes. His father died, and he went home to collect things. I didn't have the name of the town where he lived, because he was based in Dontonbori. He never mentioned the dam project. In his second scene, a stranger showed up at his father's house as he was collecting things; it was very creepy."

She turned in a circle, taking in the house. Now that she considered it, the house felt familiar. She had written the scene shortly after Simon's abrupt end. Had the stranger been Simon or someone else? She hadn't connected the stranger with Simon—but then Simon had been simply "he." She hadn't even been able to nail down Leo's name; all references to Leo had been "his son" until what she wrote this morning.

"I need to reread Kenichi's sections again."

Nikki sat on the back porch of the empty farmhouse with her laptop. Looking back, Kenichi's first scene should have been a huge clue-by-four to the head that what she was writing was real. Like all her characters, he'd sprung fully formed onto the page, already in motion. He was, however, the first where she could investigate the reality of what she had written.

Her knowledge of host clubs had been limited to manga. In them, the "club" was a sugary sweet version that high school boys put together, serving nothing stronger than instant coffee. She had been dismayed when Kenichi's story spilled out onto the page, detailing a harsh reality of manipulating women with champagne, flattery, and lies. The men would do anything, say anything, in order to get their female customers to spend every penny they had on overpriced alcohol.

Since Kenichi lived in the glitzy Dontonbori district of Osaka, one short subway trip confirmed that everything she had written was true. The nightclubs were as shallow, exploitive, and gritty as she had depicted them. She had gone home worried about her sanity. Of course, even if she'd found the real Kenichi, she wouldn't have believed he was her character.

She could barely believe that this was his family's house. The one he had left when he was eighteen. The one he had never thought he would go back to. But after he learned that his father died, he'd returned. And while he was here, he had met someone . . .

It was no longer the house that Kenichi had grown up in. The old man had wiped out every trace of that house. Kenichi's bedroom had been stripped of everything he had left behind and filled with medical supplies. His mother's only presence in his childhood had been her compulsiveness neatness. Now grime coated every surface, blotting out all trace of his mother. There was railing installed that someone who wasn't the raging giant of his father needed to keep from falling.

What was he doing here? Everything Kenichi really wanted he took when he fled when he was eighteen. He drifted through the house, looking for anything he might want to keep. There wasn't much; his standards were higher now. His shirt was Armani, his jeans were Gucci, and his shoes were Prada. He filled a box with grimy items and then abandoned it.

Really, there was nothing he wanted. Let the water take it all. Ironic that with all the arguments over the question of whether or not he would take over the family farm, when the time finally came, it was a moot point.

He stopped at the back porch, its sliding door standing open. He frowned as he took out a cigarette and lit it with his brushed gold lighter. The front door had been standing open when he arrived. Who had left the house open? There were fresh footprints in the mud of the garden path, heading toward their terraced fields.

As he tucked away his lighter, he spotted someone at the far edge of the garden, walking slowly toward the house. Dusk was setting in and mist was rising early from the river.

There was something familiar about the person, but as they drew nearer, Kenichi grew sure that he didn't know this tall stranger. He could sense his rage. Kenichi was so used to his father's fury that he could nearly see it in others, shimmering like heat off the person. For a moment, he was five and wanted to flee this angry giant. He had learned, though, that the house had no safe refuge. Nor was he a five-year-old farm boy. He was twenty-five now, a full-grown man. He lived in the gritty big city in an apartment that looked down on glittering lights. He answered to men with guns, tattoos, and missing tips of their fingers.

He pulled on false indifference, and breathed smoke like a dragon, as the stranger closed on him.

"Kenichi," the stranger greeted him. "You're all grown up."

"Do I know you?" He peered through the gathering dusk, fairly sure he didn't know this person. But if he didn't, how did this stranger know his name?

The stranger stepped up onto the porch beside him. "My, my, you've stayed a pretty boy. Not like your father, all puffed up with anger like a toad." The man reached out and cupped Kenichi's face with a fever-hot hand. "You have your grandmother's eyes."

"What do you want?" Kenichi tried to pull free without seeming to struggle. His heart was banging in his chest. There was no mistaking the towering rage within this stranger. It was safest not to fight, but to wait, and then run.

"I want to travel. I want to see all that I've heard rumors of. The cities that gleam like jewels at night. I want to hear the ocean again— not this damn endless river murmur. I want to drink deep, eat my fill, and then destroy my enemies. And you're going to help me."

"Me?"

"Your family has always been good, obedient, and useful. No need for that to change."

Nikki realized that Leo was leaning against her back, reading over her shoulder.

"This stranger," Leo rumbled. "He does not sound like my father. He had never been to this area before. He would not have known this family."

"This is the first scene I wrote after your father's last scene. I didn't link the two because Kenichi only makes the one veiled reference to the dam. Originally Simon didn't mention this house at all. I tweaked his section this afternoon." She showed him the writing on the notebook. "He came to the house."

Leo frowned as he realized the implication. "This stranger might have done something to my father while he was here."

"Yes. Maybe. Wait." Nikki pulled up Simon's section and started to add in the tweaks. She started by typing up the short paragraphs and then shifted the block of text around. Simon noticed the house halfway through his scene. In the last paragraph, though, he was standing on a hill, looking at the construction in the distance.

"He took the garden path up to the fields." Nikki pointed at the narrow beaten path. "I think it was his footprints that Kenichi saw leading away from the house."

"I haven't been up there." Leo stood, suddenly a thunderstorm embodied. "I did not think Simon would walk so far from the dam."

"He did." Nikki shut down her laptop and put it carefully into her backpack. "I need to see what's up there to figure out why his scene just ended in midsentence."

The path led up the side of the steep hillside, with worn stepping stones as testament to how long the Inoue family had farmed the terraced land. The fields hadn't been tended for a long time, growing thick with tangled weeds.

Halfway up the hill, there was a path leading off to the left.

"You can't see the construction from here. He might have gone down this path. He would be able to see the dam from around the hill."

Leo blocked her from stepping forward. "Let me go first."

She hadn't considered that there was any danger lingering on the hillside. She nodded to him. He took out his pistol and slipped down the path, silent as a cat. She removed the fabric case from her shoulder and took out Atsumori's *katana*. She felt the heat of the *kami*'s presence. Gripping tightly to the wooden sheath with her left hand, right hand on the hilt, she followed Leo.

The path led through the brooding woods. The silence grew thick and oppressive.

Deep in the woods, far from the fields, lay an ancient landslide. The side of the hill had given way, creating a tumble of rocks and dirt. The path ended abruptly at the edge of the rubble.

Suddenly Atsumori was beside her. "Careful. This place is holy, but it feels—it feels wrong."

She was shivering from the creepiness of the place. A shaft of sunlight shone on one large boulder sitting apart from the rest of the landslide. There was a strand of rope around it and paper streamers hung from the rough cord to signify that it was a *shintai*.

"There's a god here? In the rock?"

Atsumori stared hard at the boulder, his head slightly tilted to one side. "No, but there was a god here for some time. Her presence is like a perfume after the *geisha* has passed."

From the clearing, the dam construction was fully visible. The bulldozers crawled like bugs in the dirt. This was where Simon's scene had ended.

"Leo, was Simon like sand?"

"Sand?" Leo echoed, his eyebrows rising.

"Atsumori can take me over because I'm like sand. Gregory Wintson was like granite. That's why the *yakuza* used him to steal the *katana*; Atsumori couldn't stop him."

Leo's face filled with dismay. "A *kami* possessed my father?"

"I think so. It brought him up here and walked down to the farmhouse where Kenichi was. The stranger that walked into the house was Simon, but it wasn't him—it was the *kami*. That's why the stranger knew Kenichi—his family had been tending this shrine."

Leo hunched, eyes to the ground, as if fighting with inner pain.

"He's alive." Nikki offered what comfort she could. "The god is keeping him prisoner because—because the god needs him. This valley is about to be flooded. The god has abandoned its *shintai*. It can't stay in Simon, because that would kill him, but it doesn't have its *shintai* to return to."

"The *kami* has to have something else," Atsumori said. "In the heavens, we can exist as pure spirits. Here on Earth, we cannot exist as ourselves without something to hold us."

"That's why it stole your sword—to have something else."

Atsumori's face filled with anger, followed by fear. "To take the sword away from me, it would have to be more powerful than me."

"Where would it take my father?" Leo asked.

"Kenichi went back to Osaka. I don't know if he's still there."

Leo snarled with anger and caught her by the wrist. "Come on. We're going back to Osaka then."

✥ 19 ✥
Semantics

"Tell me about this Kenichi," Leo rumbled dangerously as they walked quickly back toward the construction site.

Nikki was half-running to keep up with him. "He's a host at a club in Osaka. This was his second scene. His first scene showed him working at the host club. He's one of the top money producers of his club, often number one in sales, making like three million yen a month."

Leo growled at the number. "So he's a well-paid whore."

The writer in her protested the semantics of the word. "His customers don't pay him for sex, just his company. He seems to be only sleeping with one of his clients, an American heiress, and he thinks he may be in love with her."

"Maybe." Leo laughed bitterly.

She understood Kenichi's problem. He'd watched his father use his mother, grinding her into nothingness, and he could recognize his father in his own relationships with women. Kenichi wasn't sure he could be a person who loved without ulterior motives, and he hated that and yet seemed helpless to stop his manipulation of his clients. Then again, it was hard to be strong when the reward for being weak was so rich.

She tried to filter through everything she knew about the man, to determine what might be important and what was needless personal clutter. Kenichi's first scene had revolved around the daily routine of

173

the club, leaving Nikki confused as to how the man would ever work into the rest of the story. He lived vampire hours, doing something looked down upon by most of the population.

"The third scene I wrote for him was set a week later. He's back at the club for the first time. Everyone has assumed that he spent the time taking care of his father's funeral. He'd actually taken the stranger to Kyushu via the *Shikansen*."

"What did they do there?"

"Spend money. At least that's all Kenichi was thinking about. They'd burned through nearly two million yen during the week. Running the numbers, he was going to be in massive debt by the end of the month."

"Did the *kami* return to Osaka with my father?"

"I believe so. Kenichi has a studio apartment not far from the club. He normally rides a bicycle back and forth to work."

The fact that the ultra-cool host rode a bike had tickled her to no end. It made him seem even more boylike, but in reality bicycles were so common in Japan that it was like saying he walked to work.

"It's a nice apartment. It's all sleek and modern, with a wall of glass that looks down on the lights of Dontonbori. The thing is: it's way too small to share. Part of the expenses that Kenichi was calculating included multiple hotel rooms in Osaka. It was in the neighborhood of two hundred thousand yen a night, counting room service."

"Multiple rooms every night?"

Nikki nodded. "I'm not sure who the *kami* recruited in Kyushu, but Kenichi was going to go broke housing them all."

"It would explain why my father is still alive."

"What do you mean?"

"He couldn't survive six weeks of being sole host. The *kami* has found someone else to reside in. Share the load."

"Kenichi?"

"No. He sounds like a minor Talent. People like him can sense the god, but they're not open enough that they can be easily possessed."

They reached the end of the road and started through the torn earth of the construction site. The bulldozers had dug a deep trench in their path while they'd been hiking up the hillside to the shrine. She stopped to eye the long trench blocking their way. With the slick mud, she wasn't sure she could cross it safely.

Leo jumped down into the trench, reached up, caught her by the waist, and lifted her across. She muffled a squeak of surprise at his kindness. She found herself looking down into his face. He really was quite handsome with his thick black mane and bold, expressive eyes. Her heart did a strange flutter in her chest, and she felt a blush start at her collar as she realized that she was staring at him.

He set her carefully on the other side of the trench and then leaped up and out with catlike grace.

What were they talking about? Kenichi. The *kami*. Sharing the load.

"Oh. Oh!"

"What is it?"

"Kenichi's last scene. The *kami* told him to call all the women on his client list and had them come to his apartment one by one. He wasn't sure what the *kami* had planned, so he picked a client he actively disliked and invited her as a guinea pig. Her name was Hitomi."

"Was?"

Nikki realized that "was" implied "dead."

"Oh, no, Hitomi's not dead. I'm just thinking in past tense because this happened three weeks ago. At least, that's when I wrote it—I'm not sure when it really happened. The sad thing was that Hitomi was all excited because she thought it meant that Kenichi was really in love with her. She was pissed off that there was this *gaijin* at the apartment. The *kami* circled Hitomi—eyeing her like she was a piece of meat— and then told Kenichi that she was useless, to send her away and call the next woman on his list."

Leo growled. "Sensitives are drawn to Talents. Someone like Kenichi in a host club would be like dangling bait. The *kami* must be hoping that some of his clients are strong Sensitives."

"She'll be able to take them the way she took your father?"

"Yes."

"Oh, that's bad. Kenichi is worried about the girl he thinks he loves, the American heiress. He thinks of her as special, like no one else, that when she looks at him, she knows the real him, no matter how much he lies. He's sure that she's the one the *Kami* is looking for."

"Then he's probably right."

"He's been trying to protect her by putting her at the end of the list."

Leo growled softly. "Then he does not truly love this girl."

"He believes that he does, since he was afraid for her. If he didn't love her, he wouldn't care what the god did with her."

"If he loved her, he wouldn't put her in danger's way. He would leave her off his list. He'd call her and break up with her and never see her again."

It didn't surprise her that Leo would do anything to protect someone he loved, even give them up. She had sensed that of him as she'd written his scenes. Despite the hardship of his childhood, Leo had grown into a strong man. Hidden under all the expensive clothes and brave swagger, Kenichi was still a fearful little boy. "When you're taught nothing but fear, it's hard to have courage. I don't know if I would have the courage to stand against an angry god."

Leo gave her a bleak look and then turned away. "You wouldn't have any choice. You're too strong a Talent to stand against this god. Kenichi, though, is only letting fear rule him."

She knew that Leo was right. Part of her, though, wanted to protest because she'd been inside Kenichi's head and knew how twisted his childhood had made him. She could sympathize; her mother had done a prime number on her, too.

"I cannot take you with me when I hunt this creature. If it is within Simon and I managed to subdue my father, it could jump freely to you."

"And I could not protect you either," Atsumori murmured.

Nikki shivered. "Been there, done that, not doing it again. You should know that Kenichi's nightclub is owned by the *yakuza*. I haven't done a lot of research into the *yakuza* yet, so I'm not totally clear on how the gangs work. I get the impression that the owner was a low-level boss. He had a dozen guys who worked with him. They come and go at the club, keeping an eye on things, because there's lots of competition between the clubs. Harada's first kill was the owner. He got rid of the body quietly, and, in the next scene with Kenichi, there was someone pretending to be the man. I think a *tanuki* took his place."

Leo growled softly. "This gets worse and worse."

✧ 20 ✧
Soba Noodle

They stopped at a little hole-in-the-wall *soba* noodle shop that looked a hundred years old. The table was a large square of rough planks surrounding an elevated fire pit. Nikki wasn't sure if she was relieved or disappointed that there was no fire going so early on a summer day. There didn't seem to be any chimney overhead, just a vaulted ceiling of rough beams and wooden planks. The menu was on wooden plaques tacked on the wall. Considering there was a McDonald's next door, Nikki was surprised that Leo had chosen the ancient noodle shop.

His choice became less mysterious after he ordered the food, he went outside to do secret agent stuff with his phone and to get Kenichi's place of employment and his home address. Nikki opened up her laptop and quickly connected to the McDonald's Wi-Fi. She hadn't wanted to use the hotel's Internet since it might have given her location away, but they were leaving Izushi after they ate.

She logged onto her ultra-secret forum. The log-in information was only linked to an e-mail account that had no data trail back to her. For this account alone, she was Mango Nana.

The first message was from Miriam as SexyNinja on Monday. "Who has the ball?"

"Incoming!" Pixii answered.

"Have fun playing with ball!" ChibiX said from the northern reaches of Hokkaido.

"Will do!" Pixii replied, but then posted an unhappy face on Tuesday. "Does someone else have the ball?"

Miriam posted minutes later with, "OMG, you don't have it? Scary-ass male came looking for the ball!"

"Not me!" Jaynaynay said.

"Me neither," Cloud said.

Nikki winced. She hated this sneaking around. "Bounce. Bounce," she typed in. They deserved more information, but she didn't know how closely anyone was tracking her movements. They'd know at least that she was mobile and checking in.

Almost immediately, Pixii posted, "Bounce!" in reply.

And on the heels of that, Miriam posted, "Guard Dog sighted at Narita."

Nikki's breath turned solid in her chest as she stared at the words.

Her mother was in Japan? Oh God. Oh God. Her life had gone completely, impossibly insane, and her mother was here to witness it all? Nikki checked the news. Sure enough, there was a CNN sound bite of her mother visiting with an official-sounding cover story to make it seem like she wasn't here to hunt down her mad daughter.

What the hell was she going to do? Her mother would be looking for her in Osaka; she couldn't go back there. She didn't know anyone but Miriam, and her mother would have people watching Miriam's place. Tokyo might be a city of twelve million people, but the idea of being that close to her mother was threatening to trigger a panic attack.

Rather than sit and scare herself, Nikki logged off, shut down her laptop, and focused on breathing again. As if he'd been watching her, the elderly chef appeared with two heavily laden trays of food. He wore a blue *happi* with an apron and a little dark blue cap. He looked at Leo's empty chair as he put the trays down.

Nikki struggled not to blurt out "My mother is in Japan!" and mimed talking on a cell phone. What was the word for telephone? "Denwa."

"You eat." The man pointed at the five small dishes of *soba* noodles he had just placed in front of Nikki, along with dishes of mystery sauces and what looked like soft-boiled egg in a shell. Nikki had been discovering that the Japanese have a certain love of raw eggs and a total disregard of salmonella poisoning. "I bring more noodle."

"*Arigato gozaimaisu.*" She bowed in her chair in thanks, and he bowed back. Because he continued to hover, most likely to be sure she understood the proper way to eat the noodles, she picked up her chopsticks and one of the little dishes of noodles and dumped them into a dark sauce. "*Itadakimasu!*" Which basically meant, "I receive this food."

Apparently she guessed correctly—he grinned, and thankfully, went away, as she had exhausted her food Japanese. The spotlight off her, she went limp in her chair.

Her mother was in Japan.

Leo came back into the restaurant and settled beside her as she stared at her tray. She was reaching her breaking point on unknowns. Her mother was closing in on her, and she didn't even know what she was eating, let alone where the nearest train station was. What was she going to do? Where was she going to go? Was the hell were these odd-smelling condiments?

"What is this?" she whispered, pointing to a white sauce.

"*Daikon. Wasabi.*" Leo named two of the pastes and pointed to the third condiment. "Not a clue, but it's good."

She could live with "good." Velveeta was "good," and she had no idea what it was either, other than a "cheese food" that you didn't need to refrigerate before opening. It remained the mysterious food of the gods; sinful yumminess that your mother never let you eat.

Oh great, she was losing it. Her fingers started to itch with the need to write. She hadn't written nearly enough during the day to satisfy the need, and news of her mother's arrival was rattling her hard. She focused on applying her chopsticks to the slippery noodles.

Apparently the noodles were "all you can eat." After Leo quickly slurped his way through the first five small dishes, the chef brought out another round.

"Big eater!" The chef grinned at Leo as he sat five more dishes in front of him. He looked at Nikki's last dish, which she had emptied by adding the noodles into the dark soy-based sauce. His smile faded slightly as she shook her head.

Two men in suits came through the door, triggering a call of "*Irasshaimase*" from the shop owner. Somehow they seemed familiar, even though Nikki was fairly sure she didn't know either of the men. It filled her with alarm, since the last person she "recognized" had been a *tanuki.* The taller of the two men was non-Asian. Something about his messy dark hair and fashionably scruffy clothing said "French" to her. The other was a slender Japanese man, so clean-cut and neat that he looked like the emperor doll in the traditional Girl's Day collection.

Leo surged out of his seat, growling in anger. The growl was deep as a lion's snarl, and it raised the hair on her arms to hear it. In a flash of heat, Atsumori flowed into her, readying for a fight. They reached under the table to grip the *katana.*

"What are you doing here?" Leo rumbled.

"You're being a bad monster, Mister Pussycat." The Frenchman swung around to the other side of the table and pulled out a chair to slump into it. "Not going where you're supposed to go. Not being where you're supposed to be."

Nikki locked down a gasp of surprise. She did know these men; they were Chevalier and Sato, the cleaners. Somehow, meeting Leo wasn't nearly as creepy as suddenly being across the table from two of her characters. Perhaps it was because she had been inside Leo's head, sensing he was a good and decent man before he walked out of the darkness. The only thing she knew about these men was that Chevalier liked to taunt "monsters" and Sato was far more dangerous than Leo.

Chevalier eyed her with puzzlement and mild concern. He seemed genuinely concerned that the nice little girl was sitting and eating with a monster.

Sato shifted his gaze from Leo to Nikki and back. It reminded her of the countless times she had been studied by doctors, their faces impassive, weighing her possible insanity, her mother's influence, and their own needs and convictions. They were always the ones who bowed to her mother's wishes.

"Who is this?" Sato said.

"I'm Natasha Deming," Nikki said the first lie that came to mind. All Leo's strengths aside, he was apparently not a glib liar. "I'm an art student at the Osaka University of Arts. I'm studying manga creation under Kazuo Koike."

Leo glanced at her with surprise and slight alarm. "We found out what happened to my father. There's a shrine on the hill behind one of the abandoned farmhouses. There are signs that something was sealed there under a rock like a *namazu,* but all the wards are broken. Simon got too close to something powerful, and it took him."

Some emotion was smoothed from Sato's face before Nikki could identify it. He drifted backwards, as if putting distance between him and Leo.

"Such devotion," Chevalier said. "Sato, if I go missing, will you search for me so diligently?"

"I would leave you in whatever hole you fell in," Sato said.

Chevalier grinned at this as if it were a joke.

Sato hit the doorway and said quietly, "She's not fully human."

Chevalier's eyes widened with surprise, but he was instantly on his feet. "She's not?"

Leo growled a deep rumbling menace. "She's not dangerous. She's helping me find my father."

"What is she?" Sato said.

Nikki opened her mouth to spin out a lie, but Atsumori said, "She is harmless. I am the one that you can sense. I am Taira no Atsumori Kami." He gave a slight nod of her head, a suggestion of a bow, and brought up the *katana* so that it was visible to the two men. "I have business in Osaka I wish to attend to."

"Oh hell," Nikki hissed. "I told you not to do that."

"He is dangerous," Atsumori said. "And the other is solid granite."

"For the love of God, will you let me deal with this?"

"I thought—" Atsumori started.

"No, you did not think," Nikki snapped. "Just—just—just let me do the talking."

Chevalier whispered "*Merde,*" and took three steps back. Weirdly, even though Nikki didn't know French, she understood he had just said "shit." It made her realize that the entire conversation so far had been in Japanese. Apparently it was some god superpower to speak all languages.

"They're cooperating?" Sato asked.

"He's benign." Leo moved sideways to stand between Nikki and the men. "He's only involved because his *shintai* was stolen by the American, Gregory Winston."

Sato turned his gaze to the Frenchman.

Chevalier gave a bitter laugh. He pulled a slender metal case out of his suit pocket and selected a dark-papered cigarillo. "Let the muscle take the sword?"

"It is your job," Sato said.

Chevalier grunted. He put the cigarillo in his mouth and let it dangle there. "Getting the sword would be easy. Doing it without hurting the girl would be difficult. Personally, I don't see the need."

"Protocol is . . ." Sato started.

". . . determined by the lead agent," Chevalier finished. "Mister Pussycat was told to find the *katana*, and he did. He is in Izushi, as he claimed, and he has a lead on his father, who is a useful agent. This is all—how do the Americans say? Win. Win."

Sato gazed coldly at Chevalier for a moment and then stalked away.

"Well, that put him in a snit," Chevalier murmured and lit his cigarillo.

Leo took out his wallet and threw money onto the table. "I think whatever is riding my father is behind the raids on the various shrines we've been investigating. The *kami* is seeking a *shintai* strong enough to hold it. It's using *tanuki* to do its legwork. There is a good chance my father is alive if it's being careful with him."

Chevalier nodded. "Do you know where it is now?"

"I think it's in Osaka." Leo obviously didn't want to explain why. "We were about to head there."

Chevalier glanced to Nikki, one eyebrow raised in question. "You're going after one *kami* with another in tow? Not the most brilliant of plans."

"I'm not leaving her with you."

Chevalier grinned with delight. "Oh, Mister Pussycat wants all the sweet cream for himself."

Leo rumbled with annoyance that only made Chevalier grin wider.

Nikki blushed hot and stalked out of the restaurant. Once safe beyond the doorway, and sure that Sato wasn't in sight, she quickly shouldered the *katana* and dug out a pen.

In the noodle shop behind her, she heard Chevalier laugh and say, "I will get Sato and meet you in Osaka. Even you should not try to face a *kami* and a pack of *tanuki* by yourself."

She fled toward the *onsen*, face still burning with embarrassment, clicking her pen. They had kept Chevalier and Sato from knowing about her writing, but they knew that Atsumori could easily possess her. Shiva would be after Natasha Deming, but how long would it take for them to realize that Natasha didn't exist? Hours? Minutes? Any idiot could guess that the American girl with the sword was Nikki if Natasha didn't exist.

Chevalier, though, seemed to be perfectly happy to label her as a "good monster." Having Shiva know about her might not be the disaster that Leo painted it. Certainly Leo and Sato seem to be waltzing around Japan without strings attached.

Her mother, though, wanted her locked up and tied down. And her mother was in Japan.

Leo appeared beside her, silent as a cat. "Are you okay?"

She considered telling him the truth, but would he understand? He loved his foster-father; could he understand that she wanted nothing to do with her mother? "I'm scared," felt safe to admit. Any sane person would be scared by now.

He went still beside her. After a moment, he took a deep breath and murmured, "I won't let anything happen to you."

It would be more comforting if her mother didn't often say the same kind of thing.

She trusted him—perhaps more than she should. What did she really know about him? That he had been a scared little boy nearly twenty years ago? That his foster-father loved him? She wasn't sure love moved him to find Simon, let alone how he felt about her.

"I need to—" Surely to him she could confess that she sometimes had to write. He would understand that she wasn't crazy. Wouldn't he? But she wasn't sure. "I need to take a bath before we take off— since I'm not sure when I'll be able to take another."

He nodded without looking at her. Only after he walked her to the hotel room did it occur to her that he must be impatient to get going. Still, he didn't complain, only stoically said, "I'll be waiting by the car."

She bathed as quickly as she could. *I didn't lie*, she thought as guilt squirmed around in her stomach. *I don't know when my next shower will be. The god isn't going to hurt Simon—he's too important to her.*

The need to write was so strong that Nikki was shaking as she pulled on the last of her clean clothes. *Oh God, don't let Leo come in and find me like this, shaking like a junkie needing a fix.* Kneeling over her suitcase, she flipped open her notebook and flicked the ballpoint pen. She breathed out in relief as the point touched paper and bled ink.

She'd just write a little bit, enough to take the edge off. One scene and she'd be sane enough to deal with rampaging gods, tattooed *yakuza,* and her controlling mother. She still had her normal resources plus her freaky new power, a boy god, and Leo. Of course, she didn't know how Leo felt about her. Sometimes she thought that he liked her, but other times it was like he couldn't stand to be around her. Not that she wasn't used to it; every guy she ever liked was interested until he got to know her and read something that she wrote. She started not showing her writing to her boyfriends, and finally not even telling them that she wrote at all. It was like being a drug addict, constantly trying to hide how addicted she was. Leo would just be the latest guy to be totally creeped out by what she wrote. Hell, he had more cause than any of the others, because he knew it was real.

She had her eyes closed, her headphones on, and was dancing to something playing on her iPod. He was trying not to watch. Her shirt had ridden up as she slowly swayed her hips, showing the softness of her stomach.

She opened her eyes and caught him watching and blushed with embarrassment. "I love this song," she said shyly.

"What is it?" he asked.

She surprised him by taking one of the buds from her ear and stepping close. She brushed back his hair and put the bud into his ear. It was a slow love ballad about golden fields of barley. She stood so close he could feel the warmth of her body nearly touching his. Every breath, he drew in her scent. She closed her eyes again, swaying to the slow beat.

"Will you stay with me, will you be my love, among the fields of barley?" she sang, eyes closed, oblivious of him. "We'll forget the sun in his jealous sky, as we lie in fields of gold."

He could imagine her lying in golden barley, her hair fanned out, her stomach bared to his kisses. He wanted to touch her. Hold her. She trusted him, though, and he would do nothing to endanger that fragile state.

Far too soon, the song was over, and he reluctantly handed back her earphone.

"Did you like it?" She was blushing again.

"Yes."

She smiled shyly and moved away, taking his heart with her.

"Wow." Nikki stared at the notebook. She had played him the song that morning, and he'd been all still and quiet, like he hadn't liked the song. Afterwards he had gotten all weird, but he was majorly digging on her. "Oh, wow."

She closed up the notebook, feeling fluttery and warm inside. She had written love scenes countless times before, but it was the first time that she was the focus. It was like a rush of a very good drug. It scared her slightly.

When she was younger, before the doctors started prescribing drugs that she avoided taking, and before her stays in the hospitals, where she had to be oh so tricky to keep from being medicated, she had written about a character addicted to heroin. It was slowly killing the woman, and she knew it, but she'd been helpless to stop. Everything paled to the wonderful bloom of euphoria as the drug kicked in. The sense of helplessness had etched so deep into Nikki's psyche that when she first felt that same warm rush, she had done everything humanly possible to flee it.

Surely, love wasn't the same.

Dusk was gathering in the shadows as the color bled from the sky.

Leo was sitting on the stone wall, stray cats roaring around him like a bored harem. The kitten played with his boot laces.

He's into you, she thought for courage. She walked down to the wall. The stray cats watched her coming as if she were enemy aircraft. *He knows all about how freaky you are, and still he's interested.*

He glanced back at her, his face poker calm as always, and she faltered.

Maybe he just wants sex. Men are like that. *They see a girl who's not too fat and with a cute smile and blond hair and they think with their dicks.* God knows, she'd written one or two like that.

"Hey," he rumbled in his deliciously deep voice.

She gave him a little wave and felt all of twelve. "Hi." She sat down beside him, deliberately getting as close as her courage allowed. At that moment, it translated to a six-inch space between them.

As usual, he had nothing immediately to say to her. She always took that to mean he didn't like her enough to talk to her. As they sat in silence, she wished she had the scene in her hands, so she could read the words again, and know for sure. He hadn't used the word "love," but surely he'd meant it by saying she that she'd taken his heart.

She didn't want to consider that he was the type who confused lust with love. But once she let the thought in, it took root. What if he just found her sexy and mistook that interest for love? Could she live with that? She peeked at his rugged profile. There was a scar on his jawbone, near his right ear. It served to remind her that she barely knew him.

Did she love him? In all warm fluttering rush, she hadn't stopped to think about that. If they were about to start throwing the L-word around, shouldn't she start with herself? Oh, the found-money feeling of unexpected love was great and wonderful until she realized she had to dig into her wallet and fork over a matching amount.

She dropped her gaze to his strong hand just inches from hers. It would be easy to cast caution aside and take his hand. There weren't any fields of barley handy. There was the *onsen* room, already paid for, and Atsumori. And no birth control to speak of.

And no, she really didn't want to just have sex after feeling the rush of knowing he might love her. She wanted it to be real. For both of them.

"We should get going," he said.

She nodded. "Yes, we should."

✠ 21 ✠
War Preparations

With her laptop, all her notebooks, a fistful of colored pens, a bottle of Coke, a box of Meiji chocolate-covered almonds, a brand-new multicolor pad of Post-It Notes, and a kitten chewing on her shoelaces, Nikki was going to war. She wanted Leo to have all the data she could write down in the three hours it took to get to Osaka. With notebooks and laptop balanced on her lap, it was easy to have an excuse to keep her arm near the stick shift so that Leo brushed her hand every time he shifted.

Unfortunately, it was distracting as hell. She struggled to keep her mind on the problem at hand. "I believe that this god is the main storyline of my novel. When I write a novel, there's all these characters scattered about, sometimes never intersecting, with the exception of the one event that touches all of them. One disaster, actually."

She had been through the cycle countless times. It had taken her a lifetime to learn what little control she had. Except when she was heavily medicated, she hadn't stopped writing since she learned how to read. Before then, she could remember telling stories as her toys met violent ends. Her mother had trouble keeping nannies for more than a few weeks. Her first written attempts were merely a last straw.

"I couldn't figure out what the connecting thread for this novel was. It's one of the reasons I created my Post-in-Note tree. Sometimes with it, the invisible thread shows up. Since I didn't connect your father to Kenichi, he seemed like an outlier, but he's tied back into what I think of as 'the Osaka' branch. But, now I think that's the trunk of the structure, not a branch."

"You can use this to locate the god, then?"

"I'm—I'm not sure. As far as I can tell, Kenichi is my only character still alive who has interacted with her besides Simon, but I think there might be others."

"Her?"

"I think the god is a she—as in goddess." She scrolled down through Kenichi's section. "In the second scene, he keeps thinking of the visitor as 'the stranger' and 'this person' as if what he sensed about the visitor's gender was conflicting with what he was seeing. After this, he just refers to her as the princess." Nikki flipped through her recent notebook. "In this passage where your father is dreaming of being trapped, I thought it reflected the fact that he was stuck, but there was a sense of being outside with dirt and water dripping. The wording leans toward female. I think he's picked up on her memories."

Leo growled dangerously, reminding Nikki that his mother was *bakeneko,* and she wasn't sure what that meant for Leo. One point in his favor: her mother would certainly hate him for his mixed heritage. Of course, she'd think he was Hawaiian-Japanese and not part monster.

"The damn bitch is burning herself into my father," Leo snarled. "Do you have any sign that she hasn't burnt him out?"

She flipped to a blank page and attempted to lock in on Simon. It produced nothing but the familiar string of dots. "At this moment, the goddess is with your father. I can't get a bead on him."

"What about Kenichi? Is he with my father?"

She flipped the page and started a scene with the pretty host boy. "Oh!"

"What is it?" Leo swung them around a tight mountain curve, brushing his knuckles against her skin as he downshifted.

She blushed at Leo's touch. "I wrote Kenichi inviting Hitomi to his apartment weeks ago, but apparently that happened fairly recently. He's on the last girl, the American heiress. I think he's seeing her tonight."

Leo's eyes narrowed. "At his apartment?"

"No, at the club."

Leo shifted back to fourth gear to take a straightway fast. "Is my father there?"

Nikki leaned back in her seat and considered the question. At one time, she thought she'd built an elaborate imaginary stage in her head to push uncooperative actors across. When she was younger, her stories had been a deluge of information about the stage and actors, losing "the plot" under a flood of miscellaneous details. She had trained herself to stay focused on weaving a good story, but in doing so, she stopped paying attention to all the other information that she could glean from the setting and people.

She had only written a handful of words, but it was like she'd opened a window to the distant nightclub. The doors hadn't officially opened for the night, and only the employees moved through the narrow, long maze of rooms. Kenichi paced in the large mirrored main lounge, for once not checking his reflection to see if his hair was styled to anime-perfection. He wore a perfectly tailored white Armani suit with elegant touches of gold jewelry. There were three *yakuza* drifting through the club, dark, menacing shadows.

She tried to focus on the *yakuza*. They refused to come into focus, staying blurs of darkness in the glitter of the nightclub. She could sense that they carried many hidden weapons: sharp knives and cold lumps of guns. Like an illusionist's tricks, she imagined that Kenichi occasionally caught sight of inhuman eyes, sharp teeth, and clawed hands in the mirror as he paced.

At the moment, though, Simon didn't seem to be in the nightclub.

"I don't think so. There are three *yakuza*. I don't think they're human; they might be *tanuki*. Kenichi thinks of them as 'the new ones,' and they terrify him. They seem to be waiting for the girl to arrive. Kenichi is acting like he doesn't notice that they're listening to his phone call, but he's very aware that the *yakuza* can overhear what the girl is saying to Kenichi. She has been blowing Kenichi off for the last few days. On one hand, he's happy about it because it's delaying the goddess getting her hands on the girl. On the other hand, he's starting to think that his girlfriend is seeing someone else, and he's jealous."

Leo made a sound of disgust.

"Yeah, I know."

The kitten pounced on her shoe, distracting her for a second.

"*Maru!*" Nikki wiggled her foot, trying to get kitten to stop, but it only encouraged him. She liked the fact that they hadn't abandoned Maru in Izushi; it made it easier to pretend that they weren't racing toward disaster. Three hours trapped in a car with a bored kitten, though, had its drawbacks.

Leo chuckled, deep and full, and the sound made delicious things happen inside of her.

I love him, don't I? More and more, she was feeling sure that she did. If nothing else convinced her, the rising panic over the thought of him walking out of her life and never coming back did.

She focused on writing. She needed to find out everything she could about Kenichi, the *yakuza*, Simon, and the goddess. In the scene, the conversation between Kenichi and the girl continued. "The heiress has been telling Kenichi that she's helping a friend of hers. She says it's a girlfriend, but he's suspecting that it's a boy, possibly another host at a different club. Oh, oh, oh!"

"What now?"

"He's trying to make her too mad to come and see him. He's afraid to start a fight with her with the new *yakuza* listening to his side of the conversation, but he's pushing her buttons on purpose."

"He should just tell her outright. If you love someone, you protect them."

She wanted to protect Leo. She didn't want him walking into this nightclub and facing the inhuman *yakuza*. Kenichi knew with certainty he loved his girlfriend because of how scared he felt for her. Nikki realized that she had the same fear echoing through her. *I love Leo, but I don't know how to protect him.*

Leo shifted, brushing her hand again, making all sorts of emotions shift and squirm inside her. Being in love was an uncomfortable thing.

She finished the scene and sighed. "She's angry, but she's still coming to see him."

"Once she's at the club, the *yakuza* will take her to see the god?"

"That's the plan."

"That's how I'll find my father."

Leo was missing the big picture. He was seeing only his lost father, not the wave of destruction about to crash down all around his father.

"I have forty main characters," she scrambled to explain. "Well, thirty-five. Five have died so far. Gregory Winston. Misa. Three others were killed by Harada. Oh, wait, make that thirty-four. I forgot about Harada."

"Who?"

"Harada was the *tanuki* at my apartment. At least, that's what I called him. Not sure what name he really used—I haven't got anyone's real name yet." Thirty-two if they didn't count her and Leo, but she didn't want to tell him that he was one of her characters.

Leo's confusion was clear in his voice. "And?"

"So far this is fairly typical story. People are living their ordinary lives when something ugly brushes up against them and kills them." She winced as she realized what it meant for Simon. "I'm sorry."

He gave her a worried glance, and she realized that he was counting her as a possible victim, too.

"Teach me to write myself into a story."

She focused on the notebook and the finished scene. "Kenichi is the only Osaka viewpoint character—other than me. The rest are scattered all over Japan. I don't know how they all play into this. When the goddess was talking to Kenichi, though, she mentioned something." Nikki scrolled down through her files on her laptop, found Kenichi's section, and read the line. "'*I want to drink deep, eat my fill, and then destroy my enemies.*' If this turns into one of my usual novels, every one of my characters is a likely target for her revenge." A connection was made in her mind. "Oh!"

"Hmm?"

"Oh, it just fully clicked that Harada was employed by the goddess. I wish now we didn't kill him."

"If you had not killed him, he would have killed you."

There was that small problem. She shivered, remembering the warm trickle of his blood running down her face. "Once a character is dead, I can't write any more about them."

"We'll find my father without Harada."

"Yes, we will, but I'm worried about the big picture. The thing is, normally, by the end of the book, *all* the characters are usually dead. Even if they do get out alive, every character has interacted with the main storyline. Half my characters have had only their set-up scenes— the goddess hasn't interacted with them yet."

"We're going to stop her before she can hurt them."

She hoped he was right, but it had been her experience that nothing she ever did stopped people from dying.

22
Love Hotel

It was nearly ten at night when they hit Osaka. Leo grew quiet and tense as they roared along the highways that bisected the city.

"I'm taking you to Umeda," he said. "There are hotels there where you won't need to hand over your passport. I'll get you into a room under my credit card, and then I'll go after my father. If something happens and I don't come back, then . . . it might be safer if you leave the country."

Hopscotch the world, one step in front of her mother. "I don't really have the money to run."

He gripped the wheel tight and took them down off the highway onto the busy streets of Umeda. "Write down this number. 19.43.47 north by 155.5.24 west."

"What is that?"

"It's a house in Hawaii. On the big island. Out in the middle of nowhere. You'll need a GPS and four-wheel drive to find it. It's off the grid, with solar power and catchment water. It's yours for as long as you want it."

Tears filled her eyes, burning like acid. This thing called love was stupid. He found a parking space and tucked the sports car neatly into the space.

Around the corner, the street was lined with neon bright hotels. The first was Hotel American and was fairly nondescript. The second was Casa Swan, with silver swans in midflight gleaming on a brilliant red corner sign. Beyond it, she could see Cupids flying down the center of Hotel Francisca's facade.

"Oh, you've got to be kidding! A love hotel?"

"They're mostly automated. No one will see you check in, so no one will ask for your passport."

"I thought they were only hourly."

"You can rent them for the night if you come in late enough."

The first three places were full. The fourth, a hotel, called Love Now, had rooms open. The automated booking panel had four photographs still lit up, showing the unoccupied rooms. The rest of the room photos were dark, indicating that they were taken.

Nikki stayed tucked against Leo's side, screened from anyone walking past. She could hear his heart beating through the thin soft fabric of his shirt.

"Not that one," she said of the room he was about to select. The bed was inside a large birdcage and there was a steel chair beside it looking like the love child of a gynecological examination table and a science lab.

"Which one?" Leo asked.

There was no wonder that these were the last rooms rented; they were obviously tailored for very specific tastes. Of the three, one was styled on a boxing ring, complete with boxing gloves hanging from hooks over the bed. Another was a schoolroom with chalkboard and steel desks. It, too, had shackles visible by the bed. She knew Leo didn't plan to stay, but she never wanted to sleep on a bed with restraints again. The last seemed harmless. It was decorated in opulent golds and creams and blue velvet drapes.

"This one."

"Belle's Boudoir." Leo read the *kanji* over the photo. He hesitated a moment and then pressed the button beside it and swiped his credit card. "Stay here a minute, I'll get the key."

He was back a moment later to walk her to the elevator. "I booked the room all night," he murmured as he kept her hidden from anyone who might be scanning the lobby via remote camera. "If I don't come back by dawn, I won't be coming back at all. Just leave."

He opened his wallet and took out all his cash. "Take this." He pushed the yen into her hands. "Use it to disappear."

Her hands were shaking as she stuffed the money away. *Tell him that you love him. Don't let him walk away without knowing. Don't let him walk away!*

"I—I—" The words caught in her throat. She couldn't stop him from leaving; the host club was their only lead to where the goddess had Simon. She had no good reason to go with him: she didn't read *kanji*, she didn't speak Japanese, she didn't know exactly where the host club was or what any of the people looked like, nor could she fight or shoot a gun. "I'll wait for you."

"Only till dawn." The door opened to the elevator, and he pulled her into the small space and leaned over her, hiding her completely from the world's eyes.

She shouldn't feel so safe with him pressed so close, but she did. She reached out and put her hand on his chest, felt his heartbeat. She wanted to slide her hand up, to touch his face, to kiss him. If she did, she wouldn't want to let him go.

Tears started to burn in eyes again, and she looked down so he wouldn't see.

The elevator stopped, and they stepped off into a narrow hallway. Their room was at the end. Muffled music and giggling came from behind the doors they passed.

She unlocked the door, opened it, and gasped slightly in surprise. Belle's Boudoir was for Disney's Belle of *Beauty and the Beast*. The gold and cream of the photograph in the lobby were from the Beast's ballroom. What hadn't shown up was a painting of Belle and the Beast waltzing. They looked so happy. Nikki gazed at it, filled with envy.

If only my problems were as simple as dealing with a handful of townspeople with pitchforks.

Leo had stopped in the doorway, holding the door open. He eyed the picture with open dismay and then hid the look away. "The door will lock automatically. You'll need to call the front door to get it open."

She turned from the picture of the happy couple to gaze up into his eyes. She wanted to kiss him good-bye, but she wasn't sure if she would be able to let him go afterwards. "Be safe."

He nodded as if she had said something deep and profound and left her there, alone.

✠ 23 ✠
Belle's Boudoir

There was a packet of condoms on the pillow of the turned-down bed instead of a chocolate.

She saw the bright red square as she dropped her backpack onto the king-sized bed. She picked it up, not knowing what it was. The red wrapper had the words Kit Sack inside a big white circle. For a moment she thought it was "Kit Kat" wafers, as the package styling was nearly identical to the chocolate bar. Then she noticed the much smaller word "condom" at the top of the label and dropped it.

"Oh geez!" She snatched the condom back up to prove she had only dropped it out of surprise. The silly thing even had the words "2 pieces" in English on the side. "Who thinks of these things?"

Having established her superiority to absolutely no one, she dropped it back on the pillow. Then, thinking of the heat of Leo's body under the thin fabric of his shirt as he leaned over her in the elevator, she picked it back up and shoved it into her backpack.

Of course, the condom would only be useful if Leo came back.

She eyed her backpack. If she tried, she probably could write what was going to happen at the club. But what if it all went horribly wrong? She had bawled uncontrollably over people she thought were totally figments of her imagination. Writing Leo's death would destroy her.

Just the thought of something happening to him started the need to write. She paced the room restlessly. Her hand crept up to her mouth and she was chewing on her fingernails before she realized it. She growled in frustration and jerked her fingertip out of her mouth.

If she did write something horrible, could she save Leo? She never could stop characters from dying, but they were always over there, somewhere, in a place she thought existed only in her mind. Her characters ignored the barricades she made up, brushing them aside as if they didn't exist. The truth was that her obstacles weren't actually there. The people were real, but her barriers weren't—because she couldn't change reality.

Not at a distance. This time she could be a very real barricade from disaster; she could go and do—something. The question was: could she actually change a story? It was just words on paper. Could she keep someone from going off to find out what the weird noise was in the woods, or to check out the local graveyard in the middle of the night, or a hundred and one other really bad ideas?

Of course, she would be the one doing the really stupid thing. What the hell would she do in a gunfight? Last time she had nearly chopped off Leo's head and gotten shot. And she had been very, very careful not to think too much about what she had done to the men who attacked them at the castle. They had been bad men who were trying to kill her, but she'd been inside the heads of "bad" people enough to know that they usually had people who loved them nonetheless. There could be parents, wives, girlfriends, and even children grieving for those men who she had hacked into pieces. She could only hope and pray that they hadn't really been human.

She didn't want to pick up the *katana* and let Atsumori carve his way through a crowded nightclub where there would be dozens of innocent bystanders for every *tanuki*.

Besides, there was the whole causality problem. If you went back in time to stop the man you loved from being killed, time would be rewritten so he never died. If your lover never died, though, you wouldn't need to travel back in time to save him in the first place. The paradox would snap time back into place like a stretched rubber band.

How fixed was her story? Would she be helpless to change things after she'd written them? If she stopped certain events from happening, would she have written them in the first place? Would there be some weird looping logic where the events she wrote were actually the result of her trying to stop something? If she wrote a shootout at the nightclub and rushed there to stop it, would she actually be the reason it started in the first place? Would she only succeed at putting herself in harm's way? Maybe something would stop her from reaching the nightclub so she couldn't change the story—maybe she would get got hopelessly lost at the train station or caught by her mother?

She fought the need to write as it grew stronger. She didn't want to see the future in full gory detail if she couldn't change it. Truly harrowing death experiences flashed through her mind—unbidden and unwanted. Gregory's disemboweling with the blender. Misa's rape and murder.

Fingers wanted either a pen or to be chewed on. She tucked her hands under her arms.

"Oh, you're being a big chicken." She flapped her arms and clucked. She strutted around the room, making chicken noises.

Fine, she'd see if Leo would come out of this safely and if he didn't, she'd do whatever it took to make sure he did.

Shiva knew about Nikki.

Leo had driven away from Izushi feeling like he'd made the worst mistake of his life. At the restaurant he had debated trying to kill Chevalier and Sato before they could report to Shiva. To do so would be to betray everything his father had taught him. Chevalier would have been easy to take. Sato's ability, though, made him nearly impervious to most weapons. If he failed, it would leave Nikki alone with so many against her and possibly considered guilty of the attack just by association with him.

In the end, he decided to distract Shiva with a pack of *tanuki* working with *yakuza* and a goddess on the rampage. He'd flooded Chevalier with the details, hoping he'd forget to report Nikki's ability. The polar opposite of Nikki, it was possible that the Frenchman wouldn't realize the implication of her being able to cooperate with Atsumori.

Sato was the wild card. He'd sensed Nikki's possession. He'd instantly put distance between him and the possible danger that Atsumori posed. It was questionable, though, that the *kami* could actually harm Sato; the man was godlike.

Sato had the experience to realize that Nikki had an invaluable ability without even knowing about her writing. Would Sato explain it to Chevalier? Remind the Frenchman to report her? It was impossible to say. The man was Shiva's most dangerous Talent. He had no reason to betray her—and no reason to protect her.

To wait and see how things landed had been the reasonable, logical decision. Yet it felt like he'd made a horrible mistake leaving the two Shiva agents alive in Izushi. When Nikki leaned so trustingly against him in the tight confines of the Love Now's elevator, the knowledge that he'd failed her felt like a white-hot iron bar shoved through his chest. She had to know that he'd failed her, and yet she continued to trust him. He had to find some way to keep her safe from Shiva.

Simon would know how to fix this. More than ever, he needed his father.

He found parking near the host club and started walking to meet Chevalier and Sato. They were going to storm into Kiss Kiss and pin that little whore Kenichi to a wall and make him tell them where . . .

He had only a second of warning—headlights sweeping over him—and then a dark car mounted the sidewalk's curb and struck him at full speed.

Nikki huddled in the giant empty bathtub for two, which was the farthest away from the open notebook lying on the bed that she could get.

"Oh my God. Oh my God. Oh my God."

She really, really hoped she could change the story, since there was an epic fail in store for Leo in the near future.

"Are you sure this will happen?" Atsumori asked.

She screamed and was halfway up the wall, defying gravity, until she remembered that she wasn't truly alone in the hotel room. "Shit! Atsumori!"

"Can you stop it?" Atsumori's voice was tense with his emotion.

"I don't know." She caught sight of her reflection in the mirror. Just her. No one else. Oh, she never thought it might be comforting to fall back to thinking she was just crazy.

"When was this?"

"I don't know." She shuddered. She could still feel the solid impact of carhood meeting flesh. The confusing tumble of Leo's body. He'd been conscious while he was flung through the air by the impact, but then he landed hard enough to knock him out. The story camera pulled back to follow his car keys flying from his pocket and jangling across the sidewalk. She'd already dropped the pen in horror and fled the notebook. She'd written more graphic accidents, but this was the first time she knew that a real living body was involved. "I was trying to write what was going to happen at the nightclub with Leo."

She felt better having someone to talk to—ignoring the fact that she couldn't actually *see* Atsumori. It was chasing out the echoes of the words in her head. She climbed out of the tub and turned on the water in the sink. Her hands shook as she splashed cold water onto her face, rinsed the hot burn of unshed tears out of her eyes. "He was heading to the host club . . . Oh God, how much time do I have?"

She needed to warn Leo. Ditching her phone in Izushi had seemed like a smart idea. Her mother had used her phone to track her twice before she caught on to the trick. Without it, though, she felt trapped in a bubble. She hurried to the room's phone and took the "OMG culture shock baseball bat" right between the eyes. The phone looked like it should be in the NASA mission control room being used to launch a moon shot. The headset was surrounded with dozens of buttons, all labeled in *kanji*.

"Why does everything have to be so complicated?" She snatched up the headset and punched the first button. The noise of a subway station blared from the speaker next to the button. She jumped and swore. It was the infamous "excuse" phone with sound effects to make lies convincing. Cheating spouses could use it to make it seem like they were somewhere else. "Only the Japanese!"

She reached over, snatched up her pen, and clicked it rapidly. "Calm down or you're going to be stuck writing again. Calm. Calm."

She closed her eyes, breathed deep, and focused on palm trees and waves against white sand. It made her think of Leo's place in Hawaii. She could almost see it: a rustic home with both Japanese and Hawaiian influences and a dazzling view of the ocean. She just needed to get through this mess, and then she could live in paradise with Leo. Okay, so there was a Japanese goddess, an international antisupernatural something-or-other agency, and her mother to deal with . . .

That did nothing for staying calm.

White sands. Palm trees. Hula girls. Surfer boys. Leo in a swimsuit . . .

Oh, yes, much better.

She took a deep breath and let it out. "Atsumori, I need help with this."

"Eh?" Atsumori gave a surprised and dismayed cry. "You do realize that I've never been to one of these places? People generally don't take portable shrines to love hotels."

"Just translate the instructions! I'll figure out the rest!"

After they worked through dialing Leo's number, the line clicked and hummed but didn't connect. She hung up, feeling like she'd just reached out and touched evil.

Glass glittered on the sidewalk. Skid marks tracked a car as it fishtailed on the cement, all four tires squealed as the driver fought to keep control of a speeding vehicle. Black paint streaked the front of white vending machines. The tire marks continued back onto the street, vanishing as the car fled the scene.

She was too late.

There was an ambulance disappearing down the street, lights flashing, siren echoing off the skyscrapers around her.

The only thing that marked Leo was a splatter of blood on the sidewalk that a tiny wrinkled Japanese man was spraying with a garden hose.

She gasped as grief uncoiled and bloomed hot; pressing against her ribs, it tried to grow larger than the confines of her body. "What happened? Was he killed?"

The old man went wide-eyed with surprise. "You speak Japanese so well!"

"A man was hit by a car?" She pointed at the wet cement. "Was he killed?"

"Eh? No. He wasn't killed. He kept trying to get up. They had to hold him down. Give him a shot of medicine to make him sleep."

The grief contracted enough that she could breath out in relief. "Where did they take him? What hospital?"

"I'm sorry. I don't know." The man apparently thought the conversation was over as he started to coil up the hose.

"Atsumori?" Nikki cried. "How do I find him?"

"I don't know. There are several hospitals in Osaka. I don't know how it is decided which one he will be taken to."

She closed her eyes and forced herself to be calm even though her hands were fluttering, looking for a pen. This was her story. She should be able to write what she needed to know. If Leo were unconscious, it would be more difficult. Generally her ability would only follow bodies to the end of a death scene—not a comforting thought—or if another character witnessed what was happening to the person. She would need a witness. An emergency medical technician—if they had those in Japan—or perhaps the ambulance driver. Maybe Chevalier or Sato; they might have come upon the accident on their way to meet up with Leo.

She needed a pen. The scene she'd written earlier had ended with Leo's keys crashing to the ground. She hadn't been able to extend the scene. Neither Chevalier nor Sato were viewpoint characters, but she might be able to make them one.

And where had the keys ended up? Usually if a detail like that stood out, it was because the item was vital later. People lived or died when such things went missing.

She scanned the sidewalk. Across the street was the bizarre façade of the Platea Dontonbori Hotel Gloria, which was how she had found the accident site. Four gigantic male heads resting on too small naked legs and feet—sans torso—held up four columns. Leo had landed in front of a traditional-style sushi place, closed for the night. On either side of the sliding door to the old man's restaurant, black stools sat under a slight overhang.

She crouched down and looked under the nearest stool. There was something dark and oddly shaped in the shadows. She cautiously reached out and touched cool, heavy metal. It wasn't until her fingers curled around the butt of the pistol that she realized what it was—Leo's gun. She locked down on a yelp of surprise and glanced around to see if anyone was watching her. Luckily the street was currently deserted. She quickly shoved it into her backpack.

How did his gun get there? It hadn't been part of the scene, so it hadn't flown off him in the impact. Had he thrown it away before the ambulance came? No, that didn't feel right. Someone had kicked it away from him, kept him from using it. The car that hit him had kept going, but there had been a second attacker.

Then an awful possibility occurred to her: the second attacker might have been disguised as the paramedic. The old man had said that they had pinned Leo down and drugged him unconscious. Once they had him helpless, they'd taken him. But why? Because hitting Leo with a car had failed to kill him?

She spotted his keys under the other set of stools. She snatched them up and then fled the spot, walking blindly. "Shit, shit, shit."

What should she do? Who had taken Leo? Why? How was she going to find him?

She had gone from flailing in the shallows to way out in deep water—in one of the really, really deep parts of the ocean—like the Marianas Trench (which, ironically, lay off the eastern shore of Japan). *Yakuza* with a pack of *tanuki*. A rampaging goddess. A secret agency of people with super powers. Her control-freak mother wielding the entire American government. And—unless one of them had kidnapped Leo—a new player.

Even with Atsumori, she wasn't able to take on any one group.

She needed a plan. A damn good one.

Miriam answered with a breathless, "*Moshi moshi,*" as if she was running.

"It's me," Nikki said.

"Oh my God, are you okay? Where are you? Wait, don't answer that! De Vil has spies out."

Cruella de Vil had been their code name for Nikki's mother since they were in high school together at Foxcroft.

"I'm in trouble. Deep, deep shit."

In the background, "the train is coming" music played, echoing through tile-lined tunnels. Miriam was running through a subway station someplace.

"Where are you?" Nikki's plan wouldn't work if Miriam was somewhere far away.

"I'm heading to Namba in a roundabout way—very roundabout. I think your mother had someone following me. A freaky, scary guy showed up claiming that he was FBI. He said you were attacked."

"Huh? Oh!" Leo and Harada. Miriam was operating on a reality about three versions out of date. "Look, I need to talk to you." Because everything would be too hard to explain over the phone. "I'll meet you in Namba."

"Meet me at Kiss Kiss."

"What?"

"Kiss Kiss. That host club we went to last month." The roar of a train pulling into the station drowned her out. "Train is here! I was going to meet Kenichi at his club. We can get a private room. Meet me at Kiss Kiss."

And the line went dead.

"Shit!" Kenichi's girl-friend! The American heiress! You didn't go to Foxcroft unless your parents could comfortably cough up nearly twenty grand a year.

Nikki slammed down the phone and snatched up the *katana*. She couldn't let Miriam walk into that mess at the nightclub!

✠ 24 ✠
Foxcroft

Foxcroft was a sprawling campus of brick and limestone buildings nestled on five hundred acres of lush, extremely private, Virginia countryside. The school dated back to 1914 and dripped with prestige. She'd talked her mother into letting her attend during a period of time when she had a set of sympathetic doctors championing her release. Her mother had enrolled Nikki under her grandmother's name. Unfortunately, Hortence Phelps had been dead for a decade before Nikki was born, so she couldn't protest the theft of her identity.

At first it was heaven just to be free of the hospitals and the drugs and the constant interrogation of psychiatrists. It was hard, though, watching the other girls build close friendships. They giggled and squealed and chattered, happy and carefree as kindergarteners. They hadn't been repeatedly told that they were crazy, drugged routinely, and tied into beds. They hadn't overheard an orderly raping a neighboring female patient. Slowly, Nikki began to feel like she was a black-and-white cutout moving through a world of color.

She borrowed stories from her characters to stand in for her real life. She told the other girls that she had loving parents. A secret crush on a popular boy. A best friend and a set of code words that only they understood.

Nikki was afraid to let her guard down. She couldn't stop writing, and every story turned dark and horrific. The fear of discovery made the need to write stronger. She shared her bedroom with two other girls, so she spent long hours alone in the library. Writing. She sat at a secluded table, books scattered around her, disguising her compulsion as homework. Unfortunately, she tended to tune out the world when she was writing. Weeks into her first term, she was writing the episodic *Fielding Deep,* about a demon-infested mineshaft. The most recent victim was scrambling through the dark with the rustle of a thousand multi-jointed wings sounding like an evil wind through a forest.

"Oh, that is so cool," Miriam whispered behind Nikki.

Nikki threw herself forward, covering her notebook. "No! Don't read that!"

"Why not? It's cool." Miriam pulled out the chair beside Nikki and plunked down on it. She had her hair up in Sailor Moon pigtails and was wearing a close approximation of a Japanese school uniform with a white button-down blouse, a string tie, and a plaid pleated skirt. (She explained later that her Jewish parents refused to send her to a Catholic private school that wore uniforms, so she improvised as best she could at Foxcroft.) Miriam was always comfortably balanced on the line of fitting in and still being completely herself.

"It's a letter to a friend from my old school." Nikki started to gather up books, using the action as cover to flip shut the notebook and shift it as far away from Miriam as she could. Putting it in her messenger bag would be too obvious.

"Wow, your old school sounds wicked. *A thousand multi-jointed wings rustling like an evil wind.* Is that bats or the other students?"

Nikki laughed despite the fact that her heart was trying to climb up her throat. "We make up stories. My friend and I. She starts a story. I add to it and send it back. Round-robin." *Someone else is doing this with me; I'm not doing some lone crazy thing.*

"What kind of story is it?"

"Horror." The lies she had ready for emergencies came out smoothly. Her voice didn't even shake. She picked up her dropped pen and clicked it. "My friend wrote the first part. I need to use her set-up."

"Can I read it?"

Nikki stared at Miriam, confounded. She hadn't considered someone that would want to read what she wrote. "It's—it's private. Besides, this is the middle of the story. It wouldn't make sense."

Miriam laughed and dug through her leather Coach messenger bag. "I read Japanese horror manga."

"Manga?"

Miriam pulled out a book and slid it toward Nikki. "Japanese comics. Only it's like a zillion times better than American comics. The characters have depth to them and the plot lines are long and involved and sometimes take decades to play out."

Nikki cautiously picked up the book. There were no men in spandex, just school kids riding the subway, dealing with bullies, and attending math class with familiar calculus problems on the chalkboard. None of the text, though, was in English. "You can read this? It's in Japanese."

"I've studied Japanese since fifth grade. I still need a dictionary to look up a lot of the words. I want to live in Japan someday and do something like buying rights to manga for American publishers or having anime dubbed into English. Be the gateway for bringing Japanese culture to the United States."

Nikki started to say something nice, something complimentary about Miriam knowing what she wanted for her life, but she turned the page and blood splattered the story panels. "Oh!"

"Isn't it great?"

Nikki flipped more pages. The body count continued to spray blood everywhere as the hero and heroine obviously struggled to understand the chaos around them. "You—you like this?"

"Yeah." Miriam settled back, looking slightly annoyed. "It's called *Araobi*, which means 'alive' in Japanese. These souls from deep space are immortal, but they've discovered that without death, life has no meaning to them. They're taking over humans so they can kill themselves. The hero has a horrible life. His parents are dead. He's bullied. He's not doing well in school. But because he's touched death, he clings to life. It's wonderfully poetic."

"That is deep. I wish I could understand the words."

Surprise replaced annoyance on Miriam's face. "I'm doing the scanlation—that's scanning the book and then doing the translation." Miriam swallowed and tentatively offered, "If you want, I can share the translated pages with you."

For the first time in her life, Nikki felt like she had found someone who might understand. Nikki pulled out her notebook, her heart hammering in her chest. "Promise you'll never show this to anyone else?"

Miriam made a noise of disgust. "There's no one else here that's into horror and dark fantasy. They wouldn't be interested."

She handed over the notebook and tried not to tear it back out of Miriam's hands as she opened it up. She sat clicking her pen and watching Miriam read.

"Wow, you're really good. Your characters are so vivid. They feel like real people. Are you going to go for an English Literature degree in college? I'm going to Princeton; they've got a very good East Asian Studies program."

Nikki hadn't considered college or career. Her life had always been narrowed down to surviving days as they came, with turning eighteen the end of her prison term. "I haven't decided."

Miriam made a raspberry as she flipped the page. "Happiness comes from knowing your heart and giving it what it wants."

"I know what I want." She wanted to be like Miriam. To know herself so well that she had a style of clothes, a favorite book, a plan for the future. She was sick of her mother stealing everything away so that Nikki was so totally helpless that even when she got a small amount of freedom, she didn't know what to do with it. Here she was—in high school—and she was hiding alone in the library, feeling like a cutout doll pretending to be a living girl.

The pen snapped in her hand as she gripped it tight in fury.

Miriam eyed the broken pen. "Okay, so make a plan and go for it."

✠ 25 ✠
Enter the Dragon Girl

Namba Station literally had a hundred different exits once you counted all the department stores and malls that fed into the underground maze. When she and Miriam visited Namba, they normally exited directly from the station, using the stairs up to street level. That still left Nikki with thirty possible options to cover. Assuming, of course, that Miriam didn't veer from her normal course.

Letting Atsumori guide her through the chaos, Nikki tried to figure out what she was going to say once she caught up with Miriam. She still hadn't come up with anything reasonable sounding when she caught sight of Miriam's familiar pink hair moving through the crowd. She was wearing black leather shorts, a black lace blouse, and tights that looked like tribal tattoos.

"Miriam!" Nikki shouted.

Miriam turned and scanned the crowd. She glanced at Nikki's face, but recognition didn't touch her eyes.

"Miriam?" Nikki reached out for her hand, and they suddenly went through a complicated dance of nearly touching hands, shifting of weight, and spinning. "Whoa, wait, wait, Miriam!"

Miriam bounced backwards, hands up in karate attack position. "Who the hell are you?"

"I'm Nikki! What the hell is wrong with you?"

"She is seeing me, not you," Atsumori murmured.

211

"Oh hell," Nikki said. "Atsumori, can you back off for now?"

Miriam moved back several more feet, eyes going wide, but slowly shifting out of attack position. "Nikki?"

"Yeah, it's me."

Miriam took another step back. "That was very creepy. For a minute, I—I—you looked like someone else."

"Come on, there's something I need to show you." This was going to be easier to explain if Miriam could actually see Atsumori. There was a tiny bus stop of a shrine just down the street.

"What happened? You disappeared without saying anything to me. I was really worried something—what are you carrying? Is that a *katana*?"

Nikki opened her mouth and closed it several times. She'd practiced what she would say, but even having lived through the events, she found it hard to believe it was true. *Oh, what the hell, this is Miriam.* "It turns out that everything I've ever written is real. Somewhere in England there is a Fielding Deep. Dupont, Louisana, was wiped off the map—or it's going to be sometime next year. And every character I've written about here in Japan is a real person. George. Yuuka. Harada. They were all real."

Miriam stared at her for a moment and then breathed, "Oh, cool."

"They're dead! They're all dead!"

"Well, that part sucks, but that's major coolness."

She explained as best she could about Gregory murdering Misa and how she ended up with the *katana*. "Harada came to my place looking for it, and he tried to kill me."

"You mean Mr. Freaky FBI wasn't lying about that part?"

"Leo? No, he wasn't lying, at least not about that."

"Leo?" Miriam nearly shouted his name with disbelief. "Leo?"

"What?" Nikki stepped through the gates of the shrine.

"You know what I mean. How did you end up on first-name basis with Mr. Freaky? There's something not right about him. He's serious scary, and you know it takes a lot to rattle my cage."

"He is a *yokai*." Atsumori appeared beside Nikki.

"He is not!" Nikki glared at the boy god in an attempt to keep him silent.

"His mother was."

"We don't know that for sure," Nikki growled. "Just because Shiva thought his mother might be a *bakeneko* doesn't mean he is *yokai*. They could have been wrong."

"He is not fully human," Atsumori stated. "I can tell."

Miriam glanced back and forth between Nikki and Atsumori, frowning. "How can you see him and yet never saw all the other things?"

"What other things?" Nikki looked around, hoping that there wasn't more weirdness lurking about.

"All the weird stuff, like Deb Brady at Foxcroft and—"

"What's so weird about Deb Brady? Other than being an official Darwin award winner?"

"Exactly. You never saw her after she managed to kill herself with the dry ice. She was haunting the second floor of our dorm the entire junior year."

"She was?"

"That's why I moved to the attic. She kept roaming the halls, muttering 'Why am I dead?' as if the danger of asphyxiation from carbon dioxide still hadn't occurred to her after she died of it."

"Why didn't you ever tell me?"

Miriam looked away, a blush spreading across her face. "I was afraid you'd think I was making it up."

Nikki laughed bitterly at the impossibility. "Like I would ever point fingers at anyone for being weird."

"You might have thought it, and that's what matters."

Miriam had a point. Either years of being psychoanalyzed or compulsively writing horror had made Nikki skeptical of people claiming to be psychic. Up to now, she'd believed that Miriam was merely a fellow skeptic. More likely, though, Miriam's skepticism came from the fact that she truly knew when something was real and when it was faked. "You could have trusted me."

Miriam blew out her breath. "You could never see weird things before. Why are you seeing them now?"

"She sees me because I want her to see me," Atsumori said. "I am a god, and this is holy ground."

"But only when we're on holy ground?" Miriam indicated the city street beyond the gate.

"It takes more effort to manifest," Atsumori said.

"Anyway, it doesn't matter that I can see him," Nikki started.

"Yes, it does. I've spent my whole life seeing shit that no one else can see. For the first time, someone else sees it."

"People are dead! Leo's been hit by a car and kidnapped. His father is tied up someplace, slowly dying, and you were about to walk into a trap!"

"Me?"

"Kiss Kiss was the club that I was writing, not 'someplace like it.' Kenichi is Kenichi." She realized that for once she had the names right, but only because she had changed all the names after visiting the club with Miriam. "And you're the American heiress."

Miriam laughed. "As if."

"You have a trust fund."

Miriam laughed harder. "I can only draw a thousand a month off it. If your mother croaked, that would be pocket change to you."

"Don't tempt me," Nikki grumbled. It had occurred to her in the past that jail would probably be better than a hospital—prisoners seemed to have more rights than mental patients. The potential lack of pens, however, was the deal breaker. "The important thing is, I've accidently written you into my novel, and you're in big trouble."

"How am I—oh! Oh shit!" Miriam connected all the dots. "So all those calls from Kenichi in the last few days are because he's got Princess Creepy leaning on him."

Miriam had come up with the nickname for the goddess so that they could discuss the mystery character in Kenichi's earlier scenes.

"Yes!" Nikki said.

"Okay, I'm on the same page now—at least I think I am. Scratch that. What does Princess Creepy want with me?"

Nikki blew her breath out. "Princess Creepy is actually a goddess possessing the Brit. His name is really Simon Fowler. Leo is his adopted son."

"Mr. Freaky, the *yokai?*"

"He's not *yokai!*" Nikki cried and stabbed a finger at Atsumori who was opening his mouth to counter her. "Just hush!"

"Oh, that is seriously creepy cool." Miriam had taken several steps away from Nikki and was watching her argue with herself. "But who the hell is the samurai?"

Nikki rubbed her face. "He is Taira no Atsumori, the *kami* from the Kyoto Shrine."

"Wow," Miriam breathed.

Nikki pushed on, explaining how Simon worked for Shiva; how the goddess had possessed him and had him tied up someplace; and how she met Leo, Chevalier, and Sato. She ended with finding Leo's accident scene. "I have a plan to save Simon and Leo."

"If it involves your mother, it's a stupid plan. All she'll do is drug you and drag you back to the United States. One of these times, you're not going to be able to get free of whatever hell she locks you in."

"I know. If I went to her first, she wouldn't help me save Leo and his father. She wouldn't even believe they existed. She'd put it down to proof that I'm crazy and ship me home."

"Right," Miriam said.

"But if I get shit deep in trouble, she'll come roaring in with the cavalry."

Miriam snorted with disgust and took off walking. "Stupid plan."

"That's not the whole plan. That's the fail-safe!" Nikki shouted after her.

"So what's your plan?" Miriam kept walking.

Giving a little scream of frustration, Nikki threw up her hands and chased after her. As they continued toward Kiss Kiss, she explained her entire plan. Miriam made raspberry noises at every point.

"Getting Shiva involved sounds dangerous for you and everyone else," Miriam said starting to point out flaws in her plan. "Last thing you need is someone else trying to lock you up because you write weird shit. And these two—Chevalier and Sato—they sound like they might kill Kenichi after they question him."

"It's possible."

"This is my boyfriend we're talking about."

"When did that start?"

"After you and I visited that one time. I went back."

"You fell in love with him?"

Miriam blew out her breath. "I don't know. Almost every word out of his mouth is a lie. It's just . . ." She sighed. "You gave me Kenichi's section to read, and it felt like I had found a male version of myself. My parents wanted a boy, and they kept having kids until they got one. I was just failure number three. And then I was so weird, always seeing things that weren't there, talking to invisible people, being mad that daily horoscopes in the newspaper were wrong. I think if they hadn't shipped me off to boarding school, my mother would have had a mental breakdown."

"Oh, Miriam, I'm sorry."

"You are the last person on this planet that needs to feel sorry for me. My life has always been easy compared to yours. I know my mother loves me—I creep her out—but she loves me. I would be a lot more screwed up if I didn't *know* that to my core. Still, I've always wanted that fairy-tale parent's love, you know the one, where we wear matching mother-and-daughter outfits, she takes me to work on daughter's day, and we talk on the phone every day for an hour."

"That would drive you nuts."

"Yes, I know it would, but there's a little girl inside of me who wants all that extravagant show of affection. The equivalence of your parents screaming 'I love you' as loudly as they can, because when I was a kid, I didn't understand love enough to see that they did love me very much. That love can be deep and quiet and still. I read Kenichi's first section, where he buys that ring and thinks about going home and flashing it in his father's face and maybe, just maybe, getting respect that he could afford something so expensive, and then getting the phone call that his father was dead."

Kenichi had taken off the ring and flung it in the Dontonbori Canal. Nikki had been slightly mystified by the act, but Miriam had cried when she read it.

"He's so much like me," Miriam whispered. "He wanted that proof that his father loved him."

"Why didn't you tell me that you were dating him?"

"Because you'd tell me I was being stupid—because I was—and you tell me the truth when I'm being stupid. It's one of the reasons we're friends."

The admission surprised Nikki. She'd never had the courage to put their friendship under the microscope to see what it was that kept them friends. She couldn't afford to be disillusioned. Nikki realized that Miriam was still walking determinatedly in the direction of the club. "I didn't want you to get involved in all this—craziness."

"Like I'm not already?"

"I just want you to call my mother if things go south."

"I'm just supposed to let my best friend go off and get killed? To just wait around until some bitch of a goddess unleashes a wave of massive death and destruction?"

"Yes! Wait. How do you get death and destruction?"

"This is one of your books. If you could write Nora Roberts' romances, your mother wouldn't be trying to lock you up in a loony bin. It's like you tune in to a supernatural event, and anyone who is destined to interact with that event picks up the same psychic signature. You tune in to radio-station freaky and write what you hear."

Miriam was taking this better than Nikki had expected. But this was Miriam, who lived for spooky weirdness. Who owned a dozen different tarot decks and a Ouija board from the 1800s, and who had dragged her out to graveyards.

"Okay, yes, this has all the earmarks of ending like all my other novels. I can't tell how yet, but you know the pattern. It starts quiet and innocent, and next thing you know, people are running and screaming and the walls are covered with blood . . ."

"And it ends with everyone dead," Miriam finished. "How am I supposed to walk away after you tell me that your characters are real people? Those two little boys we saw at Yasaka Shrine, the *Chigo* and the boy in street clothes, that was Haru and Nobu. And the kid we've been cheering during the high school baseball championship is Chitose. We know these people; we can't abandon them."

"I don't want you to get hurt because of me."

"Maybe I don't want to be protected. And that works both ways. Do you think I could live with myself if I just walked away and let you fall?"

Nikki knew Miriam enough to know the answer to that. "I'm not letting you walk into that nightclub alone to be kidnapped."

"How are you going to stop me? Do I need to remind you that I'm a black belt in aikido, jujitsu, and tae kwon do?"

There was that; Miriam been taking various martial arts classes since first grade, fed by a love of Power Rangers. Nikki suspected that Miriam wouldn't actually hit her, but she did have a point.

"Besides, I'm not going in alone." Miriam grinned. "You're coming with me."

✠ 26 ✠
Kiss Kiss

Like most of Japan, Dontonbori was weirdly huge and small at the same time. It was a single street that ran beside the Dontonbori Canal. The street started out open to the sky and looked much like Times Square, with every square inch covered with neon billboards. A block or two later, a roof spanned the street, creating a mile-long indoor mall—with cross streets carrying automobiles. At one time, it had been the pleasure district of Osaka and had barely shed its origins.

The boys trolling the streets for women marked the various host club entrances. They were easy to spot. Their hair was bleached and ironed and then spray glued into impossible spikes. They slouched on the curbs, hands in pocket, scanning women for signs of wealth as they walked down the street. The expensive manicure with jewel-studded fingertips, the Gucci purse, the Prada shoes, and the glitter of jewelry. With smug smiles, the boys would glide in like sharks smelling blood in water. They would flatter, tease, cajole, and beg, trying to entice the women into the club.

Kenichi's scene was one of the first that Nikki wrote after arriving in Japan. Nikki had scouted the host clubs in the gray early morning, avoiding the boys.

Miriam had read the scene and then insisted that they visit one of the clubs for authenticity's sake. "The more research you do, the better the scenes get."

They'd made one pass through Dontonbori, dodging the boys and giggling over the impossible hair. They studied the head-shot photographs posted outside all the clubs, rating the boys on their looks. Nikki chose the club that "felt right" and picked the boy to "stand in" for her character. As Miriam led the way to Kiss Kiss, Nikki realized that she had led her friend straight to the very real man who was already tugging at Miriam's heart.

Nikki paused at the door into the building's lobby to scan the dark street. Where were Chevalier and Sato? She couldn't spot them. She thought Leo had told them to meet him here. Had they given up? Gone looking for him? Or were they already inside?

"Elevator is here," Miriam called.

Nikki's heart was banging hard in her chest as they rode a tiny elevator that smelled of cigarette smoke up to the third-floor nightclub. She could feel Atsumori shimmering inside her, making her skin feel glove tight. "It's never good when the heroes go up against the villains. It's like they're like matter and antimatter. They usually mutually destruct. Violently."

"But see, they don't want to hurt us," Miriam said. "And we are quite willing to hurt them."

Nikki wasn't sure if this was as comforting as it sounded. She found herself nodding as Atsumori agreed, but she wasn't sure which of them he was siding with.

The door opened to the lobby of the third floor. A drunk woman was lying on the ground, laughing at the pretty young man trying to coax her to the elevator.

"No, no, I'm not ready to go," the woman cried, clinging to the host's legs.

"You're out of money." The host pried her free and got her up as Miriam and Nikki skirted around them. "I'll have to pay for all your drinks if you stay."

"But if you loved me, you'd pay for . . ." And the elevator closed on her protest.

Inside the club door, there was a tiny cubbyhole office and the club's greeter. "Welcome," the greeter said in Japanese. "Who is your main host?"

Miriam slapped down a hundred-thousand-yen bill, paying their cover, and said in loud English, "Hi, there, I just want to see my boy for a minute. I'm just going to go find him." And plunged into the nightclub.

Nikki scurried after her. "Aren't we supposed to wait?"

"Let your plans be dark and impenetrable as night, and when you move, fall like a thunderbolt." Miriam quoted something that sounded like the *Art of War*.

Atsumori grunted in agreement.

They darted through the nightclub. There were dozens of booths, their high backs forming bubbles of privacy. Safe from prying eyes, well-dressed women were courted by handsome hosts.

Halfway through the club, Miriam ducked into a booth, yanking Nikki in after her. "*Yakuza.*"

"There are at least three here, and they're not human." Nikki slipped the *katana* off her shoulder and undid the lacings of the bag.

Miriam eyed the *katana*. "Let me be attackman. You play defense."

Nikki nodded. Those were the positions they'd played on Foxcroft's lacrosse team. Miriam's aggression made her a star player, but Nikki had discovered a secret love of full body check on snobby girls to bleed off life's frustration.

Miriam peeked over the top of the booth. "Okay, he moved. Let's go."

They found Kenichi in the far back with a woman who was having a champagne toast. He and several other hosts were gathered around her with microphones, shouting compliments and urges to drink as a bottle of champagne was opened with a loud pop.

"Drink!" the hosts shouted as a towel was held under the woman's chin and she chugged from the bottle.

Kenichi was in the fine white suit from the scene that Nikki had written. Unlike many of the other host boys, he hadn't bleached his hair, and his black hair and dark eyes were accented beautifully by the white fabric. The top buttons of his shirt were undone, showing off heavy gold chains.

Last time Nikki saw Kenichi, he had seemed as rich and polished as his gold chains. Compared to Leo, though, he seemed as fake as jewelry from a gumball machine.

Kenichi was in mid-shout when he saw Miriam bearing down on

him. His eyes went wide, but he kept shouting until his gaze moved to Nikki. He froze in mid-shout.

Oh, yes, there is an angry god bearing down on you, scumbag.

"I need to talk to you." Miriam caught him by the wrist. "Now."

"Miriam-chan, I—I'm doing a call. I can't . . ."

Miriam applied pressure to some pain point, making him yelp, and twisted his arm up behind his back. "Yes, you can."

They started back through the nightclub, heading for the front door. Despite the fact that that Miriam still had hold of him, Kenichi kept focus on Nikki.

Miriam suddenly shoved Kenichi into an empty booth. "There's a *yakuza* at the door."

If they didn't find out anything before the fighting started, this was going to be pure stupidity on their part. Scratch that—it probably was already pure stupidity.

"Where are they?" Nikki snapped, surprised when it came out in Atsumori's deep growl of Japanese.

Miriam's eyes went wide at the fluent Japanese, but she said nothing.

"Where's who?" Kenichi seemed genuinely confused by the question.

"The goddess that your family worshipped and the *gaijin* she is possessing." Nikki said.

Miriam twisted Kenichi's arm a bit more, making him wince. "We know that you called me here to turn me over to her."

Shame washed across Kenichi's face and was hidden away. "She would have killed me."

"No, she wouldn't have," Atsumori stated. "A god is duty bound to protect those who worship them. You are the one person that she will not harm."

Kenichi gasped and looked to Miriam. "I didn't know. She's just so angry all the time."

"Tell us where she is!" Miriam said.

"They're at the Imperial Hotel in the Kita district. She's got a small army there now of *yakuza* and shrine maidens."

Nikki frowned, thinking of the shrine maidens at Inari's Shrine. "If she has shrine maidens, why does she need Miriam?"

"She's looking for someone like the *gaijin*, who she can take over easily and stay with most of the day. She can only stay in the shrine maidens for two or three hours at most. If she's not careful, she kills them." Kenichi's hands were shaking as he took out a pack of cigarettes. He fumbled through lighting one. "She collects *Maneki Neko* statues. At first it seemed cute, like a girl who collects dozens of statues of cats. Then one day, she was using one of the shrine maidens to scream at me about my failings. Mid-curse, the girl just collapsed." He took a deep drag on his cigarette. "The dead girl stared up at me, slack jawed. The silence was blessed. For a minute, I thought, 'I'm free of her.' And then the nearest statue started to tremble. I realized then that she knew she eventually would kill her shrine maidens and had gathered those statues there to take her spirit when one died. I stood there, wanting to scream, as all those cat statues stared at me with unblinking eyes."

He took another deep drag on his cigarette. "I didn't want to get you involved, Miriam. I've seen what she's doing to that *gaijin*. He looks like death when she finally lets him go. It's only a matter of time before she kills him. She's killed two girls so far, and every day she destroys at least a dozen statues. It's to the point that everywhere she goes, she leaves a trail of fine dust."

That would explain the dust that rained down on Simon in his scene. If things continued the way Nikki's book normally went, the destruction of the statues was just the beginning of the chaos that the goddess planned.

"What is she planning to do? What's her big picture?"

His laugh was bitter and edged on hysterical. "You're asking me? I don't know. She tells me nothing. According to her, I'm the least useful thing she's found in the world so far."

"You have to be able to at least guess," Nikki suggested. "Your family worshipped her—you should know who she is—what she wants."

"She's Iwanaga Hime," Kenichi said. "She's the daughter of Ohkuninushi. My grandmother used to tell me stories about her. I never believed any of them."

Nikki had felt Atsumori cringe at the names. He had recognized them; she would ask him to explain later. "Who does she want revenge on?"

He took another calming drag on his cigarette and sighed out smoke. "It's one of those stupid legends. Like Amaterasu hiding herself away in the cave, plunging the world into darkness. To lure her out, Ama-no-Uzume did a strip dance on an overturned washtub, making the other gods laugh until Amaterasu looked out to see what they were laughing at. When she saw her reflection in a mirror hung in a tree, she came out of the cave."

Amaterasu was the Japanese sun goddess. Nikki had always assumed that the legend was on par with the Greek legends of Apollo and his sun chariot; entertaining but in no way true. Her brain boggled slightly in the sudden awareness that there might be a being named Amaterasu somewhere in Japan and that the story had some type of truth attached to it. Surely the idea that the sun vanished when Amaterasu went into hiding was still just a story.

"Just tell us about this Iwanaga Hime," Miriam said.

"When it was decided to send Ninigi to Japan, the gods gathered in a great hall to celebrate his departure and to gift him with presents. Susanoo, the god of storms, gave him the sword Kusanagi. Amaterasu gave him the mirror that had been used to lure her out of the cave and her necklace to prove that he was her grandson. After the banquet, Amaterasu realized her father Izanagi's spear was missing. Iwanaga Hime came forward and said that she had seen Ninigi with a spear. Amaterasu was furious that Iwanaga had accused her grandson. She claimed that Iwanaga was only trying to cover her own crime by blaming Ninigi and demanded that Iwanaga produce the spear. When Iwanaga couldn't, the gods punished Iwanaga by locking her in a massive stone, deep in the heart of a mountain. There she stayed for hundreds of years until a landslide freed the stone."

"That would seriously piss me off." Nikki shivered at the thought of being locked in the dark for so long.

"Her rage seethes around her like flames," Kenichi said.

"So, how did she get out of the stone?" Miriam asked.

"The seals were broken long ago," Atsumori answered. "Most likely she was freed in the landslide but marooned without humans to give her a way to leave the rock."

"We were the only ones in the valley that prayed to her." Kenichi laughed bitterly. "Everyone else was smart enough to stay away from her. Our land was said to be cursed. She complains that we were all too dense for her to take and that it's our fault she was stranded so long."

So she stayed trapped until Simon had accidently freed her to have her revenge. She was angry with the sun goddess. What did that mean for the human race? Whatever she planned, Kenichi was clueless. They needed Simon, who hopefully had picked up more than what Nikki was able to learn from Kenichi.

"We have what we need," Nikki said. "We should get out of here."

Miriam peeked over the top of the booth and then slid down low in the seat. "The *yakuza* are still in the way. Is there a back door?"

"It's by the restrooms, but it's chained so that women cannot leave without paying."

Which probably made it a huge fire hazard, but the *yakuza* owners were thinking bottom line, not who could get out in an emergency.

"Shit," Miriam hissed and bounced to her feet.

One of the *yakuza* stalked up and made a grab for Miriam. She backed out of his reach. Atsumori blazed to fully engaged within Nikki, whiting the edges of her vision.

"Come with me and you won't be hurt." The *yakuza* started to reach for Miriam again.

"Get away from her, dog." Atsumori shifted Nikki to block the grab.

The *yakuza*'s eyes went wide, seeing Atsumori for the first time. "*Kami!*" He backed away, reaching into his coat to pull a pistol from a shoulder harness.

Miriam caught the gun with her left hand, jerked it up, and hit the *yakuza*'s wrist with her right hand. Like a magic trick, the gun was in Miriam's hand.

Atsumori snarled, jerking the *katana* half out of its sheath to slam the butt of the hilt into the *yakuza*'s throat. The man staggered backwards, choking, as Atsumori finished unsheathing the blade. The *yakuza*'s features blurred, and suddenly a human-sized raccoon dog stood in its place, its lips curled back to show off a muzzle full of sharp teeth.

Atsumori slashed downwards with the *katana*. The *tanuki* gave an inhuman yelp of pain, abruptly silenced as the blade sliced him open. Hot blood sprayed across Nikki.

"More are coming!" Miriam cried. "Run!"

Miriam headed for the entrance.

"Let me block," Nikki cried.

Miriam answered by veering out of the narrow walkway, stepping up onto the booth's seat and then leaping up onto the high back. They raced forward, side by side, Miriam bounding the valley of the booths in running jumps. In their wake, the normal noise of the club erupted into the terrified screams of women.

Atsumori surged ahead, blazing against Nikki's awareness until she was sure that her skin gleamed with his power. The *tanuki* saw them coming and opened fire. The bullets struck the leading edge of his power and flared into swallowtail butterflies, wings brilliant gold and wet-ink black.

The *tanuki* felt like nothing more than tissue before the *katana*, shredding into pieces of a paper doll as Atsumori sliced through the *yokai*'s body. It fell, part human, part dog, part something unrecognizable.

Beyond the booths was a long bar and then the narrow entrance with the cubbyhole office. Nikki collided with a *tanuki* in the tight space. He ducked Atsumori's swing and caught Nikki by her wrists and slammed her up against the wall, feet dangling.

"Your vessel is too small to be useful to you, lord." The *tanuki* pressed against Nikki, pinning her with its body. Its face was still fully human, but sharp pointed teeth filled its mouth. "But she'll be the perfect size for our princess."

Miriam leapt from the back of the last booth onto the bar counter and came skidding along the length of it. She snatched up a huge sake bottle as she went sliding by and used it to club the *tanuki*.

The male staggered, and Atsumori twisted it to his advantage, tucking up his legs and kicking it in the chest with both feet. Nikki yelped in dismay as the *kami* landed and beheaded the *tanuki*.

"Run!" Kenichi had followed them. "They're not the only things here."

"Shit!" Miriam caught Nikki by the left wrist and dragged her into the tiny elevator. "Something is coming."

Nikki glanced back the way they had come. Something large skittered across the ceiling. She got the impression of impossibly long, thin, yellow-stripped legs and a huge hourglass-shaped body before the doors shut.

"Oh my God, what the hell was that?" Nikki punched the lobby button even though it was already lit. Atsumori slipped out of her, leaving her feeling hollow and rubber kneed. She was panting and trembling, and there was blood splattered across her face and chest. She felt weirdly elated; they might be running, but that had to classify as kicking butt.

"*Jorojumo.*" Atsumori's voice sounded as winded as her own.

The elevator thankfully started to drop, albeit with painful slowness.

Apparently Kenichi wasn't sensitive enough to pick up Atsumori's voice. "I don't know. All the new *yakuza* look normal, but there's something strange about all of them."

It was telling that despite looking terrified of Nikki, Kenichi trapped himself in the tiny elevator with her instead of staying behind.

"What's a *jorogumo?*" Nikki whispered. A loud bang echoed down the elevator shaft as something hit the club's lobby doors.

"*Yokai,*" Atsumori said unhelpfully. "A man eater. Very dangerous."

"*Jorogumo* translates as 'binding bride' or 'spider whore'— depending on what kanji is used," Miriam explained completely. "It's a *yokai* that can take the shape of a beautiful woman, but its true form is a giant spider. And yes, it eats men that it traps."

"This does not bode well," Atsumori said. "Iwanaga Hime must have promised something dear to have gathered this many *yokai* who are willing to serve her."

✥ 27 ✥
Night at the Imperial

Kenichi fled the first chance he could. He unchained his bicycle and paused only long enough to say, "Come with me to Tokyo." When Miriam shook her head, he rode off without another word.

Atsumori muttered darkly about the cowardice of whores as Nikki and Miriam ran through the nearly deserted streets.

"You just hacked three men to pieces in front of him." Nikki felt responsible for the betrayal of Miriam's heart. She had written the scene that made Miriam fall in love with Kenichi.

"They were *tanuki*." Atsumori missed the point entirely.

"They looked like men to him." She understood the fear that moved Kenichi. If things were slightly different, she'd be heading to Tokyo, too. She'd spent a lifetime being made helpless; the *katana* was the only thing that was allowing her to believe she could actually help someone else.

Atsumori snorted with contempt. "Kenichi knew they weren't men."

"We're probably being chased by a giant *geisha* spider," Nikki pointed out. A thought that had her jumping at odd shadows.

"They are web-hunters," Atsumori said calmly. "She will not chase us out into the open."

"She won't?" Miriam stopped running. "Good."

"Kenichi knows that there are probably more *tanuki* with the goddess." Nikki winced as the statement felt very true.

"He's not going to understand." Miriam turned in a circle, getting her bearings, and then set off in a purposeful walk.

Nikki lost track of who "he" might be. "Kenichi?"

"Taira no Atsumori!" Miriam used the kami's full name. "The Genpei War was between the Minamoto and the Taira—both clans were descendants of imperial family members who been demoted to the rank of samurai. One of the Minamoto Clan allies was the great warrior Kumagai Naozane."

"What?" Nikki wasn't sure why Miriam was suddenly giving her a lesson on ancient Japan. "Where are we going?"

"You said that Leo drove his car to Dontonbori and parked it close to the Platea Dontonbori Hotel Gloria."

"Yes, the hotel with the goofy head statues."

"We're going to rescue a man who is nearly dead and currently tied up. A car would be useful for a quick getaway. I don't really want to try to carry him around on our shoulders through the subway. Especially if we're being chased."

"Oh, good point."

"Anyway, before the battle of Ichi-no-Tani, Kumagai heard the sound of a flute being played in the enemy camp. He had been impressed at how refined the player must be—a true noble."

"What does this have to do—"

"Just listen," Miriam snapped. "The next day the Minamoto Clan stormed the Taira fortress and set it on fire. The only survivors were those that fled to their ships. Kumagai spotted a samurai swimming toward the ships that were already sailing away. He taunted the samurai, calling him a coward. Despite overwhelming odds, the samurai returned to prove his courage. Kumagai defeated the samurai easily and struck off his helmet for a finishing blow. To Kumagai's horror, his opponent was a handsome boy the same age as his young son. Even as he realized that he had lured a boy to his death, there was no way to forestall it. The Minamoto were killing all who they found. Weeping, Kumagai beheaded the boy. When he searched the body for some way to identify the boy, he found a flute. The boy was the flute player that Kumagai had admired. He was so grieved by what he had done that he gave up his sword and became a priest.

"The boy was Atsumori."

"Oh!" Nikki turned to look at Atsumori with new eyes—but of

course there was nothing to see. The boy was dead, and all that remained was a powerful spirit.

"Anyone as stupidly brave as Atsumori is not going to understand Kenichi," Miriam said.

"I was not stupid," Atsumori grumbled. "Odds were that I would have drowned; I was in full armor."

Miriam stopped at the edge of a parking lot. "So, what kind of car are we looking for?"

Nikki dug out Leo's keys and tapped the "lock" button on the key fob. Distantly a car chirped. "That one."

Leo had parked in shadows, backing into the spot like any Japanese driver would have. Just seeing it made Nikki want to cry. She knew that saving Simon was what Leo wanted, but it felt wrong to be doing anything but looking for Leo.

"Oh! A BMW Z4! Okay, Mr. Freaky just gained serious style points for his car! Oh my God, I think I'm in love."

Nikki unlocked the car with the fob and then realized that she was on the wrong side of the car to drive. Japanese drove on the other side of the road. Her driving experience was limited to automatic transmission and a mall parking lot in New Jersey. "Can you drive a stick?"

"Oh, yes, I can," Miriam said with obvious relish.

Nikki tossed Miriam the keys.

Miriam slid into the driver's seat and then yelped as Maru scrambled into her lap before she could close the door. "Jesus fucking Christ!"

"Maru!" Nikki snatched up the kitten before Miriam could hit him out of pure knee-jerk reaction. He purred at the attention but chewed at her fingers with razor-sharp teeth. "Ow, ow, ow, stop that."

Miriam scooted the seat forward so she could reach the pedals. "That's not your *bakeneko*, is it?"

"No, it's Maru from Atsumori's shrine."

"Oh!" Miriam's eyes went wide. "Okay, that's cool and weird. The actual kitten."

"It gets weirder when it's people."

"Considering some of your characters, I'm hoping to avoid meeting any of them."

✤ ✤ ✤

They swung down off the Hanshin Expressway onto the city streets. The Imperial Hotel rose in front of them, a tall building at the edge of the river, its reflection gleaming on the dark water. It looked easily thirty stories tall, meaning that it would have hundreds of rooms, all with locked doors. Nikki had no idea what name the goddess was checked in under; she doubted it was Iwanaga Hime. If the goddess had been using Simon's credit cards, Leo would have found him ages ago. And writing out scenes wouldn't solve the problem either—so far all her names had been wrong.

But it would tell her if Iwanaga was currently possessing Simon or not. She juggled the *katana*, the kitten, and her backpack to find a notebook and pen.

"What do you think? Hotel parking? Across the street?" Miriam drove slowly past the hotel, its lobby a gold-lit cave in the night.

"I'm checking."

Something had happened. The pattern of Simon's hell had changed. He was bound and gagged on a hotel bed, but night cloaked the room. Instead of facing the window, he faced the door. Cat statues covered every surface, half-hidden by the darkness, faint streetlights reflecting off unblinking eyes. A gleaming line in the darkness showed that the door to the connecting room had been unlocked and left cracked open. In the room beyond, a woman was speaking what seemed to be Japanese, her voice hard and angry.

Exhaustion weighted his body until he felt like he was made of stone. He was too weary to move. Just breathing seemed too much effort.

"Iwanaga's not within Simon right now." Nikki closed her eyes and focused on the unwritten sections of the scene. "He's alone in the room, but there are several people in the adjoining room. I think the female speaker is the goddess housed in one of the shrine maidens; I think Simon's picking up on the fact she's speaking old Japanese. The maid at Izushi said that Atsumori uses a style of Japanese that seems out of a samurai movie.

"And you're right." Nikki closed her notebook. "We're going to have to carry him out."

"Hotel parking then." Miriam pulled up to the entrance of the underground parking grarage. She rolled down the driver's window and took the ticket that the machine fed out to her. "And we'll have to find a luggage cart or something."

Nikki clicked her pen nervously, her mind racing through what they would need. In theory, she knew how to pick locks, but most hotels had gone to a magnetic key system. Some had mechanical override, but still it took her minutes to get through a single lock. There were hundreds of rooms, which meant hundreds of locks. If they went around, blindly opening doors, someone was bound to call the police.

How could they safely find Simon at the hotel? Had there been anything in Simon's scene that would indicate which room he was in?

"The goddess was using beckoning cat luck statues as backup *shintai*," Nikki said.

"Yeah." Miriam was focused on finding a parking space. "So?"

"In an earlier scene I wrote of Simon, he knew he was about to be taken over because the statue exploded and dust was settling on him. It was a pattern; it happened enough times that he knew what was coming. The statues are too weak to contain Iwanaga, and when they explode, she has to move to a new container. Kenichi said that Iwanaga leaves a trail of dust wherever she goes."

"Dust, eh?"

"Yeah, I think we might be able to follow them like breadcrumbs."

The hotel lived up to the name "Imperial." The lobby was an expanse of cream-colored walls, a soft butter-colored ceiling, and a geometric carpet of blacks and reds, looking properly regal. They scouted for a luggage cart while acting out "we're debating our plans" complete with one of Nikki's notebooks standing in as a tourist book, pointing at things that didn't exist on the page and making random remarks like "I want to see Osaka Castle at night" and "I want to go to Dontonbori."

They'd just found the nook where the carts were stored when Atsumori suddenly flooded into Nikki, caught hold of Miriam, and pulled her into the darkness of the storage alcove.

"What are you—?" Miriam started to ask.

"Hush," Atsumori murmured.

For a minute, Nikki wasn't sure what Atsumori was reacting to. Then she realized that far across the lobby, the left-most elevator had opened up and men in dark suits were spilling out. There was something very strange and feral about the way they moved. They tipped their heads up as if sniffing something floating on the air.

They were *yokai*. Nikki pressed her hand to her mouth to stifle a cry of dismay. Was the goddess taking Simon away? Surely he was too weak for her to use again.

The men conferred quietly and then split into two groups. Some continued to walk toward the doors while the others waited, watching the display over the right-most elevator. The car was stopped on the tenth floor. After a minute, it started to descend, counting down the floors.

She gripped Miriam tightly. "If Simon is on the next elevator, we're going to have to follow him."

"Will you be able to recognize him? I don't want to mess with them if we don't have to."

Would she know Simon? She had recognized Leo instantly. Chevalier and Sato had looked familiar. "I think I will."

The quiet chime of a bell announced the arrival of the center elevator. The door slid open. A woman in a beautiful crimson and gold kimono stepped off. Behind her were three shrine maidens in their traditional loose red trousers and white half-length kimono jackets.

"Holy . . ." Miriam whispered. "It's her."

Nikki swallowed hard as her stomach turned cartwheels. If this female got ahold of her, there would be no escaping. The goddess, at least, didn't glance in their direction. She moved toward the hotel's front entrance so smoothly it seemed like she was gliding on ice. Was she even moving her feet?

A black luxury car slid up to the curb. The dark-suited *yokai* opened the back car doors and stood waiting for the women.

"Where do you think they're going?" Miriam whispered.

Nikki shook her head. The mind boggled about where a goddess might go after midnight.

"We should follow her." Miriam tugged at her hands.

"No." Nikki shook her head again. "We need to save Simon."

There was a faint trail of dust from the elevator to rooms 1049 and 1050. Both doors had signs hung on the doorknobs, forbidding housekeeping from entering.

"She's sealed the door against me," Atsumori murmured.

"Just one?" Nikki glanced at the two identical doors. "Not both of them?"

"Just this one." He flickered into sight beside room 1049 and traced the door's outline. "I cannot cross into this room. There is another door and a window into the room, but they are barred, too."

"I think we hit the jackpot." Nikki took out her lock picks.

"Maybe," Miriam said. "Or she has a very nasty surprise locked in there."

"Is there anything in 1050?" Nikki knelt in front of the door to 1049 and started to work the metal carefully into the lock.

"It is empty." Atsumori vanished.

Nikki could feel him pressing close to her as she felt her way through the lock's tumblers. It made her uneasy, because it seemed dangerously addictive to know she could become nearly invincible at will. As with any addiction, though, it was a matter of stepping out of your skin and letting something else take control. She had always thought she would fall to Valium or Xanax. Somehow she never suspected that she'd get hooked on a teenage Japanese god.

Another mistaken assumption was that she would need to know how to pick locks to break out of a room, not to break in. Preparing for a totally different set of disasters, she'd practiced on handcuffs, filing cabinets, supply cabinets, and hospital doors using everything from paper clips to ballpoint pen parts. It only took her a minute to work quickly through the tumblers of the mechanical override lock on 1049. When the lock clicked open, Atsumori stepped into her and together they swung open the door.

The room was exactly as she had expected.

Only the gleam of city lights from the window lit the room. The rectangle of light from the hallway door revealed a chocolate-brown carpet coated with white powder and pieces of ceramic statuary. Dust hazed the air. She breathed in the talc dryness.

Statues of calico cats, paws upraised in the lucky beckoning gesture, sat on a dresser, on the nightstand, on the table next to the window, on the floor clustered tight around the bed and lining the walls.

"Seriously creepy," Miriam whispered behind her.

Tacked across the doorway was a folded paper *shide*.

"I cannot enter with that there," Atsumori said quietly.

Miriam reached up and pulled it down. "What about now?"

"Yes, I can enter. Thank you."

Nikki stalked forward, *katana* ready, the grit from the statues crunching underfoot. Miriam followed, pulling the luggage cart into the room, shutting the door, and turning on the lights.

Simon lay bound on the bed, wearing only boxer shorts. The heavy jute rope elegantly crisscrossed his body, tying him with rough beauty. He was gagged with a ball on a leather strap. His skin was so pale it seemed translucent; his veins running vivid blue, creating a roadmap of his fragile condition. Harsh rope burns marked the days of his captivity.

This could be me. This could be me. Nikki realized suddenly.

She fought to control the fear that the sight of him triggered. She tightened her hold on the *katana*. Atsumori was with her. She wasn't helpless.

"How do we know it's just him?" Miriam whispered. "Maybe there's something other than the goddess in him."

Simon jerked. His eyes opened, dark brown that faded to stunning blue just before they closed again.

"He's alone in his skin," Atsumori said.

"Did you just . . . ?" Nikki cried, pointing down at Simon. "Possess him?"

"It is the only way I could be sure," Atsumori said. "I did what I could to strengthen him. He is very fragile."

"Maybe we should just call the police," Miriam whispered.

If the police became involved, Shiva would be close on their heels. Was this a good thing or a bad? Shiva would do nothing to save Leo from whomever had taken him. Simon would be in no condition to force them, and Nikki wouldn't be able to talk to Simon.

"Will he survive being moved?" Nikki asked.

"Yes," Atsumori said. "He cannot take another day of Iwanaga Hime using him."

"We take him then." Nikki swallowed her fear and forced herself closer to the bed.

If it were me on that bed, I wouldn't want the one person who could help me be too afraid to move. Go!

Reluctantly, she laid the *katana* on the bed beside Simon and, with shaking hands, struggled to undo the leather strap of the ball gag. She couldn't understand how the knots were tied. Unable to untie Simon, she finally slipped the *katana* under the ropes and sawed upward.

"Don't break my *shintai*," Atsumori said. "Or we'll be in the same mess as Iwanaga Hime."

"Don't you dare ever try this with me. I won't bear it. I'll kill myself first."

"I swear to you, I would never try to hold you against your will. If you were not willing, I would rather perish."

"I don't know how Iwanaga could do this to someone after being tied herself. I could never do this to another person."

"She has never been human," Atsumori said. "Her father is one of the heavenly *kami*, older brother to Amaterasu, goddess of the sun, and Susanoo, god of the storms. While she is an earthly *kami*, she is no more human than the flowering tree or a great rock."

"And Simon is nothing more than a sword or a cat statue to her?"

"Nothing more."

The ropes finally gave. She pulled them off Simon and flung them aside as if they were snakes.

Simon was a tall man—nearly a foot taller than Nikki or Miriam— and even though he was slender in build, he was going to be difficult for them to muscle around. She glanced to the luggage cart and realized that Miriam wasn't even in the room.

"Miriam!"

A muffled curse drew Nikki to the connecting room, *katana* tightly in hand.

Miriam was ransacking the dresser drawers of room 1050.

"What are you doing?" Nikki cried.

"We're in her lair!" Miriam shook a newspaper at Nikki. "We should try and find out everything we can!"

Nikki stammered a moment in surprise and dismay before managing, "No!"

"You don't make a big production out of leaving if you're coming back in a few minutes. We should find out what Iwanaga is planning."

"No! I don't know if the two of us can even move him. We don't have time to dick around looking for something that might not even exist. There's not going to be a map with a big 'x' on it and the words 'ultimate secret weapon' written on it. Hell, even if there was, it would be in Japanese—I'm not going to be able to read it!"

"I could translate . . ." Atsumori started to offer.

"We don't have time!" Nikki caught herself before she shouted so the words came out as a hoarse whisper.

"She is an Oracle," Atsumori pointed out.

"If there's something here," Nikki said, "we could pick it up, read it and not even know what we have in our hands."

Miriam frowned, still shaking the newspaper. "Right. Right. Okay. This is your book. What is in this room that is important to the heroine?"

The question surprised her at first but, then she considered it. Yes, she might be able to use her ability that way. Nikki glanced around the room. Unlike the other bedroom, this one had the earmarks of being lived in. There were piles of newspapers and books, bottles of *sake*, every type of nail polish and makeup imaginable, shoes by the door, the closet hanging open showing off a dozen hand-painted kimonos. Obviously while 1049 was a shrine to house the goddess, her *tanuki* goons and the shrine maidens interacted with her in 1050. If she were tweaking Simon's earlier scene, what would be important for her to add? What would save the heroine or doom her if she missed it?

She turned in a circle, paused, and pointed to a school bag lying on the bed. "That. That's important."

Miriam pounced on the bag and snatched it up. "Okay, let's go."

Nikki wavered. There was something more. She turned again, looking. Not in here. She walked back to 1049 and quickly checked the drawers of the dresser. At first glance, they were all empty, but then she found a man's leather wallet and a red diplomatic passport from the United Kingdom. A quick check confirmed that they belonged to Simon. "Okay, now we go."

☩ 28 ☩
Into the Mountains

It wasn't until they were wheeling Simon through the garage that they realized one small flaw to their plan. They stood in silence, eyeing the sports car.

"It doesn't feel right to put him in the trunk." Nikki broke the silence.

"I have to drive." Miriam said. "Him or you."

"Right. Trunk."

Still it felt very, very wrong to close the trunk on Simon after they had muscled him into the small space. They were bad American *gaijins* and left the luggage cart sitting in the garage like no Japanese native would and fled the underground parking lot.

"Where are we taking him?" Miriam asked when they stopped at the first red light. Maru was on Miriam's lap, paws on the steering wheel, watching the light with her.

Nikki stared wide-eyed at Miriam. She hadn't planned that part out. "Umm."

"De Vil has my place staked out. I don't want to explain to the FBI why we've got a Brit stuffed in the trunk. And if we start talking about Japanese gods and raccoon dogs, we're both going straight to the loony bin."

"Both Shiva and Iwanaga know where I live," Nikki said.

"She will know that I was there," Atsumori added. "She will assume I will go back to my shrine. It is where I'm strongest."

Amazingly the cup holder had collected a half-dozen pens at some point. Nikki snatched one up and clicked it, thinking. Where the hell did they run to? Any hotel they checked into would log their passports and instantly put them on the radar for her mother.

She hated to show up on anyone's doorstep with so much trouble, but their options were limited. "Do you think Pixii would be okay with us showing up—like this?"

Miriam laughed. "She'd probably be pissed if we left her out."

Much to Miriam's joy, a good part of the drive to Pixii's place was on highways where she could play—cautiously—with the power of Leo's car. The last thing they needed was to be pulled over for speeding.

Nikki examined the bag that they'd stolen out of room1050. It was a school bag of the kind that every Japanese high school student carried. A student would buy a sturdy leather bag in seventh grade and use it until they graduated. Nikki thought of the shrine maidens and shivered. She hadn't realized that the girls were so young.

Inside was a collection of books, not surprisingly all in Japanese. At the very bottom of the bag was a student photo ID card in a plastic holder. It showed a teenage girl with the bowl-cut of a shrine maiden.

"Her name is Umeko Kuroki." Atsumori read the kanji that had mystified Nikki. "She's a second-year student at Kagoshima Prefectural Kirishima High School."

Tucked behind the card was a Shinkansen train ticket from June. She couldn't read the station they departed from, but she recognized the kanji for Osaka. "What does this say?"

"Kagoshima," Atsumori said. "It is a city in Kyushu."

The girl didn't look familiar. She wasn't one of Nikki's characters. "Did you see her with the goddess?"

"I did not," Atsumori said. "None of the shrine maidens seemed to be the correct age to be this girl."

"The ticket suggests she came from Kagoshima to Osaka," Nikki sighed. "Where is she now?"

"Maybe she's one of the girls who died. Kenichi said that two died already," Miriam said

It would explain why she hadn't been with the goddess. What had the *tanuki* done with her body? Certainly she and Miriam had just proved how easy it would be to get a dead body down to the garage and into the trunk of a car. Nikki tucked the ID back into the bag and studied the books.

One of the books was clearly an atlas for a young child. Bright smiling children in traditional clothing stood next to maps of countries, waving flags. Oddly, Hawaii was treated separately from the United States, with kids in hula outfits and waving the state flag as well as the American Stars and Stripes. The boy reminded her of Leo, with black hair and dark eyes.

The second book was a history textbook. The third seemed to be child's science, explaining things such as electricity, gasoline engines, and airplanes.

"This is one weird collection of books." Nikki frowned at the last book, which was a thick Frommer's guidebook on Japan. The statue of a god frowned back at her from the cover.

"Iwanaga Hime knows nothing of the world as it stands now," Atsumori said. "My shrine is at the edge of Kyoto, but from it I have been able to watch the world change. I saw them lay the tracks for the first train. I was mystified when they strung the first electric lines. I was awestruck when the first planes flew overhead. I have had not only my priests and my shrine maidens devoting their lives to me, but an endless parade of people visit my shrine. From the neighbors who have owned the local bakery for a dozen generations to the Americans who come with their short pants and bug-bitten legs. How do your people get so bitten up?"

"I don't know." Nikki flipped through the books, trying to figure out what was important about them. "We taste good?"

"On that mountain, Iwanaga would have seen nothing but trees and river and farm, and the one family that served her were farmers, not priests. They would have come, prayed, and left her alone."

Had Iwanaga been lonely or was that just a human trait? She certainly had been angry when she finally managed to get free.

While the first three books seemed fairly new, the tour book was dog-eared and heavily annotated. It was in Japanese, but Nikki could guess the locations being discussed from her own research and accompanying pictures and maps. Sections of text had been underlined, circled, and crossed off. "She's looking for something. All the notes are around shrines, not hotels or restaurants and such. She thinks what she's looking for will be at a shrine, but she's not sure which one."

"A *shintai* to hold her?" Miriam guessed.

Nikki curled up against the thought. Of all the things she hated most about mental hospitals, number one was being tied helpless to a bed while the chance of rape loomed huge. The hospitals tried to prevent it, but it only took one orderly who slipped through their background checks, one patient with kinks, one visitor who saw an opportunity and took it. Her fingers twitched, wanting to write. It reminded her, though, that she didn't write little personal tragedies.

"She has to be looking for something more. She's angry, but she has to be scared that the other *kami* will find out she's free and imprison her again. She's vulnerable now, so, yeah, she wants Simon and you and the *katana*, but she's probably looking for something— something like a weapon. She'll fight before she lets herself be bound again, and the body count will be high."

"Bigger than Dupont?" Miriam asked.

Nikki nodded, clicking her pen. "Dupont had only twenty characters, and most of them knew each other. This time, I've got dozens of people scattered all over Japan, and none of them are connected. She's going to do something big—something—something that will affect them all."

Pixii lived on a mountain somewhere in Nara Prefecture. Nikki had the directions to her place memorized, but they were from the Nara train station. From there, she was supposed to take a bus to a remote bus stop and then walk the rest of the way. While Pixii had provided Nikki with detailed instructions on how to find the correct bus and method of paying the fare, they were devoid of road names, distance, and landmarks until the section on foot. Nikki fought with the GPS, trying to target Pixii's location, but failed. In the end, they used the system to get to Nara while Nikki tried calling her on Miriam's phone.

"She's not picking up," Nikki said.

"She tweeted that they were firing the kiln. She needs to stoke the fire like every fifteen to twenty minutes, so she's probably in and out of the house a lot."

In the end, they stopped in Nara at the bus station and found a map that described the bus routes and took a picture of it. After that, they drove carefully through dark, winding mountain roads, trying to find the correct bus stop.

For the first time in her life, Nikki desperately wanted to write without her hypergraphia pushing her. Where was Leo? Was he okay? She gripped her pen tightly, wanting to put it to paper, but Miriam needed her to copilot. It was taking all Miriam's concentration to drive the dark, twisting roads. According to Pixii, the bus stop was merely a collection of small markers alongside the road, showing that five different buses stopped at that location. With headlights raking through the darkness, she kept her eyes focused for the signs.

Luckily, it was near dawn when they reached the correct section of road, otherwise she would have never seen them. Each sign was only the size of her palm.

They stopped and stared at the signs.

"There's the bakery with the red roof." Nikki pointed to the building just ahead. A wall of trees climbed the steep hillside behind it, mist rising off the trees as the sun paled the sky. "Take that right."

The road rose and narrowed as it wound its way up the flank of a mountain. Farms nestled in the small valley between the hills, a dozen rice paddies reflecting the pale sky like pieces of a broken mirror.

A mile beyond the bus stop, they turned at one of the small roadside shrines so common in Japan. It was nothing more than a miniature wooden house with offerings sitting before it. The narrow dirt lane there went a hundred yards back and ended in a wood-lined yard. The smell of wood smoke hung heavy in the air. The only sign of the modern day was a cell tower in the distance.

"Well, this is the place."

Nikki cautiously got out of the sports car. The kitten hopped out and trotted off to do its business in the dirt of the road.

The smoke poured from a chimney rising out of a lean-to built over a long, crudely made wood-fired kiln. Next to it was a traditional-style farmhouse with a steep-pitched thatched roof. The door opened and Pixii padded out onto the wooden porch, pale gold hair in two messy ponytails, rubbing at her eyes. She had on a plaid sleeping shirt and bunny slippers and looked all of twelve.

"*Ohayou gozaimasu.*" Pixii yawned, hand over mouth. "*Nani o osagashi desu ka?*"

Nikki twiddled her fingers in greeting. "Bounce?"

Pixii squealed and bounded off the porch in surprisingly high hops and leaps and more squeals. She hugged Nikki, almost knocking her off her feet. "I was so worried! You said you were coming and then you never called! And Sexy hadn't heard from you either."

For a minute it was impossible to speak since Pixii was hugging her so tightly. Finally Nikki got enough breath to say "I'm sorry."

Miriam popped the trunk. "Things got really crazy. We're in trouble. Big trouble."

Pixii laughed. "Is there any other kind? Oh my God!" Pixii spotted Simon curled inside the trunk, wrapped in a sheet so only his face showed. The taut fabric made it obvious that he was nearly naked under thin white linen. Pixii leaned in, pressed a hand to his neck, and checked his eyes. "Oh, he's cute—very Lawrence of Arabia."

"It's a long story," Nikki said.

Miriam started to giggle.

"And it's been a very long night." They had discussed ways to explain it all to Pixii, but the story had gotten sillier and sillier as they drove. The last version had flying turtles and Mickey Mouse. "We need a place to hide from some really bad people."

"Okay-dokay. Let's get him inside and his feet elevated. I think I have something to rehydrate him." Pixii giggled and bounced in place. "This is going to be great!"

Nikki glanced to Miriam, who grinned largely.

"Told ya," Miriam said.

It took all three of them to lift Simon out of the car and carry him to the farmhouse. The home was more rustic than the one at Izushi. Massive, rough-hewed timbers made up the vaulted ceiling. The walls were white stucco, but still it was nearly cavelike except for the pale dawn light filtering in through *shoji* doors. The smell of clay and cut grass and wood smoke filled the house in a way that felt like it was filled with life. The only nod toward present day was a single outlet that powered Pixii's laptop and was recharging her cell phone. There were only two rooms, one with worn wood floors and the other with *tatami* mats. Off to one side was a step down into a kitchen with a wood oven and dirt floor.

Two futons were spread out on the floor of the second room, both rumpled from sleep.

"Here, put him on my futon." Pixii indicated the futon with rabbits printed on the duvet. The other was a somber navy befitting an older man. The two were an arms-length apart, indicating that sleep was all that the two shared.

"Where's your teacher?" Nikki asked. "Are you sure this will be okay with him?"

Pixii laughed as she took Simon's pulse. "Sorry, I've been up every twenty minutes for three days—so I'm kind of wired." She elevated his feet and covered him up with her blankets. "There, that will keep him nice and warm."

The far wall of the farmhouse was a large closet with four sliding doors. Still talking, Pixii slid the doors open to peek inside until she found a section that was mostly full of cosplay costumes. She took two duffel bags from the bottom.

"Let me tell you, at three in the morning, when you're trying to feed wood into a kiln without getting third-degree burns, you truly question all your life choices. Very much 'what the fuck' time."

Pixii had taken a hammer out of one bag. She was now pulling medical supplies from the other. She waved a bag of saline for emphasis. "You're a highly decorated combat medic. You have a doctorate in Asian art. You could be teaching at a women's college like Bryn Mawr or Wellesley, or at least someplace warm like Berkeley or Caltech. If you put 'women studies' into the title of the class, only girls will sign up for it. But no, you're up on a mountain with a crazy old man potter who smells of dirt making little mouse-sized sake cups using techniques that haven't changed for a thousand years."

"Mouse-sized?" Miriam asked when Pixii paused to hammer a nail into a post a few feet from the floor.

"They're freaking tiny!" She used hand sanitizer while she described the process to make the sake cups. "You take a ball of clay about the size of an egg, push in your thumb, and pinch as it rotates, holding it just so. I could make them in my sleep if I could make them perfect." She dropped her voice to a man's deep gravel. "Perfection is for machines, soulless things that do not understand beauty."

She unwrapped an IV needle, cleaned the back of Simon's left hand with a sterile wipe, and plunged the needle home as she continued in the deep-pitched voice. "Creation is focusing heaven.

Become the god of the cup. Reach deep, find the divine inside yourself, and shape the raw clay. You must recognize that beauty is the reflection of the universe. Nothing is perfect. Nothing lasts forever. All things come to an end."

"So you are listening," a man said from the kitchen, his voice deeper and richer than Pixii's imitation. "I was starting to wonder."

There was a flash of movement out of the corner of her eye, and she was aware that Atsumori was beside her, tense and frowning.

Pixii had snatched up the hammer. She checked a swing at Atsumori. "Whoa. Who's this?"

"That is what I would like to know." Pixii's teacher stepped up onto the worn wood of the other room. Snow-white hair, gathered into a ponytail, and the wrinkles on his face marked him as an old man. There was nothing old, though, in his bearing. He was tall for a Japanese man and strongly made, with wide shoulders and large, powerful hands. He was barefoot and in shorts, showing off legs corded with muscles.

"I am Taira no Atsumori." Atsumori bowed low.

Nikki eyed Atsumori humbling himself and then warily turned to the master potter. What exactly was this man? One of the few words she knew of Japanese was *yama*, which meant "mountain." All the old legends spoke of mountain gods, suggesting that every mountain had its own god.

Pixii seemed oblivious to the tension between the two males. She hung the IV bag from the nail she hammered into the post. "Yamauchi-sensei, these are the friends I told you about. ThirdEye. SexyNinja. And, um, Lawrence of Arabia."

Simon was British, just like Lawrence of Arabia, and a member of a government intelligence agency. Leo had mentioned that Sensitives were attracted to Talents such as Nikki. She could only stare in dismay at Pixii.

The others ignored her as her world tumbled head over heels.

"The kiln?" Yamauchi said.

"I stoked the fire for the last time . . ." Pixii checked the watch on her wrist. "About twenty minutes ago. So, unloading should be able to start on—God, what day is it?"

"In four days, regardless of what today is." Yamauchi sighed. "I heard of what happened in Kyoto."

"These two are under my protection," Atsumori said. "Will they be safe here?"

"Not this one?" Yamauchi knelt beside Simon.

"He has not been conscious since we found him. He has not entrusted his safety to me."

Yamauchi nodded his understanding. He studied each of them in turn. Atusmori waited, tense. "They are safe here," Yamauchi said at last. "But you will do nothing more to bring danger to what is mine."

✠ 29 ✠
Betrayal

Nikki slept. She hadn't meant to. Pixii's yawns proved to be contagious. They yawned through a breakfast of boiled rice, miso soup, and grilled fish. Gravity became impossible to resist, and they ended up sprawled out on the *tatami*, trying to explain the last few days. One minute she was listening to Miriam explain that she had been avoiding Kenichi because of the creepy scenes featuring the character "based" on him and the next she was cracking open her eyes to late afternoon. She, Miriam, and Pixii were curled around each other like a litter of puppies, covered up with blankets. Simon had been shifted to the far side of the house, the *katana* lying between him and the sleeping girls.

Maru was sitting on her chest, patting her gently on the nose. When she opened her eyes, he gave a nearly silent meow.

She sat up, cuddling the kitten.

Yamauchi's futon had been rolled up and stored away for the day, leaving no sign of the man who might be a mountain god. Simon was still sound asleep but had been shifted to the far edge of the *tatami*. The *katana* lay beside him, as if Atsumori was keeping watch over him.

The *shoji* doors were pushed open to let mountain air and sunlight to pour into the room. No smoke rose from the kiln's chimney. The car sat on a patch of grass; during her sleep, the dirt road they'd followed had been erased. Nor was there any sign of the cell tower on the far hill.

Shivering, Nikki padded to the porch and scanned the clearing. Ancient trees surrounded the farmhouse without a break. It seemed fairly safe to assume Yamauchi was a god. They'd found safe refuge in the mountain god's home.

But what about Leo? It had been hours since he'd been hit by a car and taken away by a fake ambulance. Who had taken him? Why? She hadn't been able to focus on him after she'd finished the scene yesterday. A few days ago, she would have been annoyed by her "writer's block." Now she was afraid that it meant something darker.

She found a pen and took out a notebook. Now that the moment was here, she was scared. What if Leo were dead? What if he had died while she was asleep?

Tears burning in her eyes, she put the ballpoint to the paper.

Was Leo alive?

Leo woke with the grogginess that told him he'd been drugged. The bars inches from his face told him by whom. He was in one of Shiva's strongholds, probably still in Japan, although the nondescript cage in the modern concrete basement full of shadows gave no clue as to which one. They could have shipped him back to the United States without him being any the wiser.

He could even guess why he'd been taken captive: after six weeks of wearing out Ananth's patience, he'd reached its end. He'd shifted to his true form while unconscious. His clothes were in tatters. His wristwatch painfully tight on his arm. It told him that he'd lost a full day since he'd left Nikki at the Love Now Hotel. Had she taken the money and run? Had she gotten safely out of the country? He desperately hoped she had, even though it tore at his heart to know he would probably never see her again. She trusted him, but she might decide that cutting all ties with him would be safer than seeking out his father's house in Hawaii. And she probably would be right. If she were smart, she'd go and lose herself someplace in the world where he'd never find her.

He was afraid, though, that when he didn't return, she would do something dangerously brave and unpredictable. He snarled with anger and grief. He'd lost Simon, and now he'd lost Nikki.

There was a whisper of movement, and he realized that Williams was standing in the shadows. Waiting. Watching.

He glared at the black man.

"Where are Sato and Chevalier?" Williams asked, his teeth flashing white in the darkness.

That wasn't what he was expecting. "What?"

There was a moment of stillness and silence from the shadows. "Where are Chevalier and Sato? They reported you sighted at Izushi."

He swore softly and rubbed his face with his hands. "You think I did something to them."

"They were told to bring you in, and now they're missing."

He was only alive because Shiva wasn't sure who had gone rogue: him or Sato. If they couldn't find a body, then they would continue to be unsure. There were other possibilities.

"I had a lead on Simon!" He wanted to roar with frustration. *"The yakuza are using tanuki. They have a host club in Dontonbori."* He growled as he realized that he had no proof to support that claim, only Nikki's word. He couldn't let them know about her. "Simon disappeared on the land of one of their hosts. Chevalier thought it was a good enough lead to follow. We were going to question the boy."

"Chevalier hasn't reported in since you were sighted."

"I don't know what happened to them! We talked. We didn't fight. Chevalier was even halfway civil."

"People keep disappearing around you. Simon. Nikki Delany. Now Chevalier and Sato."

It took all his control not to react to Nikki's name. Shiva knew about him discovering the *tanuki* at Nikki's apartment and nothing more, otherwise they would be asking about the *katana*.

"Something ancient and powerful was buried on that land," Leo said. "It was causing all the problems with the dam. And when my father went there alone, it took him! And the damn boy was home that day, clearing the house before the flood took everything. The *kami* used him to gain access to the *yakuza* and then it started to collect *yokai*. We're looking at a major outbreak."

Williams breathed in the shadows. Silent. Thinking. Weighing. "What's the name of the club?"

"Kiss Kiss."

✾ ✾ ✾

Nikki flopped back with relief. Leo was alive and seemingly unharmed, although judging by his emotions, far from safe. As long as Sato and Chevalier remained missing, Shiva would suspect him of the worst.

Maru took advantage of the fact that she was lying on her back to make himself comfortable on her stomach. She petted the ginger kitten absently, wondering what had happened to Chevalier and Sato. There had been no sign of them at Kiss Kiss. They must have been considered "missing" long before they were supposed to meet Leo at the host club, otherwise Shiva wouldn't have had time to find Leo and capture him. The two agents must have fallen out of contact before leaving Izushi.

They were in her story. They were her characters. Could she actually write a scene from their perspective? It was a scary idea; it meant she could possibly crawl into anyone's head that crossed her path and know what they were thinking and what would happen to them in the future.

Could she push her power to include anyone?

She sat back up, pen and notebook in hand. Chevalier had been lead agent, so where did he take his team?

Because Chevalier was Impenetrable, people often thought he was imperceptive and insensitive, too. But he was a Frenchman, and so, when it came to love, he saw things perfectly clear.

Mister Pussycat was in love.

Chevalier found it endlessly amusing. He sauntered through the ancient streets of Izushi, retracing his steps to his car, grinning hugely.

Secretly he liked cats. Perhaps it was because the French were like cats. They did what they wanted and didn't care if it pissed people off. If a cat didn't like you, it left. Dogs wouldn't leave. They had to come over, see what you were doing, and usually decided you needed to be chased off, especially if you were Impenetrable. Big dogs bit. Little dogs barked, barked, barked and waited for your back to be turned, and then bit. He hated dogs.

Just because cats didn't care what you did as long as you left them alone, it didn't mean that they weren't loyal. Others thought Simon's fierce kitten was dangerous, but it was clear to Chevalier from day one that Leo's sun and moon circled around his adopted father. Nothing got the little tomcat growling and hissing more than something threatening Simon. Chevalier used to take pokes just to get him to spit; teasing him had gotten to be a dangerous habit, though.

So, yes, secretly, he actually liked Leo. He had been worried that their kitten was going to go rogue after Simon vanished. But Leo was in love with a strong Sensitive. And, more importantly, the girl obviously loved him back, and that changed everything.

Sato was waiting by the car. By the lack of emotion on his face, the Talent was clearly upset. The man was a clam; the more vulnerable he felt, the more he withdrew into himself. It was only by years of association that Chevalier had learned to read him.

"You're just leaving him?" Sato's tone suggested that he didn't care one way or the other, which meant he cared very much indeed.

"We're going to go kick some pretty-boy butt at a club called Kiss Kiss in Dontonbori." He opened his car door but didn't get in. In a mood like this, Sato probably would just stay standing on the curb. "There will be pretty boys for me to smack around. *Yakuza* for Mister Pussycat to bloody. *Tanuki* for you to vanish into thin air. It will be fun. Come on. Get in."

"You're going to attack a human nightclub based on what he says? Without checking that what he claims is true?"

Chevalier stood tapping on the roof of the car. He had planned on going without double-checking. He trusted Leo to move the world to find Simon. But there was the girl—her motivations were unknown—and a boy in love is easily swayed. God knows, the boy wasn't experienced in the dangers of romance. It was possible that it wasn't even the girl that was moving the pieces on the chessboard, but the god of the sword.

Sato stood unmovable on the sidewalk. "You know what Ananth will ask if you call in and tell him where we're going."

Yes, Chevalier did. He checked his watch. They still had time before they needed to check in. He rapped twice on the roof. "We'll check it out."

So off across the torn earth of the dam construction they went, the noise of the bulldozers deafening close up. Five minutes of walking from there, they reached an abandoned farmhouse. It was a seedy old place where obviously the owner had spiraled downward before dying without anyone remaining who cared to clear out the space.

Sato walked through it and out into the overgrown garden beyond. There was a muddy track that led up a hill. The prints of Leo's boots and the girl's small tennis shoes went out and returned. Without even glancing down at the footprints, Sato led the way. Dusk was starting to gather in the far eastern sky.

"Do you know where you're going?" Chevalier asked.

Sato stopped and nodded. "Yes, I know." He turned and shot Chevalier. "I've known for two months now." Sato stepped over Chevalier's body and started back toward the car. "But that damn cat just made a mess of things."

Nikki jerked to a stop, dropping her pen and staring at the notebook in horror. She hadn't written of the bullets hitting Chevalier and the moment of incredible betrayal he felt as he died. He'd known that Sato was dangerous, but after years of working together, in a vague way, he thought they were a team. Friends. A thousand tiny freedoms he'd given Sato in the name of that friendship, all suddenly used against him.

She snatched up the pen, clicking it rapidly as she realized that Sato had stopped Chevalier from calling Shiva until they could "double check" Leo's story. He didn't want Shiva to go to the Kiss Kiss club and find out where Iwanaga was holding Simon. He'd probably been part of the Shiva search for Simon. Judging by his last comment, he'd found Simon and Iwanaga months ago and hidden them away from Shiva. Since he'd been familiar with the farmhouse, he had probably found the shrine that Leo had missed and then tracked down Kenichi, just like Nikki had. Only he had erased all the evidence in the process.

"Oh, this is bad!"

Sato had killed Chevalier to stop Leo from rescuing Simon. He knew that Shiva would go after Leo when Chevalier didn't check in. Shiva only had to track Leo's phone to find . . .

"Oh! Oh!" The first time she called Leo, he arrived minutes later at the Osaka Castle, and yet they were attacked almost instantly by *tanuki*. After Harada's attack, Atsumori's kidnapping her and the weirdness at Inari's shrine, she had taken the inexplicable assault for granted. Leo probably assumed that the *tanuki* had followed her, but she'd been at the castle for hours. She was filled with sudden certainty that Sato had found a way to monitor Leo's calls, just in case Leo found the *katana*.

She remembered when she tried to call Leo from the love hotel, the horrible sense that she had reached out and touched evil. The call hadn't gone through to Leo, but it had connected to someone. Something.

Shiva had been subverted by one of their own monsters.

No wonder Iwanaga Hime was being so successful at quietly gathering power when Kenichi hadn't been providing any information and limited cooperation. Sato had spent years cleaning up messes for Shiva; he put all that he'd learned to use for Iwanaga.

The question was, what did Sato want out of the deal?

Nikki picked up her notebook. Time to find out.

"There's a plane, Grandpa."

The newly repaired watch in Denjiro Sato's hands read 8:10. Breakfast, his own included, from a dozen kitchens scented the air. The cicadas were starting to stir with the heat of the summer day, threatening to drown out the radio playing softly on the shelf behind him. His four-year-old granddaughter was standing across the street at the river's edge, pointing toward the sky over the distant Aioi Bridge.

"A plane?" Planes weren't unusual; Hiroshima had a number of military camps after all.

"It's high up."

Which meant it was an American bomber, because the Japanese planes couldn't fly so high.

"Just one?" There had been another plane earlier, cruising high overhead. It had sent them scurrying toward the air-raid shelters, but that had proven to be a false alarm. The all clear had come before they scrambled from bed, gathered up the baby, and reached the shelter. Maybe this was the same plane, returning. They'd heard stories of other cities being carpeted with bombs, of firestorms razing neighborhoods, buildings going up like tinder wood. So far, Hiroshima had been blessed; not a bomb had been dropped on it.

"Just one plane, Grandpa. It's so high; it's tiny—like a toy."

He ducked into their kitchen that was off his workshop. His daughter Kayo was frantically assembling breakfast on the table in the small dinning room beyond the kitchen.

"There's a plane . . ." he said.

"Breakfast is done." Kayo brushed past him carrying the rice. "It's just one plane. They haven't sounded the siren. And if they do, it will be a false alarm like earlier. I'm going to be late for work."

So like his wife. She never let anything scare her, not even his unnatural ability to mend anything. He was not so sure, though, that there was nothing to fear. He had already lost his son and son-in-law. What was here in this house was everything dear to him. One direct hit could destroy it all. He wavered in the doorway, heart leaping in his chest like a fish on the line. Surely the Americans would send more than one plane to bomb a city. But what did he know of planes? He had been born in a time before men even thought of flinging themselves through the sky in metal cans.

"Rieko!" Kayo called to his granddaughter. "Come! Eat!"

And his granddaughter was much like her mother. "I'm watching the plane."

From his blanket on the floor, his grandson started to fuss. Kayo made a small cry of exasperation and gave Sato an imploring look.

"I will get her." He hurried out of his workshop. The street was full of people heading to work. He scanned the sky as he wove his way through the crowd to the river's edge. The one plane was up so high, it was just a dot in the sky. It was turning in a hard circle that would lead it back to the sea.

"See it, Grandpa?"

"I see it." He gasped as something came falling into view. A single black teardrop of death. It was going to hit near them. "Oh no! Reiko! Run! Run to the shelter!"

He started to reach for Reiko, and there was a massive, brilliant flash of light. It seemed as if he'd been dropped into the heart of the sun. Light sheered through him and a second later, a burning hot hand slapped him into unconsciousness with the roar of a thousand dragons.

He came back to awareness in burning rubble. Night seemed to have fallen until he realized that a great cloud filled the sky, blocking the sun. All around him was nothing but broken, burning rubble. It was as if, in one instant, the entire city been smashed to nothing. There was a low crackle and growl of fire all around. Otherwise, the world was eerily silent.

"Reiko?" He tried to get up and gasped in pain. His right leg was pinned under a heavy piece of wood. He couldn't even guess where it had come from; it seemed to be a rafter from a house, but he was down by the river, twenty feet from any building. He struggled to push it off him. "Reiko? Where are you, Reiko?"

He didn't have the strength to push the timber. Each time he shifted it, pain shot through his leg. Old-man strength. Old-man fragile bones. He cried in frustration and fear. What had happened to Reiko? She had been beside him. All around him was a mad confusion of broken lumber, roofing tiles, and bicycles. Flames licked on the wood, found it dry with summer heat, and leaped higher.

The thin wail of an infant rose from the wreckage, and his heart lurched as he realized that he couldn't tell where his house had been standing. The confusing jumble of broken timbers continued as far as the eye could see in the unnatural darkness. Was that his grandson crying? Where was his daughter?

As if drawn by the baby's cry, the fire reached out with questing fingers.

"Kayo!"

He needed to get the timber off his leg.

He tangled his fingers in the spiderweb of possibilities and yanked hard. He screamed as the pain became unbearable. He was aware of the timber slipping back along the path that had brought it to him, a thousand splinters and shards leaping up and tunneling back to what was to reform the Fujii's house halfway down the block. The house stood seemingly untouched, a sole upright building in a sea of shattered houses.

The leg underneath was a massive wound, gushing blood. He clamped a hand on the wound, suddenly aware of the fine mesh of possibilities. He'd never noticed them on humans before. Head swimming, he pulled on the lines. The blood seeped back into the wound, the flesh merged back together, and his trousers mended.

He stumbled to his feet, vision blurring and pain like a knife cutting into his skull. "Kayo!"

"Papa!" His daughter's voice came from the wreckage, trembling with fear. "The fire is coming closer. Papa! Help me! I can't move! Papa!"

Darkness surged in, and the last thing he heard was his daughter screaming as the fire consumed her and his grandson.

❋ ❋ ❋

Nikki stared at her careful neat handwriting in confusion. She'd written several scenes from Kayo's point of view, mystified as to how the events of World War II were going to affect her novel. The bombing had happened on August 6, 1945. Kayo's father had been an elderly man in his seventies, having outlived his wife and various younger siblings.

How could this be the Sato that Nikki had met? It had been impossible to judge the age of the man at Izushi. He could have been anywhere from his early thirties to well-preserved late forties, but he certainly hadn't been in his seventies, or nearly a hundred and forty.

But what if he somehow reversed his age in his desperate attempt to heal himself so he could save his daughter? What if he was the same man who had lost everything that day? Daughter. Grandchildren. Home. Business.

The entire city blasted away in a blink of an eye.

She had wanted to know what Sato planned. It was terrifying to think that this was the answer.

She had to contact Shiva and let them know that Leo hadn't killed Chevalier and that Sato was planning something awful.

✠ 30 ✠
Needle in a Haystack

Simon was younger than Nikki had expected. Even with his face pale and etched with exhaustion, he seemed only in his mid-thirties. He must have been only in his early twenties when he'd adopted Leo. He was tall, lean, and fair-haired with laugh lines at the corners of his mouth and eyes. Despite weeks of imprisonment, he was clean-shaven and well-groomed. Iwanaga apparently did not want to appear disheveled when she was hosted in his body.

Nikki shifted the *katana* to one side and knelt beside the sleeping man. She had never seen anyone look so fragile before. The hotel room and the garage had been full of shadows and fear, otherwise she would have never been so cavalier about sticking him into the trunk of the sports car. If she had seen him clearly, she would have taken him straight to the hospital.

But then Shiva would have been alerted and Sato's people might have arrived first. Trying hard to believe she was doing the right thing, she tentatively shook Simon by the shoulder. "Simon. Simon. Wake up."

His eyes flickered as he awakened. He shifted, moving as if he was trying to sit up.

Atsumori flooded into her, snatched up his *katana*, and had the blade to Simon's throat.

"What are you doing?" Nikki cried. "Stop that!"

"He was going to hurt you," Atsumori said.

259

"I don't care. What the hell would I tell Leo? Good news is I found your dad, the bad news is I killed him?" She struggled a moment to lower her hand. "Atsumori, back off!"

"You're greatly overestimating my ability at the moment," Simon said quietly. "I might have planned on attacking, but I don't think I can move."

Atsumori eased back cautiously and then loosed his hold on her body.

"I told you not to do that," Nikki growled, shaking away the feel of him on her.

"I am sorry, Nikki-chan," Atsumori's voice murmured from somewhere behind her.

Simon gazed over her shoulder, eyes narrowing. "I don't know you." He shifted his gaze to Nikki. "Either of you."

She glanced behind her. Atsumori stood watching tensely, fully visible and not looking apologetic at all. She glared at him and turned back to Simon. "Yeah, we got into this game late. Long, complicated story, but here are the important parts: Sato is working with Iwanaga Hime. She's the goddess that has been holding you captive. He killed Chevalier and framed Leo. Shiva hit Leo with a car and locked him in a cage—somewhere. Sato and Iwanaga are planning something really, really big, and it's going to be bad."

"Sato." Simon gasped as if he'd been handed a piece of a puzzle. "Of course."

"Huh?"

Simon lifted his hand as if it weighed a hundred pounds and dragged it over his face. "He's been drifting on the edge of my awareness. I knew there was something tugging at me, like a song played so faintly that you can barely hear it, and yet the chords are so familiar that you still recognize it. Sato has been meeting with Iwanaga. I think he's the reason I'm still alive; she would have worn me out weeks ago otherwise."

Apparently Sato could extend his ability to heal.

Simon's eyes drifted shut, and his breathing deepened.

"No! No!" she cried, shaking him again. "Don't go back to sleep!"

Across the room, Miriam bolted into a sitting position with a gasp. She looked around, confused by her surroundings. "Where the hell . . . ? Oh, Pixii's place."

Nikki waved her to silence as Simon's eyes fluttered open. "Simon, we need to save Leo, but I don't know how."

"Call Ananth," Simon whispered. "Tell him that Iwanaga Hime is looking for Amenonuboko."

Across the room, Miriam cried, "She's what?"

Nikki waved harder as Simon closed his eyes again. "Oh shit! Simon!"

"He is very fragile still, Nikki-chan. It would be best to let him rest."

Nikki wanted a pen.

No, she didn't want a pen. She was afraid of whatever else she might write that was utterly, horrifically true, and that she was way too late to change.

What she wanted was to grab Simon and shake him until he coughed up the location of all the Shiva strongholds. In the world. With detailed drawings of how to infiltrate them to the detention block.

She suspected that she'd kill the man if she shook him at this point.

She might be able to choose Ananth as a character and narrow down his phone number like she had with Leo, but the moment she dialed in, whatever mechanism Sato had in place would be screening the call and running interference. So much she didn't know.

Miriam climbed out from under her blanket, blurry with sleep. She must have borrowed clothes from Pixii, as she was wearing a sleeping shirt that barely fit her. She stared a moment out the open door and then came to cuddle up to Nikki. It was very unlike her.

"Are you okay?" Nikki asked her.

She shook her head, face pressed to Nikki's shoulder.

"What's wrong?"

She took a deep breath and sighed. "Stupid dream. I think my subconscious hit me with every one of my insecurities in one majorly fucked-up nightmare. I was naked at a final exam in a class I forgot I had, and these sixty-foot ninja clown turtles were chasing me."

"Ninja clown turtles?"

"I wake up and the road is gone and I'm at the house of a

mountain god who likes to make pottery. Real life isn't supposed to be weirder than your dreams."

Right.

What exactly is Ame—Ame—" Nikki stumbled with the Japanese word. "Amenonuboko?"

"The heavenly jeweled spear," Atsumori and Miriam both said.

Miriam added, "It's the spear that Kenichi said was stolen. Why Iwanaga was punished. If she's looking for it, it means that it's real . . ."

"Of course it's real," the boy god said.

"Yes, I know," Miriam whined. "I just didn't get that until now. Somehow it just stayed mythical in my head up to this moment."

"I take it that we're talking a spear with jewels on it?" Nikki said. "Is it a *shintai* like your *katana*?"

Atsumori shook his head. "My *katana* is nothing but a hollow reed to the Amenonuboko." He frowned a moment, and then started slowly to explain better. "In the beginning of all things, the universe was a sea of chaos, without shape, sunk in silence. Then there was sound, and with the sound, there was movement, and the particles that made up the universe separated."

Atsumori lifted one hand above his head. "The pure, light particles created the heavens." He held out his other hand at his waist. "The rest of the particles gathered into the dense and dark mass of the Earth. That is the difference between humans and *kami*. Why most humans cannot see the *kami* and your machines cannot register our existence. Why even the *yokai* see us as separate and above them. We are not wholly of the Earth."

"And this relates to the Amenonuboko how?" Nikki was still lost.

"My *katana* was made by humans and blessed by Inari, which is why I had you seek him out."

"Wait. You met Inari?" Miriam asked.

"I—I'm not sure what we met."

"We met Inari," Atsumori stated firmly. "If you took a reed and dipped it into gold, while it shines brightly in the sun, it is still just a reed."

It took her a moment to track the conversation back to what the reed represented. "Your *shintai* is made from common elements." She followed that much. "And the spear is . . . ?"

Atsumori thought a moment before answering. "When the first gods decided that Earth should be perfected, they called forth into existence Izanagi and Izanami. They gave the two the heavenly jeweled spear and commanded that they make the first land.

"Izanagi and Izanami took the spear to the bridge that floats between the heavens and Earth. Standing on the bridge, they stabbed the spear into the endless sea and churned the dark water. When they lifted up the spear, water dripped from its blade and became Onogoro Shima, which means the self-forming island. Izanagi and Izanami then crossed the bridge and made their home on the island."

Nikki saw the point that Atsumori was trying to make. "The spear was created in heaven by the first gods. It's not of the Earth."

Atsumori nodded.

She considered the implications of something that was more like Atsumori than his *katana*. "Does that mean that most humans can't see the spear? That cameras won't register it?"

"I believe so," Atsumori said.

"What about *yokai*? Can they see it?"

"I don't know," Atsumori admitted. "Before I was called into my *shintai*—I existed, and yet I did not. As Inari told you, *kami* are like water. We exist, we have substance, but we are not with form until we are given shape by human faith. I have faint memories of that time before the blessing, but it is like sunlight on water, shifting and bright and yet unsubstantial. I was what was desired—a noble warrior spirit—but I was without a name or sense of self until I found myself in the *shintai*. I am not Atsumori, and yet, I am.

"It means that what I know is limited and perhaps flawed. Yes, I am a *kami*. I have existed for hundreds of years. But in the grand flow of the universe, I am like a child, with a child's knowledge of the greater gods."

Miriam held up a finger and tapped it as if trying to pin down an elusive thought. "I—I don't think *yokai* can see the spear."

"Why not?" Nikki said.

"The most famous mythical weapon is Kusanagi," Miriam said. "It's like Excalibur. It's the magical weapon of Japan. The name gets used in everything."

Nikki shook her head. "I don't get the connection."

"According to legend, the god Susanoo found the sword in the tail of an eight-headed serpent. He gave it to his sister Amaterasu, goddess of the sun, as a gift, and she gave it to her grandson, the first emperor, to be part of the imperial regalia."

"That's the same guy who Iwanaga said stole the spear, Ninigi."

"Yes. There's dozens of stories about Kusanagi. According to legends it's been copied, stolen, recovered, lost at sea, recovered again, yada yada yada. It's stored at the Atsuta Shrine in Nagoya. Since the sixth century, it's been part of the imperial enthronement ceremony. It was used as recently as 1989, when Emperor Akihito ascended the throne."

"So it's real?"

"Odds are good for it being real."

Nikki felt as if someone were rewriting reality around her. The world had become a place with magical weapons. "Really?"

"No one actually saw it in 1989," Miriam admitted. "It was shrouded during the ceremony."

"Kusanagi is not wholly of the Earth," Atsumori said. "Only the heavenly gifted would be able to see its true nature. It would appear to normal people as something quite different."

"They would see a normal sword?" Miriam said.

Atsumori nodded and said firmly, "Yes. It is not wholly of the heavens."

"And the *yokai* would see a regular sword?"

He gave an uncertain "Yes." Obviously, he didn't like being unsure. He shifted uneasily and added, "At least, I believe so."

Miriam waved aside his doubt. "That's why there're so many legends about Kusanagi. Everyone can see something, even if it seems quite ordinary."

Nikki and Atsumori looked at Miriam, unsure of the point she was making.

"The spear is only mentioned in the creation section of the *Kojiki*." Miriam saved her from having to ask. "The *Kojiki* is a collection of songs and poems that tells the history of Japan. It was recorded in the eighth century, but it represented over a thousand years of the imperial rule. Or at least, it's believed to cover that time period. There's no way of telling myth from historical fact, and it's possible that the first fourteen emperors were legendary. The fifteenth, Ojin, is reported to have been born three years after his father died."

"I'm sure that's a mistranslation," Atsumori murmured. "He's been deified as Hachiman Daimyojin. We could ask him. One of his major shrines is in Yawata in Kyoto Prefecture. It's not that far."

"No, we're good," Nikki said quickly. She had more than enough gods running through her life.

"That's why I was so surprised that the spear is real and it's in Japan. If all the *yokai* could see it, then eventually stories from them would have drifted into the main consciousness."

Atsumori nodded slowly. "So only the heavenly gifted can gaze upon it."

"That counts me out," Nikki said.

"You would be able to see it. Your gifts are divine. You were born with a connection to the heavens."

Nikki wasn't sure if this was a good thing. It made her feel weirdly like Joan of Arc. Things did not end well for Joan. "But I can only see you when you will me to see you."

"That is a failing within me, not of you," Atsumori said. "I am kunitsu-kami, a god of the Earthly realm. It takes effort for me to manifest in a form that is visible to the divine gifted. Those who are not gifted could not see me no matter what."

Considering how much time Atsumori was spending visible, the farmhouse must be considered holy ground.

"So," Miriam said. "Iwanaga Hime is looking for an invisible needle in a very large haystack. How does she hope to find it?"

"I don't know, but she will," Nikki said. "This is one of my stories, remember. She'll find it and use it—or Sato will use it."

She got up to root through the pile of things from the car. "Divine gifted can see the spear. I'm betting that sometime in the past, one of them found it. He or she didn't know what it was—because otherwise it would show up in stories—but they recognized that it was dangerously powerful. And they did what Japanese always do. They marked it as holy and prayed to it." Nikki found the tour book from Iwanaga Hime's room. The book was dog-eared from obvious close study. "That's why this tour book is important. She knows that if the spear surfaced, someone would have built a shrine around it."

"Still a needle in a haystack," Miriam said. "Kyoto alone has a thousand temples. I think we're safe from world destruction."

"Still my story," Nikki stressed, shaking the book at Miriam. "People are going to die in masses."

Nikki flipped through the pages. The text was written in *kanji*. She recognized a handful of photographs, but otherwise the books were unreadable. Even if she had Atsumori translate for her, would she even know what she was looking for? As Miriam had pointed out, the spear had vanished out of myths. It wouldn't be written up in a tour book as one of the famous attractions of some obscure little temple.

Still, for some reason, Iwanaga hoped to find the spear within the pages. Nikki noticed that the book's spine been broken from being laid facedown while open. She felt a weird déjà vu; she'd written a scene with Kenichi, the goddess, and the book. In the scene, the goddess scanned a page, shook her head, and put aside the book, facedown, without reading further. In a glance, the goddess had known the information she wanted wasn't on the page she'd just read.

Nikki flipped the book open to the page indicated by the broken spine. She couldn't read the town's name in *kanji*, but she recognized the pictures. She'd researched the city after writing the scene. The goddess had been reading about Kamakura, which was south of Tokyo. It had served as the country's capital for over a century during the Middle Ages. By modern Japan's standard, it was a small town with only a handful of major attractions. The Zeniari Benten Shrine, with its cave for washing coins for good luck. The great bronze Buddha, nearly forty feet high. The giant camphor statue of Kannon that had been cast into the sea to find its own place of worship. It had drifted three hundred miles, been hauled out, found to be unlucky and thrown back in, and washed ashore in Kamakura.

A minor snakelike *kami* and two Buddhist gods. No wonder the goddess had been shaking her head; she could tell at a glance that the spear wasn't in Kamakura.

Nikki frowned and flipped through the rest of the book. In all the towns, only some of the various shrines were highlighted. "She knows who stole the spear. She knows, and she's guessing that it will be at a temple dedicated to that god."

Miriam laughed bitterly. "Oh, that narrows it down. You know there's eight million gods?"

"Yes, I know."

"And if it's Inari, there's like—what—ten thousand shrines in Japan."

"I know."

"I think we can safely assume that she's going to be at this for a long time and focus on saving Mr. Scary Cat Dude."

Leo, the tourist information, and the goddess all coalesced into one memory. "Wait! I think I know who stole the spear. I had a flyer on the Gion Festival, and I had written a note on it that Leo saw. Iwanaga is pissed off about the festival, but I never understood why. I think the reason she's mad about it is that it's dedicated to the god that framed her. All these humans gathering together for hundreds of years in a blowout celebration for the being who caused her to be trapped, alone."

"The Gion Festival is dedicated to Susanoo," Atsumori said.

Susanoo was the brother of the sun goddess, one of the three major gods in the Japanese mythos. "Why would Susanoo take it?"

"Why does Susanoo do anything?" Miriam said. "He's the original loose cannon. He got in a fight with Amaterasu and decided to fill up her rice paddies and palace with shit and vomit. Then he flayed a horse and threw it through the roof, breaking her loom and literally scaring one of Amaterasu's attendants to death."

"It's a reflection of his nature," Atsumori said. "He is the tumultuous summer storm. Wild and fierce and unpredictable."

Not a god you want to meet face-to-face, then.

31
Gion Matsuri

"Oh, yeah," Pixii said when they woke her up and pointed out that the road had vanished. "It does that. That's why I told you to stop at the shrine if you couldn't find it. Hungry? I'm starving."

"We need to go to Kyoto," Nikki said.

"Cool! Road trip!" Pixii stripped off her clothes. Under the sleeping shirt, she was all wiry muscle. On her left shoulder blade was a tattoo of a caduceus staff, the snakes both vipers ready to strike. She slid aside one of the closet doors to reveal her colorful cosplay costumes.

"The Gion Matsuri is going on! So, problem of clothing—solved. Cherry blossoms!" She pulled out a pink *yukata* with white blossoms and tossed it to Miriam.

"Pink?" Miriam checked it for length. Pixii was shorter then either of them, but the hem came to Miriam's ankles.

"It goes with your hair. Butterflies for Nikki."

A rose red *yakuta* got tossed to her. Swallowtail butterflies rose in swarm. Nikki wondered what odd gifts Pixii had that she had reserved Atsumori's family crest for her.

"And *yuri* for me!" Hers was done in mountain green and white lilies. "This is going to be great! Festivals have the most awesome food! Crepes. Grilled corn. *Yakisoba*. Have you tried the candied fruit? They dip all sorts of things into the same stuff you use on candy apples.

269

The strawberries are iffy—they end up as so much mush after the hot sugar hits them. Japanese grapes are golf-ball-sized and oh so good candied. I get sick of my own cooking. At least I've gotten better. Oh God, I don't know what I used to do that made the rice like that, but it was horrible."

"I do not want you to go." Yamauchi suddenly stood just outside the open sliding doors. "It will be dangerous."

Pixii paused in the middle of pulling on her *yukata*. Chin up. Boy flat in the chest and a web of scars on her strong shoulders and arms. For one brief moment, she looked very much a combat veteran. "I am not a child."

"You could be twice your age and still be a child to me," Yamauchi apparently didn't know how to deal with women. He couldn't have picked a worse thing to say.

Pixii finished pulling on the *yukata*. "I'm going."

"This is not mortals who are feuding. This is *kami*. The greatest of the *kami*. The sun goddess, Amaterasu, and her brother, Susanoo, god of the storms. Even a powerful god like Inari will not interfere with this directly."

"All the more reason for me to go," Pixii said. "I am not going to let people die when I can stop it."

Yamauchi gave her a sad look. "You may not be able to stop it."

Pixii pointed calmly at Yamauchi. "You should know by now that I will not be stopped."

The mountain god actually winced, but he sighed and nodded. "Yes, I know. I do not want to see you harmed."

"We will be careful. And, even better, we'll be sneaky!"

"Will Simon be okay?" Nikki caught herself before adding "alone," because in theory Yamauchi would be there.

"He will be fine," both Yamauchi and Pixii assured her.

Dusk was already starting to fall on Kyoto when they arrived. They parked the car at the outskirts of the city and took the subway in. Nikki felt like everyone at the station was staring at them. At every stop, six or seven teenage girls in *yukata* filtered onto the train with them. The girls traveled in bouquets of two or three, keeping close to each other and giggling. Nikki realized then that people were glancing at them, but also at the other girls, because they were all pretty.

They carried little fabric purses called *kinchaku*. Pixii had supplied Miriam with one but had given Nikki a slightly larger bag to hold emergency pens and a notebook along with her wallet. Because Nikki had the bigger bag, she ended up with the car keys and a carefully wrapped jade comma-shaped bead that Yamauchi had given them. It was an empty *shintai* that he had carefully crafted "when he was young." From what Astumori had told her earlier, it was more heavenly than what a human could craft and thus superior to any random luck statue that they could pick up.

The other girls had festival *uchiwa* fans tucked into the back of their wide obi belts. Pixii had tucked a pair of black batons into her obi. Nikki had the *katana* slung on her shoulder. Miriam had considered bringing Leo's gun with them, but in the end they had left it locked in the car's glove box.

The trip from Nara had been taken up with talk of battle strategies in case they came face-to face-with *yakuza*, *tanuki*, Sato, Shiva, or Iwanaga Hime. They were at a disadvantage because Nikki could recognize only Sato; the rest were all dangerous strangers. Luckily, they should be equally unknown to their enemies.

"It's really an ultimate game of blindman's bluff," Pixii said. "This is our stop."

It was obvious that almost everyone on the train was attending the festival. The doors opened and people surged forward. They trailed behind the crowd, what lay before them looming larger and larger.

"If the spear was easy to find, Iwanaga has probably already found it," Nikki said. "Gion Matsuri is one of the three largest festivals in Japan, and it's been going on for a thousand years. There's not a single Japanese person who doesn't know that the entire festival revolves around spears."

"It does?" Pixii flinched under their joint stare. "Well, I wasn't really paying attention last year and my Japanese isn't as good as Miriam's. I mostly ate the food and watched the girls."

By walking slow, they fell behind the crowd moving quickly through the tile-lined underground hallways of the subway station. Posters for current and upcoming events adorned the walls in typical orderly Japanese fashion. The Gion Festival featured the massive floats that were wheeled through the city. Nakki paused before a poster.

It had the same picture as the flyer that Leo had found in her apartment. She pressed her hand against it, hoping desperately they would find some way to him. This felt too much like running away from him. Abandoning him.

But if the world ended, it would take him with it.

"What is today?" She'd lost track over the last few days.

Pixii shrugged. "First day after firing the kiln."

Miriam pulled her phone out of her cloth purse to check. "The sixteenth. Damn, I wish *yukata* had pockets. I hate purses."

"Okay, it's *Yoiyama*." Who turned away from the poster and headed for the exit marked Yasaka Shrine. "Tomorrow is *Yamaboko Junko*."

"*Yoiyama?*" Pixii frowned. "That means light on the mountain. Dawn. It's dusk now."

"The fourteenth is *yoiyoiyoiyama*, the fifteenth is *yoiyoiyama*, and the sixteenth is *yoiyama*. It's a countdown to the parade."

"What the hell does *yoiyoiyoi* . . . ?" Pixii paused to count the yois. "Whatever, mean?"

Miriam shrugged. "Real fucking early?"

They reached the cement steps leading up to the street. Pixii trotted up the stairs ahead of them. They'd decided that since Pixii was a total unknown to Sato's people, she would take point. At first Nikki wasn't sure about this; Pixii seemed unaware of Yamauchi's status. Pixii, though, maintained that she knew perfectly well what her teacher was; just that she was unimpressed by that part of his abilities.

"He's playing the reality game at the easiest setting: god level. I'm playing at the hard setting: five-foot tall female bisexual combat medic. Now, if he was playing hardcore he'd be an African-American lesbian midget Marine."

Seeing nothing unusual, Pixii waved them up to the street level.

One of the main reasons they'd parked so far out was that the festival screwed up any reasonable attempt to drive through the city. The wide four–lane *Shijo-dori* had been blocked off for twenty or thirty blocks. A small stage had been erected in the middle of the street and a *taiko* group was performing. The big drums throbbed in the afternoon air like a massive heartbeat. Several hundred people stood listening while masses of people continued to stroll up and down the street, roughly a quarter of them in bright-colored *yukata*. Here and there little stands were set up, offering a wide variety of food and festival items.

At Pixii's insistence, they stopped at the first food booth and bought *yakitori*, one skewer of BBQ chicken fresh off the grill for each of them.

Pixii proved that work on the kiln had made her impervious to heat. She took a bite without seeming to notice that the meat was steaming hot. "So, what's this about Gion Matsuri revolving around spears?"

Nikki blew on her chicken to cool it down. "In the ninth century, something like the black plague hit Japan along with several earthquakes and tsunamis. It was decided that evil spirits were the cause, and the Emperor created a ceremony to beg Susanoo for help. He sent an envoy to the Yasaka Shrine to arrange that portable shrines holding the *kama shintai* be carried to the palace. In the meantime, he had sixty-six spears erected around a pond at the palace gardens.

"Jesus," Miriam muttered. "This isn't going to be needle in a haystack, but a needle in a pile of pins."

"Why sixty-six spears?" Pixii said.

"Because at the time, there were sixty-six provinces in Japan. When the shrines arrived at the garden, the spears were dipped into the pond. The basic idea was that a spear represented a particular province, so as that spear was cleansed, the corresponding area was rid of evil spirits."

"Did it work?"

A week ago, she would have laughed at the idea of it "working." She had thought it was a successful publicity stunt and nothing more. "Well enough that they've been holding the festival for a thousand years."

"And you know all this because it's part of your book?" Pixii asked.

"Yes," Nikki said. "The thing is that the festival isn't completely the same. About six hundred years later, one of the shoguns stopped the ritual with the sixty-six spears, but the *Yamaboko Junko* continued."

"So what is *Yamaboko Junko?*" Pixii said.

"It's the parade with the floats," Miriam said.

"Oh!" Pixii rolled her eyes. "D'oh! Yes, I watched it last year. The carts are amazing."

Nikki finished her chicken and glanced around for someplace to throw the stick away. Miriam pointed out an overflowing cardboard box between two food booths.

Nikki licked her fingers clean of the BBQ sauce. "The cart at the head of the parade is the *Naginata Hoko*—the spear float."

Pixii frowned. "So, the heavenly jeweled spear might be at the shrine or on the float or could have been one of the sixty-six spears that disappeared four or five hundred years ago?"

Nikki shrugged. "Or it's somewhere else entirely. It's a wild guess that Iwanaga Hime will find it here in Kyoto—if she hasn't found it already."

They reached the shrine as night fell. By then they had stopped for chilled pickled cucumbers on a stick and grilled corn dipped in soy sauce.

"If we're running on empty, then our blood sugar will drop." Pixii rationalized out the delays. "And then we'll get stupid. Oh! Candied grapes! You've got to try them."

The shrine was full of pools of bright lights and deep shadows. More little stands lined the walkway into the shrine. Nikki wasn't aware at first that they'd crossed over onto holy ground until Atsumori took hold of her hand.

"Oh." She glanced behind her and saw that, yes, there was a *torii* marking the entrance to the shrine.

"There are many gods here tonight, on the eve of this festival." Atsumori tightened his hold on her hand. "The air trembles with their presence. You should be careful."

"Iwanaga Hime?"

"Hush." Atsumori waved her to silence. "To say a god's name aloud is to call their attention to you. Tomorrow, all those enshrined here will be escorted through the city. They have been awakened and readied for their journey."

He meant Susanoo, his wife, and children, who were all enshrined at Yasaka.

"Maybe we should have come up with code names," Nikki said.

"So on top of everything else, we've got—" Miriam caught herself before saying Susanoo's name aloud. "The locals to worry about?" She sighed. "Code speak it is."

"I don't suppose asking where—it—is would be smart." Pixii had gotten a chocolate-covered banana while Nikki wasn't paying attention. "It would be like accusing—him—of stealing—it."

They all nodded—that seemed particularly unwise.

At the foot of the hills surrounding Kyoto, the shrine's grounds sloped gently upwards into woods. Trees screened off the city, and it suddenly felt like Yamauchi's mountain—as if they'd stumbled into a god's private pocket world. The buildings were all frame and stucco, freshly whitewashed and trimmed in brilliant orange. Details of the molding in the eaves were all done in gold leaf that shone in spotlights, seeming to be islands of tranquility in a sea of darkness.

The *kaguraden* was lit up by hundreds of paper lanterns, strung into three tiers around the roof of the open stage. Only as they drew close, and the crowds parted, did Nikki realize that the *mikoshi* were out for display on the dance floor. The three portable shrines were elaborate gold-leaf miniature houses with little bell turrets, domed roofs and festooned with red tassels. A stylized phoenix crowned the *mikoshi*, tail spread like a peacock's to make a sunburst in gold. Tomorrow after the parade, the three *mikoshi* would be taken through the town, giving the gods a tour of the city. By now, surely Susanoo, his wife, Kushinada, and his sons were enshrined in the little golden shrines. She couldn't tell them apart; they looked identical to her. The centermost one seemed like it should be the one that would hold the most honored position.

"Are they home?" she whispered to Atsumori.

"Depends on your definition of home. This is their shrine."

He meant the entire shrine, not just the tiny portable ones.

"Oh." She scanned the courtyard. When Atsumori had said that there were gods present, she had thought he meant in a less active method than out walking around. There was a line of people at each of the pull-ropes to ring the prayer bells. There were children darting through the crowds, intent on their own missions. The vendors shouted their wares as they expertly cooked their food. Noh actors were on a smaller side-stage area, in the middle of some story that involved a warrior hero and an old couple imploring him for help involving their beautiful daughter. The audience all had video cameras held up so they could capture the action.

With a flash and a puff of smoke, the daughter disappeared. The hero picked up a huge elaborate hair comb that sat in her place and showed it off. Nikki realized that the play was Susanoo fighting the eight-headed serpent. He'd just transformed his wife into a comb to put into his hair. He wanted her to see how brave he was in battle, even though his plan was to disguise himself as her and get the serpent drunk before fighting it. The whole comb thing took the fight from clever to insanely screwball.

Maybe we should go and come back tomorrow night, when the mikoshi *are housed at the city center.*

Someone suddenly caught hold of her free hand and tugged her through the crowd.

"Hey!" she cried and tried to pull free, but she was held fast. Then she recognized the person dragging her through the crowd. He—*she* was wearing a *yukata* instead of a schoolboy uniform and her hair was longer, but the face was the same. It was Inari. "What are you doing here?"

Inari laughed. "Do you not know anything with which you're meddling?"

"No!"

Inari laughed again. "I have big ears, and I've been hearing all the trouble you've been stirring up. I know both of you are young, but you need to act with more caution. Do not disturb my father."

Nikki opened her mouth and then snapped it shut as she realized who "father" had to be. Inari meant Susanoo. They reached the great gate, and Inari surprised her by continuing down the steps to where bronze foo lions stood guard.

"Go." Inari pointed at a Lawson's Convenience Store across the street. "Go."

And while she was trying to come up some reason to stay so that Miriam and Pixii could find her, Atsumori went and she found herself crossing the road.

"Yes, yes, I know I said I would not do this, but listen to me, Nikki-chan. I did not sense the weapon within the shrine. There is nothing great or holy beyond that which resonates with those who are enshrined there—which the spear would not. There is no reason for us to stay and argue."

Nikki fumed but realized that the crosswalk signal had flicked on the moment that Inari had pointed across the street, clearing the way for her. She sighed but finished walking to the other corner. There was an actual glass phone booth just a few feet from the crosswalk. Wondering if Inari had somehow magicked it there, she stalked to the phone booth.

Miriam was keeping her phone turned off so Sato and his goons couldn't track her with it. Luckily, Pixii was still off the radar.

Pixii answered her phone on the first ring. "*Moshi moshi?*"

"It's me."

"Where the hell did you go?"

"I got kicked out of the shrine by a cross-dressing god."

There was a long pause. Then, "Are you okay?"

"Oh, I'm fine. I'm across the street at the Lawson's. Atsumori says . . ." Nikki paused, remembering that Pixii was still inside the shrine grounds and thus the need for code speak remained. "Atsumori says what we're looking for isn't there but everyone is out and about, enjoying the crowd—so you should be careful."

"Eeek, okay. I'll grab SexyNinja and be there in five."

Nikki hung up and stared at the phone. While they were here in Kyoto, she should try to call Ananth. No. Not yet. They still hadn't found the spear. They shouldn't use a phone so close to Susanoo's shrine. It would blast "we know what you're doing" loud and clear to Sato as he intercepted the call. And certainly not right after calling Pixii.

✠ 32 ✠
Shrine Maiden

Nikki went to Lawson's to wait for Miriam and Pixii. Apparently being across the street from a major shrine made the entire area vaguely holy—or maybe it was Kyoto in general—or maybe Atsumori was somehow god of convenience stores. Either way, Atsumori would randomly appear as she moved through the store. She tried hard to ignore him.

The store was doing a brisk trade in drinks, reminding her that while she'd eaten, she hadn't had anything to drink yet. The bottled water made her think of Leo. While fumbling through her cloth purse for money, she ended up holding on to a pen.

She could write. Just a little bit. Just to see if he was okay. That he wasn't thirsty.

There was a startled squeak behind her. She turned to see a girl staring at Atsumori as he set a Weebles Wobble doll rocking.

"Stop that!" she hissed without thinking.

The girl glanced to Nikki, and her eyes went wider with fear. She started to back away.

Nikki looked behind to verify that no monsters were creeping up behind her. Nothing. At least that she could see. What was so scary about her?

"*Sumimasen.*" She apologized, although she wasn't sure for exactly what. The girl was still backing away, looking horrified.

And then it clicked. The only group of strangers looking for her was Sato's people. Well, Shiva and her mother—but they wouldn't be using a teenage girl with a shrine maiden's bowl haircut. She had the same too-pale, faintly bruised look as Simon. She had to be one of the girls who Iwanaga Hime was burning through. It might even the owner of the bag.

Nikki pointed at the girl. "*Umeko Kuroki desu?*"

The squeak of fear seemed to confirm Nikki was right. Umeko dropped the bag of chips she been holding and bolted for the door.

"No!" Nikki dashed after her.

The poor thing was staggering before she got a dozen feet down the street from Lawson's. She whimpered as Nikki caught up with her. There was an opening to a courtyard beside the store. Nikki dragged the weeping girl into the darkness.

"I'm not going to—oh damn—Atsumori! Help."

"I'm trying to, but she's more solid than I expected. She would have to invite me in."

Which meant that probably all the girls Iwanaga had burned out had volunteered.

"Why?" Nikki's horrified question came out in Atsumori's lower pitch. "Why are you helping her?"

"We have to!" Umeko dropped to her knees and sobbed out the words. "She came to Kirishima Shrine and talked with Konohana Sakuya Hime. She scolded her younger sister, berating her for not helping her all these years. Konohana Sakuya Hime gathered us together and said that we were to serve her older sister as if she was her. She said we were like blossoms, fated to grace the world with our beauty and then fade much too young."

"She gave you to her sister?" Nikki would have to have a long talk with Atsumori about family trees. Who exactly was Iwanaga's sister? For that matter, was Susanoo really Inari's father? Was all this nothing more than a family feud of epic proportions?

"It is the only help that Konohana Sakuya Hime could risk," Umeko said. "If she did more, Amaterasu Omikami would be angered."

"And you went along with this?" Nikki cried.

"I had to! My family has served Konohana Sakuya Hime for a hundred and ten generations. My mother couldn't conceive a child, so she came to Kyoto and visited Umenomiya Shrine and prayed to Konohana Sakuya Hime for a child and stepped over Matage-ishi.

That's why I was born—because our princess blessed my mother with a child. I owe my life to Konohana Sakuya Hime."

"You don't owe anyone! It's your life. You don't just give it away! Iwanaga is going to kill you."

"Because you took the *gaijin* away!" Umeko wailed. "She had him and she barely needed us."

"He wasn't hers to take," Nikki snapped. "She was killing him. It was just a matter of time."

"Give the girl to us!" Umeko caught hold of the skirt of Nikki's *yukata*. "Please, *kami*, she only had to call your name and you stepped right into her. Let us have her in the *gaijin*'s place. You have your sword—you have no need of her."

Nikki pressed her lips tight on Atsumori's snarl of anger. *Think! The girl is off-guard and talking. What do I really need to know?*

Doubtful this girl knew where Leo was, but she might know about the spear.

"Where's the heavenly bejeweled spear?" Nikki asked.

"I don't know! We've been looking everywhere for it. We've been checking every one of his shrines. One of his priests carried his *shintai* from Hiromine to Kyoto in the eighteenth year of Jogan. A hundred years later, the Emperor devised the ritual of the spear. It has to be here in Kyoto!"

Still, they were talking about a thousand years where the spear could have been shifted by anyone. Well, someone who could see it, which made the numbers fewer. Kyoto was a city full of shrines; surely it was equally full of divinely gifted people. Then again—Susanoo was probably fiercely guarding his prize.

At least Sato and Iwanaga were at the same point as they were.

"Go home and tell your goddess that her sister is going to destroy the world."

"She knows! She says nothing in the world lasts forever, not even the world itself."

Nikki wanted to scream in frustration and anger. This wasn't helping Leo! With the spear still lost, he was all she could think about and yet she wasn't getting any closer to him. She wanted to know he was okay, that she hadn't killed him with neglect.

"We should kill her," Atsumori said.

"No!" Nikki snapped.

"She will tell them . . ."

"That we know what they're doing. Yes, yes, but they're already looking for us."

"That we are in Kyoto on Shijo-dori," Atsumori finished. "*Tanuki* can track with their noses, and they cannot be that far away. We would have to fight or flee the city."

A sword fight in this jostling crowd of people? And if the *tanuki* had guns again?

"And you can't take her over?" Nikki asked just to be sure.

Atsumori was silent a moment before answering. "I cannot take her over without her consent, but I believe I can make her forget this conversation, that she ever saw us."

"Will it hurt her?"

"Not as much as beheading her."

Point taken.

Nikki stood in the shadowed courtyard with the teenage girl sobbing at her feet. How did it all come to this? She didn't want to hurt this girl. Their choices were "bad" and "worse."

"Make her forget," Nikki whispered.

It started to rain gently, as if the sky were weeping along with Umeko.

Atsumori took the girl's head in their hands, tipped it back, and leaned down to kiss her forehead. She smelled faintly of flowers. She was trembling within their hold, tears slipping hotly over their fingers. Nikki closed her eyes, not wanting to see Umeko's fear. She felt her lips touch the shrine maiden's feverish dry skin.

Umeko jerked and gave a quiet high whine. Nikki whimpered in sympathy. The trembling became shaking. And then the girl gasped—more from surprise than pain—and went limp.

They eased her onto the ground. Atsumori tried to turn away, but Nikki forced them to stay and check her pulse. It beat strong at the column of her neck.

"She will awake momentarily," Atsumori whispered. "We must be away quickly."

She found Miriam and Pixii at Lawson's. She was trying to keep her face neutral, but they both hugged her tight without a word.

"We need to get away from here, now," she said.

They didn't ask questions. They nodded and they went.

✣ 33 ✣
Naginata Hoko

A mile down Shijo-dori, across the shallow Gion River, and in the heart of Kyoto center, they found the *Naginata Hoko*. It sat at the intersection of Shijo-dori and Karasuma-dori, a few blocks from where the parade would officially start in the morning. It was a three-story-tall wooden cart. The black wooden wheels alone were taller than Nikki. Painted bright red, it was hung with rich colorful tapestries showing *kirin* galloping through clouds. Tucked up under a peaked roof, a dozen musicians clad in white and blue *yukata*s perched on the edge of the cart, their backs to the crowd. They were playing chimes along with drums and a shrill flute. There were ribbons attached to their instruments that trailed down over the sides of the float to large bells and brilliant-colored tassels that jumped and leaped like fish on a line with every bright chime of their instruments.

A sixty-foot-tall halberd towered straight up from the roof into the dark night.

They stood staring at it as the crowd moved around them.

"It's not the real one," Miriam said.

"Nope, it's just a big old pole," Pixii said. "Right?"

Still they turned to Nikki, or more accurately, to Atsumori, for confirmation. "It is merely a decoration."

"Thank God," Nikki breathed. There would be no way they could move it. None of the photos that Nikki had seen had captured the size of the float. In order to get the entire spear into the frame, a photographer would have to be nearly a city block away. Up close, the scale was intimidating. "Is the real one that big?"

"I do not believe so." Atsumori didn't sound sure. "Kusanagi was used by . . ."

Three pairs of hands slapped over Nikki's mouth. "Omph!"

Cautiously all the hands retreated as Miriam and Pixii promised more violence with their eyes.

"Code speak!" Pixii growled.

Atsumori huffed slightly. "He who shall not be mentioned and was not going to be mentioned used Kusanagi as a sword. As did several other less heavenly figures. It is part of the imperial regalia, and there has never been any mention of it being outlandishly large."

"Point taken," Pixii said.

"*Tanuki*. A pack, I think." Miriam caught their arms and started them down Shijo-dori toward the other floats staged for the morning parade. Each was lit by a pair of metal frameworks supporting seven strands of large paper lanterns. Everything was discreetly sheeted with plastic to protect against the rain.

As they moved down the street, Nikki realized that a set of stairs and a walkway had been built beside the three-story float so festivalgoers could tour it. Some of the *tanuki* were already climbing the steps to search the *Naginata Hoko* from the inside.

"Are you sure it's not there?" Nikki asked.

"I am sure," Atsumori said.

There were thirty-two floats in all, spread throughout the heart of Kyoto like little keyholes into the past. Nikki had been in Kyoto the week before to see them being constructed from scratch. At that time they'd been nothing but big frames of lumber and coils of jute rope as no nails were used in building the floats. In a week, they'd been transformed. Elaborately carved and gilded pieces had been added to the framework. Rich silk tapestries hid all the rough wood. Paint, statues, small trees, and a multitude of rich finishing touches had changed them in ways she hadn't imagined, despite her research.

Somehow she'd missed the existence of *Fune Hoko*, a massive wooden boat on wheels. Its bow had a golden phoenix larger than her with wings outspread. There was a tree on the roof of the *Minami-kannon Yama* that looked twenty feet tall. *Houka Hoko* had a wind-up doll that could dance. *Kamakiri Yama* had a giant praying mantis that moved its legs and spread its wings. There were dozens of larger-than-life statues, some of them five or six hundred years old.

The floats all had aged wooden boards explaining the story behind the float. Neither Nikki nor Pixii could read the text, which left the translating to Miriam. The sign for *Kakkyo Yama* had Miriam shaking her head.

"What?"

"Oh, what I've always liked about the Japanese is that they acknowledge it's all real. In the United States, if I talked about a ghost roaming the dormitory, everyone would think I was making it up or I was crazy or something. I was afraid to even tell you. Here, it's like they've never closed their ears to the truth and refused to listen to the people who could see what's really there."

Miriam's obsession with Japan suddenly made sense. Nikki wondered if it was the same reason Pixii was in the country. If so, then all three of them had a secret sisterhood of escaping to Japan so they wouldn't be labeled as crazy.

"Why are you shaking your head?" Nikki said.

"This float tells the story of Kakkyo. He was too poor to feed his mother in a manner that he wished, so he and his wife decided that they would bury their three-year-old alive in the mountains. That way they could afford to take care of his mother. Their reasoning? They could always have another child, but they only had one mother. Luckily, as they dug a hole, they found a golden axe."

"Oh my God." The float had two statues, one man in a dark kimono and the other a smiling child. Did the scene show the two before or after daddy tried to kill the little boy?

"It makes me wonder," Miriam said. "Is it really a good thing to glorify magic like that? Take your kid into the mountains, dig a hole, bury them alive—you might get a rich reward."

"The danger of belief," Pixii said.

Miriam nodded. "Of all the countless stories to tell, why pick this one?"

"Someone loved their mother more than I do," Nikki said.

Each float had stalls run by the neighborhood that sponsored it.

They were selling good luck charms and talismans wrapped in bamboo leaves. The *Housho Yama* were selling love knot charms. Nikki bought one shyly despite being teased by Miriam and Pixii teasing her.

They crossed and re-crossed Shijo-dori, weaving through thick crowds, to hit all the floats. It felt like they'd walked for miles as the rain sprinkled on them lightly. Judging by the density of the crowds and the distance they walked, there had to be hundreds of thousands of people in Kyoto, all celebrating the event. Eventually the rain started to come down more heavily.

They stopped under an overhang, soaked to the skin. Pixii surprised Nikki by pressing a hand to her neck and then tilting her head down to look her in the eye.

"He's all that's keeping you upright, isn't he?"

"Huh?" Nikki stared at her, not understanding.

"She was shot a few days ago," Atsumori said.

"Oh, shut up." Nikki knew the reaction that was going to get.

"Shot!" Pixii made a noise of disgust. "And you didn't tell us about that part? That's it. We're getting someplace to stay for a few hours."

Nikki shook her head at the possibility. "The parade is tomorrow morning. Every place sold out months ago. And if we use our passports to check in, Shiva and Sato will know where we are."

Miriam laughed. "If you've forgotten to add your mother to that list, then you're really out of it." She held out her hand to Pixii. "Let me borrow your phone. I don't call myself SexyNinja for nothing. I am Master of Google Fu! If it's out there, I will find it!"

"I'll check in with my *gaijin* card," Pixii said. "They don't need to know you're in the room. Find a big place with lots of people coming and going—not a small family run place."

"Bingo!" Miriam said after several minutes of muttering. "There's one opening at Hotel Granvia Kyoto on the top floor. Someone must have cancelled. We'll have to pay through the nose, but it will be worth it."

The name sounded familiar. "That's at the train station?"

"Yes, it will be perfect. Lots of coming and going."

✠ 34 ✠
Third Eye

Pixii checked in. Miriam and Nikki waited for a crowd of returning festivalgoers to come hurrying in from the rain and walked through the lobby with them. Pixii met them on the elevator, squeezing in. She used the room key to get them to their floor after the other guests had gotten off at lower levels.

Nikki whimpered as she pulled her notebook from her purse and discovered it was waterlogged, the ink smearing on the page. "I want to write about Leo. Make sure he's okay. Try to find him."

"There should be paper in the room," Miriam said.

"I'll run out and find another notebook," Pixii promised.

The room was a blur as they hunted for the hotel stationery. It was a mere two sheets and two envelopes of creamy, amazingly rich paper. She sat at the desk and lost herself to the writing.

The goods news was that he wasn't dead yet, which meant Shiva wasn't sure what was going on. Williams had gone off to investigate and hadn't come back. Somewhere much chaos had to be ensuing, but he wasn't sure what it meant for him except he had gone a day now without water. Surely this time they didn't mean to kill him through just locking him up and walking away. He didn't know which stronghold he was in, but normally they were all manned well enough that prisoners didn't die of neglect. Beheading? Silver bullet? Stake through the heart? Cremated alive? Yes. Dehydration? No.

What was happening in the levels upstairs? Why hadn't been anyone been down to check on him? Leo tested the bars. The cage had been built with someone like him in mind. He couldn't break free. Growling with frustration and anger, he settled in to wait and pray that Williams would actually come back with better news.

Nikki clicked her pen, re-reading what she had written, trying to find clues that weren't on the page. By his wristwatch, it was tomorrow, either nine in the morning or nine at night. He was in a bare cell without a toilet. There was a three-inch drain cemented into the floor; he'd been forced to piss like an animal. He had no access to water. The door was electronically locked, requiring a key card to open. His cell was lit by a lone spotlight, the fixture outside the cage, beyond his reach. His mouth was dry as sandpaper, and his eyes were gritty from dehydration, but he was ignoring the symptoms.

Miriam came to read over her shoulder. "You're getting more control."

"What?"

"When we first met, you'd scribble for hours before you could stop. And the prose would be all over the map, stuff about the how the steel of the axe head had been forged, about the tree that grew in the woods before it was made into an axe handle, and oh yes, how the axe itself is now buried in the head of the main character. This is light years beyond what you could do then, but it's even more controlled than two months ago."

Nikki could laugh about that now. When they first met, writing was something her fingers did of their own accord, flooding her mind with insanity. All the doctors had focused on the fingers moving. Miriam was the first to help her focus on the story, weed out the insanity and leave something more than just disobedient digits. To find the truth in the madness.

"Knowing what you're doing," Miriam said. "It helps, doesn't it?"

Nikki laughed slightly. "Oh, it didn't seem like it at first—with dead bodies, gods and *yokai* popping up everywhere—but since then, yeah, actually. The world is more off-kilter than I suspected, but I'm not crazy. I'm better than not crazy. I'm not helpless. I can see through time and space and know the truth." She spread her hand on the paper. If she focused, she could still sense the rhythm of Leo's angry breathing. "And somehow, I will figure out how to save Leo. Save everyone."

"Cool." Miriam grinned. "Do you know what would be really great? If you could figure out how to do it without writing everything down."

Nikki squinted. Could she? Certainly there had been moments in Leo's car when she didn't have to be moving her pen to see the characters moving across the distant stage. Could she wean herself from needing the pen and paper? Could she stop moving her fingers completely? After a lifetime of fighting it, was the answer to embrace the ability totally?

Miriam hugged her tight. "Why don't you take a hot shower and a nap? You're not going to be able to save anyone if you collapse."

There was a flash of lightning outside, lighting the night. She looked out the rain-smeared window. Leo was safe for now. A few hours rest and then what? She needed to fix this somehow. If she didn't upset Iwanaga and Sato's plans, her novel would barrel on, taking out every single person she had written about and thousands, if not millions, of others. Finding the spear first might derail Iwanaga, but she didn't know what she would do with the spear if they found it.

Proving that her friends truly knew her, Pixii returned with ten Campus notebooks, two pens of every color, Post-In Notes in a dozen different colors, four Cokes, and a fistful of Snickers bars. Nikki woke to find them spread across the foot of her bed like Christmas presents. She fingered the trappings of her hypergraphia with mixed emotions. A divine gift, Atsumori called her ability. It seemed to imply that she was channeling the power of the gods. It felt good to know she wasn't insane. That she wasn't helpless.

Yet she wasn't even sure where to start.

"Okay, it's a novel. I've been doing this all my life. Writer's Block 101: re-visualize the storyline. Post-It notes or colored pens?" Taking a long swig of Coke, she considered her weapons. "Post-It notes!" She tore open a Snickers and bit savagely down on the candy bar. "Plain yellow only!" She drained the first Coke and picked up a red pen. "Time to channel the divine!"

She quickly wrote the name of a character on the top sheet of the pad, pulled it free, and stuck it to the wall. Gregory—dead. Misa—dead. Harada—dead. Kenichi—fleeing to Tokyo, hopefully—no, he *was* safely in Tokyo. Simon—safe but exhausted. Dozens of names—most of them wrong, but all of them representing real people.

When she was done, she studied the wall, looking for some hidden connections, some clue where the story was going, how to change it, how to stop it.

It still didn't help.

She paced back and forth, glaring at the pieces of paper. She had forgotten Leo. Reluctantly she added him, and then herself, and then even more reluctantly Miriam.

"And me." Atsumori's voice made her jump.

She swore softly and added him to the wall. "Wait," she whispered. She was missing a lot of characters.

Pixii. Chevalier. Sato. Ananth. Williams. Umeko.

She went to add Yamauchi and realized she was running low on plain yellow and used dark blue and black pen for the mountain god. And then she swapped Atsumori to blue too. Inari. Iwanaga. Konohana Sukuya—mistress of the doomed shrine maidens. He that couldn't be mentioned.

She paused a moment and started to re-sort the yellow notes around the blues. She was with Atsumori. Pixii with Yamauchi. Simon? With Yamauchi. Sato with Iwanaga. Umeko joining together the two goddess sisters.

The twins with Susanoo . . .

She stopped and then slowly backed away from the wall.

She'd put the twins and Susanoo at the center of a hurricane. Everything spiraled in toward the two little boys.

"Oh shit."

She supposed it could only be expected; the twins had both been in the running to be chosen as the celestial child. In a few hours Haru would cut a rope that stretched across Shijo-dori to start the parade and then ride in the *Naginata Hoko*. The thousand-year-old float was the center of the entire celebration, and it was believed that it would cleanse the country of evil spirits. The *tanuki* had already checked it out at least once. The girls had narrowly missed being seen by the pack that obviously crawled all over the float looking for . . .

Narrowly missed.

"Oh! Oh! Oh!" She dived at the stuff from her wet purse laid out to dry.

"Is that a good *oh* or a bad *oh?*" Pixii mumbled from the bed.

"It's a bad *oh!*" She had brought Simon's passport and wallet with her to Kyoto on some off chance that she had to prove to someone in Shiva that she knew what had happened to him. "Possibly a very bad *oh.*"

There was a grunt from the lump that was Miriam.

Nikki had discovered that people were like dominos. If they were too far apart when they fell, then they didn't influence the path of characters you expected them to impact. If a body were dumped in the woods, it could be months before someone found it. A husband on a business trip wouldn't realize his wife and children had been butchered until he got home. A serial killer could choose a victim and stalk her, but a grandfather's death on the other side of the country could yank her out of danger.

It was one thing for characters to meet if only one of them was in motion; if both were moving, it was like trying figure out when subatomic particles collided.

Simon was very well traveled; there were dozens of stamps showing him entering and leaving countries around the world. At the end was the stamp that showed him entering Japan. Leo said that Simon had disappeared two months ago . . .

Miriam and Pixii came to eye the wall.

"What did you find?" Pixii said.

"Simon landed on June first late in the day." Nikki waved his passport as proof. "According to the scene I wrote, he waited until the next day to go to Izushi by train, and he didn't get there until nearly dark. The next morning was when he called Leo from the construction site. It means that he was taken by Iwanaga on June third."

She took out purple Post-It Notes and started to number them. "Three." She slapped it onto the wall slightly above her head. "Iwanaga's at Izushi's at dusk."

"Four." She put the next one at shoulder level. "She's in Osaka with Kenichi."

"Five." Nikki stuck the note nearly at floor level. "She and Kenichi go to visit her sister in Kirishima Shrine—which is at the foot of Mount Kirishima on the island of Kyushu. Kirishima, which I only know since the silly thing erupted a few years ago, is one of the farthest points south you can get short of Okinawa. It takes her the whole day to get down there by train. I don't have a scene of this, but Kenichi bitched about it later because she used his money to get them there and back."

"Six." It, too, went near floor level. "Her sister gathers together her shrine maidens and tells them that they're going to Osaka. She gives them a day to get ready. Seven. The shrine maidens head north, taking all day to return to Osaka. Proof: the *Shikansen* ticket that was in Umeko's student ID holder."

Nikki put the purple seven at waist level to indicate travel. She took out one of the orange Post-It Notes and wrote seven on it and put it at eye level. "Also on the seventh is the first event of Gion Matsuri in Kyoto."

Miriam shook her head. "I still don't get the—Oh! Oh, holy shit!"

"The light goes on," Pixii said. "But I'm still in the dark."

"After the seventh, Iwanaga sends out all but one of her shrine maidens to every shrine that she thinks has a remote chance of holding the spear. They've had over a month to cross off hundreds of possibilities. They would have started with his shrines and worked down through his kids' and anyone with half a chance of maybe holding onto it for him as a favor. But they didn't find shit."

Nikki tapped the orange Post-It Note. "Haru is picked to be Chigo, the celestial child for the *Naginata Hoko* on the seventh. It starts a five-week-long ordeal for him and his twin brother, Nobu. Haru is fitted for clothes and taught what to do in half a dozen ceremonies. He goes through multiple purification rituals. He's isolated from their mother and sisters. At a certain point he's not even allowed to touch the ground—he's carried like a god."

"The thing is—they're always in motion. A moving target is difficult to hit. The shrine maidens search all the Kyoto shrines, but they don't find anything."

Pixii nodded, seeing her point. "Because the boys are never in the same place they are."

"Inari probably made sure of it," Nikki said, remembering how Inari practically flung her at Umeko. He'd dragged Nikki out of the shrine and pointed across the street at the store where Umeko was shopping. How many other times had he influenced her prior to that moment? Was their first meeting really at Inari's Shrine or had the god been manipulating her life longer than that? The biggest weird coincidence had been Officer Yoshida sitting down beside her after being at Gregory's murder scene and overhearing her talk of George's murder. Had Inari engineered that collision point?

"We know that the spear isn't on the *Naginata Hoko*," Nikki said. "But the legend says that the float defeats evil spirits as it is paraded through Kyoto. Not before the procession. Not after the procession. During. Assuming that the spear in question is the heavenly bejeweled spear, one has to reason that it will be on that float."

Miriam gasped. "Haru is the only thing that isn't on the *Naginata Hoko* tonight that would be on it tomorrow!"

"Right."

"Couldn't it be just the clothes?" Pixii said. "They dress him up like one of those dolls. There's the gold phoenix crown and the makeup and the entire ceremonial Shinto robes."

"Or he who can't be mentioned might have just replaced Haru," Miriam said. "He had this contest of power with his sister. Each took an item belonging to the other and 'birthed' people out of them. She created three women out of his sword, and he formed five men out of her necklace. If that wasn't freaky weird enough, one of the men was the grandfather of the first emperor."

Nikki winced and tried to not let that little data point distract her. "I would know if he had replaced one of the boys. Something would have changed in my book. Either I wouldn't have been able to write Nobu's point of view or there would be all sorts of foreshadowing that something really weird was going on with Haru."

"Okay, that's spooky weird," Miriam said. "But yeah, Nobu didn't read any different, and he didn't notice any change in Haru."

"And it's not the clothes," Nikki said. "If it was just the clothes, they'd put them in a box and parade them around."

"Yes, that's the Japanese for you," Pixii said.

Nikki tapped Haru's name on the wall. "For a thousand years, they've gone through the bother of picking a child from some of the oldest and most powerful families in Kyoto. And then they treat them like gods for a month."

"So—what—he who won't be mentioned hides it on him?" Pixii guessed. "Where? Why?"

Miriam picked up a pen and notebook. "Couldn't—couldn't you just write and find out?"

Nikki considered the pen and paper. "I guess I could."

Haru's stomach was full of crazy looping butterflies of fear. It was dawn on a weekday, and the Yasaka Shrine had been completely empty when they entered. The trees had screened off the streets and muffled the noise of the traffic. He found the silence unnerving, like the god had gathered them close and now held them lightly in the palm of his hand. He tried not to be scared when the priest told him to go into the *haiden* and wait alone.

Haru pressed his hands together as if he were holding his cell phone and was texting his twin. He did it in class sometimes, since this year they weren't in the same room and they weren't allowed to use their phones in school.

Wish you were born first, Haru pretended to text his brother. *It's silly that I get everything because of five minutes. You're much braver than me. Why was I picked for this? You would have been better at it.*

Of course, his brother would text back a collection of *kanji* that was nonsense but made a funny face. Nobu didn't like to admit that he didn't know something, so it was the only answer he could give.

Haru moved his fingers on the phantom keypad. *I'm scared.*

"There is no reason to be scared," a man said.

Haru looked up. He hadn't heard the man enter the worship hall. He was a tall young man in a regal kimono. He settled in front of Haru with the rough ease of a farmer. He had big strong hands and wide shoulders, but his face was as handsome as a model's. Maybe he was an actor.

"I'm not," Haru lied.

The man smiled. "That's good. Tell me, do you know the story of the eight-headed serpent?"

Haru nodded. He'd been carefully coached on how to answer these questions since his name went into the pool of possible celestial children from his neighborhood. "Susanoo was in Izumo when he came across an old man and woman crying over their daughter. When he asked, they told him that they had eight daughters, but all but the youngest had been eaten. Soon a great serpent would come and eat her, too, and there was nothing they could do."

"Nothing that they could do," the man whispered. "What an awful thing, to be so helpless. Do you not think?"

Haru had not considered it before. He slowly nodded.

"To lose all your siblings that way. To know that your death is approaching. To hear it move in the darkness. To know it's coming for you. My beloved still has nightmares of it."

Haru wasn't sure what they were talking about anymore. The man had the blackest eyes he'd ever seen. "Eh?"

"When you save someone, you don't really fully save them. They stay afraid because they were helpless before you arrived, they were helpless while you saved them, and they were helpless after you killed the beast. The only way you can truly save someone is to let them save themselves."

Somehow this seemed to suggest something awful for him. "What exactly am I saving myself from?"

"Monsters," the man whispered. "I know that you can see them. Some of them act like people. Wear clothes. Buy smokes. Walk the streets at night. You know they're real."

Haru froze.

"You don't have to be afraid of me," the man said gently. "The festival is so all the monsters that cause earthquakes, tsunamis, flood and famine and diseases can be quelled. They want me to do it."

Haru realized in the depths of those dark eyes, lightning flickered. He looked down and struggled to breathe. This was Susanoo himself right here beside him. Talking to him.

"If I do it," Susanoo said, "it will solve nothing."

Haru forgot his fear. "You're not going to do it? You have to! They say that the Great East Japan Earthquake and the tsunami were because the festival went wrong that year."

Susanoo grinned and reached out to tap him on the nose. "You are going to do it."

"Me?"

"You." Susanoo tapped him again on the nose. "You are not as helpless as you think. Heaven shimmers within you. It's why you can see the monsters when no one else can. It is why I chose you and not your brother. All you need is a little boost—so you know what it feels like not to be helpless."

Haru's heart felt like it was trying to climb up his throat and run away. "I don't understand."

"You will." Susanoo pressed his finger against Haru's left check. "Left is for the girl child. The right is for the boy . . ."

Haru blinked furiously. He was alone in the *haiden* of Yasaka Shrine. The conversation that had been so vivid was fading at the edges, like he had just woken from a dream. His right eye burned slightly, but as he blinked, the feeling went away. He didn't feel any different. Had he just imagined Susanoo?

Nikki lifted her pen from the paper. "Oh my God, he hid it in his eye."

"It's just like how Inuyasha's father hid his sword." Miriam named the famous manga character. "But I think it was the other eye."

Nikki nodded. "If Susanoo has done this to every celestial child since the start of the festival, he's been at it for a thousand years. Someone is bound to have picked up on it."

"Oh yeah, and that one clan in Naruto," Pixii said.

"That's . . ." Miriam motioned at her eye and then caught herself before going off on a fangirl rant. "That's totally different."

Nikki looked at the wall and back at the paper. "This was weeks ago, just after their names were picked. All my other scenes with the twins are from Nobu's viewpoint. There wasn't any mention of this."

Miriam nodded. "Nobu was all about learning the stupid dance."

"Oh no," Nikki cried. "That's right. They were going to switch places. Nobu was learning the dance so he could take Haru's place."

"But if Haru has the spear . . ." Pixii said.

"Then the spear won't be on the float," Nikki said.

Had the twins switched places? Was it Nobu on the float, the unknowing target? She knew him better. Nobu was a boy with an irrepressible smile and fierce protectiveness of his brother. Nikki realized now that part of Haru's "fearful nature" was the fact that he could see the monsters that roamed Japan freely while Nobu couldn't. And like Miriam, Haru had chosen not to tell even the person closest to him about what he saw.

Nikki clicked her pen, considering Nobu. Thinking of him was filling her with unease, the kind that normally accompanied a character's death. "Something is going to happen to Nobu."

Miriam glanced at the clock between the beds. "The parade just started. If the boys switched, then Nobu is being carried to the float. It would be a good time for Iwanaga's people to grab him."

If the boys switched. Nobu assumed that they would, but he didn't know that Susanoo had put the weight of Japan on Haru's shoulders. To Nobu, the entire festival was supposed to be nothing but an extended party, and he was miserable that his brother wasn't enjoying it with him.

Nikki pressed the tip of her pen to the paper, and a window opened in her mind's eye. Nobu was watching the parade from the deserted community hall, sulking. He'd been there as everyone involved with the *Naginata Hoko* prepared for the parade. The two-story storefront tucked between two tall office buildings had seethed with nearly a hundred people scrambling to get ready. It had been controlled chaos as almost everyone involved had been part of the preservation committee for generations. All the gear possibily needed to roll the ten-ton cart several miles through the city was readied and double-checked. The musicians climbed through the second-story window and into the cart and started to play. The men who had positions on the cart's roof scrambled up like monkeys. The pulling team drank water, went to the bathroom one last time, and then assembled out on the street.

Nobu had tried to take his brother's place. In the confusion, it would have been easy. Not even their father could easily tell which one was which when they were pulling a switch. Haru stepped forward when they held out the ceremonial clothes and let them dress him up and apply the heavy white makeup until he looked like the dolls that all the other floats had instead of real children. When they were done, their father carried Haru away on his shoulder.

Nobu watched alone as the floats went past, following after the *Naginata Hoko*. He was going to be scolded later for not moving to where he'd be able to see Haru do the Taihei-no-mai dance that they'd practiced together. Nobu's phone was silent, but he *knew* that Haru would be still nervously tapping away messages, trying to tell him how scared he was, up on the high float, with hundreds of thousands of people looking at him.

✳ ✳ ✳

Nikki lifted her pen.

All seemed peaceful—just a little boy sulking in an empty building. If it were a movie, however, the music would already be ominous, warning that a monster lurked in the shadows, tensing to strike. What was going to happen?

Her writing was a divine gift. She could see, if she tried hard enough. She just needed to jump forward in time. She lowered her pen again.

Nobu cried out as the claw caught him under the ribcage and tore upwards . . .

Nikki jerked back from the paper. "Oh no!" She dropped the pen and the notebook. She could feel the pain, the fear, the hot spill of blood . . . She whimpered, holding on to her stomach where the claw had struck.

"Easy." Miriam caught her and held her. "Is it Nobu? Is he at the parade?"

Nikki pointed at the paper and then realized she had only written the single sentence. "He's at the community center."

"The what?" Miriam said.

Nikki pressed palms to her eyes and forced herself to think past the flash of death to the peaceful scene that she had seen moments before. "The community center on Shijo-dori. It's like the *Naginata Hoko* clubhouse as far as I can tell. Something happens after the parade starts. Something comes after him."

"If we hurry, we can save him."

Nikki wasn't sure—so far she'd never been able to change a scene once it had been written.

✠ 35 ✠
Display of Faith

The subway was packed, and everyone got off at the Shijo-dori stop. As a solid wall of people, they moved out of the subway station and onto a sidewalk even more crowded. They were only a few buildings down from the community hall, but they had to push and shove their way through the crowd to reach the building.

The door was shut but wasn't locked.

The room beyond was still set up as a stall for *Yoiyama*. Unsold charms and tickets to tour the *Naginata Hoko* were scattered across tables and the floor. A dozen children in dark *yukata* were rooting through boxes and closets in the back of the room. They jerked about to stare at Nikki with black eyes.

"Nobu!" She called out, weirdly sure that none of these kids were him. They seemed too young, barely more than toddlers.

"They're not human." Atsumori drew his *katana*.

The children leapt to the walls and ceiling and scurried like a black wave up the stairs to the second floor. They moved with a loud rustle of claws on wood that raised the hair on the back of her neck.

"Oh holy fuck!" Pixii gasped.

"What are they?" Nikki charged after the monstrous children. Where was Nobu? What had they done to him? Was he dead already? In the scene, he'd been on the second floor.

"Spider-whore young," Atsumori said. "Careful. Their mother won't be far."

"If she hurts him, I'll kill her," Nikki snarled.

The second floor was one room with a large open window looking out over the street. A *hoko* was rolling past, the upper deck level with the window. Nikki caught a flash of something large disappearing up onto the roof of the building. The rustle of claws went overhead as the monstrous spiders ran across the roof.

Nobu was pinned to the wall with strands of silk. He was making frightening little whines. She cut him down, and he clung to her, still making the noise.

"Are you okay? Are you hurt?" She realized she was speaking English. "Atsumori, ask him if he's hurt."

It took several minutes to establish that he wasn't hurt, just scared to death.

As they tried to calm him down, she realized that she'd managed to alter his ending. She had saved him. She could see the future and then change it.

When Nobu finally started to talk, he bawled "I told her!" over and over again.

"Told her what?"

"She wanted to know if I'd ever seen any monsters before. I—I— I told her Haru saw monsters all the time. Then she asked if he'd ever seen any gods. And I told her—I told her that Haru had seen Susanoo."

Shijo-dori was completely blocked off and the crowd filled the sidewalks, held back by low wooden fences in some places, yellow tape in others. Of course the good Japanese people were allowing the flimsy barrier to actually hold them in check while *gaijins* stepped over it to take their pictures until police shooed them back into place.

Atsumori shimmered inside of her, leery of possible attackers in the crowd. Nikki could understand all the random comments around her that she knew had to be in Japanese. She pushed her way through the thickly packed crowds to the curb and then realized she'd lost the others.

The parade had already started. One of the big floats was stopped before an official who stood in full ceremonial robes under a bright red umbrella. A boy marched up to the official. He wore the pale blue *kamishimo* over a white kimono that functioned as the parade's official uniform. He cut a cord wrapped around a small box that he was holding. Stiffly, the boy put away his dagger, opened the box and held it out to the official while bowing.

Nikki gazed upwards. The pole that rose up from the top of the float had a crescent moon at its tip. This was the *Tsuki Hoko*, dedicated to Susanoo's brother, god of the moon.

The official had taken a scroll from the box, read it, and nodded. The boy took a fan from his belt, flicked it open, and signaled the crew on the float that they were cleared to move. Two teams in white shoes and shorts, a white festival *happi* and straw hats, over twenty men on each team, had been crouched on the ground. They stood now, picking up two massive pull ropes. Bracing themselves, they waited for two men standing on the front of the float holding fans. Together the crew leaders waved their fans. "Not yet." They called to signal the teams to get ready. "Okay, here we go!"

The pullers heaved on their ropes, and the great float shuddered and then creaked slowly forward on its wooden wheels. Once moving, Newton's first law took over and the massive cart rolled down the street.

Miriam caught up with her. "Atsumori has to be doing something to let you go through the crowd like that. I think we lost Pixii."

"I'm here!" Pixii pushed her way out of the crowd, a small package of fury wrapped in a colorful *yukata*. "Damn, Japanese might be polite to your face, but my God, they get handsy in a crowd."

"This is *Tsuki Hoko*." Nikki pointed up to the crescent moon. "*Naginata Hoko* is somewhere ahead."

Nikki started to turn back to merge back into the crowd. Atsumori, though, had her step over the yellow tape that was strung at knee level.

"We do not have time to go that way," he said. "Come. I will deal with anyone who objects."

"No killing people! There're ten thousand cameras on us right now, and we haven't even unsheathed the *katana* yet."

"Cameras will not see us," Atsumori reminded her as he took off in as long a stride as the *yukata* allowed. "I wish we were in your normal garments. This is not what I would chose to fight in."

"I did not pick these clothes," Nikki reminded him. "Beggers cannot be choosers."

"We look sexy." Pixii trotted to keep up.

"If we get into a fight, I'm stripping," Miriam growled.

Pixii laughed. "You strip and there's going to be a whole lot more cameras than ten thousand trained on us."

"I at least have a bra on," Miriam pointed out.

"Like anyone would even look at me with the wonder twins out to play."

"I am not big-chested!"

"We're in Japan!" Pixii said. "Everything is smaller."

"Can we not have this discussion now?" Nikki cried, throwing up her hands.

They passed a smaller float, one being led by a troop of child musicians wearing headbands, lime-green *happi* and colorful shorts. For some reason they reminded Nikki of frogs. Miserable frogs, as the sun was baking off the asphalt, pushing the temperature toward the mid-nineties, at least.

Beyond the children, they were intercepted by a police officer with a black cap and white gloves. He waved them toward the curb with his pristine hands.

"Go back behind . . ."

"You are to let us pass." Atsumori reached out and put a hand on the officer's chest. "We have important business, and you will not delay us."

The police officer swallowed hard and bowed slightly. "I see. Go on your way then."

"These are not the droids you are looking for," Miriam murmured as they continued.

They passed two small *yama* floats and reached the intersection of Kawaramachi-dori. There was a big *hoko* being prepared to make the ninety-degree turn. Slats of bamboo were being placed under the massive fixed wooden wheels and made slick with water. The pullers had looped the heavy rope around the front of the float and moved up the street. With the team leaders shouting instructions and coordinated fan waves, the crews dragged the front of the great cart sideways.

Nikki stared upwards at the tall cart, trying to tell which one it was as it slewed through the turn. There was a doll in place of a celestial child, face painted white, robed in a rich kimono and wearing a massive gold crown.

"This is *Kanko Hoko*," Atsumori stated. "It is always the fifth float."

She glanced ahead. There were another three small yama floats and, far in the distance, the *Naginata Hoko*.

Nikki strode forward, eyes locked on the lumbering cart ahead. She felt like she was chasing an annoyingly fast-moving, massive turtle. They were gaining on it, but slowly. What was she going to do when they caught it? Climb up onto it and try to search Haru for the spear? Yeah, yeah, that would go over well. There were probably twenty men on the float, not counting the four on the roof. Another forty were pulling the cart, and at least a dozen were overseeing the movement of the cart. In other words, there was a small army between her and Haru. Add in the facts that the silly thing was three stories tall, moving at a steady clip, and she was afraid of heights. Scaling it was so not going to happen.

So, follow and protect him until Susanoo took back the spear? When would that be? After the parade? Tonight when the *mikoshi* were carried to the center of the city? When they were returned to the shrine at the end of the festival? Next year when another celestial child was chosen?

She couldn't spend a year of her life protecting Haru. She couldn't even stay in the country legally for more than thirty days.

And she needed to find Leo. Tell Shiva what she knew. Get him out of the cage. Get him some water. Tell him that she loved him. Then flee the country before Shiva or her mother could nail her down.

"Three o'clock." Pixii picked up her pace.

Nikki frowned. No, it wasn't even noon yet. Then she saw the dark knot of men pushing their way through the crowd to the right. There seemed to be a never-ending wave of men coming up from the subway station. "Oh shit!"

She started to trot, closing the gap, though she didn't want to get into a sword fight in front of half of Kyoto.

The cart that been proceeding at a snail's pace decided at that moment to stop. The pulling crew started preparations for the elaborate turn. The musicians were still ringing their bells and playing flutes. No one on the float seemed to be aware of the oncoming attack.

"Game plan?" Pixii pulled two short batons from the back of her obi.

Like she had one. "Protect Haru. Don't get killed."

"That's it, I'm stripping," Miriam muttered.

"Wait." Atsumori checked Miriam with a wave of the hand, and suddenly they were all wearing different clothing. Miriam and Pixii were in shrine maiden uniforms of red *hakama* pants and short white kimono tops. Nikki was in red *kamishimo* over a black kimono. Atsumori drew his *katana* and faced off against the wave of dark-suited males.

The watching crowd burst into applause.

Half of the oncoming men faltered. Obviously they were human *yakuza* and hadn't been warned about needing to face an angry boy god.

"Halt!" Atsumori thundered, and his shout rolled over the crowd and echoed off the distant hills.

"No, we won't," the largest of the *tanuki* snarled. He flicked his hand, and an unsheathed *katana* appeared in it. It reminded Nikki that they weren't true creatures of flesh and blood. Their bodies were only solid illusions. "Humans aren't willing to share this world. They've grown powerful enough to hunt us down, one by one. They kill us for no other reason than we're not one of them. We've had enough. It's time for a change. Stand aside. This is not your fight, *kami*."

"You made it my fight when you murdered my people and burned my shrine!" Atsumori charged. Power surged into them, like they'd drunk down the sun. Nikki shouted in surprise and fear.

"When they grow strong enough," the leader *tanuki* yelled. "They'll turn on you!"

Atsumori's *katana* struck the *tanuki*'s sword and sheered through it with an impact that Nikki felt up her arms. The leader's howl of pain was cut short as the blade continued, slicing through the male. There was no impact this time. The *katana* cut through him like paper. He shredded into pieces and blew away on a rising storm wind.

The crowd clapped again.

The rest of the *tanuki* surged forward. Pixii flicked her batons, and they extended out into long clubs. Miriam shifted into a defensive position. Nikki leapt to meet the *yokai*, determined to take the brunt of the attack. Out the corner of her eye, she saw three cops rushing into the fray, and then all she could see and think about was the *tanuki* she was fighting. They were trying to overwhelm her with sheer numbers.

The escort for the *yama* float, all in the light blue *kamishimos,* reached the edge of the fight and waded into the *tanuki.*

"Nikki!" Miriam's shout caught Nikki's attention. "The float!"

Nikki whirled, slicing through the *tanuki,* and looked to the *Naginata Hoko.* The men on the cart were ignoring the fight, or maybe just trying to get the cart away from the growing mob of fighters. The *hoko*'s team was focused on the front axle as they worked to slide the cart sideways on the wet bamboo slats. Two *tanuki* had mounted the rear axle. A long red tapestry fringed with bright blue tassels hung down from the roofline nearly to the massive wheels. The *tanuki* scrambled up the back as if the edge of the tapestry were a rope.

"I do not know how we're going to get up there with just one hand," Nikki shouted at Atsumori as they raced toward the float. "Unless you're suddenly able to make us fly."

He held out his *katana,* and the sheath leaped from the pavement to slide onto the blade. The sheath then tied itself to their belt.

"Or we could do that," Nikki said.

The music grew erratic as the *tanuki* reached the top. All the musicians sat facing inward, the loud chimes drowning out the fight. Now they suddenly had a stranger in their midst.

Nikki scrambled up the spokes of the back wheels, trying to think only of Haru and not the fact that she was about to climb up the outside of a mobile three-story structure. As she grabbed the edge of the tapestry, the entire cart suddenly jerked and swayed hard to the left. They'd made the turn! She squeaked in terror as she dangled from the tapestry and the right-side wheels lifted off the ground. For a sickening moment, she thought the cart was going to keep falling to the left, crushing her.

"Get right!" someone shouted overhead. "Right!"

She glanced upwards to see the men on the roof scrambling to the right side. The wheels thudded back to pavement, and the cart shook hard.

The music stopped altogether, and one of the musicians suddenly went flying down to land heavily on the ground. Haru started to scream, a thin and panicky sound.

Nikki swallowed hard on her fear and scrambled up into the cart.

One of the *tanuki* was holding a gun on the remaining musicians while the other held Haru pinned to the ground.

"Stop the *kami!*" the one pinning the boy growled.

The one with the gun opened fire.

Nikki flinched out of instinct. The bullets flared and became butterflies.

"That doesn't work!" Nikki shouted and leapt at him.

The *yokai* had height and weight on her. As they grappled, the other covered Haru's face with one hand and pulled. The shaft of a spear appeared, and the *tanuki* grasped it tight and yanked upwards. Haru wailed in fear and pain.

Lightning suddenly whitewashed Nikki's vision. She was vaguely aware of flying backwards out of the cart. She landed hard and lay for a moment on the hot cement. Black clouds boiled in the previously clear sky.

"Nikki-chan?" Atsumori shimmered within her.

"Oh, I think he knows."

"He definitely knows."

There was a flare of brilliance and an immediate crack and boom as another bolt of lightning struck feet from Nikki. A *tanuki* vanished in the flare of brilliance.

"Nikki-chan, I do not think I can protect you from him. Leave me and go."

"No," Nikki snapped and scrambled to her feet. She needed him too much. She couldn't hope to save everyone by herself. People were running in all directions. Ten thousand people trying to get away with no idea which direction "away" lay. The *tanuki* with the spear was nowhere in sight.

"Damn it. Which way did he go?"

"I don't know. I'm not sensing the spear."

"Shit!" Another bolt of lightning struck a nearby *tanuki* that been grappling with five men in pale blue parade *kamishimos*. The *tanuki* vanished, instantly dissipated, and the men were flung back, dazed.

The effect on the crowd was amazing—instantly everyone fled away from the float, and Nikki found herself nearly alone in the intersection.

✠ 36 ✠
Mother Dearest

Leo heard her coming. High Heels. Strong stride. The angry walk of a well-dressed woman. He sat up, trying to wet his mouth. He was so damn thirsty that it was hard to think. The need for water was making his head pound in time with her footsteps. It was nearly nine again, but he still didn't know if that was morning or night.

The far door boomed open, and a woman marched up to the cage. She was dressed in an expensive business suit and highlighted with diamonds. She had three-inch heels that looked like they could be classified as lethal weapons. Leo stared at her in confusion. Who was this? Certainly he'd never heard of anyone in Shiva like her.

Williams ghosted in behind her and hid in the shadows, probably out of habit.

The woman glared at him. "Where is my daughter? What have you done with her?"

"Daughter?"

"Nikki Delany. You checked into an *onsen* in Izushi with a woman matching her description. Where is she? What did you do with her?"

He could see the family resemblance now. He had thought Nikki had gotten the chin from her father; it had seemed too strong for a woman. When she was angry, like this woman was now, she stuck it out, almost daring the world to take a swing. The same honey gold hair but bobbed short. The same striking blue eyes, but in her mother, they were laser cutting beams.

All his senses were telling him that this was Nikki's mother, but it warred with the knowledge that he was still in a cage in one of Shiva's strongholds. "What are you doing here?"

"I'm looking for my daughter. Where is she?"

"I don't know," he was able to say truthfully enough. Nikki would have left the love hotel long ago. Maybe days ago. He'd lost track of time. "How did you get here?"

"I'm asking the questions."

"I don't know." He realized he'd already said that. He scrubbed at his face.

"You were supposed to bring her in."

Obviously it didn't occur to her that he might have good reason not to trust Shiva with anyone's freedom. "I was focused on finding my father. He's dying. I need to save him."

The woman started to pace, her footsteps loud on the cement floor.

"The staff at the *onsen* said you had a *katana* with you. Is that the one from the Kyoto shrine?"

How much did this woman know about what her daughter had been plunged into? Normally Shiva operated on a strict need-to-know policy. He'd been far more up-front with Nikki than most operatives would have been.

"Answer me!" the woman shouted. "Was the *katana* at the *onsen* a *shintai* for a *kami*? Your Sensitive rating is high enough that even as a half-blood you would be able to tell."

She knew what he was? How did she know all this when Nikki been so naïve?

"What are you?" Leo sniffed deeply. She had wrapped herself with Chanel No. 5, but her scent was wholly human.

"Senator Delany is head of the United States branch of Shiva," Williams murmured in the shadows.

Leo stared at the woman. Nikki had been wholly ignorant of everything that dealt with the supernatural. She hadn't even been aware of her own power. What was this woman thinking, keeping such basic information from someone who was so helpless against possession? Such things ran in family lines; surely her mother knew what Nikki was—or did she?

"Does the *katana* have a *kami?*"

"Answer her." Williams moved forward. He had a cattle prod in his hand; he had left the shadows so Leo would see that he had it.

Leo considered the woman and Nikki's wall of privacy. It was obvious now that Nikki had been hiding from her mother. But why? If Nikki didn't know what she was, then it wasn't to stay out of Shiva's control.

"Yes," he growled out. If Shiva thought that the *kami* was in control, they wouldn't be expecting Nikki to take off for Hawaii.

"And the *kami* is possessing my daughter?"

"Yes," he growled, hating himself. "The *kami* wants revenge for the destruction of its shrine."

"You left my daughter possessed by it?"

"The *kami* was helping me find my father." He couldn't save Simon, but he could at least shield Nikki. "It's probably taken her to a shrine somewhere in Izushi. I got a lead on my father; I was going to Dontonbori to find him."

"It took her to Kyoto. Why?"

"What?"

"A small religious war broke out during the parade. Susanoo got involved. There are a dozen people dead and a score more in the hospital. What is the *kami* planning?"

"Is Nikki alright?"

"What is it planning?"

"What happened to Nikki?" Leo roared.

She stared at him.

"I don't know," Leo rumbled. "Please tell me. What happened to Nikki?"

Coldness went over her face as she realized why he was desperate to know. She leaned in close and whispered, "You know what she is, don't you?"

Did her mother know what Nikki was? Talent ran in family lines. But surely, if she shared Nikki's ability, Nikki would have known what she was.

Nikki stared openmouthed at her notebook. Pixii was helping with the wounded and Miriam was translating for some poor American tourist caught up in the confusion. Nikki's hypergraphia, of course, had dragged her to a quiet corner to write.

She'd opened a window to Leo but had seen more than she could ever imagine.

Nikki had known that her mother was treating her unfairly, but that injustice paled in reality to the truth. How could she subject Nikki to drugs and hospitals again and again, all the while knowing that she wasn't insane? Tied up. Helpless. Half-convinced that what the quack doctors said was true.

Her whole life unwove itself, leaving her in free-fall. Her mother knew that all this strangeness existed—the *kami,* the *tanuki* and everything—and yet considered her insane? For not being able to stop writing?

"That bitch," Nikki whispered. "That motherfucking bitch. She knew. She knew—and she never told me. She just locked me up, told everyone I was crazy."

She needed to write. Now.

Laverne hated visiting her mother. Under the antiseptic smell was the stench of urine. One of the other patients was a screamer. She clutched her purse close, wishing that she could pretend that her mother had died a long time ago, just like she'd told everyone. She could have forged her mother's signature; she'd done it for school papers all through elementary school while her mother scrawled on the walls. It was too important, though, to have the authenticity questioned.

She came to her mother's room and paused at the door. Just once, she wished she could walk in and find a neatly dressed, sane woman beyond the door. A woman like her grandmother had been, all pressed linen, ever-present pearls, and neatly applied lipstick. Her grandmother had the patience of a saint, dealing with her crazed daughter and fatherless granddaughter, calmly forgiving them both.

Laverne curled her fingers against the painted steel of the door. God, she missed her grandmother so much. If only she could go back to that time, so much blessed quiet and sunshine and the smell of lavender water and fresh-pressed cotton.

The distant screamer wailed, reminding her that her childhood had been lost years ago.

She braced herself and pushed open the door.

Her mother crouched in the far corner, rocking in place as she hunched over a piece of paper. There must have been a change in staff. The walls were covered with mad scribbling. Starting with pens, then pencil, and finally crayons as writing implements were used up and no one had yet thought to clue in the new orderly to keep her mother supplied with paper and pens. The highest bit was all feces-covered fingerprints as madness drove her mother to use anything at hand to continue writing.

At least they had caught her before she resorted to blood.

Laverne sighed. She stepped into the room and let the door close behind her. The room smelled a hundred times stronger than the hallway, but at least the screamer was muffled to barely audible. She focused on breathing through her mouth to lessen the stench.

"Mom?"

No response. Not surprising. She'd spent most of her childhood shut out by her mother's madness.

"Mom?" She moved reluctantly closer. The smell was worse near her mother. They must not have cleaned well under her fingernails after she wrote with feces. She glanced at the wall, amazed at the ineptitude of the staff. Her mother wasn't a tall woman—she would have had to balance the chair on the bed and then stand on tiptoe to reach so . . .

Laverne's name seemed to leap off the wall at her, catching her eye. The letters were smeared, but a lifetime of reading her mother's madness made the words clear to her.

Laverne listened to the creak of his footsteps coming up the stairs. She held tight the knife. She wouldn't take any more. She wasn't going to let him touch her again.

She stared at horror at the words that trailed off to smears that even she couldn't read. She had been so careful. She had planned every detail down to the last and then scrubbed away the evidence. He was gone, and no one questioned it. Yet it was there, on the wall, for everyone to see.

"Mom? What did you do?"

They hadn't given her mother a tablet but a sheaf of paper. They littered the floor like dead leaves, every square inch covered with the careful tiny handwriting that her mother used when she had actual pen and paper. Laverne snatched one up and scanned over the words.

. . . Laverne lay panting over his still body, blood warm and wet between them. Not for the first, but this time it was his blood, not hers, and it was for the last time . . .

. . . she curled in a ball on the shower floor, weeping as the water turned cold. It drizzled over her like the rain at her grandmother's funeral. He'd stood there, the proper son, but his eyes on her had been hungry . . .

She crumbled the paper into a ball, shaking. This was exactly what she had done. Exactly what she had thought. All laid bare for everyone to see. She snatched up another sheet of paper and scanned it.

. . . so much blood, everywhere. It'd soaked through the bedding and into the mattress. How was she going to hide . . .

She crumbled it and grabbed another.

. . . she going to tell people? Certainly he'd left town before without so much as a note, but would people believe he'd run off, leaving his niece alone? Or would they search the house, looking for clues . . .

She started to snatch up all the pages, crumbling them without even glancing at them. Damn the woman! Bad enough that she had left Laverne alone in that mess, now she was betraying her while she tried to cope with it by herself.

Her mother crouched on all fours, utterly focused on the paper she was currently writing. She muttered softly a litany to the paper. "Yes, yes, that's smart, girl, keep your head, think it through . . ."

Laverne stared in horror as the pen moved across the paper, revealing her darkest secret.

. . . crypts were for holding dead people.

"No!" She caught her mother by the hair and jerked her back from the paper. "Stop it! Stop it!"

Her mother wailed in dismay and pain but her hand kept moving, spilling damning secrets.

. . . No one else would have the key to her family crypt. Part of her couldn't bear the thought of disturbing her grandmother's body . . .

"Stop!" Laverne flung her mother away from the paper. Some tiny part of her was amazed at how light as a bird her mother was. Did she ever stop writing to eat?

"I have to see!" Her mother scrambled back toward the paper. "I have to be sure! Is it safe for her? She shouldn't have been left alone with him. He was all twisted and dark inside. It wasn't the sex, it was the pain for him. He liked to hurt things, it made him feel powerful. It's why she sent him away."

"I wouldn't have been alone if you'd just stopped writing!" Laverne cried as her mother hunched over the paper again.

"Things you bury don't always stay buried. I have to see."

. . . of seeing her as anything not neat and clean, of putting him in with her as if stuffing him back into the womb that . . .

She stomped down on her mother's hand. Heard something snap. Felt it give. Savage joy and self-hatred tore through her. "I said stop!" Laverne grabbed her mother and flung her again across the room.

Desperately Laverne gathered up all the papers, cramming them into her purse. Only when the last dangerously shameful page was hidden away, did she realize that her mother hadn't moved.

"Mom?" She crept to her mother's side, still shaking with anger and shame and fear.

There was a gash on her mother's forehead. Blood was trickling down her face. Her eyes were open. Unfocused.

"Oh God. Oh God." Laverne crouched there, panting. What was she going to do? It wasn't like she could stuff her mother into the family crypt, too. The staff was going to know that she had killed her mother.

Could she make it look like an accident? How could her mother possibly hit her head on the bed? She looked frantically around the room. Her name on the walls shouted her guilt. She'd killed her mother. She'd killed her uncle, and now she'd killed her mother.

The words drew her eyes upwards. The only white space left in the room was the ceiling. The staff would probably believe that without paper, her mother would try to write on that, too. She grabbed the chair and put it lying on its side in the center of the bed, tipped toward her mother's body. Her mother was still clutching a pen; she felt weirdly relieved to see it was the pen that was broken, not her mother's fingers. Why was it so important to know that she hadn't hurt her mother before killing her?

Trembling, she considered the crime scene, trying not to think how much easier it was to clean up the second murder. So much calmer.

Should she call the staff? Explain how she found her mother already dead? No. No one saw her come in. She could slip out quietly, and no one would even know she was there.

✤ ✤ ✤

"Nikki-chan."

She whimpered as Atsumori called to her, pulling her out of the writing. Wide-eyed, she clutched the notebook to her chest, hiding the awful scene. It couldn't be true. Her mother couldn't have killed her grandmother. Could she?

"Who is this person?" Atsumori asked.

She laughed shakily. "I'm no longer sure." She forced herself to scan the words again. Everything fit. Her mother was Laverne. She had been raised by Nikki's great-grandmother because her grandmother had been "ill." She had been left orphaned when she was seventeen, years before she'd met Nikki's rich and powerful father. Nikki had never heard of an Uncle Billy, alive or dead, nor did she know anything about a family crypt.

If her mother had killed two people, it would make sense why she was so desperate to keep Nikki labeled as insane and too drugged to write. She had secrets that she wanted to keep hidden. Motivation was also easy to map out: Why protect a child who was going to end up as dangerously crazy as her grandmother?

Her mother knew that her ability was real. That's why she was so insistent on locking Nikki up. Any other person would have seen the proof that she could take care of herself—the fact that she was safe with friends every time her mother tracked her down—and washed their hands of the responsibility. She was twenty and not hurting anyone, not even herself. Her mother had carefully never told her about her grandmother's ability. Carefully made sure that Nikki never knew that her stories were true. Carefully kept her locked up because she was scared that if Nikki knew the truth, she could write out all the secrets her mother had to keep.

She'd betrayed Nikki as a mother to protect herself. Somehow, Nikki was going to make her pay.

✠ 37 ✠
War Paint

"I don't know how to drive an automobile," Atsumori stated somewhere between Kyoto and Kinosaki. One of the joys of having a famous mother was that she was ridiculously easy to track, especially when you had a secret elf talent of being able to write from her point of view. Between that and the car's GPS, her mother couldn't stay hidden from Nikki's anger.

"You don't need to know how." Nikki winced as she did something wrong again with the stick shift. The car never made that noise when Leo or Miriam was driving it. "I can drive."

"Obviously not well."

"Well enough."

"This anger will only destroy you. If you go storming into her stronghold, ranting with righteous fury, she will have the upper hand."

"Why can't you shut up?"

"Because you've stopped listening to your own common sense. You must find a weapon against her."

"A sword will work."

"Once a sword is drawn, it is not easily sheathed. Are you willing to kill your mother?"

"Yes!" she shouted.

"Truly? Strike her head from her shoulders and see it roll upon the ground like pumpkin? Bloody stump for a neck?"

"Shut up!"

"Once done, it cannot be undone."

"I want—I want her to just leave me alone. I'm tired of running and hiding like I've done something wrong. I hate it. And what I hate most is being so utterly helpless because I have to stay hidden to stay safe."

"Then you must find a weapon against her that is not a sword."

"I know what she's afraid of. She's afraid that people will find out what she's done."

"Fear is a dangerous weapon. It is difficult to wield."

She considered how the scene would go if she were writing it. For a moment, the car vanished out from under her and she was standing in front of her mother.

"You knew! You knew the truth, and all this time you've pretended I was insane. You kept me locked up and drugged so I couldn't get out and tell your dirty little secrets."

"You're clearly insane."

"So if I call up a reporter and send them to our family crypt, he's not going to find Uncle Billy shoved into the casket with great-grandma?"

"Do you think I couldn't get that quietly cleaned up before any reporter could get there?"

"And you fixed your birth certificate? Did you make sure that Uncle Billy wasn't listed as your father?"

"The name on my birth certificate isn't William Phelps."

"And your DNA? You're going to change that, too?"

"Nikki!" Atsumori shouted.

She blinked and yipped in fear as she realized she had drifted to the wrong side of the road out of habit. She jerked the car back into the left-hand lane. "Okay, so fear is bad and writing while driving is really bad."

By the time she reached Kinosaki, she'd gotten her anger under control. Leo was dying of neglect. Sato had the spear but Shiva didn't seem to realize it yet. They would know soon enough what she'd done at Kyoto but nothing she had written indicated they were aware of why there had been a battle. She had to save Leo and mobilize Shiva against Sato.

Still unaware of the battle in Kyoto, her mother was playing the part of visiting dignitary, touring shrines under some bullshit lie about tourism recovery after the tsunami. Kinosaki lay next door to Izushi. Her mother was looking for her in places where Atsumori would feel safest. There was the mild problem that Kinosaki and Izushi weren't known for their shrines.

It was Japan, so there were small shrines and temples everywhere. Nikki picked out Kyo-o-ji Temple in which to corner her mother because its garden was backed by a bamboo forest. A tall wall surrounded the grounds, but Atsumori scaled it with godlike ease.

Nikki dodged three bodyguards in dark suits and found her mother alone in the garden.

Her mother's eyes went wide at the sight of Nikki. She still was in the black kimono and blood-red *kamishimo*. She had the *katana* sheathed and tucked into her belt.

Her mother reached for her pocket where she kept the radio that linked her to her bodyguards.

"Don't," Nikki said. "I need to talk to you about things you're not going to want other people to hear."

"Nikki?"

"Yes, it's just me. Mostly." Nikki put her hand on the *katana*'s hilt. "The *kami* is here, but you're talking just to me."

"Nikki, put the sword down and back away from it. It's dangerous."

"No, I'm not putting it down. I need you to listen to me, and if I put it down, you won't."

"I don't know what the *kami* has been telling you . . ."

"It's telling me not to kill you for the shit you've put me through!" Nikki snapped. "Really, what the fuck were you thinking about, you selfish bitch? Your grandmother would be ashamed of you. She took good care of you. She gave you everything you wanted. I've seen the pictures. A bedroom painted pink. A princess bed with a canopy. Tea parties in the garden. She did everything to keep you safe and happy. Everything clean and neat and sane. And what did you do for me? I was eight the first time you checked me into a hospital and walked away. I was ten and tied to the bed when the girl across the hall was raped. After everything your grandmother did for you—that's how you treat me?"

"My mother . . ."

"Your mother was trying to protect you when you killed her! She was trying to make sure that no one would find the body you'd hidden."

Her mother had gone ashen and still.

"You knew what it was like to lie in bed, scared shitless, listening to a man move through the darkness, waiting for him to open the door to your room and hurt you. I was ten! I was ten, and you had me tied up, drugged, helpless, and alone. What would your grandmother have thought? She protected you. She kept you safe up to her dying breath. And what did you do? You killed both of her children, and then you didn't even take care of your own child."

"I did take care of you."

"No, you didn't. You realized the day you killed your mother that she wasn't crazy. You've known all this time that I was like her—that everything I wrote was the truth. You've known that this isn't some insanity that a shrink and the right cocktail of drugs will cure. And yet you kept me locked up in the hospital so *you* would be safe."

"My mother was insane. She wrote on walls with her own feces."

"Obsessive Compulsion isn't insane. It's a disorder, but its not insanity, and you know it. And every time a doctor had the guts to tell that to your face, you'd fire him and get someone who would agree with you."

Atsumori suddenly shifted them sideways, and a black man ghosted out of the shadows. He was a tall, solid man all in black. She had written about him enough times to recognize him. He was the one she really was waiting for.

"Williams." Nikki kept to her script, talking fast so her mother couldn't interrupt. "Sato has taken the Heavenly Bejeweled Spear from Susanoo, and he plans to use it to remake the world." That said, she could slow down. Her mother might be a bitch, but even she understood the dangers of a rogue operative armed with a powerful magical weapon. "Sato has Shiva's phone tapped, so he's been able to stay one step ahead of you. He found Simon the day after he'd gone missing; Simon had been possessed by a *kami* named Iwanaga Hime. Sato has teamed up with Iwanaga and a large number of *yokai* looking to take back the world. "

"And you know this how?" Williams asked.

"Because I'm an Oracle. With the annoying exception of things like *kami*, I can 'see' what anyone has done or will do, years in the past or in the future. Leo doesn't want you to know, because he doesn't trust Shiva. Being that you have him locked in a cage without water, it seems to me that he has good cause."

"And you saw *this* meeting?" William asked.

"Yes." Actually dozens of variations of it. This was the most successful storyline. "We want Leo out of the cage. We'll cooperate to make sure that happens. I know that we can take you." She put her hand onto the *katana* hilt. This was partially a bluff—Williams was scary fast and strong—but it was generally a successful bluff. Williams was used to being an attack dog, but he always waited for an order to attack.

Atsumori took his cue and stepped fully into her. "I am Taira no Atsumori. I will not be taken by force. My shrine maiden was murdered. My shrine was set on fire, and my priest was killed trying to save it. I want Iwanaga Hime and this dog Sato stopped."

Her mother's eyes went wide, and she stepped back behind Williams.

The black man nodded in understanding. "A very strong Talent if you two can cooperate in that manner."

"Let me see Leo. Give him water. Clothes. If you allow that, I'll give up the *katana* and tell you where Simon is." Getting Simon off Yamauchi was going to be their problem.

She'd run out of time writing out scenarios. It became apparent that if she didn't meet her mother here, Leo would die in the cage before she could arrange another halfway successful meeting. She only knew that she could save Leo and get the huge machine that was Shiva lurching after Sato.

After that, she had no idea what would happen.

✠ 38 ✠
Cages

The stronghold turned out to be just down the road at the rebuilt Izushi castle. When they'd rebuilt it, they'd dug several levels of additional basements to make a secret base where strangers coming and going would be unnoticed.

In the end, they demanded that she give up the *katana* before seeing Leo. Apparently scenario number fourteen—where she used Atsumori to cut open the cage—was too obvious.

They had a small shrine built into one of the underground rooms. Atsumori appeared beside her as she ducked through the low door.

"It's tiny." She hated it. There were no windows, and once the door closed, it would be coffin dark.

"Relativily speaking, it's huge." Atsumori eyed the room. "A nice place to dream, so to speak."

Her disbelief must have shown on her face, because he smiled gently at her.

"You cannot see it with my eyes. The comforts of a *kami* are different than those of a human."

There was a wide shelf in the back of the small room. She laid the *katana* on the shelf, feeling like she was doing something horribly wrong.

"This is how it needs to be," Atsumori whispered. "I learned the

321

hard way that the mind is the greatest weapon. Being clever wins the war—else I would have never died on that beach."

Nikki stood with fingers pressed to the polished wood of the sheath, not wanting to break contact with it. The *katana* had made her feel strong and capable. Without the sword, she'd go back to just Nikki, the girl who kept finding herself locked up and helpless. The girl who can't even speak the language . . .

A squeak of dismay slipped out as she realized she wasn't going to understand any of the conversations going on about what Shiva should do about the goddess.

"What is it?" Williams asked.

"I don't speak Japanese."

Williams breathed out something that might have been a laugh, and then amazed her by kindly saying, "We'll just stick to English then."

The other guard shifted impatiently and said something in Japanese. The words tumbled past her with no meaning—Atsumori had left her already.

Completely alone in her mother's stronghold, she let them lead her away from Atsumori. She could only pray that they were taking her to Leo and that she was there in time.

The thing in the cage wasn't wholly human. It looked like the fever dream of a cat or a mad painter's attempt at a silver tiger, its fur a wild mottling of white and black. It cringed as she looked at it, backing into the shadows. She glanced around the room and recognized it. This was the room in Leo's scene. That was the cage in which they were holding Leo captive. It was Leo's watch on the creature's wrist.

The thing in the cage *was* Leo.

No wonder he didn't like the name Scary Cat Dude.

This was what Miriam had sensed about him in the subway. Why he had frightened Miriam so much in a sea of people.

"You're spectacularly not coping," she whispered to herself and forced herself to see Leo crouching on all fours, panting raggedly with dehydration. It made it easy, then, to hurry to the edge of the cage. "Leo, I brought you some water."

He was trying not to look at her.

Williams gave the bottles of water only a cursory glance before turning his full attention to the clothes she'd brought for Leo. She pushed the bottles through the bars, trying not to show how anxious she felt.

"I'm sorry, I only brought two. I know that's probably not enough, but I was afraid they would take them off me if they weren't in my bag. I brought you some clothes, too, but you didn't have any spare shoes. We got Simon away from the goddess . . ."

He had hold of her hands before she even realized he was moving. It was definitely Leo's human eyes gazing at her from the beast face. It seemed unreal—like he was wearing a very good mask. "You saved my father?"

"Yes." She squeezed his hands. "He's exhausted, though, and we couldn't get him to wake up or we would have had him call in and explain everything to—to—whoever."

"But he's safe?"

"He's safe. Drink."

He let go of her hand to fumble with one of the bottles of water. The two-liter bottle was large and unwieldy, still slick with condensation. His fingers ended with great black claws that clicked on the plastic as he tried to carefully work the cap. She took the other bottle, twisted off the lid and pushed it into his hands.

"Drink it all. I'm not sure what comes next, but it feels like the shit is going to hit the fan. The creepy music has started. The monsters are coming. You need to be ready."

The guards steered her through a maze of hallways. She clung to her backpack, afraid that they would take it from her. She had come prepared for all-out war, but she'd be left nearly defenseless if they took everything from her. The need to write was growing like a wild fire. The fear that they would take away all of her paper and pens only threw fuel onto that blaze. She had minutes before the need became utterly uncontrollable. The scene with her grandmother haunted her. How quickly would she be reduced to that?

She closed her eyes even as she walked. Seashore. Palm trees. The roar of the ocean. The white foam of the surf on the sand. Leo, out of the cage, wind blowing his dark hair.

Williams promised that once Simon had been found and Leo's innocence established, they both would go free. She'd been inside his head. She knew that he would keep any promise he made, one way or another. He was a man who kept his sanity by clinging to a code of honor. His word was his form of pen and paper. If Sato and her mother weren't in the equation, she'd have nothing to fear.

The guard pulled her to a stop and said something in Japanese.

Beyond the solid door was a windowless room that seemed like a closet, minus any shelves. The floor was *tatami* and big enough for her to lie down on. A single lightbulb housed in a sturdy cage lit the cell. In the very back, there was a miniature sink and toilet, so it was a true proper cell.

The guard gave her a nudge forward.

She stepped into the tiny room, glad that she wasn't claustrophobic on top of all her other instabilities.

All that vanished as the guard tugged at her backpack.

"No!" She clung tighter to the bag. "Don't take it. I need it."

He said something that she didn't understand.

Her mind blanked on how to say "no" so she just howled it in English. "No! *Kudasai!*"

The guard jerked the bag free and slammed the door in her face.

"*Baka!*" She shouted one of the few Japanese curse words she knew. She crumbled down to the floor, cursing in English. Keeping the backpack had been a long shot but she had hoped that they wouldn't take it. "Damn it."

She needed to write, and she needed to write now. She fumbled with the front of her jeans and pulled out the folded sheets of paper that she had tucked into her panties. She had dissembled a pen down to the ink cylinder and steel point and had tucked it into her bra so it lay against the wire support. She had purchased the pen and hidden it and the paper just prior to tracking down her mother. An old pen would have leaked but this one still had a plastic glob over the tip.

She was trembling as she frantically pried the plastic off. So little paper. She had to be careful or she'd use it all up.

Leo was shaking with anger and disgust. Under the label of the water bottle was Simon's Shiva key card. She'd given him all he needed to save himself. Leo gripped the card, hating himself.

All his life he'd wallowed in pity that he'd been captured by Shiva and forced to be an operative. Listening to Williams explain Nikki's deal that the cold bitch of a mother, Leo realized now how lucky he'd been. Simon had been a good caring father who'd protected him at every step. Since Simon had freed him in Hilo when he was seven, he'd never again been tied up, caged, or restricted in any way. From what he'd gathered in the last few hours, Nikki had spent most of her life imprisoned by her mother. It was her mother that she'd been hiding from, protecting herself with her wall of secrecy.

Nikki had given up her freedom for him. She had seen his beast form and hadn't been afraid. And they had locked her up. The one person who had less than he had given up everything for him.

He wasn't going to let them keep her locked up. Williams might promise her freedom, but the man didn't have the authority to keep Nikki's mother from dragging her back to the United States, drugging her senseless, and locking her up in a mental hospital. Leo needed to free her and find some way to hide and protect her from her mother.

He forced himself to be human again.

He dressed, shivering from the change. He drank the second bottle of water that she'd brought him. When he was ready, he swiped the key through the cage's lock. With a quiet click, it opened.

He slipped out of the cell and crept barefoot to the door out of the detention area.

Beyond the access door was a freight elevator to the surface so larger creatures could be muscled easily to the detention cages. It was standard Shiva layout. The prison cells for humans would be up a level.

There was a great hollow space where the access door to the prisoner cells should stand. Around the edges of the ceiling were strands of silk from a *jorgumo yokai*. The giant spiderlike monster was deadly by itself, but it couldn't have taken down the door.

Sato had been here.

Leo hurried down the hall, fear churning in his stomach. The spider-whore was a man-eater.

Around the next corner was a huge splash of blood and flesh like someone had exploded outward with massive force. There wasn't enough to identify the person but he recognized the scent and the high heels. It had been Nikki's mother.

Around every corner were signs of Sato's passing. He'd gone straight to the temporary cells.

The cell door had been ripped from its hinges. Sheets of paper with careful tiny handwriting and splattered with blood littered the ground. Leo stared at them in grief and dismay . . .

Nikki stared in horror at what she had written. Not only had she written it, she'd written it in ink. There was no erasing it. She started to frantically cross out the words when she realized it was useless. She had no power to change what was rushing toward her—she was trapped in the closet, and everything was already happening.

She flipped the page and wrote what any sane person would at that moment.

Leo, I love you. I wish I'd kissed you and held you tight and kept you from leaving me at the hotel. I wish I had kept you safe.

She heard the soft scurry of claws, and a shiver went down her spine. It was coming for her now. The door rattled, and she whimpered in fear. She wanted to be brave. The door rattled again as sharp claws dug at the edges, and then suddenly it jerked open as it was torn from its hinges. She hated that she screamed as the creature reached for her, but she knew it was going to hurt her. There would be blood. Maybe a lot of it.

✠ 39 ✠
Churn the Dark Waters

Nikki woke in the backseat of a car driving through the night. An echo of a headache and a parched mouth told her that she'd been given Ambien. The streetlights flashed overhead in a steady beat while the wheels whistled and whined on the grooved highway.

Sitting in the passenger side was a beautiful Japanese woman who looked somehow familiar. As her elaborate hairstyle shifted unnaturally, Nikki realized there were gleaming black spiders hidden within her hair. Nikki recoiled and the woman laughed, clicking her teeth; it was the sound that Nikki remembered first and then her face. The monstrously large spider had worn this face as it loomed over her, eyes staring into hers hungrily.

Nikki clawed at the handle to the car door and jerked on it. The door didn't open.

Sato said something in Japanese.

"What? I don't understand. I don't speak Japanese."

Sato breathed out a laugh. "Of course, the giant's child comes to our land and we are the ones that must speak its language. So it is— the victor stands triumphant at all levels."

She frowned, confused, and then realized he was referring to the idea that the United States was the sleeping giant awakened when the Japanese bombed Pearl Harbor. "Why are you doing this? Why are you helping Iwanaga Hime? You know what will happen. This is your homeland. This will be like Hiroshima."

"Exactly. The Americans wiped the slate clean and built what they wanted on that scorched earth. I learned that lesson well. The best way to remake the world is to completely level the old one first."

"But—but your family died."

"Yes. Humans are like cherry blossoms. They bloom, they shower you with their splendor, and then they are gone, only to come again. I have lived for nearly two hundred years. I have lost track of all the flowers that withered at my feet. And that is the fault of Amaterasu's grandson, Ninigi no Mikoto."

It took her a moment to grasp that he was talking about the sun goddess and her grandson who had founded the imperial bloodline. "Huh?"

"Amaterasu's grandson, Ninigi, was to marry Iwanaga Hime, the eldest daughter of Ohoyamatsumi. On the way to meet his bride, though, he happened onto her younger sister, Konohana Sakuya Hime, on the seashore and they fell in love. He refused Iwanaga Hime and took Konohana Sakuya Hime as his wife."

"I don't understand."

Sato laughed bitterly. "Of course not. It's all just random sounds to you. Iwanaga Hime means the Rock Princess and Konohana Sakuya Hime means Flowering Trees Princess. If Ninigi had married Iwanaga, humans would have been as enduring and long lasting as stones. But he had chosen the goddess of blossoms, so human lives are short and fleeting as cherry blossoms."

The car was stopped at the edge of a cliff. The earth fell away in a sharp line. Clouds gathered below in a rumbled blanket of gray.

Sato got out of the car, saying something quietly in Japanese.

The spider-woman climbed out of the front and yanked open Nikki's door.

Nikki yipped in fear, scrambled into the front seat and out Sato's door. The spider-woman scrambled over the car on all fours and leapt at her, tackling Nikki to the ground.

Nikki screamed and flailed but the woman pinned her easily.

"If you fight her, she'll hurt you," Sato said calmly. "She knows I can heal you from near death."

Nikki forced herself to stay still despite the fear that was choking her. A lifetime of dealing with orderlies made it possible.

The spider was just like a gorilla orderly, leering at her like she was prime beef.

A second car pulled up, headlights cutting through the predawn gloom. It was the big black luxury sedan that the goddess had been using.

Slender feral men got out and stood guard as a girl wearing the golden kimono of the goddess drifted out of the backseat. While the woman they had seen the night they rescued Simon had seemed slightly older than Nikki, this girl seemed only about thirteen. She was a tiny little thing lost within the folds of the kimono. Blood was streaming from her eyes.

The girl drifted toward the cliff's edge. The hem of the golden kimono trailing behind her made it painfully obvious that she was a foot too short for the garment and that she wasn't moving under her own power. It was possible that the girl wasn't even fully conscious.

She floated off the cliff and paused there, a dozen feet out and hundreds of feet up. Nikki whimpered slightly. What was Iwanaga planning? Nikki didn't want to see this girl die.

The girl jerked like a puppet whose string had been pulled, then she crumbled into a heap. As if the girl had been a skin that was shed, a tall woman in a shimmering kimono of white and gold stood in her place. She looked mournfully down at the girl's body and then walked on. The girl lay there a moment and then dropped silently downward into the clouds below.

No other women got out of the car. Where was Umeko? Had Iwanaga burned through all her shrine maidens? Was that why Sato kidnapped Nikki—because Iwanaga would need a vessel after they remade the world? Or would they just throw her off the edge of the world to make sure she wasn't revealing his plans to Shiva?

The spider-woman hoisted Nikki up and carried her to the edge of the cliff. Only as they neared the edge did Nikki see that the air was distorted beyond the crumbling face. They stepped off, and she locked down on a scream. She could see down through the wispy clouds to the shrine maiden's body like a small broken doll on the rocks below.

And then under them, there appeared a bridge, of gleaming white as if sunlight had become solid.

The need to write had been nibbling at the edges of her awareness, pushed aside by her fear. As the spider-monster carried her up the steep arch of the bridge, heading to where Sato stood waiting with the jeweled spear, the need surged up, drowning her. She writhed against the spider's hold, her hands fluttering madly. She knew, though, that she didn't want the relief that a pen and paper would provide. All that was left of the story was death and destruction. All her characters—every single one of them a real living person—Miriam and Leo and Pixii and Simon—was about to die in a massive tsunami. Riding the madness of her OCD, her mind was filling with the images of bodies thrashing in dark waves.

"No!" she wailed. The more she struggled, the worse the OCD rushed through her, threatening to sweep her utterly away into mad writing. She'd be totally helpless if she became trapped in her own insanity. She needed to get free and stop this, somehow.

She flailed desperately, clawing at the spider-whore's hands that gripped her tightly. The hands looked like smooth white flesh but felt like hard, cold china under her fingers. There were sharp, hard points of chitin under the illusion, like invisible thorns. The spines stabbed into her fingers. She screamed in pain and frustration, welcoming both as they pushed back the need to write. Blood, hot and sticky, flowed from the wounds.

"Let me go!" she shouted. "Go curl up and die someplace!"

She smeared the word "die" on the spider-woman's upper arm.

The spider spasmed in pain and released her. It staggered backwards and collapsed to the gleaming deck of the bridge.

She stared at it, panting. What had just happened? Had she actually killed the monster with her writing? Atsumori said her powers were divine in nature. He had said that heaven and Earth were made of different particles. Could it be that as she got closer to heaven, her ability got stronger?

She turned toward Sato and the goddess and gasped. The two held the brilliantly gleaming spear like a solid ray of light and were raising it upward.

Crying out in dismay, she rushed toward them. She had no plan, but somehow she had to stop them. She slammed into the goddess and, amazingly, the female staggered to the side, letting loose the spear. Nikki reached out and grabbed hold of it. It felt no more solid than sunlight. She would have thought she'd missed her grab except for the tingling potential. She yanked hard, and the bridge shook as the spear point struck the deck.

"Idiot!" Sato shouted and tried to pull the spear from her hands. He succeeded only in pulling her off her feet so that she dangled from the shaft. "Let go!"

"Never!" Ripped from the bridge, the trembling potential surged through her, filling her. "If I do, you'll kill them all."

"They'll die anyway! They always do!"

She seemed to be fraying at the edges from the power of the spear. She clung to it, terrified that it would burn her out, but even more afraid to let go. "Even the stars die and you can't stop that! You don't have the right to kill all these people because you're some kind of immortal freak of nature! You selfish motherfucking prick!"

"I'll set everything right!" Sato let go of the spear with his left hand and caught her by the hair. She knew with awful certainty that he was about to unmake her.

"Denjiro Sato died at Hiroshima on August 6, 1945," she shouted as her vision hazed to brilliance. "He gasped as something came falling into view. A single black teardrop of death. It was falling straight toward him. There was no escaping it. He cried out, and his scream was swallowed by an Earth-bound sun."

She saw the brilliance of the bomb going off. Heard the sound that was louder than the sky was big. Felt the shearing pain and then nothing.

Her vision snapped to normal. She felt like she had been blown up a hundred times her normal size and then deflated. She panted, blinking, her body weak and light as a tattered paper doll's.

Iwanaga had hold of the spear. The power of the spear was filling the goddess—her eyes gleamed with brilliance.

"No, no, don't!" Nikki cried. "I know that you're angry enough to kill. I understand completely. My mother—she killed my grandmother and great-uncle—and to keep that crime hidden, she kept me locked up all my life. I know that when I realized how much she betrayed me, I wanted to kill her. Yes, I was angry. But I was more scared than anything. I was scared of being helpless. But destroying everything isn't the answer."

"They blamed me and locked me up and left me there."

"And now you're free and you can make your life anything you want. You can be with your sister. Share her shrine. Be a beloved goddess who protects her people. Wipe it away and you lose your sister, your father, Kenichi, all the people who had nothing to do with your punishment."

Iwanaga laughed bitterly. "Even if you were willing to sacrifice yourself, you would not last long enough for me to reach my sister's shrine safely."

Nikki reached into her pocket and pulled out the jade bead *shintai* that Yamauchi had given her. "I have this. It will hold you."

Iwanaga gasped, delicate hands going to her mouth. "It's perfect." She shook her head. "But they'll only try to punish me again."

"By now, everyone knows that Susanoo took the spear. He and his sister can settle it out. You're clearly an innocent bystander. You have nothing to fear."

Iwanaga continued to shake her head.

"All will be good." And Nikki *knew* that she had said true words. "I can promise you that. I have that power."

Iwanaga started to weep. For a moment, Nikki was afraid that she would have to fight the goddess, but then Iwanaga bowed low as tears streamed down her face. "Please take care of me."

✢ 40 ✢
White Sands, Blue Skies

Only when war broke out at the far end of the bridge did Nikki remember the *tanuki* that had driven the goddess. Someone had caught up with Sato and had been greeted with a hail of bullets. Who was it? Leo?

She raced back toward the cars, fear jolting through her every step of the way. It was like she was running on air, the rocks hundreds of feet down, and the dead shrine maiden a constant reminder that the bridge didn't support everything. The only reason she could keep moving forward was that the thought of staying on the bridge terrified her more.

She arrived at the cliff's edge a quivering, panting mess to see Leo break the neck of the last standing *tanuki*.

"Leo!"

Joy and relief flooded his face. Then horror washed in as he realized that he was surrounded with evidence of his deadly nature. He dropped his gaze and started to back away.

"Help me." She put out her hand to him.

He looked at her in confusion, but came and took her hand. "What is it?"

She gazed down at his warm strong fingers lightly holding hers.

She didn't want to ever let go. She leaned forward to rest her forehead against his chest. She was trembling so badly she felt like jelly. "I left the spear out on the bridge and I'm afraid of heights."

He breathed out a surprised laugh into her hair. "You are?"

She nodded. "I don't think I can go out alone again—but I'm not sure it's safe for you."

He put an arm around her shoulders and she pressed close to him, listening to his heart beating. "If I can, I'll get it for you."

She looked up and read his heart in his dark eyes. He loved her. He didn't want to scare her. She reached up to press her hand to his rough cheek.

His eyes widened in surprise and slowly, tentatively, he lowered his mouth to hers. It was a whisper of a kiss, murmuring the secrets of his heart. What was she laying bare to him? She tried not to think of other times with other men that went awkwardly and ended badly. What did it matter when this may be all they had? Life was as fleeting as cherry blossoms. One night, and then either one or both of them might be dead. She wanted to know him completely, hoard away every little detail so she would always have him, no matter what happened.

They kissed until she was breathless and he tore reluctantly away.

She couldn't watch as he tested the edge of the bridge. She stood with her hands pressed over her eyes, whimpering in fear that he'd misjudge his step and fall. Only after she couldn't hear his footsteps anymore did she realize that the spider-whore's creepy black-eyed kids could be sulking about the cars, looking for revenge for their mother.

She jerked her hands off her eyes and nervously scanned the area around her. Most of the dead *tanuki* looked like they'd been hit by a freight train. Leo was impressive when he was angry.

Leo's sports car sat behind Iwanaga's sedan. The driver's door was open, a chime announcing that the keys were still in the ignition. Atsumori's *katana* rested in the passenger seat, along with her backpack. Nikki jerked open the door and snatched up the sword.

"Nikki-chan." Atsumori hugged her close. "I'm so glad we found you."

"How did you find me?"

"Where else would Iwanaga Hime take the spear but to the floating bridge of heaven?"

And of course, as a god, Atsumori had known where the bridge connected to Earth. Leo must have taken the *katana* from the stronghold's storage so Atsumori could act as a guide.

Leo came trotting back, carrying the spear. "Let's get out of here."

It rained buckets as they drove toward Kyoto.

"Susanoo is angry," Atsumori said.

"We'll take the spear to his shrine." Leo drove with the fingers of his left hand twined around hers, reluctantly letting go when he had to shift.

"He's not there," Nikki said. "After the parade, they carry the *mikoshi* from the shrine to the center of town. He stays there until the end of the festival."

"Then we'll go there." He reclaimed her hand.

She wasn't sure of the wisdom of returning the spear to Susanoo when they reached the tiny storefront display area with the three *mikoshi*'s tucked behind a half-wall. They stood under the awning as an ocean of rain poured out of the sky.

"Good, you brought it back." Inari suddenly stood beside her, dressed in a beautiful *yukata* of cherry pink with delicate white blossoms. "Father will be happy."

"Atsumori, is this who it looks like?" Nikki asked.

"Yes, this is Inari."

"Oh good." She held out Iwanaga's *shintai*. "Can you make sure she makes it to her sister's shrine?"

"Yes." He took the jade bead and then the spear. "Thank you for putting things right." He pointed up the street. "Go to the Kinmata." Inari pointed up Shijo-dori toward the corner of Gokomachi. "Ask for a room and they will give it to you."

The hotel was a traditional *ryokan* with *tatami* rooms and futons. As Inari promised, the staff asked no questions, simply led them to a room, laid out futons, and gave them privacy.

Nikki's heart hammered in her chest. This was not like all the times with the other men. Leo knew all about her weirdness and even now her silly fears. This wasn't some guy she'd met at a coffee shop or at a bar. He wasn't her friend's brother, either. This was Leo, who would risk his life to search for someone he loved—and he loved her. And there was no question in her mind that he would die to protect her.

And yet she was trembling as she pressed against him. What was this fear? For once in her life, she was sure that the man she was with wouldn't hurt her. Was it because she finally had something irreplaceable and she was scared that it would slip through her fingers and be gone? She clung to him tightly, shaking.

He didn't put his arms around her. His hands hung by his side, clenching. "You're frightened of me."

"I'm frightened of losing you. You—you haven't seen me at my worst. I can't stop writing. If I don't have paper and pen, I'll use blood and—and—whatever I can to write with."

He breathed out and gathered her tight to him. "Whatever you need, I will give it to you."

"I need you."

He kissed her temple and whispered, "You already have my heart."

She fumbled with his shirt, trying to find a way to his skin. He moaned against her lips as her fingers found bare hard muscle. It got easier as they lost pieces of clothing, as if with each piece they shed away their fear.

He leaned over her, and her heart tried to jump up her throat.

"Wait."

He pulled back, concern on his face.

"I—I don't like being on pinned . . . on the bottom. It kind of freaks me out."

He sat back and wordlessly guided her onto his lap.

"Oh yes, this is good." She groaned as he kissed her throat. One last whisper of doubt remained, reminding her that she wasn't on the pill. She wanted her own place, a trustworthy man and children, but not all at once.

"Wait, I have protection." She fumbled through her backpack, shaking with nervousness. How would he take her wanting to use a condom? Normally it was where her relationships unraveled, as most guys were dismayed to learn she wasn't on the pill.

He eyed the package of Kit Kat look-alike condoms, one eyebrow raised.

"They were on the pillow at the love hotel. I kept them so we'd have some—something."

He smiled hugely at her and tore it open with his teeth.

Dawn came too soon, slipping quietly into the garden. The light woke her and made her shy as she realized that the dark no longer hid all her imperfections. She gathered the sheets tight around her. Leo lay beside her, beautiful in the fragile light, and unmistakably male.

She sat watching Leo sleep, hoarding the moment. His breathing changed and he opened his eyes to look up at her. She yelped and pulled the sheets up higher.

"I've never done this. Sleep with a guy."

He sat up. "You were a virgin?"

"No. I've had sex, not that it was anywhere as good as last night." She blushed and pulled the sheet up to her nose. "I mean I've never woken up with a guy. They always leave."

He reached out and touched her face. "They were fools."

Her mother's death was in the news. Not the truth but a carefully fabricated story about a car accident on an isolated road. Nikki wasn't sure how to deal with the news. She had, of course, known about it before it actually happened. It was somewhat ironic that if her mother had given Nikki freedom to write instead of so determinedly trying to keep her quiet, Nikki could have warned her.

But how should she feel? Perhaps relieved, but that seemed somehow callous and wrong. She could not bring herself to feel anything. Not yet.

Leo silently wrapped his arms around her and said nothing. He understood what a bitch her mother was, but Leo would hurt anyone who spoke badly of his father.

Shiva had also doctored the news about the fight during the parade. According to CNN, there had been a freak storm that heralded the end of the festivities. The dead and wounded were blamed on lightning. Nothing was said about the samurai girl or the transforming *tanuki*. There would be no photo evidence of her. Whatever been filmed of the *yokai* had been carefully digitally sanitized. News footage only showed the crowds fleeing the lightning.

What had happened to Miriam and Pixii after Nikki had stormed off in a rage? It only took a pen and a paper napkin to find out that they'd searched for her and discovered that the car was missing, too. Guessing that she'd ditched them to do something dangerous, they'd returned to Nara to pump Simon for information. The three of them spent the night combing for information about her and Leo. Everything they'd managed to learn had been alarming. Thankfully, though, Shiva seemed totally unaware that Miriam and Pixii were strong Sensitives.

"We should go," Nikki said.

Simon was halfway down the driveway to Yamauchi's kiln, ginger kitten in hand, when they drove up. He was dressed in a borrowed *yukata* and still looked pale and worn. Leo slammed the car to a stop the moment he saw his father and leapt out. Apparently remembering that the *tanuki* could shape change, Leo paused by the open car door, nearly vibrating with his joy and suspicion.

Simon held up Maru as if to explain his presence. "He'd gotten himself stuck up a tree, kind of like another kitten I know."

"Is it really you?" Leo rumbled low and anxious.

Simon gave a dry laugh and then said warmly, "This is my family. I found it all on my own. It's little, and broken, but still good."

It was odd to hear the quote from *Lilo and Stitch* done in a rich, warm British accent.

Leo breathed out in relief and pounced on his father.

Simon laughed and caught him in a rough hug. "You little idiot. I knew you wouldn't stop looking until you found me."

Leo nodded against his father's shoulder.

She gave them privacy to reconnect, hoping for the same. She knew that Miriam and Pixii were going to ask embarrassing questions once the scolding ended.

They were sitting on the porch of the farmhouse, *shoji* doors opened behind them, frowning at laptop computers. Pixii saw her first and yelped. Only habit got the laptop put *gently* aside before Pixii tackle-hugged Nikki with a squeal.

"You're okay! You're okay!" Pixii cried.

"You idiot!" Miriam wiped tears from her eyes and hugged Nikki tight the moment Pixii released her. "What the hell were you thinking?

I told you that getting your mother involved was a bad plan. At least you're free of her now. Good rid—ow!"

Pixii had smacked Miriam in the back of the head. "I know you're probably still trying to cope with everything that's happened. I know you probably don't want to talk about it right now, but at some point you will and you should. But the important thing is you need to let go of all the hate and fear and anger. If you hold on to it, it will poison everything. It's over. It's done. Focus on the life you want to make for yourself."

"We'll help you," Miriam promised. "We'll be there anytime you need us."

She understood now why the goddess had wept. Up to that moment, Nikki hadn't realized how free she was. She didn't have to hide anymore. She didn't have to worry about being dragged away from any life she tried to build. She could do anything she wanted. The possibilities overwhelmed her.

She hugged them both as she started to cry. "I love you two."

"Love you," they said and held her as she wept.

After she was done crying, they grilled her on her relationship with Leo in the disguise of gently teasing her with cat puns. Luckily, Yamauchi had running water and a garden hose.

What kind of life did she want? What did she want to really do now that "to stay hidden" was no longer the foremost of her needs? Not even Shiva was looking for her; in rewriting Sato's history at Hiroshima, she'd changed her own past in a thousand little impossible ways so that everything was the same and yet completely different. With her mother dead, she was sole heir to her family's massive wealth. She could pay back her advance and never have to write for money again.

Of course, she couldn't stop writing; the *need* would always be there. All that had really changed was that she now knew the truth: she had power to know the future and to change it. Perhaps the compulsion was heaven's way to make sure she owned the responsibility of having such a god like ability.

She became aware that Leo was watching her with quiet intensity. Wanting her. Afraid that completely free, she'd walk away from him.

She went to him and hugged him tight. "I love you," she said just in case he didn't know.

"I love you," he whispered fiercely. "What do you want to do?"

She picked up Atsumori's *katana*. "I want to go to Dupont, Louisana." Leo raised an eyebrow in confusion. "There's a demon there that I need to kill."

"We need to kill."

"And then Hawaii. There's someplace I've been wanting to go." She reached out to take his hand. "It's been my refuge for a very long time. I just didn't realize until recently that it's a real place. It's where I live with you."

Wen's Not Completely Accurate
GLOSSARY
of Japanese Terms

Amaterasu—Sun goddess

Arigatou—Thank you

Baka—Stupid, an insult, obviously.

Bonito (flakes)—Fish that has been dried in a cave, allowed to grow mold, hardened to the consistency of wood, and then shaved off into tissue-thin wafers. Very odd but tasty stuff, has the weird habit of wiggling when on steaming hot food.

Chigo—Celestial child, sort of a envoy to the gods.

Chotto matte kudasi—"Wait a moment, please." Sometimes uttered as "*chotto*" if the person is being super informal.

Cosplay—Dressing up as your favorite manga or anime character.

Desu—Handy Japanese word that Americans can abuse by assigning the meaning of "is" to it.

Doko iku no?—"Where are you going?"

Eh?—Not so much a word as a question mark sounded out.

Fukuro Shinai—*Shinai* is the name of the bamboo sword used in kendo. *Fukuro* means bag, but when combined with *shinai*, it means a bamboo sword wrapped with leather or "in a bag." No, I don't understand it.

Gacha—A company whose product is vending machines that dispense random toys inside of hollow balls. One ball is a variable price per machine, some as cheap as 100 yen ($1), others more expensive. (Since the one-hundred-yen coin is as common as a quarter, it's simple to have the change to do this.) The toy is usually a figurine from anime. Each machine will have a common toy and a mix of more rare and sought-after toys, to encourage people to buy many in an attempt to get the one they want. It's common to find an entire wall of these machines where manga, anime, and related products are sold. The toys are usually surprisingly well made for being only $1.00 US. I have one sitting on my desk, Akira-sama from *Lucky Star*. Do a YouTube search on "Lucky Channel Akira." Be sure to watch it in original Japanese with subtitles—the voice actress is brilliant!

Gaijin—Anyone not Japanese. The term means "outsider" and reflects a core philosophy of Japanese thinking. In almost every part of the Japanese life, a person is part of a group and anyone not in their group is an outsider. The "group" might be their class, or the people they work with, or their neighborhood. Whenever a group of Japanese takes a picture, they always take it twice, once with everyone but the initial photographer, and then the initial photographer and someone else taking the photo, because it would imply that the initial photographer wasn't "part of the group" if he didn't appear in the picture. This is also reflected in the language—how you address someone is completely dependent on if they're in your group or outside of your group. Americans living in Japan—if they're not working for a company—discover quickly that it's very difficult to socialize with Japanese because they're not part of a group. One reason Miriam attends the office drinking parties is that it's one of the ways that company employees display that they're part of the same group.

Geisha—Counter to what Westerner believe, Geisha are not prostitutes but very skilled trained entertainers. From a very early age, they're taught everything from the proper way to open a door elegantly to elaborate traditional dances. They take music lessons and dance lessons. Corporations consider it a status symbol to provide geisha to serve drinks and dance and play music at business meetings. However, it should be noted that when you bring rich and powerful men together with beautiful women, affairs do happen.

Gion—At one point the Buddhist priests tried to replace the native Shinto religion. They took over Shinto shrines and claimed that the gods enshrined were actually Buddhist gods of different names but similar aspects. Gion is the name of the Buddhist god who they chose to represent Susanoo. The Yasaka Shrine for a time was known as Gion Temple. In the 1800s, however, the Emperor allowed the Shinto temples to return to their names and their original gods' name. By this time, however, the area where the Yasaka Shrine stood had become known as Gion. This section of Kyoto is world famous for its geisha. (Inari is actually the Buddhist god of rice who could be male, female, or both. He was chosen to represent Susanoo's daughter Uga-no-Mitama and son Uka-no-Mitama, who were gods of agriculture. Since Inari was more popular than the Shinto gods, he remains Inari.)

Hai—Yes.

Haiden—Hall of worship.

Happi—Lightweight jacket worn during festivals that usually has a unifying symbol on it. At one time the symbol was the mon of the samurai family that the person worked for. Over time it's been replaced by other *kanji*. Sometimes it simply says "*matsuri*," which means festival. Sometimes it has a sponsor name in *kanji*. Since this is very traditional, it's almost never anything as crass as a "corporate logo," but the idea is the same.

Honden—A small upraised building with a steep gabled roof where the actual god is housed. This area is off-limits to all but the priests of the temple, and the doors are generally kept closed except during special festivals.

Inari—The god of good luck in business. Inari uses *kitsune*, or fox spirits, as his messengers and thus most of Inari's shrines are littered with statues of foxes. The statues are usually in pairs, representing male and female. They often hold an old-fashioned key to a granary in their mouth. It is believed that a third of the Shinto shrines in Japan are dedicated to Inari and total thirty-two thousand plus countless little roadside and field shrines.

Irashaimase—"Welcome." All employees of business shout this out as soon as they see anyone enter the store. It can be amazingly annoying if there are several employees and a large number of people entering the store.

Jogan—The Japanese only recently started to use the European method of telling time. Prior to that, the date was based on the year of the reign of the Emperor in power. The eighteenth year of Jogan, thus, means that it was the eighteenth year of the reign of Emperor Jogan.

Kaguraden—*Kagura* is the sacred dance of the shrine maiden, thus the *kaguraden* is the stage on which the shrine maiden dances.

Kami—A powerful spirit which is often worshipped as a god. Reflecting the structure of the Japanese society, there are greater and lesser *kami*.

Kamishimo—A two-piece outfit. The top piece is a vest with wide stiff shoulders. The bottom piece is a *hakama* (pleated pants that look like skirts) of the same material. The two pieces are worn over a kimono, usually of a contrasting color.

Kanji—Japanese writing.

Katana—A samurai sword.

Katajikenai—"Thank you," Its origin is from the days of samurai and isn't used now. It means more like, "I'm grateful and indebted."

Keitai haizara—Portable ashtray. Because the Japanese wouldn't think of throwing their cigarette butts on the ground.

Kendo—The martial art that uses wooden practice swords in lieu of *katana*.

Kirin—An Asian flying horse with a horn. Like a unicorn but way more cooler.

Kudasai—"Please."

Kunitsu-kami—A god of the Earthly realm.

Kusanagi—Grass Cutter. One of the three imperial regalia. A sword passed from the Sun Goddess to her grandson, the first emperor of Japan. Last used in 1989.

Maneki Neko—Literally "beckoning cat." A statue of a cat, normally a calico bobtail, with one paw upraised. It's believed to attract and house a lucky spirit that will bring you good fortune and money. There are several legends that explain how this belief came into existence. The earliest known statues were given out at a temple in Osaka. One of the most common legends is that a wealthy man was standing under a tree during a rainstorm when he saw a temple cat seemingly beckoning to him. He dashed into the rain to investigate, and a moment later, lightning hit the tree he been standing under. The wealthy man then heaped riches upon the temple in repayment for his good fortune. There is an elaborate iconology attached to the statue, including which paw is upraised, the color of the cat, and anything it's wearing, such as a belled collar. I frequented a Japanese restaurant in Massachusetts and they gifted me with my favorite *Maneki Neko*, a ceramic Weebles Wobble statue with both paws upraised. It has a little bell that rings if the cat wobbles.

Mansion—A no-deposit apartment building. Normally, a Japanese landlord requires a large non-refundable deposit called Key Money. There are no housing laws so landlords can and will refuse to rent to *gaijin*. Mansion are more expensive because they don't require Key Money and will take *gaijin* renters.

Matsuri—Festival.

Mazu—"Almost" (I think).

Mikoshi—Small buildings and boxes that can house the gods so they can be carried about. Many festivals feature parades of the gods through town so the gods can "visit" the area.

Mizu—Water.

Mon—This can be considered the family crest of a clan. It is circular with a stylized symbol in the middle, most often flowers, leaves, and insects. It was used often in warfare on flags so you could see in a glance who was where on the battlefield. The mon is quite beautiful in a simple, elegant fashion.

Moshi moshi—The standard Japanese way to answer a phone. Basically it's "hello" but best if you kind of think of it as radio-speak for "over" because it's not something you say to someone face-to-face.

Nani—"What."

Nani o osagashi desu ka?—A phrase used by salesclerks to ask if you need help; basically, "What is it you need?"

Noh—A traditional type of Japanese theater.

Nomikai—A social event requiring all employees to go out and drink with each other. Everyone is seated at one table at a restaurant which is often dedicated to this kind of gathering. There is bar food available, and the beer is often low-alcohol content because it's expected that everyone will drink at the same rate regardless of age, sex, or weight.

Noren—A curtain that usually hangs from the top of a door frame to part way down. Sometimes it only hangs low enough that a customer needs to duck under to enter the shop. Sometimes it will hang down to almost waist level. Usually found only at businesses, it often has lettering in *kanji*, either being the name of the shop or a greeting. Other times it will feature art. Traditionally, the *noren* meant to keep out dust and wind, but in modern times it is often used to create the illusion of privacy. It is are hung up at the start of the day and taken down when the shop closes.

Obakemono—A word used to group all shape-shifting *yokai* together. These include *bakeneko*, *kitsune,* and *tanuki.* All three can be benevolent as well as dangerous.

Obi—A wide belt used in wearing kimono and *yukata.*

Ohayou gozaimasu—"Good morning." Very formal version of it.

Ojamashimasu—"I intrude on you!" It's the ritual greeting that one calls as they enter the house of someone else. It stems upon the fact that, traditionally houses had a small "foyer" area that wasn't really considered part of "the house" and that guests would enter without knocking. In this sheltered area, guests could be out of the rain, take off their shoes, etc., all the while shouting that they've come for a visit. It's because of this custom that apparently staff at *onsen* will pop in and out of guests' rooms with very little warning.

Okonomiyaki—A fried cabbage pancake topped with BBQ sauce, mayonnaise, and any number of possibilities. The name literally means "what you want" to indicate the freedom to chose what you like to top the pancake. It's usually considered Japanese "pizza" in that regard, and can be found at restaurants where

it's cooked on a barlike counter, or on grill-topped tables,
or on portable grills at festivals.

Onsen—A hotel that features hot-spring baths. These are very
popular with the Japanese. The "baths" are fed by water heated
via the volcanic nature of the Japanese islands. The hotel
provides bathrobe-like *yukata,* all meals and access to baths that
are a mix of single gender, mixed gender, indoor, outdoor,
private, and public. I'm told that the staff often follow
the Japanese habit of entering a room and then announcing
that they're there.

Otaku—"Fan" with the implication of extreme.
What the person is a fan of can vary even though in the US,
otaku is used as a fan of anime/manga.

Oyakodon—A rice bowl with sautéed onions, chicken and egg.
Sometimes given nicknames like "mother and child," generation
bowl, etc., to indicate that both the chicken and the egg are the
same creature, just different stages of its life. (And yes,
this is one of my favorite Japanese dishes.)

Ryokan—A bed and breakfast where the rooms are traditional
Japanese with *tatami* mats and futon bedding. The style of the
rooms and method of dealing with the guests is what makes it a
ryokan versus a hotel. It may or may not have a hot spring bath.
If it does, then it's a *ryokan onsen.*

Sake—Rice wine.

Salaryman—A cobbled-together English phrase to mean
someone who earns a salary, but typically refers to a man
who wears a business suit.

Seme—The aggressor or "Pitcher" in a yaoi manga. The related term, Uke, is used for the "Catcher."

Shide—A streamer made of paper that has been folded into a zigzag shape. It isometimes they are tacked on to objects to create a ward or mark the item as holy. Other times they are attached to wands and used in rituals. The wand is called a *haraegushi,* or lightning wand. When it is waved, it makes a rustling noise. The wand is often used by Shinto priests and shrine maidens in cleansing rituals.

Shikansen—Bullet train.

Shintai—The vessel of a Shinto god, or physical object serving as a repository for the god.

Shoji—A door consisting of paper covering a wooden frame. Because the paper is nearly translucent, a great deal of natural light is able to shine through the door while still being able to block out dust and insects. The paper is sold in sheets and routine maintenance on the door is to remove the old paper as it is torn and glue new paper into place.

Soto soto!—"Outside, outside."

Sumimasen—Basically means "I'm sorry," but in the nature of "I'm sorry to bother you" or "Excuse me."

Tabi—Traditional socks that have a notch between the big toe and the second toe so that the foot fits easily into a sandal.

Taiko—Large drums usually played by anensemble group. The drums are made from wooden *sake* barrels with skin stretched over one end. They're played with two wooden sticks.

Takoyaki—Fried octopus dumplings, a very common "street" food often found at food courts, train stations, and festivals. It's topped with a BBQlike sauce and sometimes mayonnaise. It originated in Osaka. It's usually found in eight packs, reflecting the Japanese sense of humor and the fact that octopi have eight tentacles.

Tanuki—A common animal found in Japan that fills the niche of "raccoon," complete with face mask but is more doglike in build. It is often referred to as "raccoon dog." (While on Miyajima Island we came face-to-face with one in a back alley one night—they are scary large despite their name.) The name also refers to a trickster spirit (*yokai*) that can transform its appearances from someone the person knows to an object. For some reason, they're the patron saint of restaurants and statues of them are often found by the front door of an eating establishment.

Tansu—Traditional wooden storage cabinets, often bound with metal. They are considered portable and designed to be easily moved. They could be used for storing food, clothing, medicine, or weapons. They were custom built for one specific item so varied widely in size and shape. Some were chests, others drawers, and others wardrobes. Occassionally they were built with a wheel-base to make them easy to move long distances. My favorite *tansu* are drawers stacked up in a manner that allow them to also serve as a staircase to a second floor.

Tatami—Straw bound into rectangular mats, which are about two inches thick. Room sizes in Japan are measured

by the number of *tatami* mats that can be laid down on
the floor, thus the room might be a four *tatami* or eight *tatami*
room. While new, they smell strongly of cut hay fields.
The scent fades over time although high humidity can renew
the scent. Japanese never walk on the *tatami* mats with shoes
on and don't place chairs on these mats. In modern homes,
only the living room might be set up with *tatami* mats. In older,
more traditional homes, the bedrooms and the dining room
will also have mats.

Toire—Toilet or bathroom.

Toire wa doko desu ka—"Where is the bathroom?"

Torii—A structure of two posts supporting a crossbeam, often
translated as "gate" although there's no swinging gate or barrier
walls involved. They represent crossing from the real world to
the spiritual world. The *kanji* for this means "Bird Rest."

Toryanse—A traditional children's song, original unknown, that's
been sung by Japanese children for generations. It is much
like "London Bridge" in that the children play a group game
which involves two people holding hands forming a "gate" and
the other children "passing through the gate" while the song is
sung. The child under "the gate" when the song ends is caught
and held prisoner. For some reason, the Japanese decided when
they first added sound to crossing lights to have this song played.
I love the melody but unfortunately the song has been slowly
changed over to a very piercing beep.

Tsuba—The hilt of a samurai sword. It is fashioned separately from
the blade and can be changed if the sword is dismantled into its
separate pieces. Generally it's a disc of metal, several inches

across, with a slot in the center for the blade. Each *tsuba* is handcrafted and has artwork painted onto the surface. The artwork often relates to the samurai's family *mon*.

Uchiwa—A fan that doesn't fold, sometimes made of plastic, traditionally made of bamboo and paper. At festivals, plastic versions are passed out, often with pretty pictures on one side and festival sponsors' names listed on the other. Fans from restaurants with pictures of popular food dishes and their prices are often given out. Because festivals are in the summer, are crowded, and have countless food stallspouring out heat, one often needs a fan and something cool to eat or drink. You see *uchiwa* tucked up against the kidneys of people wearing everything from yukata to blue jeans.

Uke—The "Catcher" in a *yaoi* manga. This is normally the character that is caught off guard by the approache of the other character. Often the *uke* is smaller and prettier than the *seme*.

Wakarimasen—"I don't understand."

Yakuza—Japanese organized crime syndicates. Like most things Japanese, they are steeped in tradition. *Yakuza* members often sport elaborate and colorful full-body tattoos, but they only reveal them to fellow *yakuza*. As a penance for failing some task, they sometimes cut off parts of their fingers, starting with the pinkie. This apology is the origin of "pinkie promise" in Japan. Such self-mutation was in order to weaken the man's ability to fight, thus making him the need·protection of his organization more.

Yaoi—Homosexual comics, graphic in nature. (Nongraphic homosexual comics are considered "boy's love.") The two main characters are divided into the roles of *uke* and *seme* in terms of which character is the aggressive personality in the relationship. Oddly, the readership is mostly female.

Yen—Japanese monetary unit. One yen is roughly a penny.
A hundred yen is roughly a dollar. A thousand yen is ten dollars.
A hundred thousand yen is a hundred dollars.
Unlike Americans, Japanese embrace coins. In addition to one-, five-, ten-, and twenty-five-yen coins, they also have a fifty-yen coin, a hundred-yen coin and a five-hundred-yen coin.
Men's wallets normally have a coin section to make carrying these coins easier. That said, Japan is quickly moving to a cashless society with pre-paid cards and cell phone payments being accepted in vending machines and many stores.
Credit cards, however, are quite rare.

Yokai—Supernatural being that generally falls into the "monster" range as opposed to *kami* which are more "god."

Yukata—A summer kimono, less formal than a proper kimono, often worn to festivals. Normally only teenage girls wear them, but there are male versions. The girls' yukatas are bright, flowery gowns, often in pastel colors. Boys' are usually much plainer and run towards tan and navy.

Yuri—Lesbian comics, sometimes graphic in nature, but not as graphic as *Yaoi*.

Yuri—Lily. Often used as an old-fashioned girl's name.
(Yes, I gave Pixii lily flowers on her *yukata* for a reason.)

�܍ ✜ ✜

And the French!

Mon Ami—My friend

Monsieur Minon—Mister pussycat

Pour penser, il faut un cerveau—for thinking, a brain is necessary